Breaking Gentle

Also by Beverly Lowry

COME BACK, LOLLY RAY

EMMA BLUE

DADDY'S GIRL

THE PERFECT SONYA

Beverly Lowry

BREAKING
G·E·N·T·L·E

V I K I N G

VIKING
Published by the Penguin Group
Viking Penguin Inc., 40 West 23rd Street,
New York, New York 10010, U.S.A.
Penguin Books Ltd, 27 Wrights Lane,
London W8 5TZ, England
Penguin Books Australia Ltd, Ringwood,
Victoria, Australia
Penguin Books Canada Ltd, 2801 John Street,
Markham, Ontario, Canada L3R 1B4
Penguin Books (N.Z.) Ltd, 182–190 Wairau Road,
Auckland 10, New Zealand

Penguin Books Ltd, Registered Offices:
Harmondsworth, Middlesex, England

First published in 1988 by Viking Penguin Inc.
Published simultaneously in Canada

1 3 5 7 9 10 8 6 4 2

Grateful acknowledgment is made for permission to reprint an excerpt from *Moments
of Being* by Virginia Woolf. Copyright © 1976 by Quentin Bell and Angelica Garnett.
Reprinted by permission of Harcourt Brace Jovanovich, Inc.

LIBRARY OF CONGRESS CATALOGING IN PUBLICATION DATA
Lowry, Beverly.
Breaking gentle.
I. Title.
PS3562.O92B74   1988   813'.54   87-40468
ISBN 0-670-82245-0

Printed in the United States of America by Arcata Graphics, Fairfield, Pennsylvania
Set in Sabon

Again, for Glenn and Colin

Sunday

· 1 ·

"*E*asy."

Dropping a hand to Hale's shoulder, Diana pressed lightly.

Hale eased up. Impatience made him push; the anticipation of a surefire Sunday morning blessing. The night had been long and jagged for both of them.

The central air conditioning switched on. In the pasture a horse snorted. Without promise or enthusiasm, the wind blew.

Thumbs at her waist, Hale cradled her hips, careful not to pull at the pale fluted gown gathered in a thousand slippery folds at her waist. When he shifted his finger to one side, gauzy pleats grazed his knuckles. When his jaw muscle threatened to cramp he closed his mouth a little.

On the first night of their marriage when Diana discovered Hale could not sleep close, she threw a small fit. Why marry, she complained, to sleep alone? Hale could offer no compromise. Body heat, he explained, smothered him. To breathe he needed a nest of empty space. Lonely in sleep, Diana chased her new husband all over the bed. Some mornings Hale woke up curled like a cat at the foot of the mattress, trying to escape.

Silk, they discovered, cooled her heat. Now they slept like

spoons. And Diana dressed extravagantly for bed, ordering lavish gowns from expensive catalogues as if for a party no one else was invited to. Her favorite saleswoman at Frost's called her up when something new came in. When the gowns were soiled she sent them to the cleaners. The Lucios treated the gowns like museum pieces.

Pressing against his mouth, she lifted her hips. When he made his first move, she'd drawn away, feigning sleep. Nothing Hale couldn't ignore, anyway he knew better. To make sure, he'd raised up and checked. As he'd thought, her eyelids were jumping.

Their nights were like music, every night the same song, to the same beat. *Guilt, remorse, regret* went the refrain. *Guilt, remorse, regret* and then *regret, regret, regret.*

She dragged her fingers across his shoulder and laid her strong wide palm on his wingbone. Pressing the tender spot beside his spine, she settled in. Her breathing deepened. Hale recognized the signs. She was serious now; she would get there. He moved to a new place, slightly off-center and over to one side.

For a horseman Sunday was like any other day. Horses still had to be watered and fed, mares palpated, hay bags hung, stalls mucked out. Most Sundays they went to the track. But when they did not, as they were not going to today, Hale took a break, slept past six, gave the stable-hands the day off. More often than not he cooked a special breakfast and dawdled over the papers; in the afternoon sometimes he even took a nap. For a man raised staunch Baptist, six days on and one off seemed an appropriate arc of time—harder on the work end, skimping on pleasure—one of those beneficent limitations which, like marriage, made a man feel not trapped but more free.

Past the end of Hale and Diana's bed, Diana's desk—a table really—sat pushed against the side wall, on the wall above the table charts and diagrams, photographs torn from books and magazines, postcards she liked—two of Virginia

Woolf, one in luminous youth, another in dark and frightened middle age—newspaper stories and pictures—an under-six-foot basketball player leaping past defenders to make a basket, a nonchalant Baryshnikov as blithely midair as if he lived there, Carl Lewis landing heels-first in the dirt to set a long-jump record.

Alongside the pictures and postcards were outdated notes to herself—snatches of torn yellow second-sheet paper written on in a hasty scrawl—newspaper stories of outrageous behavior, headlines she found either ironic or shocking, fashion pictures from glossy magazines, models in unwearable clothes posed in impossibly contorted positions. Tiny holes dotted the wall where other odd scraps and messages once had hung.

Diana played tricks on herself, made lists, devised mental bribes. She did not want to be like her mother. One of her most vivid childhood memories was of Gloria in the car, rolling down the window, tossing the Sunday papers out onto the Gulf Freeway, never looking back. In the backseat, Diana and Fanny watched as the papers flew by. Fanny, only five, maybe six at the time, giggled behind her hand. Diana, older by five years and by far the most serious member of her family, ducked down and hid. At the wheel, Duncan Dubard, Fanny's father and Gloria's third husband, said nothing. Duncan just drove.

Diana had bought one of those time-organizing diaries; it was all but blank. Hale used to lecture her about the pleasures of daily routines. The lectures only depressed her and did no good; anyway he'd given up trying to be her teacher.

Books were piled on the work table like a fortress around her typewriter, stacks of white paper and yellow second sheets wedged between the piles. Beside the second sheets, a blue enamel cup was filled with pens and pencils. Next to the cup sat a black coffee mug with two fingers of stale coffee left in it. Under the table, the computer Hale had bought Diana, still in its box.

Playing a game with herself, making believe she was on a road going nowhere, nothing called orgasm to expect or hope for, Diana moved her hips more slowly, in circles, then side to side. *Play,* she reminded herself. With her fingers she pressed Hale's back, relaxed then pressed again. No longer impatient—this was the moment he cherished, just before she came—Hale stayed where he was.

Downstairs, beneath them, their son, Roger, lay sprawled across his high school twin bed. On his bedside table, a small radio played all-night rock and roll. He had left his light on. In a motel ashtray beside the radio were piles of gray ashes. He'd been to Austin the night before, alone, gliding from bar to bar. Home at three, he'd smoked a joint to get to sleep. Gorgeous face turned to one side, cheekbone resting on a tanned and very muscular arm, the boy slept unshakably, the deep nightly blackout of a child safe at home with his parents.

It began to happen, the folding, unfolding, layer after layer, lapping over and under, making slow curls which turned to peaks, then rose. How Hale envied women the complexity of their unraveling, how privileged he felt to play a part in it. The tradeoff was plain enough. Men got speed and reliability, women mystery and distance. He did not move, did not push but made her come to him, ask for more.

Cradling his ears with her hands, she pressed down, opened up, made her sounds. Of all the men she had been with, only Hale moved her this strongly, only with her husband did it happen this quickly, a fact she neither understood nor particularly liked but there it was: after twenty-six years she still dreamed of the two of them, straining away in a public place, the children and others watching. Without his plastic Baggies of secret weed, not even Jesse could find the last door within her.

Hale changed neither his rhythm nor the intensity of his pressure. For twenty-six years he had pursued this woman, his wife, Diana Beauchamp Caldwell—pronounced Beechum in the Louisiana way—waiting as she turned zombie in his presence and then, for no apparent cause connected to time or reasons, came back again. Proximity guaranteed nothing. He could be in the same room with Diana and not know where she was. But here, now, she was with him. Here, now, he had her, with or without her approval or her permission.

When she could take no more, she lowered her hips, slid her hands to his jawbone, laced her fingers around his chin and lifted it.

"Rest."

"I'm not finished."

"It hurts."

"How can it hurt?"

She covered her pubic bone. "I don't know, I can't explain. Come up here."

He moved up the bed until they were face to face.

"Morning, glory."

She wiped his mouth. "I was asleep."

"You were not."

"I was trying."

"You were playing like."

"How do you know?"

"Your eyes were jumping."

"You smell like me."

"Nectar of the goddess."

"Put it in."

She threw her arms up over her head and curled her hands, palm up, on the pillow. Along the fold of a lifeline lay a pale pubic hair. Taking both wrists in one hand Hale found a Y-shaped callus between the index and middle finger of her right hand and rubbed it. He shifted his hips and, without using his hands, did as he was told.

Her palms were wide, her wrists frail, her knuckles so large she wore a man-sized ring. Peasant hands and royal wrists were a combination which in a way defined Diana, that blend of frailty and strength, as if one had been wrongly attached to the other, like the box game children play, making points by adding anatomical parts to the picture of a skeleton until an entire, mismatched body has been created. She was strong in the major areas. Only her connections failed her: joints, knees, spine, a tricky elbow she'd learned to put back in place when it dislocated.

Keeping a low center of gravity, his movement eased and sweetened by her pleasure and his saliva, Hale slid against her breasts and stomach and the bunched folds of her gown until the bunched-up knot of what he thought of as his very *self*—his restlessness and the tedium of the long night, sleeping, not sleeping, watching the green numbers of the digital clock, thinking about what he always thought about in the middle of the night, Red, Bethany and money, money, Bethany and Red—poured out of him.

He let his weight drop and released her wrists. Diana locked her arms around his back, held him, cupped his buttocks, bent her head, briefly sucked his tit, let him go.

Downstairs Roger stirred, turned over. The radio had drifted from the station. Without opening his eyes, he turned it off and dove back down into black sleep.

He was twenty-four. He had come home from California to spend Christmas with his family and help out with Bethany. That was seven months ago and Roger still had no plans to leave. As for Bethany, who knew?

On Diana's bedside table, more books. A hardcover Volume 5 of the diaries of Virginia Woolf and a number of paperbacks, all except one mysteries. The exception was *Change Partners and Dance,* a book about shifting psychological patterns in the American family. Although the book had come highly recommended, so far Diana had found nothing in it she didn't already know. On the floor, a stack of magazines. *Vogue, The New Yorker, Texas Gardener, Horticulture,* a *Farmer's Almanac,* a literary journal, still in its plastic mailing wrapper. Angled across the magazines, a yellow legal pad, clipped to it a blue felt-tip pen.

On Hale's table, the last few issues of *Quarter Horse Track* and several *Time* magazines—one of them two months old— the new *Blood-Horse* and several copies of *Quarter Racing Record,* a thick hardcover book about fads and the madness of crowds which he read a bit of every night. Last night he had finished the chapter on the tulip craze. The mania for bulbs reminded him of some of the schemes he had gotten caught up in himself, the strip shopping center, gold, the dish antennas, the motorized water skis. From history Hale was trying to learn, even though he knew that mostly history did no good. On the floor, mysteries, biographies—one of Jeb Stuart he'd been meaning to get to for a year—also a stack of easy-to-read paperbacks about espionage and adventure in which games played for high stakes were won by the bold- est player.

Every night they read themselves to sleep. Some nights they pretended, lying side by side staring into the darkness. Often Diana gave up. In her nightgown she roamed the house, reading, folding clothes, drinking from small brown bottles of mineral water.

Beyond their feet, a large bay window framed the coun- tryside. Directly beneath the window lay the slope the house was built on, then the vegetable garden and deer fence, on the other side of the fence the pasture, beyond the pasture the famously beautiful hill country of central Texas. Rib- boned with the first streaks of dawn, the sky had barely begun to brighten, shifting from its nightly blue-purple to a pale, watery mauve.

The air was cool, a tease. By ten the charade would be over. By noon the July heat would have clamped down on them like a jar on a grasshopper. Afternoons, sidewalks and backyards all over the hill country were deserted, as people went inside to take naps or watch afternoon soaps in air- conditioned living rooms, sitting in the dark, waiting out the hottest part of the day.

From two ranches away, a peacock screamed.

Hale rolled lightly across Diana's hipbone and found the floor with his foot.

Diana stared at the ceiling and tried to recall a dream. With her hands she pressed her gown, refolding the pleats.

On his side, the boy took up most of his bed. The sole of one foot rested against the other knee, the knee crisscrossed in scars. He had not heard a thing. As their room was directly above his, sometimes they woke him. He was old enough not to mind but after all they were his parents. It didn't matter how old he was. He didn't want to hear them.

· 2 ·

*H*ale pulled back his foreskin and without waiting for the water to warm, splashed himself, moving the loose flap of skin back and forth, making certain to wash in and out of every crevice. Mimi Caldwell had drilled advice into her son earlier than he could remember: pull back your foreskin, eat vegetables, brush your teeth, wash your hands. Hale could not remember a time when his mother's lessons hadn't been as much a part of his life as the color of his eyes and hair.

He used no soap. Sometimes even Ivory inflamed his delicate skin. He'd been to dermatologists; some said stress, others allergies or contact dermatitis. After reading in a health magazine that aluminum residue caused skin rashes and Alzheimer's disease, Diana had made holes in the bottoms of all her aluminum pans and put plants in them. They had replaced the aluminum with cast iron and stainless steel. Hale washed new clothes before wearing them. They used baby detergent and double rinses in the laundry; he wore no polyester or wool.

Nothing worked. Lotions eased the dryness. Drugs and salves soothed the fiery attacks of itching. But there was no prevention and no cure.

"I've never known how you could stand that." Diana sat on the toilet.

"Stand what?"

"That cold water. Why don't you wait?"

He stood back from the sink. "Gotta be a pro, my dear." He did a charming and awkward little dance step. His penis flapped. "Gotta be a man in this world."

Diana rolled her eyes. "Oh, you" was all she could think of to say.

He was forty-eight but looked younger. His belly was flat, his hipbones a hatrack, the muscles in his long legs like planks of wood. Bottom, Hale called his strength. Without bottom, he said, a man—like a horse—could never let down or slackness would catch up and take him.

He turned back to the mirror and, as if he did not give two cents for the way he looked, casually brushed his sandy hair off his forehead. The lift of his eyebrows gave him away; the angle of his face as he greeted the mirror with what he thought of as his best look.

Diana went to the sink and stood beside him.

People said they looked alike. People said they looked so much alike they might be brother and sister. It wasn't true, not feature by feature, only in build and general bone structure, tallness, thinness, fair-headedness. But in those ways yes, there were similarities.

They'd met in college, Austin, the University of Texas, he an engineering major who did not make a grade less than A his first two years, she an honor student in accelerated English. Perfectionists both, they were known on campus as icebergs, too rule-bound and repressed. Diana and Hale thought the same thing but so what? People were different then; it was a different time; people believed in destiny and character and fixed personality, in fate and beneficent limitations. Nobody thought you could make up your mind to be some other kind of person and then just go out and be it, nobody.

In imagination before and after the fact, neither of them

would have expected to have fallen for the other. Until Diana—
and since—Hale was drawn either to small doll-like girls or
to what he thought of as the after-hours bloomer: large,
mildly slovenly women with big breasts and an easy, raucous
laugh. Diana had envisioned herself in love with an ethnic
type, small and dark, a little neurotic in a citified way. Hale
was the only light-haired man she had been attracted to,
Diana the first brainy woman Hale dared ask out.

He had that abstracted look—still did—as if he knew more
than he was saying. Those huge blue eyes, that Dick Tracy
jawbone, that chin of his, stiff as a cup. As a girl Diana was
pale and ribbony. She kept her long, naturally ash-blond hair
off her face with two serviceable tortoise-shell barrettes and
wore careful clothes: A-line skirts, soft sweaters, thin socks
and loafers.

Neither dated much. Hale occasionally, Diana not at all.
They met at the library, both having rushed in near closing
time to check out a source book for a research paper. Reaching for the same drawer at the same time their thumbs touched.
Surprised, they gasped, drew back their hands and began to
apologize, a whispery you-take-the-drawer-no-you routine
which went on until they felt silly and had to laugh. At that
point, they looked more carefully at each other and thought
they saw, behind the blue eyes in his case, the gray-green in
hers, something in the other that was the same as themselves.
Their first date was like bumper cars on Saturday night car-
nival ride, slam-bang. All spring, in Hale's car, bony legs
entwined, they explored lust, secrecy, sex, and each other.
He wooed her with chocolate-covered graham crackers, she
charmed him with her hidden passion. During summer school,
they married—at the J.P.'s house, not church, for which blas-
phemy Hale's mother still blamed Diana—hoping, believing
actually the way so-called good young people did in those
days, that lust between two such upstanding citizens would
be transformed into the better thing, into whatever love turned
out to be.

With one finger, Hale dabbed expensive prescription lotion on a recurring itchy spot on his chin. He worked his jaw. The tiniest patch could drive him crazy. The lotion was cool. It smelled medicinal. He shivered.

Although he had given up on external connections to church, Hale was as hard on himself as his upbringing demanded. Even though as a boy he'd gone every Sunday, once he quit he didn't miss church, only the singing; once his voice changed and deepened he'd been an undistinguished if dependably on-key baritone. The third Sunday of every month he and the others in the choir used to pack into a schoolbus and go to a county singing convention, at which some twenty or more choirs sang a cappella outside all afternoon and afterward had dinner on the grounds, then went back home on the buses, stuffed. That was a fine time. The music lifted Hale's spirits and made him feel, uncharacteristically, a part of the oneness of the universe. Some Sunday evenings even now he took his portable radio up to bed with him and listened to an all-night gospel show broadcast by a far-off border station he could get only late at night. Eyes closed, wearing spongy earphones, he sang along.

Catching her looking at him, he shrugged. "What can I tell you?" he said. "You gotta be a pro." His blue eyes flashed. Sex—success—made him bold.

Diana nudged him with her hip and reached for her hairbrush. Hale went into the bedroom.

Her hair was a bird's nest, her skin drawn and pale. She'd turned forty-seven in April. Until this year she had not allowed herself to think about age, but now she could not escape it. There was the physical evidence—droops around the eyes, the lined neck—but physically she felt about the same. It was the loss of spirit that got to her. The emotional downslide. Guilt and remorse drained out hope. Regret sucked juices from the glands. With age she'd gained a certain amount of command over the way she looked for the first time in her

life, but confidence and stylishness hardly seemed a fair ex-
change for the rest.

Tender-headed, she laid one hand alongside her scalp to
keep from pulling at it. Her haircut was new, short and lightly
permed. She'd also let her beautician talk her into lightening
the color, taking it from its now natural mousy brown a few
shades closer to what it once had been, that lost pale ash
blond.

She stretched her neck and ran her fingers down the edge
of the lace strap of her gown. From within the branches of
her collarbone a blister of skin crept out, a tiny place, only
a nick. The scar had healed strangely. Instead of turning white
it had retained its raw pinkness, like a wad of chewed
bubblegum. Diana gently pressed the scar with her finger. A
not unpleasant chill ran through her.

"You want to give Red a go?"

She lifted her finger. Like Hale, she was thin. She kept her
weight below 120 so that she could ride the two-year-olds.
With the babies she had a touch, light but sure. Even Pito
had to admit it. She went to the bathroom door.

"Now?"

Hale pulled on a knit shirt, frowned and put on his glasses.
When he ground his teeth, a muscle near his temple came
up, a small egg moving in circles.

"Do you have time?"

"You make the coffee. I'll be right down." She went to
the sink for her toothbrush.

In his time, Pito Badillez had been a real race rider; he had
the pictures from Columbus, Evangeline and Ruidoso to prove
it. After suffering several bad wrecks—a broken collarbone,
bruised liver, hoofprints on his thigh, pin holding bones together—he'd lost his nerve. Pito had a family now. He thought
too much to be a jockey. At the track, Hale used someone
either younger or just naturally brasher. Pito trained for Hale,
taught his horses to rate and how to hold their heads, to

behave in the gates and break. Pito had great hands. His rubdown mixture—a secret recipe of vinegar, alcohol, Absorbine Jr. and coffee—worked better on a horse's sore shins than any expensive cure-all on the market.

But Pito was touchy. He didn't like other people riding his horses. Diana rode either early before he came, late after he had left, or on Sundays.

Ducking his head to miss the star light over the landing, Hale went down the stairs. On his way to the kitchen, he straightened the painted metal Haitian sculpture hanging over the fireplace.

He did not want to be the kind of person who thought in terms of luck, fate and portents, for ill or good. He couldn't help it. Fatalism was a reflex. There were times he couldn't keep himself from thinking that whatever was up there—whoever, whatever—had it in for him. Fate, God, luck, whatever.

When he let the Haitian sculpture go, it swung back crooked again.

Illuminated Red 1 had been the most promising two-year-old Hale had had since Dash Too. Casey Koenig, his horse conditioner and best hand, said that Red was a perfect filly, just perfect. Then in March she'd shinbucked.

Hale whirled the rheostat to high. A rectangle of track lights came on, lighting up the kitchen like a chicken coop.

In the quarter-horse racing business, the big money was in futurities, and two-year-olds. Red had been a February foal. When she was a full two, the vet pronounced her sound. They'd taken her to a schooling race in Goliad. When the gates opened, Red flew. Early speed was in her background and so her performance in the starting gates was not surprising, but there was no way to know if the speed would hold. Red didn't stop flying until she crossed the finish line. After another schooling race, they ran her in a 300-yard futurity at Manor Downs. Red won by daylight. Then in

March, after running a 93-speed index in Bandera, she came up sore. The vet said maybe it was because of a soft spot in the track and maybe she was just too young, maybe her knees hadn't closed up after all. At any rate, coming out of the gates, she'd bucked her shins, that sheath of muscle covering her shinbone having peeled from the bone as easily as wrapping paper from a Popsicle.

Hale had had Red blistered, Casey nursed her. By late April the blisters had healed. Physically Red was fine. But she'd gone spooky on them. When they tried to put her in the gates, she went crazy. Hunting boogers, Casey said. Red was as intelligent a colt as any Hale had ever been around, and that was the problem. She remembered too much.

He took yesterday's paper cone of grounds from the coffeemaker and dumped it in the compost pail. The pail was full, its contents rank. He replaced the top on the pail and fastened the latches that held it shut.

They'd had the kitchen renovated and outfitted with fancy new equipment. Diana was uncomfortable with such grand efficiency but Hale loved it, the icemaker, the hidden ventilator hood and under-counter lights, the double ovens that switched from radiant to convected heat. He liked to work the appliances for people, to show them off. The romance of purposeful shabbiness, so adored by Diana and her friends, escaped his understanding altogether. He'd lived with shabbiness enough to last him a lifetime.

He washed the coffeepot.

In the middle of Red's weanling year, Hale's money man and partner, Marvin Thoede, had nominated the filly for the quarter-horse Triple Crown. Because most of the purse money came from owners, the nominations had picked a fair amount of cash from Marvin's pockets. Then Red got hurt. Languishing in her stall, she'd already missed the Rainbow and the Kansas Futurities. But the All-American was still ahead. Marvin had not only paid Red up in that one, he'd nominated her in advance, to take the discount. He'd been that sure of her.

Hale spooned decaffeinated coffee beans into the grinder. The All-American was run on Labor Day, the purse a cool million dollars. To adjust to the altitude, Red needed to be in New Mexico six weeks before the preliminary trials. At least Labor Day was late this year; even so, she'd barely make it.

But barely was going to have to do. Red was going to the All-American. With oil and real estate down the tubes, a million-dollar purse at stake and Marvin already some $2,000 into this race—not to mention the other two thousand for the Kansas and the Rainbow—if there was one sure fact about Illuminated Red 1's short life it was that she was leaving Texas to go to Ruidoso, New Mexico, by the end of the week, spooky or not.

Hale put the ground-up beans in the filter cone, filled the well of the machine with water and turned on the switch.

Locating a pair of jeans in the bottom of her closet, Diana shook them, then gingerly directed a foot down into one leg. Before moving to the hill country she'd never seen a scorpion in her life. One day she'd put on a pair of shoes she kept by the back door without checking. One sting was enough to make her cautious forever.

The jeans were properly tight. Hurriedly she zipped them, slipped a green T-shirt over her head, pulled her jeans' leg up, put her boots on, pulled her jeans' leg down and knotted a bandanna at the base of her head. She had started down the stairs when she remembered her legal pad. She went back for it.

When Hale awakened her she was entertaining herself with one of those halfway fancies on the surface of the conscious mind. The dream had been about Bethany, the two of them engaged in a chatty conversation—school, clothes, the latest fashions—like a TV-sitcom version of mom and daughter.

She started down the stairs. The dream had made her hopeful. She could smell the coffee brewing and hear the electric drip pot growl. She wondered if Bethany was still sleeping.

· 3 ·

*A*fter Hale sold Dash Too and made up his mind to leave Houston, he and Diana had looked for a house for more than two years, each with certain, not always compatible priorities in mind. Diana wanted windows, a view, proximity to city life and a college, a decent grocery store with decent lettuce and bread, not just iceberg and Mrs. Baird's. Hale needed improved land, a flat area for a training track, if possible an existing barn. They agreed on topography. Having grown up in unyieldingly flat land—she in midtown hopeful Houston, he in the unforgiving plains of West Texas—they longed if not for a hill then at least a slope; some roll to the land, a sense of the difficulty of the upward climb, the ease of the downhill run.

There were the children to think of—five and twelve when Hale proposed the idea, seven and fourteen when they finally moved—schools, transportation, the effect of the move on their lives. But Hale and Diana had no set child-rearing philosophy—no real ideas about being parents—and so they did not consider the children's needs first. Caught between the authoritarianism of the preceding generation and the increasingly free-thinking methods of the present, they waffled, shrugged, then went along with the new.

If pushed, they would have said they believed in a basic neighborhood upbringing and public schools—school as more a process of socialization than pure learning, public education as a fair way to give all children the same chances. As parents Hale and Diana took each crisis as it came, with no particular overview. Hale was busy, first with his work, then his horses, Diana with her books, her papers, her love affairs. They loved their children, read to them, overindulged them. It seemed enough. When Diana read *Summerhill* she thought she'd discovered certain truth: they would let the children decide for themselves when and how fast to grow up.

After an uneventful, fifteen-year career as a designing engineer in the offices of an offshore drilling rig company, Hale finally escaped Houston and his job by cashing in on the fruits of an educated guess. He knew about racing quarter horses, having been around them all his life. For something to do as much as anything, he bought a mare from the backyard of a jakeleg trainer serving time on an income-tax-evasion rap. The mare had run a little. She looked promising.

"Mamie Rae's a good brood mare," the trainer's wife told him. "She's got Top Deck on one side and Go Man Go on the other, so she ought to be. My husband, Sidney Mouton, you know Sid? Everybody knows Sid, he started jockeying over to Lafayette when he wasn't but forty-nine pounds. Sid said keep her but I can't." The trainer's wife stood in the back door, her arms folded across her chest in a helpless way. "I just can't," she repeated. And then, as if to warn Hale not to try to take undue advantage, she narrowed her eyes. "Top Deck on one side," she reminded him. "Go Man Go on the other." Hale paid the woman on the spot.

The first two years Mamie Rae bore decent offspring. Hale sold the colts as yearlings.

The third year, he bred Mamie to a classy stallion in Seguin named Dash Ahead. Having injured his cannon bone in a freak pile-up of green colts, Dash Ahead had been retired to stud before going to the track, and so his fee was low. When Dash Too was born Hale held on to him. When the colt was two he hired a trainer.

They all used to go see Too run. Diana fixed picnic lunches, took books to read between races. Roger never liked the track much but Bethany loved it. She could always find kids to run with, games to play, who could jump the highest, the fastest, the farthest. In winner's-circle pictures Roger is usually frowning. Bethany, blond and chunky, in somebody's arms, is all smiles. When Dash Too showed what he was made of, Hale paid the colt's entry fees in futurities outside of Texas, in the states which had parimutuel betting. Dash Too blazed holes in track records all over Oklahoma and New Mexico.

Before the All-American, Hale sold the colt to a syndicate for a quarter of a million dollars. Too did not win the All-American but he showed. Third place won back the syndicate's original investment; the next year the colt won the derby and the next the syndicate retired him to stand at stud. Dash Ahead's stud fee went up tenfold. Everybody profited.

Hale's father thought he was crazy to give up a steady white-collar job for the insecurity and the unpredictable dailiness of horses.

"It's stupid," Claude Caldwell said with the incorruptible certainty he brought to any discussion, whether he knew anything about the subject or not. "You get a college degree and look at you, back with those damned horses. You'll be sorry, Hale," he warned. "You'll have a fire. They'll all burn up alive. Some damn virus will come along and take every last one of them. Foal pneumonia will smother the life out of your colts. And by God, you'll be sorry."

Hale's father had quit school in the fourth grade to go to work in a belt-buckle factory. When he was old enough he got a better job at an oil refinery where he stayed, doing shiftwork—days one week, three-to-elevens the next, then graveyards, double shifts when he could get them—for forty-seven years. During the Depression he'd made fifteen cents an hour—Hale had heard about that often enough—and when Claude's older brother, Alvin, couldn't find work at all, he'd come to live with them. Claude Caldwell thought a man ought to embrace security like the Prodigal Son. The only risk he ever took was horses. Sunday afternoons after church they used to load up the horse trailer and drive to a town called Mindeola together, Hale, his father, his uncle Alvin.

There were no grandstands at Mindeola Downs, just folding chairs. The bathrooms were so dark you could not see the drain in the urinals. The track was slightly canted. Inclined toward the finish line, during rainy seasons it drained fast. In the concession stand, ladies from town fried hamburgers, greasy and delicious. Match races were put together as the afternoon went on: my horse against yours, so many yards. Beside the track was a dance hall, painted bright orange. From the horse barn you could hear music from the Mindeola Ballroom jukebox: country for cowboys, salsa for the Mexicans, zydeco for Cajuns. Hale was thin as a spear in those days, with long arms that hung to his knees and hands like a catcher's mitt. He stuck close to his father, stayed away from knife fights and listened to the men, most of them poor and uneducated like his father, as they leaned on fences trading dreams and lies. At the rail and around the paddock, gamblers circulated. "I like the one horse," a bookie would say. "I like the one," in a kind of chant. "I like the evens, who wants the odds." "I'm taking number three, giving light. Taking three. Giving light."

When his father worked days, Hale and his uncle Alvin took over. Together, they hauled whatever horse they were running to Mindeola. Hale never got it right, not once, not even if the horse won. Claude Caldwell refused to give his only son his blessings, however hard his son tried.

Ignorance was a curse. For the injustices in his father's life

Hale had sympathy and some understanding. But he couldn't help it that he had not had to work for fifteen cents an hour himself. And that was the only way, he'd finally decided, he could prove himself man enough to please Claude Caldwell.

Difficulty and risk suited Hale's temperament. He liked to have his feet set within the unforgiving click of time: seasons, weather, gestation periods, birth, death. There was always something. A barn to build, a horse to buy or sell, some new virus to watch out for. As his mother often—regularly—told him, "Whatever *can* happen with horses *will*."

But those were the risks. A shot at a big score made the risks worthwhile. Wasn't anything better than forty-seven years of shiftwork? Hale's mother had never been to the track in her life. She had never seen Hale's horses run and would never. She was a Baptist.

When Hale and Diana finally found the house—set on sixty-eight acres, twenty-two miles from Austin on a farm-to-market road between Kyle and Driftwood—it satisfied them both. There was space for barns, a flat area for a training track, a great house. Much of the land surrounding the house had already been cleared of scrub brush and planted in coastal and buffalo grass.

On the advice of an architect friend, Diana had had the house opened up, walls ripped out, replaced with glass. Now the walls were mostly windows. From any room she could look out and see the ghostly landscape of the surrounding hill country, the dark, stunted wind-gnarled trees, the pale whiskery buffalo grass and white limestone, the dangerously spined cactus and fields of white poppies. In winter, clumps of mistletoe hung like Christmas stockings from wet, leafless black limbs. In spring, fields of wine cups, as startlingly colored as a rock star's lips, all but stopped her heart.

They'd bought the house from a former blackjack dealer who'd moved his family from Reno to what he'd been told was the garden spot of Texas. The blackjack dealer had switched from playing cards to smoke alarms. He'd also dab-bled in real estate and imported cheeses. When Hale and Diana came to see the house, a ruby-colored Porsche was still parked out front, even though none of it had worked out, not real estate, smoke alarms or cheese. Judgments were raining down on the blackjack dealer's head like hill country spring storms. His family had left. The house was being foreclosed.

A fault line ran through the countryside nearby, dividing it sharply. The house was on the hill-country side, where streams ran clear and topsoil thinned. Risky business, the gambler said, stroking his honey-blond beard and looking out over the countryside. When the earth splits, he warned them, anything can happen.

The blackjack dealer went back to Reno, where he said odds were easier to figure. He came back once, gunning a Harley-Davidson, a slim, dark-haired girl holding him around the waist. Were they, he wanted to know, interested in selling? Hale said no and the blackjack dealer went off again, not by the road but across the field between fences, spooking horses right and left.

When Hale and Diana moved in, Diana found aluminum TV-dinner trays in the garbage cans and books of leftover food stamps in the kitchen drawer. Doors to bedrooms had all been kicked in. She wondered if the blackjack dealer still had his Porsche.

· 4 ·

*T*he stairs were bare wood. With no carpet on the living room floor and no curtains on the windows, against the tile floor Diana's boot heels made a clicking sound which echoed.

She slapped her legal pad against her leg.

The center of the house—living room, combination kitchen and dining room—was large and open with high, vaulted ceilings and exposed dark beams. The fireplace had hearths on two sides, one for the living room, the other for the kitchen. The stones forming the fireplace had been gathered from around Wimberley and Blanco. They varied in color, from buff to gray to a pale, fleshlike pink.

Diana had had the wall-to-wall carpeting replaced with Mexican tile, the kitchen ripped out, the walls stripped and painted white to best display her Mexican masks and bark paintings, the brilliantly colored rugs and molas from Guatemala, the Day of the Dead clay pieces and tree-of-life candelabra from Mexico, the cheap papier-mâché dolls with glitter for earrings and a painted blank facial expression. Diana had no desire to be a collector and no nose for authenticity. Many of the pieces were the cheapest kind, readily available at any bordertown marketplace.

Hale stood by the coffee machine, watching it work.

Diana tossed the legal pad on the table. Hale ground his jaw.

"I only made two cups but it's slow. Have you vinegared this thing lately?" She did not answer. Hale lifted the pot, poured two cups and opened the refrigerator.

"Thank you." She accepted the carton of cream he held out to her. "We can make more later." She dumped in enough half-and-half to turn the black liquid pale brown, then put the carton back in the refrigerator. Holding her cup high to steady it, she started for the door. As she passed him, Hale reached for her.

"Wait." He took her by the shoulder. She lifted her cup, making too much of the gesture.

He set his coffee down. "Can you stop one minute."

"Of course." She widened her eyes to let him know she meant it. "What?"

There were rules, unspoken but firm. *You remind me of your mother* was off-limits, so was *of your father;* also, *when you do that you look just like your* . . . either parent.

"There's a worried look you have." Hale ran his hand across her forehead. "Here. You keep it most of the time." He lowered his hand to her jaw. "Except times like this morning. And horseback. When you ride, your face is free." He kissed her where he said the worried look was.

"Age. I'm old."

"Not age."

The wide eyes again. "Then what?"

"Hey." He held her face between his hands. "Ease up. It's me, remember?"

Diana leaned against him for a second, closed her eyes, pressed her forehead into his chest.

"Red." She straightened.

"Let Red go. We can read the papers. I'll fix breakfast tacos."

"We have to. I'm ready. You can cook later."

The lying between them was no more dense or complicated than between most people. They lied to keep things as they were; lied to each other with not half the intensity and willed ignorance with which they lied to themselves. Diana's *of course*—so like her mother—was breathy and impatient. It meant *if I must,* but this was a fact too thorny for her to acknowledge or even begin to admit to, and so she ignored it.

Last night's argument still lay between them. They were being careful with each other because of it.

Hale switched off the coffee machine and followed Diana out into the gray morning air.

"Come on, rain," he said to the heavens, although there was no sign of any.

On the porch, Rufus raised his big bony head and beat his tail against the floor. When Diana shot a glance in his direction, the lush red dog got up and went with them.

· 5 ·

Bethany-Belinda Beauchamp Caldwell sat by her window looking out. Not that there was anything to see out there she hadn't seen a thousand times before. Looking out was just something to do.

Mostly she was thinking. About names, the important ones. Gloria, Diana, Mimi, Fanny. She had changed hers but she was having a hard time remembering. When people called her Bethany she still turned around.

She was in her pajamas, pink and short with ruffles around a scooped neckline. By seven-thirty she was supposed to be dressed, down to socks and shoes. In twenty minutes she would be breaking the rules.

Diana said Hale sent the pajamas but that was a lie. Cedar Hills was the garbage dump as far as her father was concerned; she might as well have that tree out there as Hale Caldwell for a father.

She slid her hand beneath the pillow covering the windowseat and felt for her prize, fingering its silver scalloped edge.

She was not sure why she had taken the knife; mostly, she thought, just because it was there.

Try telling that to Diana. Or Hale. Everybody else in her family was too white-swan perfect to understand that stealing was reverse process, an act that stemmed more from an inability *not* to do a thing than the other way around.

She lifted her legs to the windowseat and, clasping her knees as close to her chest as they would go, grabbed hold of her toes. For a special treat, she'd painted her nails a bright blue with a white dot in the middle. She liked to look at them, ten far-off tiny skies with a moon in the middle.

Her parents didn't care about names or family, they acted like they'd invented themselves from out of the blue. That was one reason Bethany liked Mexicans. When there was a family gathering Mexicans turned out in droves, everybody drinking beer and having fun, the weddings with the dance after, the sweet-sixteen parties with the flower arch and the tiara. When Mexicans got together, they got together.

Other parents would arrive at noon on the dot. Not Diana. Maybe twelve-fifteen, twelve-thirty, a quarter to one, whenever she got around to it she'd sashay down the walk, skirt going *swish* like Rose Narcisco.

Cedar Hills was not called what it was, prison or the Nutty-Brown Nuthouse. It also did not look like its real self but a high-class resort hotel. The only thing missing was a swimming pool and they were talking about building one, if they could figure out how to blast through the limestone without blowing the place to bits. There was no truth in Cedar Hills Therapeutic Community anywhere. It was all pure baloney.

The buildings were arranged like a wagon wheel, in the center the administration building, dining room and kitchen, all fake-Spanish adobe white with red clay roofs and brown trim around the windows. Ranging out from the center were smaller buildings in the same style, decks, plants, big windows. Inside, white walls, modern furniture, aquariums in the walls. Each unit housed eight wacko kids and a resident shrink. The wackos were supposed to feel like brothers and sisters. This *arrangement,* as it was called, was supposed to create a *normal* feeling of family. As if normal existed. Or family. The kids sat around watching the cartoon-colored fish going back and forth inside the glass, as bored and restless as the bored wacko kids.

Kids were not fooled. Maybe parents but parents were easy. Hang up a few plants, use words like enlightened and progressive, parents fell all over themselves. Kids were smarter. Whatever it looked like they were up to, the kids at Cedar Hills were all doing the same thing, waiting to go home.

The creek was bone-dry; even Bethany had noticed, who couldn't care less about nature. She and her friend Bobby Neuhaus had gone down to look. Bobby had taken a sip of what water there was. He said it tasted funny, like skin. Skin? she'd said. *Skin?* Sometimes Bobby could be very Nutty Brown.

The footpath to her unit—14—was made of rocks from the nearby hillsides, sunk into the ground. The rocks were supposed to look like they grew there. The grass around the path was Astroturf and so it stayed green with or without rain.

A girl came down the path, Tiffany Leberman, known at Nutty Brown as Miss Boo-hoo. Tiffy wiped her eyes on her sleeve.

She'd have on one of those blouses she liked, sheer with puffed sleeves, maybe embroidered. Diana spent a mint on clothes, so did Hale, but not on himself. Hale liked to see his Di dressed up. Bethany liked blue jeans and T-shirts, cut-offs when it was warm. Alex liked the way she dressed. If anybody in her whole life had ever loved Bethany Caldwell it was Alex Hurtado.

Tiffany came up the steps, spraying Binaca on her tongue. With permission from home Cedar Hills allowed kids to smoke but since most kids didn't want their parents to know, they sneaked. The front door opened, closed.

Bethany ran her hand down her breasts to her waist, up and down and in and out. She'd gained a lot of weight since she'd been at Cedar Hills. Diana hated fat like a cockroach.

Bethany wasn't crazy about it either. She would like to be rid of the extra weight but it would take too long. The food was always there. At night she made vows, in the morning she ate. If Alex was around, well then. She'd be down to bones in no time.

She squinted her eyes. Whenever she started to go at herself, she pressed on her lids until everything went double and dark. Somehow when she did that the bad things moved back outside herself. Sealed off, she became indestructible again, rolling down the halls of Cedar Hills like a tank.

She smoothed her long straw-blond hair behind her ears. She'd already gotten word from the kitchen. Before seven, a furious woman in a hairnet stormed in.

"Me?" Bethany had said, pointing at her own chest. "A whole cake?"

She'd gone after midnight, not to steal the cake in particular, not to steal anything really, only to see if she could get in. There it was, on a butcher block, covered with aluminum foil, Happy Birthday Cedar Hills and a big "3."

The sky outside was blue, not a cloud. Beyond her unit, the rocky footpath veered off into the woods. In among the trees were private conference nooks. The P.C.N.'s had cement benches arranged inside a cleared space between trees with fake cement tree stumps for tables.

She'd rather be beaten up and put in solitary confinement. There were no bars or locks but even if you did get out there was nowhere to go except ten hot miles down 290 to Austin. Then what? Alex had gone to Mexico, so the Hurtados said. Bethany had heard he was in Del Rio. There was no fairness in the world, not anywhere. Maybe Russia but probably not.

She dropped her legs and kicked at the windowseat with her heels.

If she could hold out until January she'd check herself right out of here. Rose Narcisco had made a big mistake telling her that they could send her to prison when she was eighteen but they could not make her stay in the nuthouse. January tenth, she was history. Maybe she'd go to Del Rio and find Alex. Del Rio was a long way. She was also thinking of going back home, getting Roger Dodger out of the house, living with Hale and Diana forever.

"Belinda . . ."

"Yes, Doc." Bethany swung easily around, pretending not to be surprised. "What's up?"

The Rose checked her watch. "It's seven twenty-five and you aren't dressed, for one thing."

Bethany groaned. "I was getting ready to." She plucked at her pajama top. "You interrupted me."

"And I hear you have eaten the celebration cake."

This was new. Usually Rose beat around the bush. Having learned about warfare from all the Dungeons and Dragons she'd played with Bobby Neuhaus, Bethany took the offensive.

"Every time somebody eats something illegal around here, who gets blamed?" She punched at her chest. "Me. Always me."

To cut down on noise, bedroom doors had pneumatic pumps which automatically steamed them shut. Rose Narcisco held her foot against the door to keep it open. Short and stocky with a big chest, she was dressed for Sunday success, navy blue suit, white blouse with a flounce, low-heeled shoes. The skirts were a help to the kids. *Swish* against her pantyhose.

"Whenever you protest like this, Belinda . . ." She smiled her phoney-baloneyest smile.

"Yes ma'am?"

"I know you are guilty. Now get dressed. You know the rules."

She left, *swish!*

Funny stuff. Ordinarily, head-on collisions were unheard of at Nutty Brown Fruitcake.

The door steamed shut. Silent doors were a major disappointment at Cedar Hills. Bethany missed the slamming doors of home.

As she slid from the windowseat, Bethany dislodged the pillows. Against the metal, her bare legs made a sound. She rearranged the pillows, making certain the knife was covered. Moving toward the chest of drawers for her clothes, she flipped her long hair over her shoulder.

· 6 ·

*H*ale and Diana came to a curve in the road. Before them, a big gray rabbit bolted from the trees.

"Bang," Diana said, pointing an imaginary gun.

The rabbit disappeared.

Every night, in search of moisture and greenness, small animals sneaked from woody hideouts to raid her flowerbeds and vegetable garden. Rabbits munched leaves, armadillos uprooted plants. Deer could decimate a corn patch overnight. Diana had tried everything, mothballs, Pet-Away, aluminum foil pie pans, cayenne pepper. She felt like a vigilante. Death to small animals. The animals kept coming.

They came to the mare barn, which Hale himself had built out of gray cinder blocks, cedar posts and treated pine. The roof was tin, the floor plain dirt lined with the wood shavings he bought by the semi-load. There were eight stalls, a tack room not much bigger than a closet, a wide cool-down area with an electric walker. The barn was watertight and sturdy; he'd done a good job building it and had enjoyed the work. By the time he needed another he was too busy to take the time.

The newer barns were prefabricated Butler buildings with

concrete flooring in the walkways and built-in electric heaters and fans. In one he kept his two stud horses and his teasing stallion, in the other the colts and fillies in training. He'd planned to have a new barn built in the fall, so that he could separate the fillies from the colts, but with money so tight he didn't know. If Red ran up close in the All-American, then maybe.

When they'd moved to the country, Hale's first purchase had been mares, which he hauled around to stallions himself. And weren't those lonely times, always on the road. Other horsemen were suspicious. He was from Houston and even though he tried to talk like them, they knew he was educated. Eventually he leased a dun stallion named Sandman for a season; the next year he bought his own. Six months later, the appropriately named Dark Prospect died in his stall. Now he had two stud horses, a bay named Dangerous Species and Enlightened, a gray. The bay was a proven producer. So far Enlightened hadn't done much, but he was young and Hale was hopeful. He liked grays.

Except for Pearl, the mare barn was empty. Pearl was new and in foal for the first time. Hale was being careful with her.

At their approach, the horses in the training barn began to stamp and snort. Clean as a hospital, the barn smelled of wood shavings, horse manure, Absorbine Jr. and the antiseptic spray they used to keep down contagious diseases.

Red's gorgeous head hung out over her stall door. When she saw Hale, she began to whinny and snort. The blaze on her face, shaped like a perfect number one, went up and down. Hale's heart lifted.

Diana pointed out a wasps' nest in the hollows of the barn door, beside the hinge. From the knob of the tack room door, Hale took a pale yellow walking cane. Diana went inside the tack room, got a can of long-range insecticidal spray and went back out to kill the wasps.

Red nodded her head. Her beauty struck Hale like a slap,

every day. She was a glory, a prize; a gorgeous, unnatural gift. In the pasture, she sometimes reared up and, pawing the air, turned in a circle just for fun. "Like Trigger," Diana said. Watching Red run, Hale felt the way he had in college when he worked for hours on an equation until finally all the parts began to fit, the only way they could.

A horse like Red was a fluke, one of nature's majestic freaks. They didn't come along often; when they did all you could do was hold your breath and hope for the best.

He rubbed her nose. She nibbled his hand. Hale spoke to the horse in baby-talk falsetto.

"Give us a kiss." She nuzzled his cheek. Diana lingered behind to pet High Wire, a four-year-old gelding whose steadiness and lack of competitive spirit made him a perfect pony horse.

When Hale shoved at her head, Red took a step backwards. From a hook on her stall door he lifted her halter and went in.

The All-American was a quarter of a mile long, over and done with in twenty-one seconds and change. When the gates opened, to be in contention a horse had to be flying. Partly a clean break from the gates had to do with training, breeding, the jockey, the horse; a lot of it was plain luck. Hale had seen races lost before they were run when at the last moment a horse decided to spook at the shadow of a cloud on the track.

"Hey, girl, hey." He slipped Red's halter down over her face, stroked her flank and knelt beside her. Diana came in.

"Hold her, will you."

She took a firm grip on Red's halter. Red lifted her head, then settled. Diana smoothed her forelock and stroked her face, careful not to touch her topknot.

Hale began running his thumb along the filly's shinbone, pushing hard against the muscle.

"Hand me that stick."

Diana passed the cane to Hale.

Having grown up in the city, Diana had had no experience with race horses until after they'd moved. She did, however, know how to ride. Gloria thought riding would help her meet the right kind of Houston girl and so Diana had taken lessons in Memorial Park. She'd learned how to post and ride English, she'd worn the garb—jodhpurs, jacket, the velvet hat. She'd even won a few ribbons. When the horse they were renting— a brave old gelding named Cinnamon—died, Diana quit. She was bored with riding, and anyway the right kind of girls did not like her.

Red nickered.

"Anything?"

"So far so good."

He began knocking against the other leg. Red looked insulted and annoyed but not in pain.

Three years after they moved, Diana rode her first race horse, a smallish gelding named Bee's Dream. Bee's Dream was never going to be great. He was too short in the legs, too skimpy in the hindquarters and, Hale said, just too damned dumb. Hale never gave up on a horse until he had to— especially a horse that didn't have blue papers—but he was on the verge of getting rid of Bee when Diana asked to ride him. At first Hale refused and then—Bee was as gentle as a cat—relented.

He showed her what to do. She took Bee onto the track and galloped him around a few times. Hale was pleased to see Diana taking an interest in the horses but at first he did not take her interest seriously.

He stood. "Don't let's push her hard, okay? Just blow her out a little." He smoothed the hair on Red's belly.

"From the gates?"

Hale went to get a bridle.

"Just warm her up, then gallop her twice around." He slipped the bit between Red's teeth and buckled the bridle under her throat, pulled her forelock out from under the headband and steadied her, telling her to *whoa* and hold up. "No gates."

"I could walk her through."

He bent to inspect Red's right front shoe. Red backed away.

"*Whoa* now, Red. I said *whoa*."

Hale smacked Red's leg. The horse grew still. She offered her foot. With a hoof-pick, he dug a piece of gravel out of her hoof, near the frog. He straightened. "Not today," he said. His face was flushed. He led Red from the stall. "We don't want to push her too fast. Here."

Hale handed Diana the reins and laid a blue-plaid blanket on Red's back. Sometimes he worried how long his strength would hold out. The stamina he'd built up as a boy could not last forever. Someday he'd start to feel old, then what? He straightened the blanket, laid the saddle on top of it. He couldn't afford to think too far ahead.

As canny as a beauty queen, Red prettily bowed her neck. The other horses set up a racket.

"They're not happy about this."

Hale bent to inspect the girth, tightened, buckled it.

"They think I'm starving them to death."

In the distance, goats babbled. Blackbirds wheeled and shouted. A cardinal whistled nonstop. From two miles away, the peacock cursed the air as if in furious response to the cardinal's incessant sweetness.

Suddenly the birds and animals grew quiet. There was no wind.

Diana watched Hale's deft, careful hands, his fingernails bitten to the quick.

In Houston before they moved, Diana had quietly begun to accumulate a scholarly reputation. She'd published a few pieces in academic quarterlies. The quarterlies were not widely read, but being in print at all amazed and pleased her. Those days, when Virginia Woolf was not as popular and feminist literary theories not well developed, a reputation was easier to come by. Even now, when conferences were held, she was sometimes invited.

"Ready?"

"Ready." She set her coffee cup on a fence post.

For the most part she did not miss scholarship. She had grown to dislike critical distance and theorizing. But writing was something she was good at—she had a knack for discovering the unexpected phrase, the unlikely connection—and she did like to teach: the students, the openness—never knowing how a semester would go—the engagement of the mind. The money, even though it wasn't much. The presence of Jesse.

Hale took the lead shank, handed Diana a leather helmet and led Red out of the barn. Diana put the helmet on over her bandanna and buckled it beneath her chin. Red nudged Hale from behind, pushing at his shoulder with her nose.

And there was Woolf herself, her quirky, cranky genius. Diana never taught *To the Lighthouse* without feeling moved, especially the gap in the center of the book representing the death of the mother. The students at the community college were often just this short of illiterate. Many worked full-time in addition to taking classes. Most were first-generation college attendants. They could not imagine why they should have to read the work of dead writers when all they wanted was a shot at a better-paying job. Often at her lectern, Diana felt like a proselytizing preacher, after their hearts and minds.

Missionary work had its satisfactions. She had actually reached some students. Some she had convinced to take their obvious intelligence seriously; a couple she had managed to arrange scholarships for, to better schools than the community college.

They cut through a path between the trees. At the opening in the low iron fence circling the track, Hale turned. In the helmet Diana looked like an obedient child, eager and expectant. He pulled Red to a halt.

When Bethany went to Cedar Hills, Diana had taken an unpaid leave, starting in the fall. She wasn't sure why; it just seemed the right thing to do. Hale said it wasn't. In June, she told the dean she'd changed her mind. Now she wasn't sure. She was going to have to let them know soon. They were stretching things to let her wait this long.

Hale held Red firmly. "Don't push too hard. See how she feels."

Money was a problem the two of them had never come close to solving. Diana hated not making any, Hale insisted it wasn't important. He wanted her to concentrate, he said, on finishing her dissertation. He could not, would never understand, she did not care two cents about finishing her dissertation.

Diana turned to the filly, placed her hands flat on Red's back, held up her left foot. Her arms were leathery brown from the sun, the muscles in her forearm ropy and well defined. Her skin was thin and papery; she would not, Hale knew, age well. She would get thinner, leaner, her joints crankier. On this score he had the advantage. But Hale had his own liabilities. High blood pressure ran in his family. People keeled over at an early age and did not come back. All of that was ahead of them.

He wove his fingers in a basket and gave her a leg up. Before Diana could get settled Red reared. Hale pulled down on the reins. Diana swung her right leg over and took hold of the reins—looping them over her right hand, knotting them the way she liked, clasped between her thumb and middle two fingers.

"Goddammit," Hale said. "Now *whoa*, Red." Red snorted, then stood still. Her ears were pricked. Diana drew her knees up and fixed her feet in the stirrups.

"Gallop her easy." Like his mother Hale never said anything just once. "Take her around once to warm her up. The second time around let her down but don't push."

Practically standing in the saddle—knees flexed and turned

in toward each other, thigh muscles clamped, butt high—
Diana secured the knot of the reins and pulled them in to
her chest. The first few times she'd ridden, she'd rubbed terrible blisters on her hands, but her palm and the crotch of
her hand between her index and middle finger were now
properly callused. She pulled the reins tight. Red liked something to move against. When one of their gallop boys tried
running her with a free rein, Red just dawdled. When the
boy got off, the filly looked back over her shoulder, gave the
boy a baleful look and snorted.

Diana felt a shudder run down Red's neck to her shoulders.
She stroked the filly's neck. "Okay, girl," she said, "okay."
She gave Red a nudge. They moved onto the track.

From her first time up—on Bee's Dream that day, with
little or no idea how and fear pumping her heart to twice its
size—Diana knew, she was hooked. Scholarship could not
begin to measure up. Not even close. Hale didn't get it. He
hadn't taken her request to ride Bee seriously and for that
matter, at first neither had she. But when she got down off
of the horse and felt her knees turn to water and the ground
go woozy beneath her feet, she knew she would not stop
riding race horses until she had to.

She held her elbows high and hummed through her lips,
loud enough for Red, who liked music, to hear.

When her forefeet hit the soft dust of the track, Red made
a soft groaning sound. Diana clamped her thigh muscles harder
and pulled back on the reins. Red protested again. Diana
hummed louder. When Pito rode warmups he whistled, his
own trilling version of "The Star-Spangled Banner." Diana
could barely whistle in the best of times, much less horseback.
Red bowed her neck and warily moved farther onto the track.
Cold prickles of sweat popped up in Diana's hair, beneath
her helmet.

When they reached the middle of the stretch, Red danced
a little sideways jig. Diana spoke to the filly and pulled on
the reins. Red ducked her head.

Hale had jogged to his place at the fence, halfway down the track at the mark they'd made for a finish line. Rufus lay beside him. The bright blue iron starting gates were behind Diana and Red, in the infield. Diana sat gently down on the saddle, keeping her back erect, as she had learned in posting class. Hale worried about her back but there was no use trying to convince Diana not to do something she wanted to do, especially for her own good, and in fact she was really adept at this, particularly with the young ones. She was firm with them but she understood them, in that way people either naturally had with horses or did not.

They passed Hale and Rufus. On the blacktop road ahead there wasn't much traffic. An old red Ford pickup, the bed filled with baling wire. A small Japanese car. They rounded the first turn. Beyond the trees Diana could see the house and beyond it, the hills. Halfway down the backstretch, Red laid back her ears and snorted. Diana stroked her neck.

After the second turn, Diana dropped down full in the saddle, drew her knees up, leaned into the filly's neck, tapped her once with the ends of the reins and yelled out, "Hah! Hah! Hah!"

Red moved into a gallop. It felt as though she'd lowered a foot. Diana kept a tight rein, pulling her hands against her chest. They passed Hale. From between Red's ears Diana saw a car zoom past on the road. With her long forceful stride, Red gathered up track, left it behind; gathered, left it behind. *"Hah!"* Diana yelled again. *"Hah!"*

She rocked with the horse's motion. This was the best part, when she leaned into the horse's neck and, taking the measure of the horse's rhythm and stride, adapted to it, went with it, made the shape of the horse's movements the shape of her own.

They made the first turn. Diana had never been on a horse like Red before. Whatever power the filly was dipping into to make her run there was more to be had. And then more.

And then it left her. Diana was leaning into Red's neck,

midway through the backstretch, when the filly suddenly faltered and pulled up. Her gait went from a gallop to a trot. Diana had to catch herself to keep from falling. She did not try to push the filly; she let the reins go slack then stood in the saddle, knees knocked. Red slowed to a walk. Her breath came fast. Her nostrils, slick with sweat, quivered.

"All right, girl, all right." Diana patted Red's wet shoulder and rode the horse to where Hale waited. Hale set his cap down lower on his head. There was a slump to his shoulders that broke Diana's heart.

She unbuckled her helmet and took her feet from the stirrups. "What happened?"

"She saw the gates."

She rubbed her left knee. "Why didn't she spook the first time around?"

"She knew you were warming her up."

"She did make a noise over there. I didn't make the connection."

"It was the goddamn gates."

Diana swung to the ground and led Red to the opening in the fence. She handed Hale the reins and lifted the helmet from her head.

"What now?"

Hale frowned. "I don't know." There was a crease between his eyebrows, deep and straight. The crease had developed in the past few years. He scratched Red's nose. "I just don't know."

They walked the filly back through the woods. In the barn, Hale unbuckled her saddle and laid it on a fence rail. He led the filly past the stalls to the walker.

"The trials are less than six weeks away. Closer to five." He took off Red's bridle and attached her halter to a latch hanging from an arm of the walker. "She needs thirty days to acclimate to the altitude. I have to think of something."

When he flipped a switch the electric motor began to hum. Red pulled back. Hale yelled and clapped his hands. As soon as Red stopped resisting, the walker forced her to move in slow circles. She gave Hale a dark look.

"Bitch," he whispered. She snorted.

Hale and Marvin Thoede had been partners seven years. Marvin's finances, like those of a lot of other rich men in Texas, had become a tangle of loss and sneaky bookkeeping, impossible to unknot. Hale wasn't rich but he was in trouble, too; they all were, and with reason. Every boy in Texas had been raised to believe in three known facts: that God would punish the wicked, that real estate would always go up and that people would never stop using more oil. If Hale had heard Marvin say it once, he'd heard it a thousand times: "Real estate won't never go down, buddy. They're not making any more of it." Claude Caldwell used to say the same thing, and he never owned a piece of land in his life wider than he could spit across.

So much for the Known Facts of Texas. Marvin had already sold his private plane. In the spring he'd held a divestiture sale to get rid of those cows Hale told him not to buy in the first place. Creditors were hounding him; bankers were keeping him afloat. But there was no way to tell a plunger not to plunge. And there was no way to know exactly how Marvin Thoede's finances stood. Three years ago, his second wife had divorced him. In the settlement, LeeAnn Thoede got four million dollars cash. Marvin offered real estate but LeeAnn was no fool.

Hale and Marvin also owned and ran a moderately successful tack-and-western store: grains, feed, bridles, some overpriced boots and western wear. Roger was running the store. Since he'd been there, their records had gone haywire. Hale planned to buy the boy a computer. Young people understood computers.

The filly nodded her head.

"Old Reddo," Hale said. "Going to Ruidoso like it or not. You got to put up or shut up, Red. Run or hit the road."

"Oh, Hale."

"I mean it, Diana. There's something to be done for this filly. So far I haven't been able to figure out diddly fucking squat."

"Let's try to think of something."

"I've tried. I've thought."

"Maybe we could take a new tack."

"You want to give Sam a go?"

Diana shook her head. "Now?"

"As long as we're here."

"Fine with me."

Carrying a bridle, he walked toward the stall of Ingratiating Sam. From the tack room, Diana lifted her favorite riding bat from a hook on the wall. Sam needed encouragement. She put her helmet back on and rested the bat on her shoulder.

She'd done the wrong thing suggesting they think of something new. Hale resisted suggestions like the plague; he liked to ride a problem into the ground until either he or it was subdued.

Besides, doomsaying and self-denigration were old Baptist tricks. Diana had learned not to take them too seriously.

In the barn door she waited for Sam. Poisonous spray still dripped from the wasps' nest. The wasps had all flown away to die. Hale led Sam out of his stall.

"Hey, Sam," he said. "Want to go for a stroll?"

Ingratiating Sam nickered. Abandoned, from her walker Illuminated Red 1 whinnied like a spurned lover.

· 7 ·

*B*ethany had not always been fat. In the eighth and ninth grades she was thin, really thin. That was when everybody kept coming at her to eat and she wouldn't.

She took a baby-blue bra from her drawer and fitted it over her chest. In some ways, fat was the same as thin. Food was the great power.

Not that she'd been an Annie Rex, not even close. There were a lot of A. R.'s at Cedar Hills. Annies were truly Nutty Brown Fruitcake.

Reaching behind her to hook the straps, she had to strain. She wondered why bra companies didn't use Velcro.

Mimi said Bethany shouldn't worry about the trouble she'd been in.

"Honey, every family has its black sheep," her grandmother had said, patting Bethany's arm. "The only difference is, usually it's a boy."

Diana had been outraged by Mimi's remark but Bethany felt curiously calmed. Her grandmother's fatalistic assessment had served to confirm her suspicions about her place in the world. Mimi was the only one honest enough to tell her the truth.

After stretching her black Motley Crue T-shirt in every direction, she pulled it over her head. She had ripped off the sleeves and the neck so that the shirt had the look she liked.

Being overweight made for problems. But she was still strong. And light on her feet. Diana asked about drugs to curb her appetite but Cedar Hills didn't believe in drugs, a big joke as far as the kids were concerned.

Bethany brushed back her hair. With each stroke, a sweep of golden strands lifted and then slowly dropped.

"Bee?"

"Hold it." She pulled her T-shirt down. "Okay."

Bobby Neuhaus cracked the door. He was wearing his usual Sunday garb, good knit shirt with a collar, real pants, polished leather loafers instead of Reeboks.

"Hey." He stuck his long, thin face through the crack. "Bee?"

"What." She looked at him in the mirror. His shoulder twitched. He was jumpy, no surprise. It was Sunday. "Would you," she said, "please come in and close that door."

He did as he was told.

He said it again. "Bee?"

Sometimes she wanted to murder Bobby Neuhaus. "How many times do I have to answer. I said *what?*"

He stepped back. "I don't know. I was thinking. You want to . . ." He pumped his shoulder. "Do something?"

The trouble with Bobby was he was manic-depressive, no in-between, if he wasn't M he was D. On Sunday when mothers were coming, Bobby was totally M; high as a kite.

"I'm out of pinkies."

He frowned. "I didn't mean pills. I meant . . ." He flopped his hand back and forth. "*You* know."

She knew what he meant. "You meant you know?"

He stomped his heel. "Bee!"

She mocked him. " '*Bee!*' Don't waffle, Bobby. You want to fool around. Am I right or am I right?"

Bobby pulled out his ace in the hole. "I have a Reese's."

Bethany stopped brushing her hair.

Staff made a big commotion about sex. They gave lectures on moral equivalency and being in charge of your own functionality. Every kid at Cedar Hills did some anyway but almost nobody went all the way, not because of functionality. Because they had a reason not to want to get kicked out.

Bethany's hairbrush had been Gloria's. The back and handle were sterling silver, scrolled with sculptured flowers. The bristles were as soft as a baby's, not much good on long thick hair but Bethany loved it. She set the brush on the dresser.

"Nah," she said. "I don't feel like it."

Bobby's face fell. His hair was a mass of frizz around his thin, angular face. When Bobby washed his hair his curls went crazy.

"So," he curled his mouth. "Some D and D?"

"You know I hate D and D." Bobby was a madman for Dungeons and Dragons, also reruns of "Star Trek." Bethany had gotten where she didn't mind "Star Trek." One Saturday they'd checked out ten videotapes from the library. They'd watched for eight hours.

"You hear about the celebration cake?"

She went to the windowseat and sat with her back to the window, facing Bobby. She motioned him closer.

The truth was, she had not eaten the cake. After only three bites, she had heaved it down the hill. Middle of the night, cake flying, what a sight. She'd crammed the aluminum foil cover so far down into the dumpster they'd have to unload the entire contents to find it. Now everybody would go crazy. She could watch them scramble like ants in an ant farm.

Bobby rolled his big dark eyes. "No, Bee, I didn't hear about the celebration cake. It's just all over the place, that's all. Everybody knows you did it." At the foot of her bed he leaned against the frame. "I can't believe it," he said, shaking his head. "A whole cake."

She shrugged. "You gotta be a pro."

They had been through a lot together at Nutty Brown.

One time they'd stood naked together in front of her mirror. "The odd couple," Bethany proclaimed. Bobby was dark and scrawny, she white and soft, the skin on her belly pearled with stretch marks, her blond pubic hair a soft woolly patch of pale fur.

Bobby was fifteen; he could pass for ten. When he caught her staring at his penis he had covered it with his hands.

"I'm a late developer," he explained. "My mother said every man in her family was a late developer."

"All right already," Bethany had said, and she'd pulled his hands away. "So give it a rest."

Two seconds later Bobby's string bean began to rise. Bethany giggled, Bobby blushed. Two seconds after that, Staff blew in. A weekend freeze was called. The other kids were so steamed they wanted to murder Bethany and Bobby.

Alex had called the night before he left. "I'm leaving town until this thing blows over," he said. "I can't come back, Blondie," he said. "I'm a Hurtado. They'll lock me up. I'll be like that Russian guy, what's his name?"

"Sakharov?"

"That it?"

"The one they exiled?"

"I thought his name was Gorky."

"Gorky's the town."

"How come you know so much, Blondie?"

"I don't know," Bethany said. "Anyway, the stuff I know is real dumb."

For grand theft auto, possession of a controlled substance and possession of stolen goods including two firearms, Bethany had been sent to Cedar Hills instead of reform school, Hale and Diana and their blue-eyed, color-blind lawyer had made that deal with the judge. If all of them had their way, she might never see Alex Hurtado again in her life.

Too bad for them. She was born to be with Alex Hurtado. She would get to Del Rio if she had to walk.

"I mean," Bobby said again. "A whole cake."

Bethany giggled. She put her hand over her mouth. She had begun developing fat-person habits, giggling behind her hand, coming up behind people and shoving, always first in the food line. She couldn't tell which was the chicken and which the egg, if being fat made you do things like that or if she was always that way underneath.

"What do you think," she said. "A freeze?"

"What I hear is they think you like freezes so they're going in the other direction."

"Paradox? Reverse paradox?"

Bobby raised and lowered his eyebrows like Peter Sellers as the Pink Panther. "Paradox," he said. "With a twist."

"New tricks. We'll have to think of something. Where's the Reese's?"

They were doing a paradox on her about the eating, letting her fill her plate and eat all she wanted. She was on to their tricks all right; she just hadn't figured out what to do about them.

Bobby checked the door.

"Bobby." Bethany hated it when he got crazy. "There's nobody there."

"It's almost time for breakfast. They'll check."

"The door squeaks. We'll hear."

"Not that much of a squeak."

"Look at me." His eyes were about to pop out of his skull. "Don't turn your head around until I say to."

When Bobby was M, only direct orders calmed him down. When he was D, forget it.

He took a deep breath.

When parents came kids went nuts. It started Saturday night. Girls did hot rollers, boys polished their shoes, everybody practiced pitiful looks in the mirror. By Sunday breakfast, the entire place was Nutty Brown Bananas.

Bobby's mother had long frizzy hair dyed as red as Rufus the dog's. Bright-colored Mexican dresses and beat-down rubber flip-flops were all she ever wore; in the winter she put a coat on and added socks. She smelled like cat and cigarettes and her name was Miami. Miami was, she said, a poet. Bethany called her The Vice. Noon on the dot Sunday, The Vice showed up with cigarettes, poems and the news—all of which was bad. When his mother read a poem, Bobby was full of praise. Last Sunday, he compared her to Walt Whitman. Today, Emily Dickinson. Bobby was no fool. If he flattered The Vice she kept reading. If she kept reading he didn't have to hear the news: The wrecks and murders and mutilated animals, the burning of small children with cigarettes. People he didn't even know.

"So who pays?" Bethany asked after meeting Miami the first time.

"For what?"

"This. Do you know what it costs to lock us up in here?"

"So we're not locked up, Bee."

Sometimes Bobby was truly boring. "Really now."

He shrugged. "We're rich, I guess," he said. "My grandmother owns about every Sac 'n Pac in the world, plus other stuff. But mostly it's Sac 'n Pacs."

"So why does your mother dress like a slob?"

He squinted his eyes and refused to answer.

"So why does she smell like cat?"

"So she takes them in."

"So cats?"

"Cats."

"So? Like off the street?"

Bobby rolled his eyes. "Only about a ka-billion. She goes to kitty-power meetings. She has an I-Brake-for-Cats bumper sticker. And like that."

Bobby reached into his pocket and brought out an unopened package of Reese's peanut butter cups. To Bethany's mind, there was nothing better than the taste of chocolate and peanut butter mixed. She would rather have one Reese's than an entire German chocolate cake twice over.

Bobby closed his hand over the candy and put it behind his back.

"So what do I get?"

"One game."

"D and D?"

"No, idiot. The other." She flopped her hand back and forth. "You Know." She turned and looked over her shoulder out the window. A tall thin man with silver streaks in his hair was getting into the Mercedes. Bethany would like to tell the man the joke about hemorrhoids and a Mercedes: every asshole gets one sooner or later. The man was not handsome, just tall. He just thought handsome.

Bethany held out her hand. "So give."

"If I give first how do I know you will?"

"Do I lie, Bobby Neuhaus?"

"Yes."

"I do not."

"Sometimes you do. Remember? The peanut M&M's?"

Bethany's cheeks flushed. "So I won't this time."

"So how do I know?"

She held up her hand. "I swear on my grandmother's grave." This was an oath Bobby had thought up. When Bethany reminded him that one of his grandmothers wasn't dead and neither of hers was, Bobby said blood oaths didn't have to be strictly true.

"You said that last time."

In a rage, Bethany slid off the windowseat. The cushion went with her. The knife fell to the floor. Bethany returned her prize to its hiding place.

Silently Bobby handed over the Reese's.

· 8 ·

"Want a Mary?"

"Not much of one. I have to make that twisty drive."

"Take the interstate."

"Too far."

"Mild then."

"You get started, I'm going to check the tomatoes."

Rufus at her heels, Diana went from the gravel road down into the yard.

"Hey."

"What."

"Think I should put Roger's name in the pot?"

"What time is it, eight?"

"About."

She'd heard the boy come in, 3:00 A.M. by the digital clock. "He got in late. Whatever you want, I don't care. I'll be back in a minute."

Hale considered his alternatives. If he woke Roger up, they could enjoy his company. Roger loved breakfast tacos. And Diana wouldn't be able to continue her silly argument. He wiped his feet and went into the kitchen. From a drawer he took out his transistor radio. Sunday mornings the local country-FM station broadcast a gospel show. The Carter Family was singing "On the Wings of a Snow White Dove." In the background, Mother Maybelle executed her usual fine harmony on the lute. Hale hummed along.

With a wooden spoon, he stirred spicy tomato juice in a glass pitcher, added black pepper and Tabasco, Lea & Perrins and a healthy dose of fresh lime juice. When the mixture was well stirred, he filled a tall glass with it, added ice, poured in a one-ounce jigger of liquor from a half-gallon bottle of vodka and stirred.

Roger woke up happy; he'd lift their spirits. On the other hand . . .

What other hand? In no other area of his life had Hale been this wishy-washy. As Bethany said, *not even close.* There were reasons. As a boy, his father had whaled him with a leather belt more times than he wanted to remember, sometimes without explaining which rule had been broken. Later, his butt raw, he would ask his mother. From her, no sympathy. "You're supposed to know the difference, Hale," she would say. "You know that."

Hale loved his children, felt for them. He had not wanted to repeat those old patterns of abuse, surely an honorable aspiration. But excessive love got in the way. He'd gone too far in the other direction.

He set the drink on the table beside Diana's legal pad. Diana and her lists. Every time he looked up, here she came with one. Pros and cons, risks and consequences, as if their life was only broken and she the handy fix-it man.

The top sheet was blank. He lifted it. On page two, number one was "Sell the house. Suggest we move." They had been through that one last night.

There was a number two and a three but Hale let the top sheet go. He poured a healthy slug of vodka from the bottle into the pitcher of Marys, not bothering to measure.

At one point in the fiasco called Trying to Do Something About Bethany, Diana had suggested they see a family therapist. They were in a rut, she said; the problem was not just with Bethany but the whole family. "Bethany," she had said, "is the I.P. The more we focus on her, the 'sicker,' quote unquote, she gets."

I.P. meant identified patient. This particular mumbo-jumbo was not Diana's. She was borrowing from some book.

I.P.'s in mind, Diana went out and found Gil Barrientos. Barrientos had gotten a master's in social work, then hung out his shingle. This was possible in Texas; Hale had looked up the law. Family therapy was not well regulated. And Gil Barrientos was not a bad man; he just had a mediocre mind. He also had the distinction of being possibly the only Mexican in central Texas that Bethany didn't go for.

He filled his own glass with ice.

"Think of your life," Barrientos had told them, "as a refrigerator." They were in session. Hale had looked up from studying his thumbs. Diana was nodding as gravely at Barrientos as if he'd just come up with a cure for cancer.

"There are no mystical problems," the therapist went on. "Only practical ones. Your goal should be to fix the refrigerator, not so that it's new again. Just so it *works.*"

They'd gone together. Bethany spent the entire session chewing her sleeve and hiding behind her hair. Diana talked a lot, focusing strictly on Barrientos. Hale waited for the time to be up. More than anything, he was impressed with the cost, ninety dollars for a fifty-minute hour. Diana had waved his complaints away. Most family therapists, she insisted, stuck to a forty-five-minute hour and many cost far more than ninety dollars, particularly when seeing a family. "If you think that's high," she said, "try Houston."

In the end, Bethany proved to be a smarter game-player than Gil Barrientos. During the third visit, she'd been so rude and surly that Barrientos said she could not come back until she apologized. "Fine with me," Bethany snarled. "You sit by your phone, doc, and you wait for that one. I'm out of here." And she stormed out.

Standing in the center of the kitchen floor, Hale held his glass in one hand. In the other he turned the pitcher of Bloody Marys in a circle, mixing the liquids. This time he was going to take the offensive. When the proper moment arrived, he'd be ready. Diana was not serious about selling the house, he knew that. Taking her at face value was simply the only way to call her bluff.

Actually, Mimi's black-sheep theory seemed no sillier to Hale than Gil Barrientos's refrigerator. One thing about Baptists, they knew where they stood. About Bethany's weight gain, Mimi had said, "Some people are meant to be fat. Born fat, stay fat." And she went on to tell about Aunt Ev, who had begun life as the fattest baby in Arp, Texas, and died seventy-three years later weighing some three hundred and fifty-odd pounds.

Hale would not have called the original cause of all this God; he did not believe people were predestined to be any particular way at all. But to a certain degree, some portion of a person's character did seem to him to be unalterably built in. A horse was either fast or it wasn't. No amount of training could change that. Bloodlines were important, drugs helped for a time, then either lost their punch or drove the horse crazy. At some point speed either declared itself or did not. People were the same.

Anyway what was he supposed to feel guilty about? He had not stolen a car, he had not forced Bethany to. How could it be his fault? When he protested to Diana she countered, saying he would do well not to think in terms of blame and fault. But the implication was there: if the problem was with the family itself and not just the girl, then all of them had done wrong to some extent. And if he did not think in terms of blame and fault what else was there? Diana slogged around in wishy-washy middle ground. And privately, he believed, she felt the same as he. She was just trying to find some way to blame anyone on God's green earth except the girl herself.

The Carters finished their song. A commercial came on advertising a local restaurant.

On the other hand, if he was so sure that none of it was his fault, why did he feel so racked up all the time? Why were his nights so jagged and uneven, why did he sometimes find himself as immobilized as if he'd turned to stone, with this burning hole in his gut?

Some nights they woke up at the exact same time, two or three in the morning. Diana would sit up, then Hale. Hadn't they heard something? The honk of the sheriff's horn when he came to tell them she'd been arrested?

As Willie Nelson started in on "Amazing Grace," Hale poured himself a drink, then put the pitcher in the refrigerator. He took a healthy sip. The Mary was excellent: strong and peppery with a satisfying citrus bite. He set his drink down and readjusted his glasses.

He tried to tell himself it didn't matter that Bethany was a girl, the situation would have been the same if she were a son, but it wasn't true. No matter how hard he tried to convince himself, he simply could not stand to think of his daughter—specifically, *especially* his daughter—spending the night in jail. In time, bad boys straightened out. The world loved a bad boy. Bad girls went from there to worse. When Diana backed him into a corner with her rhetoric on this particular subject, he felt like he might explode.

From the windows looking out over the slope, he could see her squatting beside her tomatoes. Squatting was hard on the knees but according to Diana easier on her lower back than bending.

Hale drank himself into bed every night but did not feel it. Never staggered, was rarely drunk. He had his rules. Ice was a comfort; before pouring in his martini, he filled his glass. Except Sundays, he never touched a drop until sunset.

He took another sip. If Diana knew how precarious their financial situation was, she wouldn't be so cavalier about suggesting they sell the house. And who was she planning on selling it to, the sultan of Brunei? In Houston, foreclosures had become so commonplace they'd lost their stigma. Chapter Elevens swarmed like mosquitoes in the summertime. Now Austin was going down the tubes.

He dug around in the bottom drawer, searching for his cast-iron skillet. The drawer wouldn't come open. The pots had been stuffed in one on top of the other at cranky angles. Hale stuck his arm in the drawer and pressed down, agitating the pots and pans until the handle preventing the drawer from coming open was out of the way.

Diana the Siamese twin. In the garden she was as meticulous as an ant; in the house, Tobacco Road. She had crammed things into drawers as if the drawer would never have to be opened again.

He took out pots and pans and stacked them on the countertop. When he finally came to the cast-iron skillet—on the bottom of the stack, unoiled—he replaced the other pots, closed the drawer and stood.

The decision to leave the city still gnawed at him. Although she denied it, Diana had been happier there. He'd offered to move to the country by himself. He would, he said, take the children with him; she could stay in Houston until she finished her dissertation, or for as long as she wanted. With the money he'd made selling Dash Too they could afford to live both places. Diana said no, she was coming with him.

As for Bethany, no lesson Hale had ever learned about strategies applying to any difficult situation he had ever faced did a dime's bit of good when he tried to apply the worth of those lessons to his daughter. When she acted up he turned into a stark raving lunatic. Away from her he vowed to hold his tongue. In her presence, he became a one-dimensional idiot. Education and intelligence were of no help. If anything, intelligence hurt. He *knew* he was an idiot.

With a paper towel he oiled the cast-iron skillet with corn oil until the rust had disappeared and the bottom of the skillet was black again.

Maybe if she'd been a son, he'd have been able to handle it better. Maybe, maybe not. Drinking helped him sleep, a little. That was the only lesson he'd learned.

Willie strummed the melody of "Amazing Grace." Humming along, Hale placed the skillet on a burner and began gathering ingredients. Onions, green peppers, cilantro, serranos, chorizo. He used what they had. There was one small potato left in the hand-painted blue bowl Diana kept on the counter. The potato looked long in the tooth but the eyes hadn't sprouted. He took it out of the bowl, wondering why when she cooked them Diana had left this one behind.

With a serrated steak knife from the utensil drawer he began to chop.

Answers either used to be easier to come by or he had not then fully understood the questions.

· 9 ·

On her knees, Diana lifted a tiny plant from the soil. The leaves drooped.

Some of the tomatoes were on their sides. Others had been tromped on. Two had vanished. Beyond the plants were the telltale signs: pointy little ditchlike holes, dredged out as if by a triangular blade. The mark of the armadillo.

She had raised the tomatoes from seed, a variety called Celebrity she'd had particular luck with in the spring. Hoping for the same kind of success in the fall, she had ordered early from Stephenville, then babied the seeds, potting them in vermiculite in trays covered with plastic to make a greenhouse effect until they germinated, then separating the seedlings, planting them in individual Styrofoam cups and for a month keeping watch, taking the cups inside and out as the weather changed and the sun grew too hot, watering every day without fail . . . just never removing her attention from the fledgling plants, one day to the next. Three days ago she'd set the tomatoes out. From old wooden roof tiles she'd made small shields, two to a plant, as protection from the afternoon sun. She'd fed the plants with Tomato Booster and mulched them heavily with wet compost and hay.

She ran her hand down into the damp, mulched earth. She had added truckloads of rotted manure and shavings from the horse stalls to the garden soil and so the dirt was loose and friable. To make the best use of water, she'd planted an underground drip-hose system so that while the surface of the soil looked dry and crusty, the roots of the plants were always moist. With the ground everywhere else baked hard as concrete, it was no wonder animals came to the garden to dig, where the ground was soft and wet and lush with earthworms.

She turned up a fist full. No ants or grubs, only a few harmless roly-polies.

She sat back on her heels. Trouble made her tired. She was waiting for life to settle back down to normal and boring again. So far not so good in any direction.

In December, the north wind and the seven-degree temperature had burst every unwrapped water pipe in the county and even some that were well protected. She and Hale had sat for hours taking turns aiming her hair dryer into dark crevices in the walls, their fingers frozen into a permanent hand grip as they waited for chunks of ice caught in elbow joints to thaw. They had even had a sticking snow, several inches, which never happened in this part of Texas.

Then spring, unseasonably, irrationally cool. Late in March, she had chosen not to believe the forecast of a freeze, a reasonable enough decision, that time of year. Her ficus, left covered with a sheet on the porch, had turned to mush, her bougainvillea to black sticks. In April, just after she planted a few annuals to get the season under way, a midnight hailstorm beat her poor frail impatiens and petunias to the ground. Chunks of ice big as thimbles bashed into windows, denting car hoods. In April.

Now it was July and the world was on fire. No end to the drought was in sight. And her horoscope predicted emotional fireworks in the fall.

She scooted down from the armadillo tracks to the shallow

pocket of mulch where the absent plants had been. As she moved, her back gave a small twinge on the left side just below her waist. She pressed a certain place low on her spine to relieve the pain. The spasm passed.

To the east of the stolen tomato plants, beside the place where she would plant spinach when the weather cooled, was a fledgling *Salvia greggii* she'd dug from a friend's pasture. The salvia had come up on its own, a small blessing in the middle of a barren patch of limestone, beggar's-lice, nettles and mesquite. There were many different varieties of salvia; the *greggii* was Diana's favorite. After a two-month struggle the bush had bloomed. Tiny red flowers had hung from its branches like small wet flags, an exhilarating shade of pure garnet red, jewel-like and tender.

The bush had been stripped.

Diana ran her hands up the branches. Ants might have taken the leaves but she saw none. That left deer and rabbits. The eight-foot aluminum deer fence should have taken care of the larger animals but these days, who could say. She inspected the damage more closely. The limbs of the salvia had been snapped halfway up, indicating the weight of an animal as it rested its paws, reaching for the topmost leaves.

Rabbits. Armadillos and rabbits in one night. If they were going to work in concert she was going to have to get serious. Mothballs were supposed to keep animals away but she hated for her garden to smell like a winter sweater. Besides, Rufus ate them.

She threw the ruined Celebrity into the dirt and, pushing her heels into the ground, slowly straightened. She slipped her bandanna from her head, shook out her hair, and without untying the knot in the scarf wiped her hands.

Except for a few patches of the delicate, blue-green buffalo grass, Hale's pasture was parched and brown. Even Bermuda grass had given up its stubborn hold on the ground and turned roots-up to the sky like so many dead bugs. Only the mesquite, the wild white poppies and the cactus looked happy.

The slight morning breeze stirred the lacy mesquite leaves like a floor fan ruffling a shawl. The lawn was dead. They'd let it go, preserving water and time for the garden. Hale had had to send all the way to Lockhart for alfalfa.

She stuffed the bandanna into her back pocket. Before she turned to go she saw the basil.

There had been eight bushes, each a good three to four feet tall. The basil had been stripped. Diana moved closer. At the base of each plant lay a pile of leaves, like an abandoned skirt the bush had stepped out of.

Basil was supposed to ward off insects, not attract them. What was out there that would take the leaves from a plant and not make use of them? Diana wiped her hands on her jeans. The world was on its ear.

Head hanging low, sleepy Rufus ambled up, slid his head beneath Diana's hand. A neurotic Irish setter, Rufus had only a few purposes in life. He ate, he ran, he begged for love. When they had him neutered he gave up barking in the nighttime, but he still went roaming.

Some mornings they heard him come home, panting lavishly, lapping water and then the Rufus Flop as in one motion he fell in a heap on the deck. One morning near dawn, Hale had seen him zooming along the edge of the bluff overlooking the creek, long ears flying, head bobbing in rhythm with the run, as focused as an athlete. Hale had been up all night, taking turns with Casey walking a colicky mare. The sight of Rufus, he said, had lifted his spirits. Soon afterward, the mare had taken a large dump. They had unhooked the lead shank and let the horse go.

Rufus's eyes were the same color as his coat, a burnished red-brown. Originally, he had belonged to a city friend, a divorced woman with a small son living in a Houston apartment. The boy was hyperactive, the dog was driving them crazy. Hale and Diana took Rufus to the country to be an outside dog. And Rufus was happy now. And if they hadn't wanted him to be a joke dog, they should not have given him a joke name.

"Ah, Rufus," Diana said, rubbing the dog's head. "Some watchdog you are. Some watchdog." Rufus closed his eyes. A long contented sigh bubbled through his trembling lips. Rufus was beautiful and that was enough. They had no right to ask for more.

The full moon was Friday. There would be plenty of time to buy new tomato starts, feed them and set them out before then. The problem was finding the starts. It was early. Most nurseries waited until mid-August to put them out. Diana liked to plant before the Fourth, so that she could have home-grown tomatoes with her Thanksgiving turkey.

Douglas might have some. She would drop by Xanadu on her way to Austin.

Gardening and scholarship were not so different; both took long hours and single-mindedness, resiliency in the face of major setbacks, a gift for tedium and a flair for the marriage of the unusual. Both strained the eyes and lower back and depended to some degree on fate, prejudice, perspective and the intuitive flash. In scholarship intellectual prejudice became theory, in the yard a personal design: if you hated hydrangeas you left them out. And while research was not prey to the night routs of the armadillo, back-stabbing was no more prevalent in the natural world than in the halls of learning. Armadillos were just odder looking.

Through the glass she could see Hale's head bobbing between the trunk and lower limbs of the hackberry tree. The deck spanning the width of the house had been constructed around the hackberry . . . a mistake according to Douglas. Hackberries were short-lived. This one was already maybe twenty years old. One day, Douglas warned, the tree would start to die from the roots up. They could only hope when it went it fell the other way.

Her adviser at the University of Houston had been more

than generous, awarding her one extension after the next on the due date for her dissertation. He liked her or he'd have already set a final deadline. Her theme was Virginia Woolf's mysticism: the transformation of fancifulness and dream symbols not into narrative—which would have been a kind of science fiction—but into the very shape of the sentences and the structure guiding the logic of the paragraphs. Mysticism as structure, mystery as legend. She'd focused particularly on *The Waves*.

The creation of clutter took a steady hand. Blue did better with white, red with yellow. Books said choose one kind of flower, one color to a bed, but Diana had a hard time restraining herself. She wanted it all. In the soft light of dusk, white flowers glowed like small stars and so she had banked flats of white impatiens in a bed to themselves for a moon garden to look at after the sun went down. She had intermixed carefully, vegetables, herbs and flowers; wildflowers next to river fern and Dutch iris, lettuce shaded by dark aspidistra, red amaryllis multiplying off to themselves, dill next to broccoli, garlic far away from green beans, jonquils and rain lilies near the trees. The slope now looked like a hodge-podge feast. As if it had all come up on its own that way, like lions lying down with the lambs.

Hale's head went away.

She'd learned from books, everything from philosophy, history, aesthetics and design to the nuts-and-bolts lessons on nematodes, root rot and the Ph factor. She often took a how-to book down to the garden with her, laying the book open as she worked, keeping a dirt-rimmed nail on the page to hold her place.

She started up the path between the asparagus bed and the empty one she would plant in January in old-fashioned roses. She'd put gladiolus in the bed last year only to remember after they were up that she hated gladiolus. After the bulbs bloomed she'd dug them up and given them away. Ruthlessness, according to Vita Sackville-West, was the first rule of gardening: if you don't like it, dig it up. Vita was right.

Large stones from the nearby hills set off beds from one another. When she'd gotten into native plants—purple cone flowers, pink pavonia, red-orange Turk's-cap, Texas purple sage and spiderwort—she'd had to be particularly careful. Maximilian sunflowers could take over the world.

Douglas Bredthauer, her landscape adviser and favorite nurseryman, had hauled in the rocks. Diana had stood halfway down the slope and, feeling like God in the beginning, told him where to put them.

As she took a step toward the house, a slight wind from the east blew across Diana's face, flipping a thread of hair into her eye. The wind smelled of smoke and cedars. With the tip of her finger, she plucked the hair from her eye and turned to look in the direction from which the wind had come.

The worrying never let up. She had tried tricks on herself, making lists, willing herself not to think of the girl until a certain time of day. "Do five things," Gil had suggested. "Then think of Bethany." In idle moments while doing the five things, she found herself going back over it again, re-staging conversations, trying to figure out what had happened and why. After *why* came *what next*. On a good day Diana imagined a happy next chapter. More often than not she predicted the worst.

Love, naturally, was at issue. Gil said Bethany loved Diana more than was ordinary for a girl, that the two of them were in some way *in love* with each other, the way girls usually were with their fathers. Diana tried to keep her wits about her when Bethany was vicious, tried to tell herself this is not hatefulness but love misconstrued, love baffled, love in artless disarray. But the deeper currents of truth were hard to hold on to when the surface reality was clawing at your confidence and calling you names.

There was an expression Gloria used to use, "hurt feelings." "I'm not speaking to you today," she would say. "You've hurt my feelings." Fanny would relay messages. "Tell your sister," Gloria would say, looking through Diana as if she didn't exist. "See if your sister wants . . . Ask your sister . . ."

Diana turned from the wind, lowered her shoulders and went up the slope. At the bottom of the stairs leading to the deck, Rufus bumped into her. She grabbed the railing and let the dog go by.

In the night, the miserable Diana would smell her mother's thick gardenia perfume, lighting her path like a lamp. A deep sleeper, Fanny would be into dreams by then. Diana would be lying there like a lump. Gloria would tiptoe in and—knowing Diana was awake—pull her daughter to her. "It's all right, Didee," she'd say. "Mama's not mad anymore." They would hug and kiss and Gloria would go off. Diana would sleep after that, with no more idea of what brought on the truce than what caused the trouble in the first place.

From above her on the porch, she heard Rufus do his flop. Behind her, morning clouds parted and began to dissipate, making room for the rainless sky. Yearning toward the clouds, the hills looked like the blue-purple bodies of reclining women. The rise of breasts, the dip of midriff, swollen craggy knees.

Going up the stairs, Diana relaxed the muscles of her face in case Hale was watching.

· 10 ·

*F*rom his position at the stovetop burners, Hale had looked down and, seeing Diana turn to stone, felt his heart sink. When she glanced in his direction, he moved out of sight. Diana did not like him to watch her. She said being watched turned her into an object, like a bug on a slide. Women could complicate the simplest act. He could not himself imagine not wanting to be looked at.

He downed his drink and fixed a fresh one so that she would think it was his first. On the radio, Johnny Cash sang "Love Lifted Me."

He did it, too. Going about his work he sometimes found himself turned to granite at a horse's stall, arms slung over the stall door, watching a mare chew her feed. Nothing going on he hadn't seen a hundred times before. Just standing there. As if he had weights in his boots and could not move.

The top of her head appeared. She was leaning heavily on the stair railing. Her back again. He had tried to get her to go to the diagnostic clinic but she refused, preferring her fruity assortment of quacks. Her chiropractor, osteopath, Gil Barrientos, that loony astrologer in the trailer park.

Hale never commented on Diana's immobility or tried to tease her out of it. Eventually she rallied.

He held a serrano against the butcher block. With the steak knife he minced it, careful to remove the seeds.

And if they were given a second chance? If he died and came back and they started all over again?

He would do the same thing again, not only go wrong but wrong in the exact same way. A man lived out the few choices open to him, did what he had to. There was nothing to do about that.

He scraped the seeds and stem of the serrano into a pile for the compost.

There were two opposing schools of thought on how to break a horse. Rough-breakers rode babies hard, holding to the belief that a colt was born with a certain amount of badness in him which had to be forcibly ridden out. If a colt was not inclined to buck, a rough-breaker used his spurs and bat to force him to; otherwise, a rough-breaker's philosophy went, the buck came out when you least expected it. Hale had heard his father say a thousand times, "You got to ride the buck out of them colts. You don't, they'll get you for it."

His father broke horses to a halter by tying them to a tree and leaving them overnight. The horse might rear up, hit his head on the tree, open his skull, scrape his chest. None of that mattered much. At some point, the exhausted animal gave in. That was the moment Claude Caldwell waited for.

Hale didn't believe in the innate buck. He gentle-broke his babies, fooled with them, talked to them, led them until they gentled to the halter, then had Pito lie across their backs until they got used to that before allowing anyone to sit on them. Casey broke them to the rein by using a hackamore, a bridle without a bit. Although in any stable there would occasionally be an incurably mean colt, for the most part Hale's methods worked. Most of his colts never threatened to buck at all. Breaking gentle was slow. But Hale couldn't stomach the other.

Finished with the serrano, he set it aside.

That was what philosophy came down to, a feeling that ran so deep a person was not aware of it, like blood. He and Diana had done what they felt was right for their children at the time. They'd been wrong but they'd given it what seemed to be their best shot.

In the middle of a dramatically protracted "Love . . . lifted . . ." Hale turned Johnny Cash down and started in on the cilantro. Some had gone slimy. He picked out the bad stalks and tossed them into the compost pail.

Why was another question. Why they had not been able to apply to their children the hard lessons they had learned the way they applied them to themselves and one another, he could not begin to say. He only knew that if they went back and started over they would end up exactly where they were now.

"Even me," Johnny Cash sang, as if surprised.

Hale turned off the radio. He never had liked Johnny Cash.

Gloomy thoughts had darkened his mood. Next Diana would start in on her list. He set his jaw, ready for the coming skirmish.

· 11 ·

*B*obby was a virgin, Bethany was sure of it; that was why he was nuts on the subject of sex. The Reese's was soft from the heat of his hand. Bethany slid her bright blue fingernail between the layers of the orange-and-brown candy wrapper.

Mexicans were different from Anglos, cooler, calmer, more self-assured. You could see it in the way they walked.

Last year, a Mexican had drowned in his car at a low-water bridge between Kyle and the road to Dripping. There'd been a flash flood. The water hadn't gone down right away and so they couldn't find the body. Bethany had gone with Alex to the low-water bridge. Mexicans were there, standing at the edge of the water. No one was saying anything. They were all just standing there, quiet and respectful, watching the water, like candles in church. Mexican friends and family of the drowned man walked the creek day and night for a week, carrying ropes and knives and grappling hooks. When the water went down the man was found, no more than a hundred yards from where he went under. His foot had caught in the roots of a cypress tree.

That was what she liked about Mexicans: they stuck together.

Alex Hurtado lived in what Diana would call a shack if Diana had ever seen Alex's house, which she never would. The Hurtados had no telephone. Four small children slept in one bed. The bathroom was a wreck. But Bethany was happy at Alex's house. The Hurtados all did the same thing at the same time, ate, played cards, watched shows on television. Nobody went off in a sulk reading books. Nobody kept his head in a bucket of vodka. Maybe somebody got mad sometimes; if they did, they yelled. When it was over it was over.

Bethany thought her long, straw-colored hair was fine but if she had Mexican hair, she could get a punk cut like Alex's, long in the back with spikes on top. She would gel the top part until it looked like a chain-link fence, get her ears pierced two more times, roll up a scarf, tie it horizontally around her head, look tough.

She popped the first Reese's in whole. The candy began to melt. The great tastes mixed and turned to a sweet dribble in her throat.

Her father loved her when she was thin but he did not love her now. She was making good grades at the Cedar Hills school but good grades didn't count for anything anymore; nothing would ever count for him again. When she was in jail that night and they came with a lawyer to get her out and Bethany saw the hateful look on her father's face, she knew she had lost his love forever. There he was, carrying her shoestrings so she wouldn't hang herself, and he had that look. If he did not love her then, he never would. Now he only loved Diana. And perfect white swan Roger. When their blue-eyed lawyer came to tell Bethany he was trying to get her out of jail and asked if there was anything she wanted she had said yes, a Coke and a Twix bar. The lawyer had never heard of Twix bars but he brought her two. Not to bribe her. He just brought them. Which Bethany thought was really nice.

Who needed Hale Caldwell? If she couldn't stop messing up, which she couldn't seem to do, she would have to learn to live without his love.

The first Reese's was gone. Bethany sucked her cheeks to draw any leftover bit of juice down her throat. She could feel Bobby's eyes burning a hole in her. She ran her tongue across her teeth.

Sometimes she looked at pictures of herself as a baby, in Diana's arms, then Hale's, then Mimi's and Gloria's, all dressed up in bonnets and drippy dresses. What a time that must have been. She wouldn't exactly say she was a beautiful baby, but she had a perky sort of button look that was pretty great if she did say so herself. There was a picture of her in nursery school she liked especially. Somebody had come to take a picture for the neighborhood newspaper. The photographer must have asked all the kids to reach up. Bethany's in the first row, hands over her head, shoulders up around her ears, bangs down in her round eyes, eyes hopeful as anything as she strains to make her fingers touch the sky.

She'd have to say, even if it was about herself, she was really cute in that picture. Kindergarten was fun. Then came first grade and she had to sit all day and watch the teacher write on the stupid blackboard. Then boom.

Things started to go wrong in the fifth grade. Teachers turned against her, the rules she made for herself started to go muzzy on her, she couldn't stop herself from testing all the time to see how far she could go before somebody told her to stop. They moved to the country. She hated the country. There was nothing to do in the country but watch TV. She wanted to go back to Houston and live with Gloria. Diana said no. Her mind started whizzing. In high school she did papers for her friends. They liked her. If she had money to spend they liked her more. She stole from her parents. They never said anything, only Hale that one time when he threatened to kick her out of the house, then didn't.

She began to think of her life as divided in two. The white

part was boring, obvious and phoney. The dark part was secret, thrilling, and real; everything her parents were not.

She took a small bite of the other Reese's. Her teeth made a ruffle in the chocolate. Slow eating made the pleasure last longer and kept Bobby on a fishhook.

She had met Alex Hurtado at a party. He offered her pills, or a smoke. In his family's car, a five-year-old Grand Prix in mint condition, they smoked dope together. Alex was the sharp-featured kind of Mexican, hawk nose, small deep-set eyes, that straight black hair, cut into a long crewcut on top, down past his shoulders in back. He'd had one ear pierced. In the hole he wore a tiny gold cross that swung back and forth when he walked.

The Grand Prix was maroon with a white hard-top and all-white vinyl interior. After they smoked the dope, he took her around to the trunk of the car and opened it. Inside was a brand new turntable, three cameras, a fuzzbuster, and a set of tools.

"This is nothing," he said.

Bethany's heart swelled.

"I can use you, Bethany." Alex had whispered. His quiet voice drew her close. "You want in?"

There was a chain of people. Nobody took all the risk. It was foolproof, Alex said. A foolproof chain.

To celebrate their partnership, Alex took her for a drive, up past Dripping on a farm-to-market road, taking forty-mile-an-hour curves at fifty-five and sixty. High on a hill overlooking a new development of houses being built, they smoked more dope and did things together.

Alex was right, Bethany was good at being a part of the chain. Straight people trusted her; she looked like one of them. Everybody thought she was great. Alex called her his Tex-Mex Blondie.

She only wished Alex had told her about the guns so that she would not have looked so shocked when the policeman asked. Then they would have been in on everything together.

Again she slid her teeth into the Reese's. Only a sliver was left.

Hurtados were well known throughout the hill country for their drug dealing and family battles. A month before Alex and Bethany were caught, a cousin of Alex's had aimed a Daisy .22 rifle through an open window and shot his uncle and that uncle's son while the two men played dominoes in their living room. One of the men died. "Hurtado business," Alex explained. Bethany asked no more questions.

She polished off the Reese's and wiped her hands on her shorts.

Being with Alex had been the last happy time she would have until she got back with him again. Alex probably would not recognize her now. In eight months she had gained twenty pounds. At least. She'd stopped weighing.

"Okay," Bobby said, folding his arms over his chest. "You swore."

Bethany wadded the candy wrapper and tossed it toward the wastepaper can.

"Missed." She flipped her hair with the back of her hand.

Bethany arranged herself and showed him. Focusing on the soundproof ceiling tiles, she thought of Alex, his deft quick fingers. The rule for Bobby was, look but don't touch, and only for as long as Bethany said.

Bobby's eyes widened and he began to breathe in that rattling way as if maybe he was about to have an anxiety attack or get asthma again, which only happened when The Vice was due.

Stealing the Trans-Am was not bad in and of itself; getting caught made the difference. After the police pulled them over they found the stuff in the Grand Prix. Otherwise the chain would have stayed foolproof, the way Alex promised, and she would not be in Nutty Brown Fruitcake.

"Time's up." She rearranged her clothes.

"No way."

"I checked the clock."

"Gah, Bee. Reese's gets double."

"So it's late. We have to go."

Bobby jammed his fists into his pockets. "You can't go like that."

"Like what?"

"Like no concert shirts on Sunday?"

"Shit."

Bethany shooed Bobby out. From her closet she got out a better shirt. In the hall, Bethany passed the candy wrapper to Bobby. Bobby put the orange paper in his pocket. He looked a little less M than before, not much.

Bethany flapped down the hall in her fat-person way, bumping people out of her path in her rush toward food. Whenever she thought of the knife, beneath the pillows in her room, she felt happy, safe and sound, like a tick buried deep in a dog's coat, softly sucking.

· 12 ·

*D*uring the week, signing up for breakfast was mandatory but eating was not. You could put your name on the sign-up sheet and then go back to bed. Sundays, you had to dress better and sit at your place at the table. Nobody could force you to eat, of course, but you had to be there.

Bethany made her entrance, Bobby close at her heels. The dining room was large and open with a dark red linoleum floor divided up in octagonal tiles. Above the tables, ceiling fans slowly turned. Bethany and Bobby went to their table.

Sundays, breakfast was served family-style. One person took the role of Authority Figure, a rotating job. The A.F. dictated when the meal began and ended. Today was Bobby's turn. Bobby and Bethany renamed the A.F. Parental Unit. P.U. for short.

A thick mountain of steam rose from the platter of scrambled eggs sitting in the middle of the table. The bacon looked greasy again. When the regulars were seated, Bobby cleared his throat. "Bethany," he said. "Would you like to say the blessing?"

Bethany stared at her plate. "No."

"Anybody?"

Two people looked at Bethany and then away.

"Tiff? Stephen? Anybody?"

Bobby hesitated. Blessings were not required at Cedar Hills but some students felt that Staff noticed. Not that Cedar Hills cared about blessings, they only wanted to see whether or not you had the nerve to push people around. Figuring all this out could be tricky, but kids who'd been there awhile knew the drill. Staff pretended there was a lot of freedom at Cedar Hills, but when they said, "It's up to you," the wiser students knew to watch out.

At the other end of the table, Mama to Bobby's Papa, Bethany drummed her fingers. There was no way she would ask for a blessing next week when she was P.U. Not even close.

Bobby looked around. "Come on, Bee," he hissed across the eggs, "just do it. The food's getting cold." He pointed at the fans.

Bethany closed her eyes, clapped her hands together and, fingertips beneath her chin, said, "Good food, good meat, good God, let's eat. Amen. Pass the bacon."

She looked up. Bobby was checking behind him to see if anyone had heard.

"Was that a joke," he said, "or what?"

"Or what. Pass the bacon."

Tiffany Leberman giggled. Bobby passed the bacon.

Bethany didn't particularly like any of this but she didn't know what else to do. She wanted to be different. People on the dark side had more fun. They knew more about what was really going on in the world.

"Rolls?" As P.U., Bobby looked like a snooty headwaiter. Bethany took three pieces of bacon and waited for the rolls.

A girl two down from Bethany sniffed. "Anybody hear about the celebration cake?" The girl kept her head turned away.

If there was anyone in the world Bethany hated it was Priscilla Marchione. Priss Marching-on, Bethany and Bobby called her. That bony look, those horn-rimmed glasses, the snooty way she pressed them back up her nose.

"No," lied Bobby. "What about it? Eggs?" He started the scrambled eggs. Already the rising steam had diminished to wispy threads.

"Well. Somebody—and"—cupping her hands around her mouth—"ahem, notice I am not saying *who*"—she did the thing with the glasses—"ate the whole thing."

Bethany leaned around Stephen Doty. "Priss," she said. "How do they know?"

Priscilla gave Bethany a quick, darting look. "What do you mean, how do they know?"

Stephen flattened himself against his chair. "What I said, Priscilla. How? What's the scoop, who's on first?" Sarcasm was a trick Bethany had learned from Hale.

Behind the thick glasses, Priscilla's eyes widened. She shrugged. "So the cake was in the kitchen last night, this morning it was gone." She blinked. "I mean gah, Bethany." She took some eggs from the platter and passed it on.

Bethany leaned her chair back on two legs, threw back her head and began to laugh. People would do anything to avoid being laughed at in this way. People brought her cookies from home and warned her when trouble was in the works. Everybody was nice to her. The other seven people at her table waited. Conversation, eating, the passing of food were by general unspoken agreement suspended until she finished.

Stephen Doty held out the egg platter. People from other tables looked over and, seeing it was only Bethany, looked away.

Bethany despised all this, every minute of every day, and all the wackos. Priscilla Marchione was supposed to be a genius, her father beat up on her, finally she had a nervous breakdown, N.B. in fruitcake shorthand. Johnny Todd was a kleptomaniac, Stephen Doty was so afraid of exhaust pipes he would not ride in a car until he had gotten down on his hands and knees and inspected the rear of the car to make sure no bomb was hidden in the muffler. Andrea "Tiny" Saunders nobody knew about, except that Tiny used to be a serious piano player and now she wouldn't go near the keys. Jason Michaels was all right. Mostly Jason never spoke. No Affect was supposed to be his problem. In some instances N.A. was a relief. And there was precious Tiffany with the Binaca and the Goldilocks curls. Tiffany's mother had gone off with an exterminator from Bugman of Texas. Tiffany hadn't stopped crying since.

Bethany straightened her chair. "Well, *gah*, Priscilla," she said. "That's the funniest thing I ever heard of." She wiped her eyes with the back of her hand. "Just because somebody took it, how do they know who ate it? Somebody could have taken the cake to the Salvation Army. Poor people could be eating that anniversary cake right this minute. There is such a thing as poor people, Priss, you know."

"Well, gah, Bethany. I know about poor people."

"Really? How?"

His arms quivering, Stephen Doty thrust the egg platter at Bethany, who took the platter and heaped her plate.

Priscilla Marchione said nothing. She stared at her food. Bethany winked at Bobby, but Bobby looked away. "Sure, Bethany," he said. "Sure they could have. Yeah, sure. Now." He looked around the table and like the father of them all said, "Shall we eat?"

Bethany bit into a roll. Bobby poured salt on his eggs. Every day was bad but Sunday was the worst.

From across the room, Carol Alexander was watching. Carol was the headmistress. She insisted the students call her by her first name, like an old pal. She wore her long hair parted in the middle, falling down by her eyes in a pageboy. Carol's big talent was the splits. When they had parties, Carol would be standing there, and then she would be on the floor, legs going in opposite directions as if somebody was pulling her apart.

She let her hair flop over in one eye, then turned her head

away. Carol Alexander was the slickest person at Cedar Hills. Her smile was a trap, just like the study room where they sent kids who made trouble. The S.R. was solitary confinement in drag. When they wanted to control you they called it Acting Out—A.O. was the fruitcake name—and sent you to S.R.

Bethany threw her own hair over one shoulder. Carol Alexander knew about the dark side of life but she pretended never to have heard of anything bad in her life. Bethany felt closer to Carol than the others while hating her the most.

Russia couldn't be worse than this.

Bethany scooped up a bite of eggs and shoveled it into her mouth. She crammed bacon in on top of the eggs.

"Stephen."

The small boy looked over.

"Here." She handed him her last piece of bacon. Stephen hated eggs but he was crazy about bacon.

Stephen Doty nodded and said nothing.

· 13 ·

Diana drew the legal pad toward her.

"This mine?" When Hale didn't answer she reached for the Bloody Mary and took a sip. "Thanks."

The muscle in Hale's jaw rose, twitched and shifted, disappeared and then came back up again.

With her finger, Diana stirred her drink, then punched the lime slice down into it and sucked the end of her finger. The drink was hot. She poured herself a cup of coffee, added cream and set the cup on the table to cool.

"So," she said. "No more Celebrities."

Hale shoved the chopped cilantro to one side and stirred the contents of the utensil drawer, looking for the potato peeler. "Really?" he said.

Diana hooked her legs over the arm of her chair. "Armadillos," she said. Hale still had not looked at her. "And a rabbit. The *Salvia greggii* is stripped. Plus something took the leaves from the basil plants and just left them. It's like a war zone out there."

"It's the drought. Animals are coming where they can find water and green."

"Not the basil. They didn't even eat the basil."

"Ants?"

"I couldn't find any." Diana flipped the pages of her legal pad.

"Diana." She looked up at him. When he called her by her name in that tone of voice, he was getting ready to lecture. "There's something we have to get straight." The muscle in his jaw came up again. "I'm not moving."

Diana flipped a page.

"Not ever." He leaned away from the stove to scrutinize his work through the lower half of his glasses.

Diana wiped her finger on her jeans. She was not serious about selling the house. Surely he knew that. The suggestion was a gauge, one play in the whole of an intellectual game. Test the waters, Gil had said. Find out how much change you can stand.

"It was just an idea." There was a shameless, weepy edge to her voice. Hale glanced up through the top half of his glasses. Diana turned away.

Hale took a carton of eggs from the refrigerator. He flipped the stove-top knob to High.

Diana considered her list. Number two was "Go to Belgium." Number three, "Tell Eureka."

Hale dropped half a package of chorizo into the pan. The chorizo started to sizzle wildly. He turned down the heat. Steam coated his glasses. He stood back and with his wooden spoon began to break the sausage apart.

Actually Diana knew a couple who had done as she had suggested; to force change on the family sold the house and moved into a college dormitory as house parents to wait out the storms, thereby finding a way to kick the baby birds firmly from the nest—the birdlings being at that time twenty-four, twenty-six and twenty-nine—without actually taking a stand or hurting anyone's feelings. Because the parents could not bear to ask the children to leave or to stake any claim on the house that made it theirs only and not equal property of the children, they sold it. Stored the furniture, moved. At first the children were furious. Eventually they adjusted.

The point about the house belonging to the adults and not the children was a touchy one. To this day, when Hale went to his mother's house, he hugged Mimi, then went straight to the refrigerator. Mimi loved this boyish habit of his. As if Hale were still a teenager eating everything in sight, never gaining a pound.

Hale took a sip of his drink. "Perfect again," he said, sighing. "Nothing but the best." His eyes were untroubled. As if no cross thought had entered his mind in days.

Diana drew a line through "Sell the house."

Define the problem, a book called *Change* had suggested. Use active verbs. Paint yourself into the picture. Suggest possible solutions. Because Hale did not think there was a problem, he could not paint himself into the obvious picture being painted. Roger had come home to help out with Bethany, which was fine but it had been seven months. Roger was in a slump. Hale knew it wasn't right. He knew the boy should go back to California.

But Roger made Hale happy. He didn't care if the boy ever left.

In the beginning they had agreed: marriage either worked or it did not. Hale mostly still believed that. Willed ignorance had its up side. If lessons were never learned, the same problems provoked the same heated response again and again. Life was guaranteed an attractive edge. In time, Diana had learned a new tongue. She now spoke of negotiations and options, agendas, alternatives and perspective. Whether the use of these new terms indicated a commitment to the negotiated life or stemmed simply from her tendency to take any stand that opposed Hale's, neither of them was certain, although Hale had his suspicions. Friction was a habit. They had made a life together, keeping the string taut, holding each other's feet to the fire, never giving in to total agreement on anything.

Hale stirred the chorizo. He was cooking too much food again. Frowning, he leaned away from the stove to keep from being popped with grease.

"Great Bloody Mary, Hale."

He ducked his head and looked at her through the top half of his glasses. "You do know why I made them."

"It's Sunday."

"And?"

"What?"

"Twenty-six years today."

They didn't make much of wedding anniversaries; still, she usually remembered.

"Of course," she said.

He pointed the spoon. "You forgot."

"No," she said, dipping her finger into her drink, "I did not."

"You wish."

Ah well, their life. Diana could not imagine herself married to, say, a medievalist, the two of them sitting around the fire, the medievalist reading structuralist theories on *Beowulf* while she studied *The Waves* for the umpteenth time.

She looked at her list. Her number two suggestion was "Go to Belgium." Roger was an excellent cook. In California he worked as a chef. Someone had offered to recommend him to a school in Belgium, where he could learn classic cuisine. Diana had thought they could buy him a restaurant, maybe in Austin. Roger didn't want to go. She drew a line through "Go to Belgium."

Hale twisted the chorizo package shut and set it on the counter. He wore a white knit shirt, open at the collar. At the base of his neck on the right-hand side, a raised red bumpy spot the size of a dime had appeared. He pulled the lapels of his shirt together.

The chorizo—freshly made by a woman in Kyle—had a pungent smell, pork and sharp spices, chiles, garlic, cumin, cayenne. He minced a garlic pod with a small slender steak knife by making a series of slices vertically, then horizontally, then down the length of the pod. He scraped the tiny bits of garlic from the chopping board and, lifting the knife carefully, dumped the pieces into the skillet.

"There are bigger knives. Also a garlic press."

"This is fine."

When the collar of his shirt shifted again Diana could see another patch of red forming on the other side of his neck. The places came in pairs, like ink blot patterns. He sipped his drink.

"I love this house, Diana," he said. "I want to be taken out of this house feet first." He paused. "In a box."

Diana flinched. She began making looping lines on her note paper, drawing balloon men.

Hale cracked an egg.

"Hale," she said. "I wasn't making a pronouncement about the house. I was just looking for . . . " She hesitated. "Creative alternatives to the situation."

A muscle in the general area of his left eye twitched.

"I hate it," he said, "when you use that word."

She could feel his annoyance growing like the red spots, which had become quarters.

"Which?" She couldn't stop. "Alternative?"

"No." Flicking his wrist, he sailed an eggshell across the room. "Creative." The eggshell went into the compost pail. He cracked another. "Whenever I hear that word, I know somebody's about to get snookered." The second eggshell missed. He picked it up and tossed it again, a hook shot. "Cords and floor."

"You gotta be a pro."

"Shit."

"What?"

"I forgot onions." He started to chop.

"Is fresh," Diana said, "better?"

"Fresh what?" His knife went *tock-tock* against the butcher block.

"You know what."

"No." He widened his eyes. "I don't."

"Alternative. Instead of creative. Fresh alternative."

"Oh." Secretly admiring her dogged tenacity, he shook his head. "No," he said. "I don't think so. No."

Diana went to the refrigerator for more cream.

"You want help?" She reached up to lay her arm across his shoulder and massage his neck.

Hale looked down at her. He was crying.

"I have," he said, pointing his knife toward the mound of chopped onion, "enjoyed about all of this I can stand."

Like the monkey said while making love to the skunk.

The joke was an old one, as much a part of the vocabulary of their marriage as their brand of toothpaste.

Tears ran down his cheeks.

"Hale, call it quits. That's onion enough."

"I'm almost finished."

She took up his spoon and began stirring the chorizo and garlic.

Hale tossed his steak knife aside.

"Okay," he said, "I'll take over."

With his hip he eased her out of the way. He dumped the onions into the skillet. Juice splattered. He stepped back. Holding the skillet up off the burner, he again lowered the heat. When the coils had cooled, he set the skillet back down and went to the sink, took off his glasses, washed them with liquid detergent and dried them with paper towels.

"Well," he said, setting the glasses back on his nose, looking out the wall of windows toward the hills. "Hello, world."

Diana put a checkmark by "Tell Eureka."

· 14 ·

*F*rom the pillow Roger could see the tops of some trees. One kind was lacy, the other sturdy and serious. The leaves were still. Above the trees, the gray morning sky was turning blue.

From the kitchen he could hear his parents talking, pots and pans clattering. The conversation went from hot to cool. He had the feeling they were talking about him.

He folded his pillow beneath his head. On the wall beside his bed were framed family pictures, himself as a child, Bethany as a baby, himself holding Bethany, Gloria as a girl, her hair in waves. In a posed studio photograph, a young Diana and Hale look soft and anxious, like clay impressions of the finished people they would become. Diana had intended for the room to become a guest room. After Roger moved to California, she hung the pictures. Then he came back.

He stretched his legs and pulled the sheet to his waist. Working out at the gym had bulked out his arms and shoulders. He was a big boy, not lean like his father but muscular and strong and not quite as tall as Hale.

He was right to have come home. It was not vanity thinking he was important to his parents but a simple, observable truth. With the weakest jokes he could lift their spirits; he had that knack. He could do it for other people too, but no one else keeled over with happiness the way his parents did.

In seven months' time things had begun to change. Hale and Diana were beginning to worry about him instead of the other way around. Gil thought if Roger could take some of the heat off Bethany, then Bethany might stop feeling the need to be bad. Roger could become the I.P. in her place.

He opened a magazine on his bedside table and from between the pages took out a package of cigarettes. He shook one out and lit it. He felt woozy. Too much wine and smoke, too little sleep. When he walked, his knee creaked. He went to the window, opened it, blew a puff of smoke out the screen. On the driveway, Rufus attacked a flea on his back near his tail, grinding at his flesh with his small front teeth.

His parents wanted him to be ambitious the way they were. They wanted him to set up goals to fit his life around, then go after those goals. He would like to have those desires, to please them if nothing else, but he simply did not. Anyway, what was their hurry?

Benicia was a beautiful harbor town north of San Francisco, a haven for artists—the light was great—lesbians, pigeons and people who wanted to live near the city but not in it, yet not in the suburbs. In Benicia, Roger had a great apartment, three floors up in a fabulous Art Deco building on the main street of town only two blocks from the water. It was time for him to go back, but he'd made a pact with himself not to until he felt his parents were safe and ready. And there was Gil. Roger had wanted to go into therapy. There was a woman he'd heard about, a Reichian in Napa, on the fringe of the wine country. He couldn't afford the Reichian. Here, his parents paid.

He tapped ashes in the motel ashtray. Diana was a maniac about cigarettes. Hale didn't like them either. If they noticed, they did not say. If they knew, they pretended not to. He remembered a song he'd listened to as a child. "You hear what you want to hear, you see what you want to see." He lay back down, enjoying his smoke while he could.

His parents had done everything for him, taken him to nursery school and a special kindergarten, to museum school before he was five. They bought paints when he said he liked to draw, a waterbed when he'd admired one, a leather jacket he'd seen in a shop on vacation in Colorado. When he brought home drawings from the museum school they hung them on the refrigerator and said the right thing, not "What is it?" but "Tell me about it. It's wonderful."

After a while, he grew nervous about expressing admiration for anything. They'd buy it. He wouldn't like it. They'd be disappointed. Again.

He did not know how to be hard on himself the way they were. They had some need to matter in the world, and he did not; his preference was to belong rather than matter. He liked to keep a group around him all the time. Hale and Diana thought his need for other people was part of a plot which kept him what they called On the California Float instead of out in the world doing things. And maybe they were right, who could say. They sounded right.

I am a glorified housekeeper, he wanted to tell them. *I like to cook and stay home. I don't care about history or making a name for myself. If I was a girl I'd have a baby.*

They would never get it. If he floated it wasn't California's fault. A floater was what he was.

In Benicia, he cooked at a coffee bar and gourmet take-out restaurant called Lana. The two women who owned the café roasted their own beans and dripped coffee cup by cup for customers. They had a huge copper cappuccino machine, always polished to a reflective sheen. *Caffè latte* was Roger's favorite: a soupbowl-size cup of steamed, frothed milk on top of dark-roast coffee, a dash of cinnamon on top. The cream was delivered every other day by a local dairy. One of the women who owned the restaurant, Patty, had decided they should grow their own herbs, so they always had fresh.

In California, this was possible all year long. Patty's partner, Jane, was the gardener. Jane had grown up in the South. Her backyard looked like *Gone with the Wind*, lush with camellias and gardenias and roses in every shade of pink and red.

He knew what the world thought of northern California. When he came home to Texas, he saw what the world saw, leftover flower children growing their own herbs, doing acupuncture, bleaching their jeans. But he liked it out there. In Texas everybody was so caught up in the ends of things, it was as if they all wanted to rush through and get it over with. Then what?

The color of the light in Benicia made him happy. He could sit on the docks and watch the pigeons, the boats and the water for hours. He had learned to wind surf, which made him feel like he was flying. He could take his mountain bike for an all-day ride and come home feeling physically used up and spiritually nourished. For a treat he and his friends took backpacks down to the Big Sur and camped out. The air, the light, the landscape swelled their hearts and left them with little else to talk about.

Everybody floats out there, Hale protested. Maybe he was right. And maybe the world needed its floaters.

He took another drag from his cigarette. The central air conditioning switched on. In the kitchen his parents had grown quiet.

They said they just wanted him to be happy. They did but not just. He'd gone to U.C./Santa Cruz for five years. With only ten credits to go before graduating, he'd moved to Benicia.

He ground out the cigarette.

Hale and Diana disapproved of the move, whether it made him happy or not. He couldn't blame them. They'd paid.

He'd thought of suggesting that Bethany come to Benicia

to live with him. Gil had convinced him not to. He could not stay here forever. Sooner or later Jane and Patty would get tired of doing the cooking themselves. Finding another job was no problem. A good cook was never without work for long. But he liked Lana.

By his bed on the floor was his notebook, beside it a hardcover book from the library. Gil had suggested the book. But Roger was a slow reader. He didn't think he could finish the book before he went back.

He'd gone to a speed-reading course; they'd finally concluded they could not help him. "You're one of those people," the instructor said, "for whom reading is not visual. You actually *hear* the words pronounced as you read them. Did someone read aloud to you as a child?"

Roger said yes, his mother had read to him long past the time he knew how.

"That," concluded the speed-reader, "is the problem. When you read you listen to the sound of your mother's voice."

Roger thought of the RCA dog with his ear to the phonograph.

His room was immaculate, his clothes neatly folded in his drawers. Hale and Diana drove him crazy, the way they never threw anything away. He had cleaned out the storeroom in the garage and the large storage closet beneath the stairway. In the closet, he'd found stiffened rags next to a box containing Diana's silver baby cup, an old suitcase filled with moth-eaten clothes Diana hadn't worn in twenty years, magazines they'd never get to, a box containing a gauzy evening gown that once belonged to Fanny.

"If you throw anything away," Diana said, "don't tell me." Fanny's gown was one of the dresses they had considered burying her in. When they decided not to use the dress, Diana tossed it in a box, then threw the box in the closet. In the storeroom, Roger had found an etching, framed and signed. The etching had been gnawed by roaches and mice. It was a nice picture. He asked why they'd kept it if they were going to leave it to be ruined. "Oh, the glass cracked," Diana said. "I meant to have it fixed. Then I decided I'd really never liked it anyway. But Hale did. So . . ." She shrugged.

Roger liked to lie in the bed and picture his socks and underwear piled neatly in a drawer, then open the drawer and find them exactly as he had imagined.

He fanned smoke away. When he got up to close his window, he slipped into his underwear.

He'd had male lovers and female. He'd enjoyed both. What he wanted was to be with women; he didn't want to die of AIDS, he did not want to be a homosexual. Much of the time he simply swore off, living alone, prowling the streets, going to San Francisco with his beautiful lesbian friends, to concerts or a movie and dinner. No one out there thought of him as a floater. He had a job. Compared to some other people he knew, he was a workhorse. As for sex, as the random pursuit of that activity became more and more dangerous, more and more single people were becoming celibate and more and more married couples were staying together whether they wanted to or not. Out here in Driftwood that fear was anomalous, like dark clouds. In northern California the threat—and the fear—were real.

Jane and Patty loved his cooking. They all had a wonderful time together. There was a girl he liked, a painter, Kim; she'd come to Benicia for the light and the water. They'd gone out. He thought they might move in together when he went back. If she hadn't found someone else by then.

Gil had suggested he tell all that to his parents. Family secrets, he said, were a cancer that ate away at the family system. Roger wasn't sure he cared that much about the system.

He put on a pair of blue jeans and buttoned them. Living at home, he'd gained weight. Not much; enough to notice. He began making up his bed.

Working at the store was interesting enough. He knew the cowboys considered him an oddball, but that didn't bother him. He could play the same joke-telling trick on the cowboys he played on his parents. The cowboys didn't know what to make of him. Off their guard, they often bought what they hadn't planned to.

He ran his hands through his hair, picked up the ashtray and poured its contents into a brown envelope beneath the magazines.

He could go back to sleep. But today was their anniversary. He'd planned to cook a special dinner tonight. If he could talk Hale out of fried chicken, he'd do an exotic dish he'd thought of during the night, breast of veal stuffed with onions, walnuts and prunes, spiced with maybe turmeric and cumin.

He fingered a small round place on the back of his head, a scar where no hair grew. When he was a year old, he'd pulled himself up to the toilet seat. His knees had gone wobbly and he had fallen against a hot water pipe and burned his head.

He thought of himself lying there, his head sizzling. Diana had been talking on the telephone when it happened.

"You did everything too soon," she said. "I couldn't keep up."

He smoothed the covers and sat on the bed. He felt no rancor toward Diana about the childhood incident. But when his hair blew she brushed it over the scar. If she touched it, she shivered. "I can feel it," she told him. "Like a razor blade, slicing me down the middle."

"Then leave it alone," he said.

"I can't," she replied. And she shivered again.

He could go out now. He was awake enough and they were not arguing.

He had hurt his knee doing stunts on his mountain bicycle. He'd had to have surgery. Maybe there were leftover traces of the risk-taking person he'd been as a child. Besides the knee he couldn't think of many. To him, his life seemed pretty tame.

He unbuttoned his jeans and lay back down. It was early. There was time for one more short nap. He tucked the envelope of ashes beneath the magazines and turned over on his side.

· 15 ·

"In Eureka Springs that time, remember? I went to that conference?"

"I do." What he remembered most was that one of the nights Diana was gone Bethany had asked to go to a movie with friends. He'd said yes, thinking by friends she meant girls. Instead, six Mexicans—four boys, two girls—showed up in a Volkswagen bug. All were older than Bethany by at least two years. They went to San Marcos.

There was never anyone to call. Bethany only told them first names. Agatha, Carlotta, Cindy. Ricky, Tina, Sugarbear. None of them had telephones. Bethany didn't get home until two in the morning. They'd had a flat tire, she explained; with no spare they'd had to wait for a tow truck. Hale was so relieved to see her he hadn't been angry. He'd never told Diana.

"We visited a house, it was on the tourist attraction list, Irene's Castle."

Hale reached for a package of flour tortillas.

"The woman whose house it was was still living there. There we all were trooping through her living room and her all the time in a rocking chair in her den watching a TV game show. She was, I mean, a dried-up little raisin of a woman, maybe ninety. She answered a few questions, but she didn't care about the house, she just wanted us to pay our money and leave her alone to watch her show."

Hale opened the tortillas. This was when Diana looked her best, when she was engaged in work or conversation. Her face came alive and she let go of that long-suffering look which she seemed to think proved her a serious person.

"The walls of the living room were completely covered with vines and plants. It looked like a jungle. Ivy and philodendron had been trained up the walls. The vines made a loop at the ceiling, then doubled up and came back down again. Only the windowpanes were uncovered. Outside, more jungle . . . mostly wild things she'd let take over, senna bean trees, giant sunflowers, Johnson grass, buttercups, milkweed, bull nettle. Wisteria and honeysuckle grew through the windows. She'd made openings in the windows like doggy-doors so that in the spring and summer, the vines could climb through. The furniture was cheap vinyl, ugly but comfortable. And there were aquariums. I remember the green lights." She sipped her drink. "Remember that time we tried one?"

"What?"

"We bought the motor, the food, the plastic grass, the tropical fish. Roger cried for two days when they all died."

Hale nodded. Diana went on. "We never could raise anything that didn't walk on the ground. Remember the bird? Christ. Anyway, Irene had these aquariums; you could look through the tanks and see the vines on the other side. It gave the odd impression of fish swimming through philodendron. Inside the tanks, there was the usual paraphernalia, but Irene didn't believe in store-bought. She had made her castles and bridges from rocks and cleaned bicycle chains and ball bearings and bottles and real seashells. On the coffee table in the middle of the living room was a terrarium made from a clear plastic cake plate and cover. Inside the terrarium were rocks, turtles, plants. Well, it was a wonder, the whole thing. An absolute piece of native folk art all its own."

Hale turned on the heat under the stovetop griddle and lifted the stainless steel covering.

"Originally Irene and her family came from I think Oklahoma. Some western state. Her husband had gotten a job in Eureka Springs. He liked the Ozarks for the fishing and so they came to Arkansas, he and Irene and some large number of children. In Eureka Springs they bought a piece of property out from town, an acre or two on the side of a hill with a shacky little house and a chicken coop. The husband promised if Irene moved in, he'd build her a better house right away and so she did."

Hale hummed a little tune.

"Hale, are you listening?"

"Right away and so she did. So go on. It's a great story."

"So Irene waited for her house. And waited. Winter, spring, nothing. Finally one day she'd had it. After her husband left for work one morning, she gave each of the kids a tool. They moved the furniture to the chicken coop. When the husband got home, all that was left of the shacky little house was a pile of lumber. Irene and the children were standing in the door to the chicken coop holding their tools. 'Now,' Irene said, 'I guess you'll build me that house.' "

Hale looked up and laughed.

"That's a great story," he said. "You never told me." He began warming tortillas. When they were soft, he placed them between two enamel-coated tin plates to keep them warm. He began handing condiments across to Diana, sour cream, chopped jalapeños, grated cheese, pico de gallo, green salsa.

"Once Irene got her house, she turned it into a live-in collage. In the dining room and kitchen instead of plants there were paste-ups on the walls, ordinary everyday things, bits and pieces of paper, snatches of fabric, bits of glass, pictures from magazines, an old valentine, hundreds of Christmas cards, anything and everything. There were no paintings and not many snapshots. I remember one of the Kennedys, Jackie and the children holding hands during the funeral. Outside, the hollyhock bed was marked off with brown Orange Crush bottles pressed neck down into the ground. The wisteria vine was ringed by a border of blue milk of magnesia bottles. There were bird feeders made from Clorox bottles, new seedlings germinating in buttermilk cartons, oh just everything."

To soak up excessive grease, Hale dabbed at the sizzling meat mixture with a wad of paper toweling. "Sounds like you," he said. He tossed the toweling aside and tore off another.

"Oh, Lord. I'm an amateur compared to Irene. So . . ." She was trying to remember the point of the story.

When she did, the studied, serious look came back. "So I was thinking. Maybe we need a fast change like that. I've been wanting to turn the downstairs middle bedroom into an office so that I could work there, what do you think? We could . . ." She began to talk faster so that Hale could not interrupt. ". . . shift the furniture, see what happens." Her voice drifted off.

"You mean wait until he's gone, then change things around?"

"Oh well, Hale . . ."

"It's a chickenshit way of dealing with things, Diana. You could just come straight out and ask him to leave. You could tell Bethany to take a flying leap. We could build a wall. We could live in padded cells."

"I wasn't . . ."

"Yes. You were."

"So could you. You could do all that, too."

"So could I, yes, but he doesn't bother me the way he does you." Hale poured beaten eggs into the sausage-and-onion mixture. He lowered his voice. "Roger is not the problem, Diana. He is not the problem. I don't know what you're after or when you will ever be satisfied."

He tossed in a thimbleful of minced serranos.

Diana made a line through "Tell Eureka."

"He's here for a reason, Hale. He thinks it's his job to be here, to take the heat off Bethany."

Hale's jaw muscle jumped. "Job," he muttered.

Diana set out plates and forks.

"We have to see this through, Diana. We just have to see it through."

"You mean wait."

"I mean . . . yes, I mean wait." He fought the urge to claw at the itchy places on his neck.

"For how long, would you say?"

"I wouldn't."

"If you had to." She took bright-colored napkins from a drawer and closed the drawer with her hip.

"As long as it takes."

"Forever?"

"It won't."

"But if it has to?"

"It won't. That's the end. It won't."

A few more flicks of the wrist and he was finished. He set the black skillet and the warm plates on the table, sat down, pulled up his chair and began to construct his breakfast taco. He took out a tortilla, piled on chorizo-and-egg mixture, added pico de gallo, green salsa and jalapeños. Diana spooned green salsa over her eggs. Hale ladled out a moderate-size dollop of sour cream.

"You know," Diana said, "I'm the one who's supposed to be doing this."

Hale rolled up the tortilla.

"Doing what?"

"Holding on too long. The mother hen. Chicks in the nest and so on."

"I didn't say hold on," he said. He took a bite.

"Roger could take the rest of his life to decide to grow up. We have to find a way to help kick him out. Otherwise we're infantilizing him."

He glanced at the Sunday papers; Diana reached over and touched his arm. He frowned.

"Do you remember when he wanted to be a city planner, how lit up he was with ideas? Remember that Christmas? Pocket parks for the poor?"

Hale wiped his mouth.

"Diana."

"Wait. Let me finish. By Easter he was back to movies. A friend of his was a friend of a friend of Warren Beatty."

Hale looked out the glass door. Rufus had come around to the porch. He was lying flush against the glass, coat flattened.

Hale began to build another taco.

"Eat," he said. "It's no good stone cold."

"He's thinking of staying, Hale. He thinks Gil is brilliant. With only ten credits to go he's talking about coming back down here and going to U.T. He says he might want to become a family therapist. He'll have to start over." She tapped Hale's arm. "Yesterday when I was on the phone he stood right over there with an open book in his hands waiting for me to finish so that he could read me a paragraph which he said would help me understand cybernetics."

Hale held the dripping B.T. with both hands. "And did it?"

"No, Hale. I'll never get it. No."

He licked a drop of salsa from his lip.

"We have to do something."

"I know, Diana," he said. "I know."

When Hale said I know I know, she might as well be talking to the walls. He polished off his taco in silence.

When he was finished, he drained his Bloody Mary, stood and stretched.

"I'm stuffed," he said. Fast eating was a Caldwell family trait. At Mimi's house they ate as if the house was burning down. Diana was always trying to catch up.

He gathered up the papers.

"I'm going to turn out the horses, then go up. Let my B.T.'s settle, maybe take a nap. You want any of this?" He held out the newspapers.

"Only the Arts."

Hale found the arts sections of both papers and set them on the table.

Diana nibbled at her taco. "Great breakfast, Hale."

"Only the best."

"Happy anniversary."

"You too."

"Hale?"

"Yes."

"We'll work it out."

Hale slid the newspapers under his arm.

"Or we won't."

On his way out, he scratched at the places on his neck, set the newspapers on a table by the stairway and opened the front door. "Goddamn son-of-a-bitching skin," he muttered loud enough for Diana to hear. He stepped outside. "I ought," he said to nobody in particular, "to be taken out and shot." He let the door slam.

As Diana watched him, a flicker of memory caught her attention—Hale between her legs, mouth smeared like a baby eating candy, eyes bright, hair a mess—then it was gone.

· 16 ·

At the sink, she pondered a custard cup half filled with grated jack cheese. The refrigerator was already full of just such custard cups covered with plastic wrap, inside each some leftover dab of something on the verge of going blinky. She set the dish aside.

It was nine-thirty. She had a new blouse to take Bethany, also a book of short stories by a writer named Alice Fine whose deadly cold tone—first person, present tense, like a list—Bethany admired.

She stacked her plate on top of Hale's and took them to the sink. Hale came back from turning out the horses. Without speaking, he picked up his newspapers, poured himself a cup of coffee and went upstairs. From above, Diana heard his shoes drop.

She tossed silverware into the sink, wrapped the leftover chorizo in plastic and put it in the refrigerator, returned the glass of cilantro to its place beside a plastic container of she could not remember what.

Roger had quietly padded in from his room. Out of the corner of her eye she saw him, in the middle of the living room floor dressed only in a pair of blue jeans. His hair was matted in curls, flattened against his forehead, as if pressed down by an iron. There were baby pictures of him looking exactly the way he did now. Soft and rumpled and very serious. He squinted. Without his contact lenses he could not see distances.

Diana turned to the sink. She dumped the grated cheese into the disposer trap but did not run the machine.

" 'Morning, Mom." He padded over and hugged her from behind. She could smell cigarettes. "Happy anniversary." He kissed her cheek.

"You remembered."

"Me, forget?"

Don't leave. She did not say it. She was not exactly aware even of thinking it. *Whatever I say. Don't go.*

He relaxed his grip.

"Well," she said. "Thanks. And good morning."

He moved away. She asked what he wanted for breakfast. The B.T. mix, she said, was cold, but she could heat it up. Or she could poach some eggs with an English muffin. There was cereal, Grape-Nuts, raisin bran or a new kind of high-protein granola, sweetened with fruit juices.

"Poached eggs would be terrific." He rubbed his bare stomach. "I feel a little woopsy for B.T.'s. I may make hollandaise." He reached for the coffeepot. "You want any more of this?"

Diana shook her head.

He turned off the machine. "I'll make caff. I need a jolt."

He empied the pot and from the freezer took out one of the bags of Patty's dark-roast special he'd brought from California. "Maybe," he said, "old Dad will have some with me." He poured beans into the electric grinder and pushed the button.

Diana wondered if she could eat anything else, maybe a scrap of flour tortilla with hollandaise; Roger loved for them to eat his cooking. He'd done some catering since he'd been home, a ladies' tea in San Marcos, a wedding in Buda and one in Kyle, some parties. He called himself Dripping Springs Food. At home, he experimented. Crabmeat pie, cold buttermilk soup, grilled rabbit with lingonberry sauce, pecan and chess pies and his Chinese specialties: cashew chicken, hot-and-sour soup, a magnificent pork tenderloin with black walnut sauce.

"Back in a minute," he said.

On his way out he turned on the radio, tuned to the university station which on Sunday mornings played jazz. From two speakers mounted high on the walls flute music came on, a high-pitched wail without vibrato. The music filled the house. Roger shuffled into the bathroom and closed the door. Already Diana could breathe a little freer, as if the boy had magically swept her bad night into an over-sized dustpan. She could hear Hale rumbling about upstairs. She snatched up her legal pad and hid it under the newspapers Hale had left for her.

Hale came down, whistling in counterpoint to the flute.

"Didn't I hear our young man?"

"You did. He's in the bathroom." Diana pulled the egg-poaching pan from the drawer, upsetting Hale's careful stack.

"Hey," he said. "I just did that."

She shoved the pans back in and closed the drawer. "I have to hurry. I have to finish in time to be there by noon."

He set the sports section on the table. "He want me to do B.T.'s? I could warm ours up if you haven't given them to Rufus."

Diana took out two eggs. "No," she said. "He wants poached."

The coffee machine growled. "He make more coffee?"

"Caff," she said. "Be careful."

"Yes ma'am."

She cracked an egg into a saucer. "I suppose two."

"At least. I'll do another round of Marys."

"Not for me. I have that drive to make."

"How many times are you going to tell me that?"

"Tell you what?"

One hand on the pantry door, the other on a can of spicy tomato juice, Hale said nothing.

Diana lifted the skillet of breakfast taco mix from the burner. "Before you do that, would you take this out to Rufus?"

Hale set the juice down, then took the skillet outside and set it next to Rufus's nose. Without bothering to get up, Rufus gulped down the mixture and licked the skillet.

"Easy, Roof," Hale said. "You'll rust the cast iron." Rufus wagged his tail. Hale rubbed the dog's ears. The look in Rufus's eyes was of pure, uncomplicated devotion.

Too bad Rufus was a dog.

As Hale picked up the skillet and stepped through the sliding glass doors, Roger sneaked up from behind him. He leaned around his father and planted a wet kiss on Hale's surprised cheek.

"Happy anniversary, Dad."

Hale looked as embarrassed and as pleased as a high school girl getting her first corsage.

Roger's hair was wet. He had combed back his curls.

"And good morning," he said.

His parents stood there smiling radiant smiles. How could he leave? With their happiness beaming warmth at him like rays from a giant toaster, how could he possibly leave them?

Hale offered Roger a Bloody Mary while Diana slid eggs from the saucer into the simmering water. She was cooking them too soon; if he was going to make hollandaise, he would have to poach more. Roger said nothing. Eggs were good for Rufus's coat.

· 17 ·

*B*ethany had switched from her Sunday shirt back to Motley Crue. She held the knife close.

Time was like a weight on her chest. Days were starting to drag. Waiting was the worst. Next to onions and liver, nothing was worse than standing in line.

Sometimes she imagined someone coming to take her away, a fairy godmother with a wand, or the space ship in *Close Encounters* when it let the lost people out and the new ones on. Or Superman. She the rescued Lois Lane flying out of Cedar Hills and down the fault line, toward home.

She wrapped her hair in a ball and fixed it under her head. Maybe if that happened she could start over. She did not mean to be bad, neither did Alex. Alex wanted to go to college. His dream was to be an architect. They made promises. Then the thing came down and they did the bad stuff again. They didn't forget their vows; it was like they never remembered promising.

Deep down, what she wanted was for everybody to be together. Happy, too. But mostly together. Christmas every day would suit her fine; she was a Christmas expert. Everybody said she gave the greatest gifts and they weren't making it up, she had that knack. One time she ordered a tiny, battery-operated fan for Gloria, so that when she sewed—Gloria was always blazing hot, that was how she said it, I'm just *blazing hot*—she could turn the air on herself and not sweat so much. Gloria cried, she liked that fan so much. Last year she gave Diana a small gold boot on a chain. Hale got a black leather vest, Roger an original painting she'd bought on Sixth Street.

A totally bad person would not be able to pick out great gifts for other people.

She ran her finger against the blade of her knife, down and up the ridges of its scalloped edge. The knife was not that sharp. She could press hard and not cut herself.

Bobby had gone to do his deep breathing. "I don't want," he said, "to have an N.B."

Bethany couldn't see that the deep breathing did any good, but if Bobby liked to think so it probably did.

She brought the knife out from under the sheet and put it against her stomach. She was lying on her side away from the door so that if anybody came in she could hide it fast.

The same when she cut Diana. She had not meant to throw the knife, it just happened. Like some great power moved her hand, zap. Then it was over. And Diana was not really hurt, it was only a nick, not deep at all. Diana had not told Hale. Bethany had thought it would be like the other things Diana knew about but had kept to herself: their secret. B.U., as Bobby said: Between Us. Then one day Hale let Bethany know Diana had spilled the beans. Probably by now everybody in Texas knew.

She'd been helping with dinner, boning chicken breasts. Hale and Diana went to all this trouble with food; it drove Bethany crazy the way they chopped and stirred and went nuts over recipes. Bethany liked regular American food, chicken-fried steak, burritos, tacos, corn on the cob, soft white bread, spaghetti with meat sauce. They were always telling her she liked something she didn't.

For example, macaroni-and-cheese. When Bethany happened to mention that she happened to like macaroni-and-cheese, nothing would do but for Diana to go out and buy Vermont cheddar and macaroni from Italy. It took an hour to put the dish together—what with Diana standing there grating the cheese, stirring the sauce, washing pans—instead of the ten minutes it took to make Kraft's at the Hurtados'.

The last straw was, Kraft's was great and Diana's tasted like glue. Bethany was supposed to pretend to like it even if she didn't, but if she did Diana would make it again and the next time she'd say, "Well, you liked it the last time I fixed it," and there they'd be.

Food definitely was the great power.

So Bethany was doing the chicken breasts and Diana was going at her about where she'd been the night before and how late she'd come in and what she was doing to her future by letting her grades slide. Bethany hated chicken breasts. As she slid the blade against the bone, the knife slipped and sliced into her finger, a clean cut, curved, like a cartoon smile.

Blood dripped on the chicken breast. Bethany felt sick and in a rage at the same time. The next thing she knew the knife was flying across the room and really if she had aimed she'd never have been able to hit her in a thousand years. Diana was wearing one of her Mexican blouses with a square neckline.

Bethany wanted to tell her to duck but it happened too fast. The point of the knife nicked Diana's chest, right at the collarbone. Her mother screamed. "You tried to kill me," she said. "You went for my throat." Blood made a red streak down the front of Diana's blouse. Bethany held up her own red finger and cried. "I'm sorry," she said. "Sorry, sorry, sorry." They cried together, then went for Band-Aids. Then nothing.

Bethany curled up, bringing her knees to her chest. She cradled the cake knife between her breasts. It wasn't her fault the nick hadn't healed right, she didn't have any say-so over scars. But wouldn't you know, wouldn't it just have to.

She slid her hands between her legs. It was a comfort to feel what Alex had felt, to imagine it was his hands exploring inside herself and not her own. She brought her knees up closer and closed her eyes.

· 18 ·

*B*arefoot and showered, Diana sat at the dresser. Her slip was one of her good ones, off-white silk with lace.

"I am an artist," Gloria used to say, sitting hunched over her sewing machine guiding slippery rivers of fabric beneath the jabbing electric needle. "My canvas is satin. Bugle beads and sequins are my oils." Looking down to find Diana at her feet, a wispy light-haired little girl surrounded by spilled chips of glitter, forgotten spools of thread, shards of shiny fabric, she repeated herself, enunciating as carefully as if she were speaking to the deaf. "I am," she said, "an artist." And Diana would nod, gathering up beads and sequins to put in a cake tin Gloria used for a scrap box.

At night she redirected her talents. In front of the mirror Gloria painted her face, drew, erased, redrew, moving so slowly it seemed the gears that had kept her going at such a frantic pace during the day had been wound down. At the mirror, patience was Gloria Dubard's middle name. She could sit there, it seemed, forever, until in her mind she looked not just attractive but young again. Drops of makeup base fell from her fingertips. Face powder sent dusty showers across the room. Nail polish dripped. Overturned bottles of gardenia perfume soaked permanently into the mahogany. Gloria saw only her own face.

The dresser—mahogany, with drawer pulls shaped like acorns—was one of the few pieces of Gloria's furniture Diana had kept. The rest was in storage. No one wanted it—there was no one—there was nothing to do with it, Gloria was not going to get out of the nursing home except as Hale would say, feet first in a box. And so there the furniture sat, at thirty-five dollars a month for the storage.

Diana poured makeup into her palm and with the tips of her fingers began to spread it across her forehead. She closed her eyes and covered her eyelids. The makeup felt cool and soothing.

When it was over, Gloria would gather Diana and Fanny to her and, holding their faces on either side of hers, bat her fabulous eyelashes and say, "Mirror, mirror on the wall, which twin has the Toni?"

Like good chorus girls Diana and Fanny answered on cue. "You do, Mama," they said. "You do."

Diana opened her eyes. Bethany's were the same, gray-green with stubby dark lashes, that one drooping lid. A Floyd Beauchamp eyelid, Gloria claimed. Floyd Beauchamp was dead before Diana was old enough to have him set in her memory. She had a couple of pictures of him, taken on the same day, with his dog, a white German shepherd. In one he is at a gate with the dog. In the other one he and the dog are walking away. There is a hopeless slump to Floyd Beauchamp's shoulders.

When they married, she and Hale had not meant to have children right away. Diana did not know what else she wanted to do with her life, they simply had thought it best not to have a child too soon. The Pill was not yet widely used. On the advice of a friend Diana used a contraceptive vaginal foam. Roger was born within two years of their marriage.

Motherhood changed everything. Diana focused fearsome attention on Roger, powers of concentration she didn't know she possessed. Roger thrived, but from the beginning Diana longed for a girl. The first baby having come with such ease, she thought a second would be as little trouble.

There were miscarriages, one stillborn; meantime Roger risked his life. Quiet in the womb, in the world he became an active baby, and later a nervous, adventurous child. He stood too soon, walked too early, careened into sharp edges. They'd had to take him to the emergency room six times in three years.

Doctors could not say what Diana's trouble was, they could only give her medicines, prescribe regimens of rest and a special diet to try to prevent the premature contractions from happening again. Challenged, she became a maniac, taking her temperature, calling Hale at the office when the time was right. She read books, meditated, studied, thought. Hale suggested perhaps she was concentrating too hard.

"Maybe," he said, "you should think about something else. How about school? You said you wanted to get your master's."

For distraction as much as anything, she went to graduate school. In two years she had her master's. Roger attended day care, nursery school, kindergarten. Diana went to work on her Ph.D.

At some point a pregnancy clicked. Her doctor told her to spend the last three months in bed. She read, studied. Weekdays Roger, in first grade, took care of her. After school, he brought fruit and saltines to her bed. Together they watched cartoons. Krazy Kat, Superboy, Astro-boy. She could sing all the theme songs. That was when Roger began experimenting with food, scrambled eggs and then omelettes, chocolate chip cookies, won-ton soup, pudding from a mix.

Hale was good with his hands. He used to sit for hours at Roger's table, knees at his chin as he and the boy made tiny clay people who could stand and sit. The people all had separate eyebrows, lips and noses—minute balls of clay rolled between thumb and forefinger—and they wore hats and boots.

When Diana came home from class or the library Hale and Roger would be sitting there, looking at the door, the clay men lined up for her to see.

That time seemed happy enough, but much of it was a blur, like the clay men at the end of the afternoon, smashed into a ball.

Unlike Roger, Bethany *in utero* was a wildcat. She thumped, bumped, punched Diana's spleen. At eight months, in the middle of a winter night, she turned. As carefully as if her stomach were made of glass, Diana reached down to see what had happened. Bethany's head was against one hipbone, her feet against the other. Hale slept with a hand on Diana's arm during that time, so that if she got up in the night having trouble, he would know. She pulled the arm away. He snapped from sleep. She took his hand and put it on her stomach. They wrapped Roger in a blanket and went to the emergency room. There was nothing to do. Diana would simply have to tolerate the discomfort for a while. In a few weeks, if the baby didn't turn, they would take her surgically.

Bethany—of course—stayed where she was.

Diana opened a mascara brush. She flicked the bristles down the length of her eyelashes, turned her face to one side and blinked. *There,* Gloria would say, patting the skin beneath her chin with the back of her hand. *That's where it begins. Right there.*

The doctor took her uterus out, along with Bethany. She had not been prepared for the after-effects, the joy of having a daughter utterly counterbalanced by the desolation of losing a part of herself she had hardly ever thought of before. She felt shockingly *defaced.*

Diana didn't dwell on aging much, but she felt it, the loss of possibilities, the long slow process of very simply drying up. None of this made her feel depressed or desperate, just sad. Being with Jesse had helped. A boyish thirty-seven, Jesse had given her a feeling of spiritedness and youth. Diana had been seeing him for three years when she gave him up.

As a baby Bethany was placid and fat, a lovable chunk of sweetness who could lie in her bed for hours, staring at a colorful mobile, holding on to her toes. Those were good times, the long quiet afternoons, Roger at school, Hale at work, Bethany and Diana together in the large dark house they had rented in the Montrose section of Houston. Her last baby. She'd been a happy child, Diana had pictures to prove it. Whatever had happened to make things go wrong later on, Bethany Frances Caldwell had been a happy baby. In pictures she was always laughing, mugging, rolling her eyes, playing games.

From the makeup tray Diana took out a small brush, outlined her lips in pale pink, then filled them in with a slightly darker shade.

Floyd Beauchamp—Gloria's second husband; she refused to speak of the first—was said to have been a sweet but ineffectual man, a violin repairman and general woodworker. He died when Diana was four. Diana had one memory of him. He was handing her something he had made, a doll or figurine carved from wood. Diana had asked Gloria about the doll but Gloria professed not to remember. Every time they moved, Gloria went into a fit of cleaning. The house was always a horrible mess until they moved. Then Gloria went crazy. *Don't think about it,* she would say when Diana came home from school and asked about something missing from her room. *It's gone.* In the memory, Diana could see her small chubby hand reach out, the carved figure being placed in her palm. She could feel the weight of the doll. And her father's presence. A large face leaning in toward her.

Her hand began to tremble. She held on to her right hand with her left, guiding the lip brush back and forth until her lips were filled in. She slid the bristles of her makeup brush back down into the case and put the case in the makeup tray.

She turned her face to the side. Gloria had had the same mole, just there at her chin below the left corner of her mouth. A hair grew from the mole. Like her mother, Diana kept the hair clipped. From the drawer, she took scissors, laid them against her chin and snipped. Without her reading glasses she could not see the hair but she felt it give.

Gloria met Duncan Dubard at a square dance party. She'd started going to church to meet someone. For the party she'd made herself a square dance outfit—gingham check with six ruffled petticoats beneath the skirt—and had done her hair up freshly blond and curled. Duncan Dubard was not the square dance type, Diana couldn't imagine him going but somehow some way he did and there was Gloria. His destiny.

Precious Fanny was born soon after. Diana took care of the new baby, fed and dressed her, changed her diapers, put her to sleep when nobody else could. Watched her while she slept, afraid to look away, thinking something might happen.

Lustrous, dark-haired Fanny. Two years after Roger was born, she had come to live with Hale and Diana. I'll baby-sit, Fanny promised. But Diana would never have left Roger alone with Fanny. Fanny wanted to be a torch singer. She was also dangerously careless.

Diana ducked her chin. Her looks were hazy, her features small, her cheekbones high and delicate. She was not beautiful like her sister. Hale said she was but Hale exaggerated.

Duncan Dubard hadn't lasted long. When he died he left college money for Fanny. "To improve her chances," he specified in his will. Gloria used most of the money for a face-lift, doubtless thinking to improve *her* chances instead.

Ten-forty, past time to go. Diana put on white sandals and a sheer white blouse, a cotton skirt striped in shades of lavender and purple with gathers at the waist and large patch pockets. The blouse was girlish, with cap sleeves, embroidered cut-out flowers on the chest, a buttoned jewel neckline. She unbuttoned the top button of her blouse and spread the corners. The scar showed. She refastened the buttons and reached beneath her skirt to pull down the tail of the blouse.

In the back of the Montrose house there'd been an extra room, empty except for a black rocking chair and a golden oak rolltop desk Hale had refinished. The empty room looked out over a cheap greenhouse tacked on to the back of the house. There was nothing in the greenhouse. A few empty pots, no plants. At night, the plastic-coated screening came loose and flapped in the wind.

In the back room Diana rocked Bethany. While the baby slept she read. Diaries, journals, *The Waves.* The screen flapped. She watched the baby sleep. She kept Bethany at the breast fifteen months. In the night when she cried, she brought her into bed and fed her there. Many nights the three of them fell asleep together, warm and dreaming, milk crusting on the baby's mouth, Hale on his side, Diana's one breast exposed.

The black rocking chair was gone. They had bought it second-hand, nothing special but they might have held on to it. When a slat came out and the legs began to wobble, Hale said get rid of it. Diana put the chair on the curb for the Senior Citizens Army but a man who mowed lawns took the chair before the truck came by. Diana saw it go and was sorry. She didn't know why she'd let Hale talk her into getting rid of it in the first place.

They had put the rolltop desk in the family room downstairs. Diana had thought she might use it to work at but, really, she preferred a table.

She picked up her purse. Sometimes the past seemed like a dream from which she'd only just awakened and could not quite remember. Other times she wished she didn't have to. She shook back her hair and, smelling of the rough brown herbal soap she bought regularly in Austin, went downstairs.

·19·

*H*ale and Roger were still at the table, talking baseball.

Hale sopped at Roger's hollandaise with the corner of a flour tortilla.

"You gone?"

Roger shook his head and whistled. "Looking sharp, Mom," he said. "Looking real sharp."

Diana tried not to show her pleasure. "It's time. And thanks. Yes, I'm going. Anybody want to come?"

Hale stiffened.

"Never mind." She took her keys from her purse.

Roger pushed his chair back. "We're fixing fence this afternoon. Watching the 'Stros and don't plan on cooking."

"I wasn't."

Hale shifted in his chair. "Diana," he said. "Do you *need* me to go?"

Ignorance was bliss. He had convinced himself he was really asking and she could not bring herself to answer him truthfully. She put her hand on his arm.

"I'm going because I want to, Hale."

He flinched, ground his jaw.

Diana waved over her shoulder and went out.

Before she closed the front door she heard their conversation resume. Last year the Astros had gone to the play-offs. Roger posed theories explaining what happened this year. Hale wondered if their luck would change.

Diana had planted pots of Texas bluebells by the front door. The plants—new to her—were strange. The flowers were lovely, a rich shade of purplish blue, but the lower leaves had curled and turned yellow. Passing the plants, she deadheaded some withered blooms. She had watered the bluebells, fed them, let the plant dry out to stress it. Nothing seemed to help. Part of the plant thrived while the rest seemed determined to die.

Rufus wandered up. Diana gave him a pat. The sun was bearing down.

As she reached for her door handle Buster jumped out. Diana brushed yellow cat hair from the upholstery. Cats were all over the place, twelve at last count. Most cats were useful; they kept down mice. Buster lived at the house and petitioned for Meow Mix.

He stood in the driveway looking stupid. Diana got in the car. Buster was a stray. They had come in from dinner in Austin one night and found him screaming in a tree. Diana hated Buster. Secretly she wished he'd disappear. Buster licked his paw.

She started the car and pushed a button. As the convertible top rose over her head, the car seat darkened. She locked the levers in place and rolled up the windows, turned on the air conditioning and started backing out. The car died. She turned off the air conditioning, pumped the accelerator and recranked the engine. The car was fifteen years old. It required some babying.

Diana backed to the wide spot where they turned around and wheeled in. Before she got there she saw Hale come out onto the doorstep. In the turnaround, she waited to see if he had something to tell her. He waved and stood there. She waved back.

The Buick was a fire-engine red Riviera with a white top and red interior. They'd had the car since it was new. Hale had tried to convince Diana to trade it in—two hundred thousand miles, he said, was far enough for a car to go—but she refused. She loved the car.

The road, wide enough for one car only, twisted past the mare barn through scrub cedar and oak and cactus and wind-whipped mesquite, past their water well and pump. Diana made the turns easily, slowing down only at the sharpest curves. Coming to the farm-to-market road, she checked in the rearview mirror for Rufus. When they first got him, the dog once followed Hale all the way to Dripping.

At the gate, she turned left onto the blacktop, pressing the accelerator to the floor. The big car responded quickly. All it took was gas.

She switched on the radio and turned down a county road which snaked through the countryside beside a creek. The drought was evident everywhere. As dry topsoil blew away, limestone rocks emerged from pastures like drowned bodies floating up from the bottom of a river. Except for white poppies, the wildflowers—usually glorious in this part of the state—had been thin and wind-weary. There was some scraggly Turk's-cap and firewheels, not many. Earlier in the summer, cactuses had bloomed their heads off, waxy red and yellow blossoms perched on thorny plants like exotic spaceships on a prickly launching pad.

An old couple in a pickup truck pulled up to the road from a driveway. Diana honked and raised her index finger. She'd learned to respect country manners. People driving the back roads expected to be acknowledged, whether they knew one another or not.

The rock-and-roll station she liked was doing a pretaped Sunday morning special about Crosby, Stills, Nash and Young. Diana listened to bits of an interview with Neil Young, then opened her glove compartment for a tape. The announcer of the program was too overwhelmed by his own importance.

So was Neil Young. She inserted the tape, Sarah Vaughan doing Cole Porter, and turned the volume up.

Before she met Jesse, she used to listen to an AM country station with loud commercials and headline-type newsbreaks. Jesse had played so much rock and roll for her, she had become something of an enthusiast. She ejected Sarah Vaughan and put in an all-rock tape Jesse had made for her. "Travel takes a heavy beat," he'd said. "Keep it in your car." Diana sped up. Jesse's idol came on, singing "Jungleland." In the car listening to loud music, going fast, she felt uncomplicated and honest. She could think more clearly.

Driftwood was no longer a real town, only a store, a church, some houses, a famous barbecue restaurant open only weekends in the warm months of the year. The restaurant used to be great, another one of those Austin landmarks people loved to be nostalgic about. Xanadu was just past the restaurant.

Diana checked her watch. Ten fifty-five. She had thirty, maybe thirty-five minutes to spare. She sped past the Driftwood general store and, after a mile or so, slowed down at the gravel drive leading into Xanadu. As she turned in, she lowered the volume of the cassette player. The back door to the house next to Xanadu was open.

In the pea-gravel parking area, she switched off the ignition. Roger had said she should never turn off the ignition without first ejecting the tape but then Roger was strict. And often, Diana forgot.

Slamming the door of the first greenhouse, she went into the second.

"Diana. Hello."

Tanned and shirtless, his hair pulled back into a long blond ponytail, Douglas Bredthauer emerged from behind a small seedling Norfolk pine. Douglas was short and barrel-chested, with a drooping mustache he liked to play with. He had one pierced ear, in it a diamond stud. His eyes were pale and blank, his suntanned skin satiny with sweat.

"Douglas." Diana put her hand to her chest. "I didn't see you."

Douglas used to teach geology in San Marcos. After five years he'd quit his job to live off the land. He'd built a cabin in the hills. A young woman went with him. When she left another came. The cabin had become something of a local attraction. One entire wall of the house was made of odd-shaped stones and fossils, some from as far away as Alaska and the Himalayas; others—Indian arrowheads and ax heads—came from San Marcos. On another wall, two huge rattle-snake skins were set into the wood, lacquered over so that they could not easily be removed. Over the bathroom mirror, deer horns were mounted in the studs.

There were stories. People living nearby said they heard screams of wild laughter. Some said devil worshipers. Most just thought drugs.

"How're your Thompsons?"

Diana held up crossed fingers. "So far so good. I haven't eaten any yet."

They'd built a grape arbor just down from the porch. The grapes were a new hybrid, a variety of Thompson seedless which was supposed to like hill country soil and weather.

"I hope the heat doesn't turn them into raisins."

"It might."

"You looking for anything in particular, or do you want me to leave you alone?"

Douglas ran his hand down his flat, muscular stomach and adjusted his belt buckle, pushing at it as if it were pinching him. The buckle was made of free-form stone the color of topaz. He wore blue jeans and rough-cut work boots, nothing else. A red bandanna hung from his back pocket.

"Tomato starts."

"I thought you were raising your own."

"I was until last night. An armadillo uprooted them, all except two. Which a rabbit snitched."

"No extras?"

"I gave them away. No good deed goes unpunished."

"I don't have Celebrities but I did get some Jackpots and a new one, supposed to be fast, called Bingo. The Garden Line's big on them."

"I'll take anything."

Douglas had finally given up on both academia and pioneering. He'd made a lucky marriage to a child of the hill country named Ethylene Vaszik. Ethylene had money, her great-grandfather having been one of the early Bohemian settlers of the area who bought great patches of land when the land out here was considered good for nothing. The Vasziks raised their own hogs, made their own soap and grew their own vegetables. Their children were pale, waif-like creatures who squinted like cave animals when brought to town. The Vasziks had drifted and dwindled. Ethylene was the only child of her generation left in Driftwood. Douglas and Ethylene and their baby Taylor Wayne Vaszik-Bredthauer lived in the white Victorian house next door to Xanadu.

Douglas squatted to take hold of the Norfolk pine. Two trees had thatched together at the root. He was separating them.

"Mothballs," he said as he pulled, "are supposed to help."

"My armadillos," she said, "walk around mothballs. Then Rufus eats them and gets sick."

"The armadillos?"

"No. Good Lord, no. The mothballs."

"Tried a shotgun?" The larger sections of the roots came free.

"Too gruesome. You have to keep killing them. They keep coming."

Douglas took a large knife out of his belt. "It's a choice all right." He lifted the knife and hacked at the roots of the pine.

Diana moved away.

"I don't have much time. I'll just look a few minutes."

"Help yourself."

She checked her watch. She could stay twenty minutes, no longer. Given any leeway she could wander about in a nursery for hours, staring at six-packs, imagining plum-colored petunias by the back door between the pinks and the daylilies, picturing yellow gazanias in a barrel on the porch, wondering how the brilliant celosia plant would look set next to flaming Red Rocket salvia.

Douglas went back to work on the Norfolk pine. Diana browsed among the marigolds. She liked the musky flower, its unpleasant aroma like broken matchsticks. Beyond the marigolds were the vegetables. The stalks of Douglas's tomatoes were not as thick or as strong as hers had been but the plants looked healthy enough. Bingo? She'd never heard of Bingo. She opened the greenhouse door and went out, feeling as though she'd stepped away from Douglas's grasp.

Between the second and third greenhouses was a big open space where Douglas mixed soils and mulch. *Dirt*, Douglas was fond of saying. *Gardening is dirt.*

Great mounds of rotting brown stuff lay on either side of the walkway. Recently dampened, the mulch smelled heady in the sun. There were three more large piles, one a landscaping mix, another potting soil, the last a recipe for roses devised by a prize-winning rosarian from San Antonio.

Diana opened the door to the third greenhouse, where Douglas kept his tropicals. A drop of sweat ran down inside the top of her slip and skated around her rib cage.

The years in the Montrose house were strange ones. There were the children, taking Roger to art class and the zoo, later tending to Bethany. Diana read, studied, healed, stared out the back windows at the empty greenhouse, wrote. There were many blank spaces she could not fill in.

Once the coursework toward her doctorate was done she dawdled, postponing writing her dissertation. Once she was pregnant she wrote fast, as if taking dictation from the work she'd already done in her mind. In three months' time, she'd turned her paper in. Her adviser had been enormously pleased.

Diana had a natural flair, he said, for creative thinking. But he wanted a rewrite. There were some theories she needed to think through. One of the members of her committee was a professor from Rice whose field was the modernists. The Rice professor would be picky. Diana had taken the paper home and shelved it. She would wait, she told herself, until after Bethany was born. After that, there were other excuses.

In one corner of the tropical greenhouse sat a large green plant in a yellow pot shaped like a chicken. The plant's long arms climbed over the chicken's back and down across its wings. Along the arms, pale green leaves grew like stacked coins.

She lifted the chicken pot.

The door slammed.

"I thought," Douglas said, "you'd given up on indoor plants." He aimed his watering wand at a dieffenbachia near the door.

"I have. I was thinking of my daughter. Is this a jade plant?"

"It is."

"I don't know." She set the plant down, picked it back up again.

"Succulents are easy."

"Says who."

"Tell you what." The spray of his wand made a gentle whacking sound against the leaves of the dieffenbachia. "That one has been around awhile. I'll knock off a dollar." Diana studied the jade plant. "As you can see . . ." He hesitated. She looked over. He gestured toward the pot. "It's in a chicken."

"Oh, I noticed." She liked animal-shaped pots.

"How is your girl by the way?" He went back to his watering.

"Oh, you know . . ." She stopped herself. She'd vowed to keep quiet about Bethany. "Fine," she said. "Not bad at all. I guess I'll go on and get this."

"Set it down. I'll bring it."

She put the chicken pot between a euphorbia and a hen-and-chickens. At the door Douglas aimed the spray away from her. She turned sideways to get past him.

"I'll get my tomatoes," she said. "Then I have to go."

With a lever on the spray head, Douglas switched off the water.

Douglas Bredthauer owned a piece of Diana about the size of a watermelon plug. Her world was made up of quiet, comforting exchanges with people she never saw outside their own small worlds. She and Douglas had worked hard together, side by side in the heat, hoeing, weeding, thinning, laughing at each other's mistakes. When winter brought needed relief from gardening or in the height of summer when there was little to do but wait and water, she missed Douglas, his boffo-masculine cockiness, their teasing camaraderie. As soon as the weather broke in either direction—usually before, like now—she found an excuse to drive to Driftwood to browse among the plants at Xanadu and visit with Douglas.

Her blouse was beginning to stick to her skin.

She checked her watch. Time was jumping.

She passed the rotting mulch piles. In their backyard, Douglas and Ethylene's pet billy goat stood with his front feet on the white picket fence, his head inside a nest of watermelon-colored crepe myrtle blooms.

When Bethany was little Diana had had more love affairs than she liked to remember: casual sex with casual acquaintances, up and off and running when it was over, making up lies on the way home, how long she'd say she'd been at the library, the grocery store, the movies. It all seemed crazy now; at the time she couldn't seem to stop. In time, she'd become choosier, less compulsive. Douglas was strange. From him she kept her distance.

She snapped two six-packs of Jackpots free and put them in one of the cardboard trays Douglas had stacked beside the vegetables, then picked out a Bingo, figuring she might as well give them a try.

Jesse was the first boyfriend she'd had in years. They'd had fun together for a time. When the fun stopped they agreed to give each other up.

Douglas had a new supply of herbs. There were large pots of rosemary, both upright and prostrate, some moss-like thyme. She had plenty of thyme and rosemary. Both had survived the winter's hard freeze. The rosemary had bloomed bright blue in the snow. Next to lemon thyme, Douglas had put a large bushy plant with lavender flowers and oblong, lacy leaves. Mexican oregano. Diana ruffled the leaves and sniffed. The pot was marked $6.95.

Carrying her chicken, Douglas came in from the other greenhouse.

"I just got that," he said.

"Pricey."

He shrugged. "Supply and demand."

"It's pretty."

She ruffled the leaves again.

"I guess I'll take it," she said. "Should I keep it in a pot or can it take winter in the ground?"

Douglas set her chicken down beside the cash register and pulled his hair back to catch it tighter in the elastic. "We'll have to watch and see," he said. "Something tells me it needs protection. After all . . ." He looked up at her. "Mexico."

She laughed at his little joke. "I need a bag of potting soil."

"Large?"

"Might as well."

Douglas rang up the sale and went to get her potting soil. Diana took out her checkbook.

"Oh. Douglas."

He turned. She held out her car keys. "Would you?"

He thrust the chicken pot toward her. "Just hang them on her beak."

She slipped the key ring on the chicken's beak. Douglas went out. When Diana looked up from writing her check she was surprised to see Ethylene peeking out at her from behind the chemical sprays. Astride Ethylene's hip, Taylor Wayne Vaszik-Bredthauer sucked his fingers.

"Good morning, Ethylene," Diana said. When Ethylene smiled, her skin color brightened and her watery blue eyes lit up.

"Hi." Speaking barely above a whisper, she shifted Taylor Wayne to the other hip. The baby was red-faced, with wispy blond hair and a huge round head.

"Douglas said I shouldn't come out right yet but there's a phone call I thought he'd want to take." Ethylene looked tentative, as if she was waiting for Diana to tell her what to do.

"He just went to put some things in my car. How's Taylor Wayne?"

Diana went to the baby and placed her index finger inside his damp hand. The baby's fingers curled reflexively. His hand was white, the skin stretched so thin there hardly seemed enough to cover him.

"Oh," Ethylene said, softly pinching Taylor Wayne's cheek, "he's fine." She looked out the door.

Taylor Wayne blinked and turned his head away from Diana. Pressing his forehead against her shoulder, he clamped his mouth firmly on his mother's bare arm and began to suck it. Diana pulled her finger away.

When Gloria was hospitalized the first time, the emergency crew had taken her to the small, overcrowded county hospital. She'd had to take a semi-private room. Her roommate was a Jehovah's Witness who'd had a stroke. During visiting hours and after, the room was always filled. The visitors preached endlessly at Gloria and Diana, waving copies of *The Watchtower* in their faces, giving impromptu lectures on the evils of liquor, meat, license and free will. One of the girls looked a lot like Ethylene.

Diana slipped her check beneath Douglas's book of sales tickets.

"All in." Douglas let the door slam. When Diana turned to say good-bye to Ethylene, she was gone.

In the Buick, she remembered her car keys. She reached for the door handle. In the greenhouse door, Douglas pointed toward the hood of her car. Diana shrugged and shook her head. Douglas pointed to the windshield. He had replaced the keys in the ignition. When Diana cranked the car, the rock-and-roll tape came on. She turned down the volume, ejected the tape, waved to Douglas, put the car in reverse and backed out.

Passing the house she saw Ethylene and the baby making their way past the billy goat eating the crepe myrtle. Diana waved but Ethylene had her head down. She ducked beneath a leaning rose arbor and disappeared through the back door, Taylor Wayne's pink mouth still glued to her arm.

·20·

*E*leven-fifty, and she was a minimum twenty minutes from Cedar Hills, longer if she got behind a slow truck on the narrow road between here and 290.

She switched the air conditioner to high and lifted her arms to let the cool air flow into the sleeves of her blouse, reinserted the tape, then ejected it, took off her watch and put it on the seat beside her, face down. The smell of oregano filled the car. The chicken pot sat safely wedged in a corner in the back seat, the jade plant's arms draped around it as if in protection.

At the intersection of 150 and 12, she turned left toward Dripping Springs. A flatbed truck stacked with round bales of hay poked along on the road ahead. Passing the Dripping Springs cemetery, Diana tried to get around the truck, but the double yellow line stopped her. She gently braked the Buick to a slower speed. From here to 290 the road twisted and curved like a dropped length of ribbon. There was nothing to do but follow along and wait.

She wondered where the hay came from. Most fields were so skimpy, farmers had begun baling milo. She turned the radio on and turned it back off again.

She passed the rock farmhouse where she had heard drug

dealers lived. Three cars were pulled up to the front of the house, a white Camaro, a black Cadillac and a silver-and-blue short-bed pickup with a silver roll-bar and chrome-framed lights on top of the cab. Behind the house on a primitive landing strip sat a small private airplane.

The house was old and sturdy with a knee-high rock wall all the way around it. Chickens ran around in the front yard. A large dog slept on the front porch. The porch sagged dangerously at one end.

Diana tapped her horn. The dog woke up. His body was white but his head was black. In the yard, a cracked concrete birdbath leaned in the same direction as the front porch. The birdbath was dry and dirty. Surely no birds came near it.

The hay truck slowed. The dog stood up and barked. He looked like a white dog wearing a hood.

The truth of the matter was, Fanny was no singer. Fanny could not stop singing flat to save her soul. When she practiced, Diana had to leave the house. But Fanny would not be dissuaded. When she couldn't get work, she took lessons.

"Waitressing is my job," she used to say. "Singing is my career." Like Gloria at the sewing machine saying "I am an artist."

Fanny could have gone to college. Even after Gloria's face-lift there was money enough to send her. But Fanny had no inclination toward the academic life, and no interest in improving her chances. She barely passed high school.

On the left, cars were pulled up nearly to the door of a gray stone church with a stone cross on top. Again the hay truck slowed. Looking up to find the bales practically on top of her, Diana pressed down hard on the brake pedal.

Eventually Fanny moved into her own place, a tiny studio apartment in a rundown apartment house just south of downtown Houston, near Chinatown. Fanny liked lowlife; would-be musicians, down-and-out bums, fly-by-night truck drivers. Diana began to see her sister less and less often. Each time she did, Fanny was thinner, paler. Her lights began to dim.

She talked all the time. Diana couldn't seem to do anything to stop the downslide.

She was thirty-six when she died, in a stucco motel in Nuevo Laredo. The boy with her could not have been older than eighteen. Tall and skinny, wearing a sleeveless muscle shirt, his punk-short hair bleached a pure peroxide yellow, the boy was a bundle of nerves. Diana hadn't known Fanny had gone to the border town. It was, the boy explained, just a weekend trip.

The cause of death was officially ideopathic bacterial invasion, ideopathic meaning they didn't know what caused it. The bacteria had hit her intestines first and then spread. She'd gone to see an American doctor who lived in Mexico. The doctor said he'd never seen anyone with less resistance.

Whatever else the boy with the punk haircut knew about how she died and why, he did not say.

When she was living with them, Fanny used to steal from Diana, clothes, earrings, five-dollar bills from her wallet, then tens, twenties, her credit card. One morning Diana had gone into Fanny's room—Fanny was asleep—and found, beside her bed, a note: "Put D's card back." Diana took her charge card and crumpled the note. If Fanny needed money that badly, she thought, she could have it.

Two-ninety was less than two miles away. Diana checked her watch. Twelve. Bethany would be furious.

By the time she died they'd left Houston. Diana went to Houston to arrange the funeral. The next fall, Gloria packed her clothes and took the bus to San Marcos. "I'm here," she said from the bus station pay phone. Diana found her a small house in Wimberley. Hale paid the rent. Gloria said the house was too small.

Physically Gloria was a wreck. Diana took her to doctors. Her blood sugar was high, she had arteriosclerosis. She should, they told her, stop eating mayonnaise and Lorna Doones. There were cataracts. They'd had them removed. Gloria hated the glasses. They went back in and inserted implants.

That Christmas, Roger came home. He was fixing Gloria's favorite dish, fresh ham studded with cloves of garlic. Gloria came into the kitchen holding her head. "I need aspirin," she said. "Do you have any aspirin, my head hurts so bad." Before Diana could find one, Gloria had collapsed. By the time they got her to the hospital she was unconscious. An artery running the length of her spine had, in the words of the attending physician, opened up like a zipper.

She was still alive but she'd left this world to live in her own time and place. She thought Diana was her sister. When she visited, Diana brought banana milkshakes from Dairy Queen. Once, she'd taken a sack of Hershey's Kisses. Gloria stuffed five in her mouth. Before Diana could pry the candy out Gloria had swallowed them, silver wrappers and all.

At 290, the hay truck lumbered off toward Llano. Diana turned in the other direction, pressing her foot down hard on the accelerator. As the car gained speed, the air conditioner shut off. Diana turned the fan to Maximum and held her hand in front of the vents. Nothing. She slapped the dash. Nothing. She lowered the window. Hot air blew in. She rolled the window back up so that it was only cracked.

The nursing home was in Georgetown; Diana visited once a month. Once a week she saw Bethany. To Bethany she brought not banana milkshakes but other kinds of gifts— books, clothes, this balloon of hope in the middle of her chest. The hope gave Diana a floating feeling: maybe this time things would be better.

Two-ninety was six lanes wide. The Buick's big engine responded easily to her request for speed, up to eighty, then back down as she released her foot. Their insurance rates had already been raised because of tickets she'd gotten.

She and Hale had looked at a house in this area, on Barton Creek. Back then, you could see across the hilltops to Austin. Now the hills had become solid rooftops, unseamed for miles, like water. Along the highway were signs announcing the entrance to suburban developments with exotic names. Cedar Trails. Deerfield Village. The Escarpment.

Beyond Oak Hill, Diana turned off the highway. She drove down a meandering road until she came to two rock pillars. She turned in. The parking lot was packed. She found a spot a long way from the front door, beneath an oak tree.

She tossed the keys into her purse, opened the car door and reached into the backseat to get the jade plant. The plant was not heavy, but its branches were long. Douglas had spread newspapers over the car seats to protect the upholstery. The chicken looked smug.

Diana picked up her watch. Twelve-forty. She got out of the car, went around to the passenger side, opened the door, drew the chicken to her chest, closed the car door.

Opening the trunk, she lifted out the sack with the blouse and Alice Fine in it. She hoped she'd made good choices. As she walked down the rock footpath winding between cedar trees, her skirt swung against her damp legs, her heart raced and she felt that misty cloud of dread forming in the lower part of her stomach.

· 21 ·

*H*ale snapped open the ironing board, set the levers in place and turned the contraption upright. Using the remote he switched from baseball to golf.

July was a bad month for sports. Too late for basketball, too early for pre-season football. The Astros weren't on until three.

From a shelf in the closet he took down the iron, a small ceramic pitcher, a can of spray starch.

Football was his favorite, the pros. Only gamblers, parents and crazed alumni liked college ball. He and Marvin Thoede had gotten into serious gambling one of their good years, the autumn before gold fell. They'd used a bookie from Dallas. Marvin had a WATS line. They watched the games on two sets, keeping track of their bets in a special notebook. A chartist, Hale kept records of past performances from which he figured odds with a hand calculator. Marvin just plunged. The bookie called every few minutes. "You want to press?" "You think they'll blitz? Punt? Draw?"

Hale set the iron on its heel and went to the kitchen for water. He'd told Roger to go on to Austin for his swim. It was too hot to fix fence. Even the horses were standing around in a daze. He'd heard an extended weather forecast. There was some chance the drought might break by the end of the week.

For their anniversary he was cooking his specialty, fried chicken soaked in buttermilk spiced with cayenne and paprika in the manner of Popeye's. Roger was doing the rest. Hale was even thinking of trying biscuits. He used to be great at biscuits, then he lost the knack. He thought he might test his skills again, to see if perhaps his knack had only gone on vacation.

He plugged in the iron and switched it to Steam/High. Plucking a shirt from the clothes basket, he shook it open and, waiting for the iron to warm, flipped channels. On the rock station, a boy dressed like a woman sang a song about a lizard. Phoney snakes crawled around the singer's feet. Hale poured water into the well of the iron.

Diana hated to iron. She said she had to keep going over the same spot again and again and everytime she did she made new creases. Hale thought she simply did not try. Anybody could iron.

The boy dressed like a woman primped his long blond hair and swung his hips. He was wearing lavish lipstick and eye makeup. His skirt swayed. The snakes circled his ankles. In the background, a black man blew on a harmonica and danced the cakewalk. MTV was comforting. Like baseball and golf it went on and on.

A cloud of steam rose from the belly of the iron. Hale laid the shirt across the ironing board. Spreading the collar wrong side up with the fingers of one hand, he shook the starch can with the other and lightly sprayed.

He should have gone with Diana; he'd had a feeling when she left something was going to happen. But if he hated hospitals of any kind—and he did—more than any other he especially hated Cedar Hills. If that was cowardice so be it;

he was old enough to have earned the right. Anyway Diana didn't like him to interfere. Whatever her pretense, she liked to travel alone.

The trick to ironing was sequence. Collars—wrong side out first—button lapels, sleeves, the body. When he pressed down on the iron, the pleasant smell of hot cotton billowed up in a soft wet cloud.

Sometimes he thought they should have let the judge send Bethany to reform school instead of cushioning yet another of her falls with sweet talk and sympathy. He had not, of course, said that but he did think it. He'd been dissuaded by the lawyer, who'd bluntly dismissed the idea before it came up. "Nobody's helped by going to reform school," he said. "Nobody."

The collar was beginning to fray. A couple more washings and he'd toss this one. Or he'd try. More than likely Diana would retrieve it, use it for a gardening shirt. Diana would not throw anything away.

He turned the collar right side out and aimed the point of the iron at the exact center of the collar, then wiggled it to the points, careful not to bunch up the fabric.

Another music video came on. A young woman stood on the ledge of a building threatening to jump while a young man reached out to her from a nearby window and sang.

He finished the collar. The shirt was western-style with pearl snaps. Stretching the lapel, he slid the iron carefully in and out of the small pearl dots, and with his thumb, switched from MTV to baseball to golf.

Fall meant the World Series, then football, winter the hoop, spring back to baseball. As a boy he had dreamed of becoming a sports hero. In spring, he stole impossible bases and hit over-the-fence homeruns. Autumns he dodged defenders like Paul Hornung. Winters he made the final winning basket. Later the dream shifted to horses. To be the one who trained the winner of the All-American.

Dreams died hard. Intellectually Hale had come to terms

with the fact that his father would never think of him as having any more sense than God gave a cedar fencepost, but in his father's presence he couldn't help hoping. To protect himself he'd withdrawn. There were times when they were together, of course, but Hale found ways to limit the duration of those occasions. His strategies did not always work. Claude Caldwell's talent for finding a soft spot was as deft as Bethany's. Once he found the place, he kept punching.

He saw his sister, Gail, now and then. All she ever talked about was her smart children. On her car bumper she'd pasted a sticker: My Child's on the Honor Roll at GHS. Gail tried to convince him to give up drinking and return to the church. So much for Gail. So much for family.

He started on a sleeve, wiggling the iron back and forth to the cuff the way his mother always did.

His dreams had lost their scope. In time they'd become domestic, almost womanish. His dream now was of Bethany back home again, going to football games, showing off a new outfit. He didn't care about grades. That went a long time ago. She was so smart. When she was nine she swore she was going to school in the East where it snowed all the time. He'd thought maybe Barnard. Or Vassar. Whatever the hell was up there. Now his hope was that Bethany not get hurt too badly and that she stay out of Goree and the electric chair.

His heart sank. Christ. The electric chair.

He set the iron on its heel and switched back to rock and roll. The girl was still on the ledge. When the tears started coming they would not stop. He set the iron back down on the sleeve and watched a wet spot spread. He ironed the tear into the fabric.

They didn't do the electric chair anymore, did they. They did it by injection, on a gurney, drop by drop.

The girl on the ledge jumped. The singer tore at his hair. He did not stop singing.

Hale flipped back to baseball. Finished with the sleeve, he sprayed the back of the shirt. The spray can sputtered. He went to the closet and got another. Dwight Gooden was pitching. What a sweet-looking kid. That long-legged, smooth delivery, the look of wonder in his eyes when the strike was called, as if amazed at what he could do himself. Dwight had been down and come back; it could happen.

Girls had been important of course, but for Hale girls were a late interest. He'd been a slow maturer. When he looked back over the earlier years of his life mostly what he saw himself doing was attending to sports: reading, listening, practicing; hitting a tennis ball against the side of the house, throwing a volleyball through the metal rim of a tricycle wheel, making up games to play alone which would improve his skills.

Once he was finished with his chores, in spring and summer he sat with his ear pressed against the radio, listening to baseball. From a magazine he learned to keep box scores. Mimi still had his old notebooks, filled with penciled records of games.

He flipped the shirt to the front.

The sides were retired. He switched to golf. A commercial. He switched to HBO. Teenagers were having a party in a hotel room. The party involved a donkey, drugs, confetti, cocaine, food and vomit. The hotel manager stormed in. The kids began to disperse. The manager tore his hair. The point of view of the movie was the kids' but Hale sympathized with the prissy hotel manager, who had fainted.

He flipped back to golf. Another commercial, for radial tires. He finished the shirt and held it up. One point of the collar needed retouching. He sprayed and pressed. The tournament came back on. The announcer pronounced Ballesteros's name correctly, Bye-es-teros, with a ruffle on the final *r*.

He hung the shirt on a hanger and went to the kitchen, got out a Lite beer, pulled up the tab, took a deep swallow and went back.

On the wall next to the television set was a framed picture of Bethany at five, hanging by one arm from the low limb of a magnolia tree. She'd been such a monkey, such a neighborhood kid, so busy. Her friends used to come over and make Kool-Aid. They'd put up a stand, plan to get rich. What happened? It was Roger they worried about then. When he got to junior high he'd become such a scared, nervous boy, always watching television, dabbling with model cars—which he was never good at—hanging around the kitchen. Bethany meantime was hard at play. More than anything she had seemed so *normal.*

Back to baseball. He picked another shirt from the basket. McMurtry threw a curve ball that went wide at the last minute. The batter, Strawberry, checked his swing, too late. Full count.

In the past few years, under Marvin's influence, Hale had been investing in ventures riskier even than horses. Now that oil was down so were horses. His money was more tied up than Diana knew. And he was more inextricably bound up with Marvin Thoede than she suspected. Diana understood money; he used to tell her everything. But there was a point at which her eyes glazed over, her attention wandered, and he knew she didn't want to know. And so he stopped telling her.

A called strike. Strawberry stared in disbelief at the umpire. A replay verified the call. Returning to the dugout, Strawberry dragged his bat.

This shirt was one of his favorites, white with pale-blue stripes. Hale spread the collar. The last time he'd worn it, a young girl at the track had come up to him and pulled him to her level by the lapels. Two snaps of the shirt had come undone. "I like that sound," the girl had said, and she burrowed her head in his chest. Hale had found the girl's aggressiveness irresistible. But then he was slightly drunk at the time.

And there was Bethany. The lawyers, the doctors, the fines. The hospital, or whatever Cedar Hills called itself, was a bottomless pit, $4,000 a month, and every month extra charges.

Insurance paid half. Hale didn't question the cost. He just paid the bills. Sometimes he thought Bethany wanted to strip them of everything so that they could all be poor together, like her Mexicans. The romance of poverty had never impressed Hale. All he had ever wanted from poverty was out.

Less than an hour after Diana left, Rose Narcisco had called. Were they coming to see Bethany? Hale had checked his watch. "My wife should already be there," he said, then remembered the tomatoes. "She may have made a stop," he told Rose Narcisco. "Is anything wrong?"

Bethany, it seemed, had hurt herself. Not badly, Rose Narcisco hastened to assure him. Only a scratch, a plea for attention, nothing to worry about, but she wanted to make sure someone was coming. Hale assured her someone was and Rose Narcisco quickly terminated the conversation.

He held up the shirt. A commercial came on. He flipped to golf. Behind the players, green grass stretched to the horizon. He started in on the sleeves.

There were other framed pictures on the wall, Claude as a young man with a cigarette hanging from his mouth, his head cocked to one side, as if daring life to come take him on, Mimi as a beautiful, scared young girl, a paper parasol on one shoulder, Gloria in a costume she'd made for an Old South ball complete with hoopskirt and ruffled bonnet. All the sad stories. Fanny's picture had been taken when she was practicing to be a singer. Dressed in a long slinky gown, she stood with her hands on her hips, hips thrust out, long legs slightly apart. Her head was thrown back and her mouth was slightly open. She looked ridiculous, like a teenaged boy in beauty-queen drag.

In Houston, Fanny had shamelessly pursued and seduced him. Eventually he'd given in. Diana had never found out and would not; Hale would lie his way into hell before he told her. Fanny was a snake. Pathetic, needy. Scary. She couldn't help being a snake.

Next to Fanny was a picture of Roger, sitting in the sand

at Galveston, making a castle, in his eyes that look of furious concentration, as if the castle might be his last chance to please them. In another the boy—maybe five—is standing at Diana's side, looking up at her. Diana's head is turned in the other direction and she has on her zombie face: aloof and unreachable. In other pictures, Bethany is running into the surf, working at a puzzle, in a sandbox digging, at Diana's breast nursing. In that one Diana is looking straight at the camera. Her face is relaxed and soft. Her hand around the baby's bottom looks like a claw.

Hale flipped back to baseball. Gooden wound up for a pitch, Hale lifted his iron. If he had a bookie, he would gamble on this one pitch, right now. Gooden let go.

"All right, *Dwight*," Hale said aloud.

The batter did not bother to question the call.

· 22 ·

The administration building of Cedar Hills sat against the Austin skyline like a cell gone mad. A white, free-form structure, the building was supposed to blend subtly into the limestone background like another rock. It did not.

Chicken pot held firmly to her chest, in huge gold reflective windows Diana watched herself. Her hair drooped, her lipstick was gone. From inside the building you could see through the gold windows clearly enough. Visiting parents in the parking lot saw only themselves.

At the end of the rock footpath she turned her back to a glass door to open it, wondering as she did why such an up-to-date building did not have automatic doors like grocery stores and K mart.

The door gave too fast. Diana stumbled, caught herself and turned. Rose Narcisco held the door.

"What happened?"

"Good afternoon, Mrs. Caldwell."

"What's wrong?"

Rose Narcisco ushered Diana into Cedar Hills with a downward swing of her arm. "Nothing is wrong, Mrs. Caldwell. Bethany is fine. Would you come with me to my office."

Diana rearranged the chicken and led the way. If nothing was wrong it had to be money. But they'd paid. Diana had written the check. She pulled her silk slip from between her legs.

Inside the building, the architecture of Cedar Hills sang a hymn to modern openness. With no ninety-degree angles, the flow of unstructured space—one room leading to the next, all the rooms connected to one another—gave evidence of a dazzling display of unity, like small tributaries pouring into a major river. There appeared to be no walls; this was an illusion. The divisions were there all right but discreet, more like interruptions than boundaries. Surrounded by half-walls of thick, translucent Plexiglas, conference areas were screened so that people sitting behind them could be seen only when they stood. The acoustics were a marvel of modern engineering. If Staff wished to call for assistance, all they had to do was stand, give certain hand or verbal signals. Help instantly appeared.

Despite the blind alleys and false leads of Cedar Hills, children were sometimes helped here. The misleading cues reminded the children of home; the phoney facades were comfortingly familiar. But this was not home. Here they did not have to contend with the anxieties and dislocations, the wildly exaggerated expectations and hurtful possibilities of love.

Diana swiveled her head to make sure Rose Narcisco was still back there. Rose smiled and indicated with a fluttery gesture of her hand that Diana should keep going.

The untrustworthy, benign face of Cedar Hills was as familiar to parents as it was to children. Faced with its plasticity and phoniness, its seeming good nature backed up by iron determination and blood-raw will, parents felt as impotent and as outraged as they did at home, trying to help, cope, deal and live with their stormy, sulky, willfully unpredictable and desperately unhappy children.

Diana made her way between divider screens. Passing one,

she heard the calm, unwavering voice of a counselor. "Our *system*," the counselor said.

The first time she'd heard the word used in a therapeutic context, Diana had protested. "You don't like *system*?" came the amazed and calculated response. "It's a wonderful word," she was informed. "All the emotional ballast has been unloaded."

Beyond the reception area, the uninterrupted flow of Cedar Hills came to a halt. Here where the real business of the system was carried on were the ninety-degree angles missing from the reception area. Here there were traditional offices with traditionally closed doors, behind them traditional desks and wall-to-wall carpeting. The doors were of thick dark oak. Each had a bronze name plate.

The first office belonged to the Headmistress, the second to the Director of Education, the third—always busy—the Bursar, then the Chief Psychiatrist. Rose Narcisco's door was ajar. Diana went in.

The office was thickly carpeted in nondescript beige with a low pile. The walls matched the carpeting. Nonassertive art—pale swirling abstracts—hung on the walls. There was a huge corn plant in one corner. In another under the buzzing blue glow of fluorescent tubes an assortment of African violets flourished.

The windows were covered with silver miniblinds, tightly twisted shut. The air was blessedly cold. The doctor closed the door.

"Let me help you with that," she said. She took the chicken.

Diana brushed at her chest. Specks of potting soil fell into the cut-out flowers of her blouse. A few drifted to the floor. Diana tried to kick the dirt beneath the desk. She succeeded only in making a smudge.

"Lord," she said to distract Rose Narcisco, and she pulled her blouse away from her skin, "the air conditioning in my car went out. I'm a puddle."

"Good Lord." Rose Narcisco set the chicken on her desk. "What a calamity." She motioned Diana to sit.

"So what happened?"

"Please, Mrs. Caldwell, everything is fine. Now please. Have a seat."

Have a sit. Rose Narcisco had a foreign accent Diana could not place, possibly Middle Eastern. There was that faint mustache over her lip, that roundedness in her midsection just beneath her breasts. Narcisco could be her husband's name. She wore a wedding ring, large diamonds in an ornate setting. Diana wondered what Mr. Narcisco did. More psychiatry? Did they sit around at night taking notes on each other?

On Dr. Narcisco's desk, a neat arrangement of supplies gave notice of an orderly mind: in-box, out-box, notepad and telephone, a burgundy leather appointment book, the chicken. The chicken looked ridiculous.

Diana crossed her arms over her chest. "I have to know," she said. "What happened?"

"Belinda is fine."

"Bethany."

Rose Narcisco rolled her eyes. "Bethany, yes, is fine. Now, please, Mrs. Caldwell, this is a busier day than usual. It's our anniversary."

"Really. Mine, too."

"Excuse me?"

"Never mind."

"It could be important."

"Today is my and my husband's twenty-sixth wedding anniversary."

Rose made a note on her pad. Diana sat on the edge of her chair cushion.

The doctor placed her hands on her desk and leaned toward Diana. Rose Narcisco had learned a great number of tricks in her years of dealing with parents: to use the desk as an advantage, to swivel in your chair while they must sit still, to make sure they sit while you stand, to close the blinds, to keep lights relatively dim. She knew how to compensate for being short.

"First of all, she's fine, absolutely fine."

"But?"

"She's cut herself."

Diana half stood.

Rose Narcisco lifted her hands in a motion that begged for calm. "It's not serious. A doctor has seen her. He did not have to take a stitch."

Diana sat back down. Mothers' intuition was supposed to be infallible. Where was hers?

"Not a stitch," Rose repeated.

"Where?"

"In her room."

Rum.

"Not the place she did it. Where . . ." Diana's voice cracked. "Where on her . . . you know, self?"

"Ah, yes." Rose placed one long red fingernail just beneath the bottom edge of her rib cage, on the right. "From here." She drew a line across her diaphragm. "To here." At a couple beats past midpoint, she stopped. "Mrs. Caldwell?"

Diana shivered. "Excuse me," she said, "is there any water?"

"I'll get it."

Rose Narcisco bustled out, her suit skirt swishing about her calves. She was moving too fast. Bad news took time to settle in. Diana took deep breaths. Rose returned holding a cone-shaped paper cup.

Diana gulped the water down. Some spilled. She tried to brush the drops away but the water soaked in.

Rose Narcisco sat back down, swiveled away and then back. Elbows on the arms of her chair, she laced her scarlet-tipped fingers together.

"This was in no way, we feel, a suicide attempt. The girl was trying to tell us something. From the look of the scratch and its position, she might even have had it in her mind to write a word. Or perhaps—this may be the more likely possibility—a name. Do you understand."

Diana downed the last of her water and crumpled the cup. "Writing?"

"Yes." Once again, Rose Narcisco pointed to the right side of her diaphragm with her fingernail. "She started here, on the right side, and was going across."

"So that whatever she wrote would be decipherable to other people."

"Yes." Rose swiveled again and relaced her fingers.

"Like a signboard."

"Yes."

"What did she do it with?"

After the initial shock, Diana craved details.

She waited. When she sat all the way back in her chair, her feet barely touched the floor.

Rose looked down at her hands.

"A cake knife," she said.

Diana flinched.

"Cake knife. How did she come by a cake knife?"

Rose looked annoyed. "She sneaked into the kitchen last night after hours."

"What was a cake knife doing out?"

"That we are not sure of. An oversight, most likely. An unfortunate goof."

Guf.

Rose Narcisco shrugged. "Accidents happen," she said.

Heppen.

She went on. "We do not lock doors here as you know, but we do position Staff at various stations throughout the system to prevent this kind of thing happening, but somehow . . ." Rose Narcisco unlocked her hands and turned her palms toward the ceiling . . . "somehow Belinda got past the stations." She looked squarely at Diana. "Bethany," she said.

Diana closed her eyes. In an involuntary gesture of failure, her shoulders curled in and down, toward her lap. Time healed nothing. Every wound was fresh. Passing the Austin jail where they took Bethany, Diana went weak in the knees. Seeing the Holiday Inn parking lot where she and Alex were arrested, her heart turned to jelly. They all toyed with her— the sheriff, the judge, the psychiatrists, the lowest parole officer and county clerk—and she could do nothing to help herself. She was as guilty as they implied.

"Mrs. Caldwell?"

Diana looked up. She hoped the doctor was not gathering her forces to deliver a message of commiseration.

Useless hope. At Cedar Hills, ruthless insensitivity came wrapped in the all-purpose lingo of false compassion. "I want you to know," she said. "I share your pain."

Diana clutched the arms of her chair. "No," she said simply. "Thank you but no, you do not." To escape Rose Narcisco's look of relentless disengagement, she toyed with the crumpled paper cup in her hands, making curving rips in the waxy paper.

"Well," said Rose. "That's neither here nor there, of course. It's best to be honest in any event. I must warn you, however, there will be consequences."

Her tone had changed. The shift was familiar to Diana. A warning from on high was in the works; either a dire prediction or a veiled threat.

"Yes?"

"Mrs. Caldwell, I don't know what we're going to do about this." She picked up a pencil and tapped it against her desk. "As I'm sure you know, at Cedar Hills we do not accept potential, ah, suicides, do you understand." She tapped the pencil. The point broke. She set it aside. "As a basically freeform, inherently family-based institution, we are not equipped to handle the more severe forms of pathology. In Bethany's case, my feeling and that of the medical doctor who treated her is that she was not in any way trying to, ah, *kill* herself, do you understand. But policy is policy. We must think of the other children. Staff will meet tonight. There will be a discussion."

"What might happen? The worst?" Diana had learned to think in percentages. Odds, handicaps. Chances for hope and disappointment.

"She could be asked to leave."

Live.

"But the judge, the legal ramifications . . ."

Rose Narcisco pursed her lips. "Please." *Pliss.* "You asked."

Diana cleared her throat. "And a step or two up from the worst?"

"We might call a freeze . . . although we've been disinclined to lay yet another one on Bethany's head. I simply cannot say at this point. She also"—Rose Narcisco swiveled her chair in a half-circle toward the darkened windows—"more than likely stole and perhaps even ate our celebration cake. She denies this, of course, but once she provided us with clear evidence she'd been in the kitchen, we were pretty certain. Of course we can't openly accuse her of *eating* the cake. Even if she stole it, we don't know what she did with it." Rose's tone was heated. "What we do know is that, one, the cake is gone; two, that Bethany was in the kitchen last night; and, three, that she is capable. I don't think we told you about another recent incident. One night after dinner Bethany stole a cooked ham. She hid the meat beneath her skirt and sneaked it into her room. There, in an orgy of indulgence, she ate it all. An entire ham." Rose clicked her nails and let the point sink in. "She invited the other children in to watch." She raised her well-plucked eyebrows. "She burned her stomach holding the meat against her stomach. Later she vomited and so we knew." The eyebrows went down. "The celebration cake was German chocolate. Bethany loves chocolate. So . . ." Rose Narcisco shrugged.

Diana envisioned the uproar. The examination of the vomit, the ham-shaped burn.

"What do you think she was going to write?"

"She refuses to say. There is a vertical line that starts at the rib cage, then goes down. At the apex of that line is the beginning of another one, angling down from the tip of the first one, I'd say at about a forty-five-degree angle. Maybe an *N*, or a *D*. An *A*. Possibly a *B*. It's hard to say."

To demonstrate, Rose drew two imaginary lines on her diaphragm. "Something," she said, "like that."

"So what do I say to her? How do I act?"

Rose relaced her fingers. "Act normally. Do not try to do therapy on her. Have as pleasant a visit as you can."

"In other words give her what she wants. Attention? Sympathy?"

"Attention, sympathy. The point is not what she wants but what you feel like giving, do you understand. Be honest."

"But if I reward her bad behavior by giving her the attention she wants, won't she feel compelled to repeat that behavior?"

"Compulsive repetition, yes, it is a risk but . . ." If Rose Narcisco had her way, a prerequisite to a child's being admitted to Cedar Hills would be that parents not read a word of popular psychology. "Our theory is no. Not if we give her what she wants, so to speak, in spades."

Spehds. Occasionally Rose used outworn expressions which made Diana think she had learned English during the fifties.

Diana sat forward. "What this ploy has to do with, I take it, is the assumption that what Bethany really needs is not food but love. She can't seem to get enough. She asks for more. If we give it to her, let her have all she wants, eventually she'll be satisfied. Is that anything like the way it works?"

"Something like. Not exactly." Rose took a quick, professionally impatient breath. "But, you see, it's not a ploy. It's a technique, based on a well-documented philosophy."

"Bethany knows about this, you know. She told me. It's called paradox. Whatever she wants, you give her the opposite."

Diana frowned. Was that right?

Rose grinned triumphantly. "But don't you see, she's got it wrong. What she is describing to you—*if* that's the way she put it and I'm not at all certain it is, these children are quite, quite clever—is not paradox but ordinary parenting. No, we give them what they *think* they want, do you understand. As *much* as they want, in her case food, in the case of an anorexic none. You don't want to eat, we tell them, you don't have to. Now." Leaning in toward Diana, Rose lowered her voice. "Bethany is overweight. She says she wants more cake and candy and so?" She answered her own question. "We give it to her. You see? She is still sneaking around to get extra snacks, but all of that will in time cease, or that is our hope. She's skeptical, which is normal. All adolescents test authority. Our responsibility is to maintain the integrity of our authority and not give in. What I am hoping is that this cake is the top of the mountain and that now . . ." She swiveled around and slapped her desk. "*Now* she will begin to think of something else. We force nothing. We allow the child's mind the freedom to change on its own. Do you understand."

"I tried that. I thought everybody ought to be able to make their own mistakes. It didn't work."

"Yes, well, perhaps we are more systematic and persistent. It's easier for us to be objective. And consistent."

"In other words you're the metaphor."

"For?"

"Good parents. Structure in the family."

"If you like."

"So tell me what to do."

"But don't you see, I can't. Do yourself a favor. Pretend you are at home and that Bethany has hurt herself. Pretend none of these other things have happened. Pretend she's a child. She's cut her finger, scraped her knee. She's crying. What do you do? You go to her of course, you minister to her needs. Remember what little children do when they have hurt themselves? They hold out the injury for you to see and once you've seen it they keep holding it out. They want you to look and look and look and then look at it again. The slightest scratch."

Diana nodded dumbly.

"That's Belinda. She wants you to *see* her hurt."

"Whether I want to or not."

Rose winked. "Of course. Otherwise the tree falls . . ." She lifted her shoulders. "Nobody hears."

"Where is she?"

Rose checked her watch. "In her room. She did it less than an hour ago. Maybe forty-five, fifty minutes."

"At noon."

"More or less."

"To punish me for being late."

"Yes?"

"I stopped to get the plant." She indicated the chicken. "I thought it might help to bring her a present."

"For your anniversary?"

Diana reached to her chest and through one of the cut-out flowers rubbed her scar.

"That, of course, does not help."

She lowered her hand.

"Some people on staff were inclined not to accept Belinda in the first place. But there were convincing arguments against a more severe diagnosis and so we relented. But now . . ." She shook her head and stood. "Bethany is waiting. Please remember, Mrs. Caldwell, it is herself she cut and not you."

Diana reached for the chicken. "Just so I'll know. Is it covered?" Rose Narcisco shook her head, as if Diana had used a word she didn't understand. "The wound. Is it bandaged?"

"Ah. No, she wanted to look at it and so we left it uncovered. The doctor said there was no harm. We've painted it with antibiotics. There's gauze and tape in the room if you'd care to bandage it yourself."

Diana gathered the plant to her chest. When she stood, the water cup tumbled to the floor. The breakfast tacos felt like lead in her stomach.

"When will we know your decision?"

"I'll get that." Rose Narcisco bent down and picked up the cup. "We'll have a staff meeting tonight after visiting hours. I'll call you at home. But do check by with me on your way out. I'd like to hear what happens."

Rose placed the crumpled cup on her desk and straightened her skirt, sweeping across the back of it with the palm of her hand.

Diana picked up the plastic drawstring bag with the blouse and book in it.

"I brought some things," she said.

The doctor smiled. "Fine," she said.

"So, I'll go now."

"Yes."

Diana was almost to the door when Rose Narcisco stopped her. "Mrs. Caldwell," she said. "We called to make sure you were coming. We spoke to your husband."

Diana turned halfway around. "You told Hale?"

"Yes."

"Did Bethany speak to him?"

"She said he wouldn't want to talk to her and so we didn't insist."

"What did he say?"

"That you were on your way. That's all."

Diana opened the door to the doctor's office. A woman waiting outside leaned against the wall. The woman's hair was shaved around the ears and as short on top as a Marine's. Small earrings outlined the woman's ears from lobe to tip. They looked like the tiny seed-ticks which gathered around Rufus's eyes. The woman looked mad enough to eat nails.

"Thanks for telling me."

"Of course. Please close the door."

Diana obeyed. The woman in the earrings stared at her feet.

Rose Narcisco threw Diana Caldwell's crumpled paper cup in the wastebasket and sat down to make notes on the conference.

Diana worked her way down the maze of halls toward the footpath leading to Bethany's unit.

*B*ushes of giant ligustrum flanked the front steps. At the top of the steps a wide redwood deck overlooked the woods on one side, the parking lot on the other. At one end of the deck, at a round white patio table with a giant multicolored umbrella in the center, Bobby Neuhaus sat with his mother. Around the table were several patio chairs and many potted plants. Beside the front door a basket of fuchsia impatiens hung from a black hook. All the plants were well tended.

Bobby and his mother faced the parking lot. In her arms the mother cradled a large looseleaf notebook. She held the notebook close to her face. She was reading aloud. Bobby paid rapt attention.

The jade plant was a silly idea. Bethany had never shown the slightest interest in plants. They had made the same mistake so many times, giving her everything she asked for and some she'd never gotten around to, the dance classes, guitar lessons, the camera with the special lenses, that rabbit. The rabbit had fleas and the mange and got too fat for his cage. One night he mercifully disappeared . . . whether eaten or escaped, they did not bother to find out.

Before Bobby and his mother had a chance to notice, Diana

tiptoed back down the steps. She set the chicken pot beneath the lowest limbs of the ligustrum, then eased the plant in closer to the trunk. A slender arm of the jade plant snapped off. Diana picked up the arm and stuck it into the potting soil. It was a succulent; it might root. Dusting her hands, she straightened slowly, to let her back come around. She brushed at her skirt and, shaking back her hair, again climbed the stairs to Unit 14.

Miami Neuhaus read on, her voice a steady drone.

The living room was packed. On the couch, three people sat side by side, hands in their laps, like bus riders. Except for the sound of the bubbling aquarium and the television set, the room was quiet. A baseball game was on. The kids' eyes were glued. As if they were all just nuts about baseball.

One man looked up. Diana smiled automatically. The man did not smile back. Parents of institutionalized children gained little from knowing other parents in the same boat; they were all too mired in misery to offer one another help.

At Bethany's door, she knocked and, without waiting for a response, went in.

Bethany closed her eyes and laid her arm lightly across her diaphragm. Ordinarily, she left her window shade raised. Today, for effect, she'd made the room dark.

She had brought things from home to make her room feel more like her own. Behind her bed she'd hung a satin banner saying "Sting" in his handwriting. Now Sting was old hat. On the wall were posters, rock-and-roll stars with their instruments, chins thrust forward, legs shamelessly spread.

From around the windowshade the relentless July sunlight in thin slats of yellow wormed its way in.

The pneumatic device let out a hiss. Diana tiptoed to Bethany's bed. A sheath of hair lay over her face. Her eyes were closed. Diana leaned down so close her lips brushed Bethany's ear.

"Bee?"

Bethany pulled her shoulder out from under her mother's touch.

"Hey," Diana raised her voice. "Miss Bee."

Bethany sat up so suddenly she and Diana almost butted heads. Diana drew back. Bethany blinked and rubbed her eyes.

"Oh," she said dramatically. "It's you." She looked at her watch. "What a surprise."

"I've been in Dr. Narcisco's office."

"For an *hour*?"

Diana's strategy, worked out with Gil, was to ignore sarcasm and focus on concrete physical tasks. *Float like a butterfly,* Gil had said, leaving out the part about the bee.

"Hi, honey," she said. She kissed Bethany's soft cheek. Bethany accepted Diana's gesture without response. But when Diana began to straighten, Bethany put a hand on her mother's shoulder and pulled her down.

"Mom," she whispered. "They said I ate the cake and I didn't. They blame me for everything. I didn't do it. I didn't eat the cake."

"It's all right, Bee." She tried to release herself but Bethany held on.

"You don't believe me either. I knew you wouldn't." She let Diana go.

"I didn't say that."

"You don't, I can tell. You're just like them." Sitting up, she could see herself in the mirror. She looked the way she felt, mad, crazy and fat.

Diana took a deep breath. Important to remember, the cake was not an issue. Make a plan, Gil had advised. Make her come to you.

"I brought you something." Diana held up the drawstring bag. When Bethany didn't look, she shook the bag to get her attention. Bethany covered her face with her hands. She didn't want to cry, but she couldn't help it. They all pushed her around. Nothing was being accomplished in her life, not a single thing.

Diana went to the bed. She knew what would happen next. After a crisis they all fussed and fumed as predictably as if the roles had been written ahead of time. Eventually somebody stormed off—sometimes Bethany, usually Hale, occasionally Roger, never Diana, who could not bear to let a fracas go—the one who left swearing never to speak to the rest of them again. The others waited. Eventually the one who stormed off came back. The inevitable reunion was tearful, apologetic and corny. Love was declared, promises made. They vowed to be more loving and honest, to make more sincere attempts at understanding one another. And—this was the pitiful part—they believed they would.

Usually these confrontations occurred in the middle of some long, horrible night, at two or three in the morning when promises come easy. They lulled themselves to sleep by convincing themselves things had been, if not fixed, patched up for a while. Beneath the certainty, however, lurked a persistent, nattering nervousness. It wasn't over, it would happen again, it would never be fixed.

Diana pulled a chair to Bethany's bedside.

"Honey," she said. "Why did you do it?" She pulled Bethany's head close. Her cheek was warm.

"I didn't," Bethany said. "I wouldn't."

"I don't mean the cake. I don't care about the cake. I mean . . . the other." When Diana tried to sit up and look, Bethany tightened her grip.

"Don't."

"Hey." Diana pulled against Bethany's arm. "Bethany," she said, trying to laugh. "You're hurting me."

The girl let her go. Diana rubbed her neck. Bethany flopped over on her back so that Diana could take a good look.

The beginning cut was the deepest. She had pushed in the knife in a soft spot just below the bottom edge of her rib cage with more strength—and confidence—than she was able to sustain. The other cuts—scalloped, like the knife's edge—barely broke the skin. They looked more like the cobwebby scratches of a kitten's claws than cuts from a knife. The skin around the puncture mark at the top of the vertical line was puffy and red. Another scratch went from that line out and down in about a forty-five-degree angle, exactly as Rose Narcisco had drawn on her own diaphragm.

What was she writing? *M* for Mother? *B* for Bethany or Bobby? *A* for Alex, *D* for Dad?

Bethany lifted her head from the pillow.

"I should have had a different kind of knife," she said. "A cake knife doesn't have a point."

"Why, Bethany? Why did you want to hurt yourself."

"You weren't here. There wasn't anything to do."

"I was on my way."

"So maybe I wanted to see what it felt like. Maybe I wanted to see if it was anything like a tattoo."

"And was it?"

"I don't know." She frowned. "I've never had a tattoo."

Diana giggled.

Bethany pulled the sheet up over her head. "I've heard about tattoos," she yelled through the sheet. "On 'Sixty Minutes,' they did a program. You think everything I say is a joke. Ha-ha, big joke Bethany. Very funny. Very, *very* funny."

Diana tugged at the sheet. Bethany drew the edges tighter.

Diana let go. She had tried to tell Hale, fight with children on their turf and you lose; Hale never listened. Most of the time Diana was not able to pay attention to her own good advice either. Again she grabbed the sheet and tried to pull it down. Bethany held on.

Diana took a new tack. "Bethany," she commanded, stepping back. "Don't be ridiculous. Take the sheet down." She felt like a fool.

"I don't want to."

"Then goddammit, just don't."

Bethany's bare feet stuck out of the bottom of the sheet.

Her toes curled, then straightened. Her short little toenails were painted bright blue with a white dot in the center. Diana let go of the sheet and went to the window. She raised the shade, squinting as daylight streamed into the room.

On the deck, Bobby Neuhaus swung his legs and held on to the seat of his chair. His mother tapped her ashes and blew out a puff of cigarette smoke. She turned a page of her notebook. Bobby looked up at the sky, the treetops, at nothing.

The sky was a picture. No clouds. Far off in the distance, Diana thought she could see the state capitol, pink against the sky.

"So?"

Diana turned from the window. Bethany had dropped the sheet to her chin. "So what?"

"So." Bethany shaded her eyes. "Are we going to finish this or what?"

"What."

"*What* what?"

"We are going to *what* instead of finishing this fight. I don't want to fight, Bee. I don't want to fight with you at all. I had this dream this morning. We were having fun together, you and me, just talking. It was great. That's what I want."

Bethany pulled her T-shirt to the edge of her bra, away from the scratches.

"It wasn't a fight."

"Sort of it was a fight."

"Because you laughed."

"Because you said something funny."

"Because it wasn't funny. It was dumb."

"I thought it was funny."

"You thought it was dumb."

"No. I thought it was funny."

"Dumb." She was having a hard time keeping a straight face.

"Come on, Bee, it was a joke. Think about it. You said you wanted to see if doing what you did felt anything like having a tattoo, and I said, 'and did it,' and you said, 'I don't know, I've never had one.' Now does that sound like a line from 'Saturday Night Live' or what?"

"How can it be a joke when I didn't mean it to be one?"

"Jokes are like that."

Bethany pouted.

Diana went to the bed and massaged her forehead.

Bethany lifted her chin and for the tiniest fraction of a second let down her guard. In that instant, the real Bethany came back, with the anxious, love-me look she used to have, back in the happy days of kindergarten.

"Okay," she said quietly. "I'm not frowning anymore."

Diana took her hand away.

"Now let's cover those cuts. Dr. Narcisco said there was a bandage?"

"It's over there."

Diana found the bandaging supplies on the dresser. When Bethany first came to Cedar Hills, Diana had asked if the mirror behind the dresser was two-way. She was told it was not. She still wasn't sure she believed that.

"I brought you a blouse." She addressed Bethany's reflection in the mirror. "And the new Alice Fine."

"Great. Do you believe me?"

"About what?"

"The cake."

Timing was everything. Without hesitation, Diana lied. "Yes," she said. "I believe you."

"Whether you do or you don't," Bethany said, "I didn't eat it."

"I said I did. Now let's do this, then maybe we'll go take a walk. I saw Bobby Neuhaus on the deck with his mother. What's her name?"

"I don't want to go outside."

"Then we'll stay in here."

"Miami."

"What?"

"Bobby's mom. We call her The Vice."

Diana took a length of gauze from the roll. "No scissors?"

Bethany pulled a long, dramatically sarcastic face. "Oh, sure, Mom. I'm sure they're going to leave scissors around after this." She pointed at her stomach.

Rather than ask Staff for a pair, Diana bit the gauze with her teeth. The threads stretched but did not give. She bit it again. Threads snapped. The tear was ragged but would do.

"Looks like they'd have gauze pads," Diana said, "instead of these old-timey rolls."

"Cheap," Bethany remarked. "Cheapo tighto Cedar Nut-house Hills."

Diana laid the strip of gauze against the wound and criss-crossed it until the wound was covered. There were moments when a parent had to put on a brave face. The trick was to concentrate on the emergency at hand.

She bit off another length of gauze. Touching the wound, she repressed a shiver.

Bethany switched modes. She had two. She could change from one to the other as fast as a lizard darting up a tree. One minute she was Surly Sue, the next Chatty Cathy. Placing an arm beneath her head, Chatty Cathy told Diana about Bobby Neuhaus's mother and her horror stories. The dead hamster, the burned baby. Once Bethany had switched, there was no stopping her. One Sunday, she had recited the entire plot of a "Star Trek" episode. When she seemed to be finished, Diana tried to change the subject, but Bethany shushed her. "Wait," she said, "that's not all." And she did an imitation of Spock lecturing a malevolent Klingon. When it was over, Diana said, "I thought you didn't like 'Star Trek.' " "I don't," Bethany replied in her best off-hand manner. "It's just something to do."

"When she leaves wait and see, he'll be totally Nutty Brown.

If they believed in pills here, you know what they'd give him? Ritalin, the same as Daddy gives horses to jazz them up. Can you believe it? It perks up horses but M-D's like Bobby take it to calm down. Weird."

"By she, you mean his mother?"

"You take a look at her?"

"I've seen her before. She's a doozey."

"Nut case is more like it. If you think Bobby's nuts, you should talk to Miami."

"I don't think Bobby's nuts." Diana pulled a length of tape from the roll and ripped it. She lay the tape over the outer edge of the crisscrossed gauze. When she did, the gauze shifted, uncovering some of the wound. She lay the tape on the bed and replaced the gauze.

"He's in here, isn't he? We're all nuts. Nutty as a Nutty Brown fruitcake."

West on 290 beyond the turnoff to Cedar Hills was a praline factory called Nutty Brown Candies. The road that ran by the candy factory was called the Nutty Brown Road.

"They don't make fruitcakes out there, you know. Just pralines."

"Okay, so a Nutty Brown praline. Aren't you finished?"

"Almost." She laid the tape once again on the gauze. This time the gauze held.

"You do know what she is, don't you. Miami, I mean."

Diana bit off another length of tape. "Seems like you told me. A writer?"

"A poet. What a jerk."

Diana secured the final strip of tape across the gauze. "What's wrong with being a poet?"

"Nut is more like it. Nobody's a poet."

Bethany pulled down her shirt.

"I'm not sure it will hold. I'm not much of a nurse."

Bethany looked down at her stomach. "I know."

"You remember the time you broke your wrist and I just about pulled your arm out of the socket?"

Bethany snickered. "I couldn't believe you did that. My own mom."

Bethany had been roller-skating. Some kids called her over to do the whip. Bethany had never played the game and so when everybody else said, "I bid not to be on the end," she lost out. Everybody held hands in a long line. The person at the beginning of the line began to skate in one direction and then another. Bethany had only just learned to skate. The whip popped. Bethany's feet flew out from under her. When she reached back to catch herself, her wrist snapped. She'd come home holding her arm. Diana thought it was only a bruise. She'd told Bethany to wash it. When Bethany turned her arm over and showed her the lump, Diana had taken Bethany to the hospital. After the doctor set the bone, he admonished Bethany to keep the cast dry. That night Diana went to help Bethany with her bath. Seeing the cast slip nearly into the water, she'd pulled Bethany's arm up by the fingers. Bethany screamed, Diana dropped the arm. They had to go in for a new cast. Later they'd had a big laugh, Diana as the Stan Laurel version of a nurse.

Thinking back, Diana could no longer consider such moments casually. Could that have been when Bethany's life cracked in two and was never the same?

"Would you like to try on your new blouse?"

"I guess. I hope it fits."

Diana took the blouse from the plastic sack and held it up. Bethany was busy smoothing a bumpy piece of tape on her stomach. Diana took the tissue from inside the folds of the blouse and began removing straight pins.

Bethany glanced at the blouse. "It's great," she said.

"I can take it back if you don't like it."

"I said it was great."

Diana did not reply.

Bethany rocked her head. "Terrific," she said. "Here we go again."

Diana took a breath.

"No," she said. "Let's just stop, okay? Now, would you like to try the blouse on?"

"I said yes." She took the blouse. Made of lightweight, long-staple Swiss cotton, it had a drawstring neckline and short puffy sleeves. In the fabric were woven tiny flowers—roses, violets, English daisies.

"Not my usual style."

"No, well, I thought you might like to try something new."

Bethany crossed her arms and lifted her T-shirt past her shoulders and over her head. She was wearing a blue cotton brassiere with a butterfly embroidered between her breasts.

She pulled the new blouse over her head. The sleeves were twisted. When she jerked them back around, a thread popped.

"Do you like it?"

"I said I did."

"But on? Look in the mirror. I think it looks great. A new you. I like it a lot."

Bethany slid out of bed and put on her sandals. The straps hung over her heels. When she walked, the shoes flapped against her feet.

At the mirror, she brushed her hair back with Gloria's silver brush. She turned to Diana. "Ta-dah," she said, holding out her arms. And there she was again, hopeful and shining. She looked beautiful.

"What do you think?" She did a small sashay.

Diana's voice wavered. She remembered Gil's *too much in love, the way girls usually are with their fathers.* "I think," she said, "it's wonderful."

Bethany flipped back her hair. "Let's go," she said.

"Where?"

"Outside, where else?"

She gestured toward the door, which Diana—who was already beginning to feel worn down from the constant effort of being tested both by herself and her daughter—obediently opened.

· 24 ·

*I*n the living room, people milled about, getting up to check the weather, watch fish, or flip through well-thumbed *National Geographic*s and *Smithsonian*s. A father drummed his fingers on an end table while his wife talked and his daughter stared at the television screen.

On the arm of a wing chair Tiffany Leberman chewed a strand of hair. Silently, she wept. No one seemed to notice. Her mother—the thin pale woman with the earrings and the Marine haircut—sat in the wing chair behind Tiffany, holding her soft leather shoulderbag to her stomach. Perched on a stool between very fat parents in chairs, Stephen Doty watched baseball. The parents watched the back of Stephen's head.

Diana went to the front door. From behind her, she could hear Bethany's shoes flap. When Tiffany saw Bethany, she dried her face with her sleeve and nudged Stephen Doty, who pulled away from his parents and gave Bethany a secret salute. Bethany glanced over but gave no indication she'd noticed the greetings.

Diana opened the door.

"Let's sit on the deck." At the sound of Bethany's voice, Bobby Neuhaus swiveled in his seat and waved.

Miami Neuhaus stopped reading. "Join us," she said, gesturing with her cigarette.

"Oh, Bee," Diana said under her breath. "Let's not."

Bethany was curiously acquiescent. "Fine with me," she said. "We're taking a walk," she told Bobby and his mother. "We like to sweat."

Diana softened Bethany's excuse. "But thank you."

Miami Neuhaus turned back to her poems.

Bethany bounced down the stairs past the ligustrum and the hidden chicken, toward a path which disappeared into the woods.

At the time of her arrest she had already been in some trouble with the law: a speeding ticket, failure to come to a complete halt at a stop sign. One night the San Marcos police charged her and Alex with public intoxication. The police didn't like Hurtados. They jumped at any opportunity to haul one in. Hale was able to get Bethany out of the ticket easily enough, but once her name was linked with Alex's, the police began keeping an eye on her as well.

Last winter, on one of those numbingly cold December nights, Bethany stepped over the line into real crime.

She'd gone out for a drive with Alex. As it was a school night, she was supposed to be in by eleven. At a little after eleven, Diana and Hale had gone to bed. They lay in bed waiting to hear the sound of tires on the gravel when she came home.

Some time after midnight they gave up. Hale went to the kitchen, made a drink. Diana stared out the window into the dark night. They folded clothes and pretended to read, saying little, hoping nothing terrible had happened, feeling scared one minute, furious the next, foolish for the fear, guilty for the anger. Hale built a fire. At two-something the county sheriff came out and, thinking they might be asleep, honked his horn. Bethany was in Austin. The police there had called him; she was in jail, so was Alex Hurtado and the charges were serious. He thought they'd rather he tell them in person than over the phone.

Hale called the lawyer who'd helped on the public intoxication ticket. Accustomed to emergency telephone calls in the middle of the night, the lawyer answered quickly and alertly. They drove separately to Austin. As Hale never exceeded the speed limit by more than five miles an hour, the lawyer arrived long before Hale and Diana. The jail was lit up and, even on a Wednesday night, as active as a downtown cafeteria at noon. Prostitutes stood in line for bail, drawing fake furs around their shoulders. Drunks came in by the carload, most of them, according to the lawyer, having provoked a policeman on purpose, in order to come in and get warm. The police sergeant was fat and rude. He made Diana and Hale feel like school children called into the principal's office. At four when the lawyer managed to get Bethany out, the three of them drove home in silence. When they got there Hale went to bed. Diana made hot chocolate and a sandwich. Bethany pulled a rocking chair close to the fire. In the corner, their Christmas tree was already beginning to shed its needles from the heat of the colored bulbs.

A terrible winter, just terrible. In her red goose-down vest, Bethany shoved her hands deep in her pockets and stared at the fire. When Diana brought her the hot chocolate and sandwich, she nibbled at the food and set the cup on the floor. She wasn't that hungry, she said. The lawyer had brought two Twix bars and a Coke.

Diana stoked the fire. She had made herself a cup of herb tea. She sat down beside Bethany and waited. Bethany rocked. They watched the fire. Finally Bethany switched modes. Her voice was calm and she spoke with cool detachment . . . as if the events had either taken place on their own or had happened to somebody else.

They had seen a Trans-Am in the Holiday Inn parking lot—the round Holiday Inn, she was careful to point out, the one next to Town Lake, by the freeway. They'd been cruising Austin when "I saw it first," Bethany exclaimed. "Brand new, not a scratch. God, Mom." She sounded like a small girl describing a new toy. "But it was fine. It had the, you know, gold bird on the hood and everything." They had pulled into the parking lot to get a closer look.

"It was Alex's dream car," Bethany said. "You just don't know, Mom. It was his dream."

They drove closer, peering from the windows of the Grand Prix into the Trans-Am. The interior was white and perfect, she said, like it had never been sat in. The dash looked like a jet plane's. They drove past the car slowly. "Now you'd have to see it to believe it, Mom, but get this, the keys were there, I mean can you dig it? A car like that and the keys are hanging from the trunk? It was cool. I mean it was really cool."

Waiting for a response, she paused.

Diana made a daring leap. "So," she said. "Why did you take it?"

Bethany looked at her mother as if she'd just gone stark raving idiot crazy.

"The guy left the keys in the trunk, Mom. It was Alex's dream car. I mean, you don't get it. You really don't get it, do you?" She snorted, and sipped her hot chocolate.

Diana had become an irresistibly easy mark. Her instinct was to jump to her own defense. She defused that instinct by taking shallow breaths and tensing her neck. She pressed on. "So somebody was careless. Does that give another person the right to steal from him?"

"No, but . . ." Bethany frowned, lifted the poker from the hook and stoked the fire. "You're such a goody-good, Mom. You always get me mixed up. Anyhow can I please finish? Or do you want to lecture me some more? If you do then go ahead, I mean everybody else has."

"It wasn't a lecture. It was a question."

Bethany side-stepped the issue. "*Any*way," she triumphantly proclaimed, "the driver didn't *own* the car. It wasn't *his*. The guy was a *sales*man. I didn't even know they rented Trans-Ams. Guy's probably a *zill*ionaire." She tapped the poker against the hearth.

Diana covered Bethany's hand with her own. "Now look. Don't get mad, Bee, but I want to ask you a serious question, okay?"

Bethany drew her hand away. "Okay." She tapped the poker.

"Deep down, do you think it was wrong to steal the car, whoever it belonged to?"

"Deep down?" Bethany dropped the poker and thrust her hands back down in her pockets. "At the time we did it?"

"Whenever." Diana reconsidered. It was important to be specific. "Yes," she said. "At the time."

Bethany turned down the corners of her mouth in an ugly grimace. "Nah."

"And now?"

She gave Diana her most disdainful look. "What do you think? We got caught, Mom. If you'd like to know, I spent the night in jail with a dirty old woman who scratched all night. I think she had fleas. Like that rabbit we had, scratch scratch. Or maybe it was lice. They came around and put orange medicine on her. It was freezing cold in there. I thought I was going to freeze to death if I stayed another minute. I mean when we were walking down the hall toward the cell and I saw a window at the end of the hall, I thought about running down there, Mom, and jumping out. We were three floors up, Mom. I mean, what do you think if I'm sorry or not?"

Gil had said they should present a united front, but Diana had not told Hale everything she knew. She had found money in Bethany's room—$360 worth of twenty-dollar bills—blank checks from the purses of friends, the wallet of a boy named Hector Contreras, a plastic pipe for smoking dope, feathered roach clips, small items possibly shoplifted from department stores, never used, a brand new portable stereo cassette player, still in a box. Diana had left the articles as she found them. They were not well hidden. Obviously Bethany meant for them to be found. Diana saved the girl from Hale's harsh ethical sensibilities. She closed her eyes to the stolen goods, crossed her fingers, hoped the articles—and the trouble— would disappear. She knew it would take a miracle but stranger things had happened.

They'd had her tested. The tests said Bethany was normal, no trace of serious pathology or psychopathy. She felt guilt, the tests said. That was one of the main areas of concern. Sometimes in life it was hard to tell.

"Do you want to hear the rest of it?"

"Sure. Go ahead." Diana sipped her tea.

After stealing the car, Bethany and Alex had driven to Lake Austin. In a parking lot they'd switched license plates with another car. "We knew," Bethany explained, "the car was rented. There was a Hertz sticker on the windshield. Alex said all rental cars have a certain kind of license plate. So," she shrugged, "we switched. The guy had left a Walkman in the backseat. We pawned it. We bought a pizza with the money." The police picked them up at a Mr. Gatti's. When Alex directed the police to his own car, they discovered the stolen goods in the trunk, the cameras, a stereo, a VCR, some tools. And the guns. A .22 pistol and a shotgun, both stolen.

"Do you know what they did, Mom? Get this, the great police, who you love. I'm sitting there eating pizza, we have the heater on—of course, because it's freezing cold outside— and so we don't hear them. They come up. Three cars." She held up three fingers. "*Three*. And they get out and one of them whips open my door—like a stupid I left it unlocked— and he says don't move and he sticks a gun here, right here." She put the point of her index finger on her forehead, between her eyes. "A big fat guy with a red face. 'Don't move,' he says." She imitated the policeman's voice and punched at her forehead with her finger. "And I'm sitting there with a wad of pizza in my mouth. Like I was a killer or something." She lowered her hand and shoved it into a pocket. "I should have thrown up on his shoes. I felt like I was going to."

To shut out the picture of her daughter with a loaded gun at her head, Diana closed her eyes.

Bethany waited. When Diana was up to it, she spoke.

"I guess," she said, "the police have been trained to do that."

"I knew you'd take their side."

"It's not a matter of sides."

What was she supposed to say? Whose side should she take? How was she supposed to be a good parent? Who should have taught her how to take care of a situation like this?

"And Alex is still in jail because he's Mexican and I'm Anglo, isn't that right, huh, Mom? And we have money and he doesn't and he's a Hurtado and my name is Caldwell. You don't have to answer. I mean I *know* the answer."

Diana managed to ask one more question before they went to bed. Did she and Alex think no one would find out? Did they have in mind keeping the Trans-Am forever?

With the poker, Bethany turned a log over so that the red side was on top.

"Who knows," she said. "Life goes away and it comes around."

They went down the path to a Private Conference Nook.

"Nice," Diana said.

Bethany kicked at the leg of the concrete bench, which had been made to look like two tree stumps and a plank of wood. On one side of the bench was a raised bed of red petunias; on the other, one of marigolds. The petunias looked exhausted. The marigolds blazed away.

Diana's response to Bethany's story had still not jelled. One side of her wanted to slap sense into the girl and make her do right. That part wanted to scream out, *Don't you get it yet? Don't you know this is what happens when you break the law?*

The other came down on her when she saw Bethany in her jeans and sweatshirt and red goose-down vest shuffling— chin on her chest, hair over her eyes—down the hall of the Austin jail. At that moment, law, morals and the responsibilities of citizens to a civilized society vanished. Diana became a savage. Freed from considerations of law and order, she might have stooped lower than she had ever thought possible, performed the scummiest criminal act, debased herself and everything she stood for to get her daughter away from jail and rescue her from the policeman with the hairy hand on her shoulder.

Through the trees they could see 290 and the traffic. The traffic never stopped. Cars, trucks whizzed by in a steady stream.

"I wonder," Bethany said, flopping down on the bench, "if there will be a freeze."

"A freeze?" Diana held her hair off her neck.

"A school freeze. Because of the cake."

Diana sat down. "It might be worse," she said. "But not because of the cake."

Bethany plucked a dead petunia and tossed it into the grass. "What else is there?"

"Your . . ." Diana gestured helplessly toward Bethany's waist. "The cuts."

"Oh." Bethany sucked in her stomach. "That. Well," she shrugged, "it's my skin. I don't know what they have to say about it."

"They don't care that much about the cake, really."

"It's my body."

"But there are rules."

"The rules say I don't own my own body?"

"You're fighting the wrong battle, Bee."

"I'm not fighting. I'm just asking. Okay?"

"Okay."

"So what's the excuse? No, wait. What's the *reason?*"

"If you do harm to yourself they think maybe . . ."

"What?"

"They don't keep kids here who . . . well, but I don't think they will. It's not as though you really tried to kill yourself, is it?"

"And if I did?"

"They could ask you to leave."

Bethany's face dropped. "They can't. No way."

"But you weren't. Were you?"

A flicker of something really ugly went through Bethany's eyes. One eyelid—the drooping one—squeezed shut.

"No," she said. "Not really. And I'm sure you're all broken up about that. The world would be better off if I'd done it, especially my dad's world, old perfecto Hale."

Diana reached for her hand. Bethany flinched but did not draw back. "What were you going to write, Bee?"

"Nothing."

"Do you mean . . ."

Bethany jerked her hand away.

"I mean it's my business." She put her hand under her blouse. "I mean it's my skin and I can do whatever I want to it."

Diana sat up straighter. "I suppose I should be grateful for the fact that it's yours this time." It was out before she thought. She was tired, that was all. Tired of floating above her feelings. Tired of strategies and pretense and trying to think of the right thing to say.

Bethany crossed her arms over her chest. Remembering the cuts, she winced broadly and dropped her hands.

It was Diana's turn to be Chatty Cathy. To cover up her mistake she told stories, about the armadillo and Red, how worried she was about Red's shins, and the destroyed garden. When she came to the basil Bethany jumped up.

"What makes you think I care about your stupid, fucking basil," she said. "I hate your stupid fucking garden. I didn't ask to come to this place, so what do I care if they kick me out. If you cared anything about me you'd have already gotten me out instead of waiting for them to do it."

"I can't. The judge . . ."

"Fuck the judge. You could if you wanted to and you know it. You don't want me to come home. Nobody does."

"That's not true."

"Well, as long as I'm here, I know one thing. I don't have to listen to this."

Once again, Bethany reached beneath her blouse. The bandage came off in one piece. She threw the gauze and tape at Diana's feet.

"It wasn't going to stay anyway," she said. "You did a lousy job."

She ran down the path.

Diana picked up the bandage and sat watching the traffic a few minutes, then stood and looked down the hill. The creek was down there somewhere.

From the deck, Bethany stood on tiptoe. That was where she'd thrown the cake, just about where Diana was. She wondered if Diana could see it. When Diana turned to come back down the path, Bethany shot inside the front door. The Vice read on.

At Unit 14, Diana went through the living room and down the hall to Bethany's room. She tossed the bandage into a garbage can. At Bethany's door, she knocked and pushed. But Bethany was standing against the door.

"Honey," Diana said, trying to keep her voice down. "Let me in."

"*Go away!*" Bethany screamed.

The living room grew quiet. Someone lowered the volume of the television set.

"Bee?"

"I don't want to talk to you anymore."

Shoe heels clicked against polished linoleum-tile floors. Diana left before Staff could greet her with their platitudes of piety and concern. In the living room the aquarium bubbled. The fish swam. Diana opened the front door and went out. On the footpath her ankle turned when she stepped on an uneven stone.

She knocked on Rose Narcisco's door. There was no answer. Diana left, certain that Rose's secretary had used a Cedar Hills hand signal to warn the doctor in time for her to get away.

In the parking lot she remembered the chicken.

She could not go back now. The jade plant and the chicken would have to fend for themselves. Maybe it would rain. Maybe the chicken would find herself a home there, beside the ligustrum. Maybe anything. Probably not.

· 25 ·

The Buick smelled of oregano and overheated tomatoes. Diana put the car in reverse and pressed down on the accelerator, sending a spray of gravel out from behind her tires.

At the highway, she turned south toward Oak Hill instead of north in the direction of home. She pulled in at the Big Wheel, a local all-night truckers' café where the coffee was strong, the chicken-fried steak hand-pounded and dredged, the biscuits tender, the pie crust thick and chewy.

She ordered a cup of coffee to go and asked if Mildred was on.

"Nope," said a thin, snappy woman in a blue polyester uniform. "Mildred's off. You need Sweet 'n Low or cream, honey?"

"Honey?"

"We don't have no honey."

"I'm sorry. Just cream, please."

When she taught, Diana stopped at the Big Wheel every morning for a cup of coffee and sometimes a biscuit. The interior of the Buick was always littered with Styrofoam cups and crumpled paper napkins with a picture of a wagon wheel on them.

The waitress brought packages of powdered milk-substitute. Mildred knew better. Diana asked for real milk. The waitress sighed and went off to the kitchen. She came back with several thimble-shaped containers of half-and-half.

Diana poured two containers in her coffee, covered the Styrofoam cup with a lid, paid and went out. There was a public telephone just outside the door. Diana inserted a quarter and dialed.

After seven rings, a girl answered, her voice fuzzy with sleep. Diana hung up. Jesse was a deep sleeper. He hadn't heard. As if the pay phone could see and hear her, Diana tiptoed away from the Big Wheel.

In her car, she let the top down and set the coffee on the seat. She drove through Oak Hill, winding in and out of lanes to dodge the traffic. At the Tom Thumb-Page she took the left arm of the Y and pressed her rock-and-roll tape back into the slot. She fast-forwarded to the next song, one of her favorites, Chuck Berry singing "Nadine."

Past the Nutty Brown Road, she turned off toward Camp Ben McCullough. She felt bad about the chicken. Succulents didn't need a lot of water. The jade plant would be all right for a time but not that long. Worse, if someone found it and showed it to Rose Narcisco, she'd know.

At the crest of the second hill after the turnoff, Diana let the car coast downhill while she opened her coffee. Hale did this thing with coffee-to-go, cut a triangle from the lid so that you could drink without spilling. It was hard to do with one hand. Ordinarily Diana used a car key but it was too late for that. She put the lid on the seat and held on to the cup.

A third hill came quickly. Near its peak, a gaunt agile fawn bolted from a clump of cedars and cleared a fence on the right side of the road. Startled, Diana slammed down the brake pedal, checking her mirror at the same time to make sure no one was behind her.

On delicately tapping feet, the fawn ran across the blacktop to the other side of the road, then leapt effortlessly over the fence over there, taking to the air with the grace of a heron. Once over, the fawn disappeared.

Between Diana's breasts, a coffee stain ran and spread. She could feel the dampness soak into her slip. At the bottom of the hill, she pulled over and mopped at her blouse with a scarf. The oregano plant had slid to the floor. She put it on the front seat, then wedged the cardboard tray containing the tomato six-packs upright between it and her purse, like children in safety seats.

She stuck her arm out the window and poured out the rest of the coffee. Chuck Berry finished asking Nadine if she was the one he saw and the Pretenders came on to sing the song about Ohio. Diana turned up the volume. Tears filled her eyes. Like Tiffany Leberman she did not wipe the tears away but let them run.

She was not a bad person, or she did not think she was, and yet she could not seem to do one right or good or useful thing in any direction. Now she had to go home and greet Hale, and decide what kind of face to put on the visit to Cedar Hills. Then the wait for the call from Rose Narcisco. She hoped Roger was home.

She blew her nose and dabbed at her eyes with the scarf she'd used to mop up the coffee. There was no need to rush, the blouse was either ruined or it wasn't, but Diana sped home as fast as if someone were after her, keeping her eye out for deer as she went.

· 26 ·

*H*ale rose from the creaking comfort of his leather chair and went back to the ironing board. He'd had a sinking spell. Too much thinking, too much regret: he'd wallowed. If Diana found him sprawled in front of the television set like some Sunday slob with his sports and beer, she'd know how his afternoon had gone.

He added fresh water to the iron. On MTV, exploding limousines were turning into men in tuxedos.

At that moment her tires crunched against the gravel. The car door slammed. He switched from MTV to golf. The tournament had ended in a tie. A seasoned player and a rabbit turned pro teed up to play a sudden-death hole.

In falsetto baby talk, Diana greeted Rufus. She had never spoken a word of baby talk to the children. When Gloria or Mimi indulged in the *goo-goo ga-ga* they were used to, Diana threw a fit. Hale remembered Gloria once offering Bethany a "tratter." "Why do you talk like that, Mother?" Diana had asked, her voice stippled with righteous indignation. "Do you want the child to grow up calling crackers *tratters*?" Gloria had thrown the saltine to the floor. "Worse things have happened," she declared. And with the toe of her shoe she had ground the cracker to smithereens.

Hale reached into the clothes basket and took out a pale pink oxford-cloth shirt. He didn't particularly like oxford cloth. But Diana had bought the shirt. And so he wore it.

He flipped the shirt open, sprayed the collar with starch.

The front door opened, slammed.

Her face was damp and flushed—she'd had the top down— her hair wild about her face. There was a brownish stain down the front of her blouse. She held out a small bush in a pot. She looked hysterical, and as radiant as a bride. Pale lavender flowers drooped from the limbs of the pot plant.

"Hi," she said, thrusting the plant in his direction.

He set the iron down.

"More salvia?"

She shook her head. "A present." She held the plant under his nose.

He ruffled the leaves and sniffed. "Oregano?"

She drew the plant away. "But?"

"Oregano's not a bush."

"So?"

"So I give up, what?"

"Remember the ceviche recipe? We didn't want to use oregano because we thought it would taste like fish pizza?"

"Mexican oregano."

"Oh, sorry." She brushed a leaf and a few specks of potting soil from the pink shirt on the ironing board.

"I thought we weren't doing anniversary gifts."

"It's not for that. It's just a present. Douglas only had a few." She set the plant on an end table, picked up the remote and flipped away from golf. "I did get some more tomato starts. No Celebrities, but . . ." She shrugged.

"What kind?"

"Jackpot, Bingo."

"Bingo? That's why you were late."

"When was I late?"

"To Cedar Hills."

Her eyes went flat.

"What happened?"

When she came to the PBS channel, Diana lifted her thumb. A lecturer was explaining the ovulation cycle of whales. The program was a repeat. They had watched snatches of it earlier in the week. Hale had got up and gone to bed. "More than I want to know," he'd said, "about whales."

"I meant," Hale said, pointing at her chest, "your blouse."

"Oh," she said, looking down. "That." She brushed at the stain. "It was stupid. I bought coffee at the Big Wheel and took the lid off when I turned onto 1826. A deer came flying across the road, I had to stop and there went my coffee. It was really stupid. I should have waited until I got past the hills. Maybe it will come out. I don't know."

The Big Wheel was in the wrong direction from Cedar Hills, toward Austin, not away from it. Hale said nothing.

Diana flipped to the arts channel. A large black woman sitting at a baby grand piano was being interviewed.

"Carmen McRae," Diana said. "She's great."

"So what happened?"

She leaned back. "What did they tell you when they called?"

"Only that she'd cut herself."

"Scratched really. Spidery marks. Like a kitten's." She flicked her hand as if to brush the trouble out the window. "It's not bad."

"Where'd she get a knife?"

Carmen McRae put her hands on the piano keys.

"The kitchen. They don't lock doors, you know. She sneaked in during the night and apparently stole an entire German chocolate cake and the knife. The knife she took to her room. The cake we don't know about. Staff came in and caught her carving on herself." Diana sighed. "She swears she didn't eat the cake and I tend to believe her. I don't know about that place, Hale. They aren't doing anything to help her lose weight. She's fatter this week than last."

"Where?"

"Did she do it?"

He nodded.

"Her stomach. Here." She pointed. "I think she was trying to write 'Alex.' She didn't say so—she wouldn't—but that's what I think. She didn't finish the A."

"Christ."

"I know." Diana concentrated on television. Hale picked up the iron. Diana looked over her shoulder and lowered her voice. "She could be sent home."

He held the iron in the air. "For how long?"

"What do you mean how long. For good."

He shook his head. "They can't."

"It's their school."

"What do you mean their school? She could go to jail. We worked out a deal. They can't."

When Hale panicked, Diana grew calm.

"Cedar Hills," she needlessly explained, "is a private institution. They can do what they like."

Carmen McRae played an introduction to "Come Rain or Come Shine." Hale turned off the iron, took the shirt from the board and tossed it back into the basket. He was not sure which upset him more, Diana's phoney show of calm, the prospect of Bethany going to reform school or the one of her coming home.

"Hale, there's no need to panic yet. Let's wait and see. I have a feeling it'll all blow over. Rose Narcisco said she'd call tonight. We'll know then."

Carmen McRae enunciated syllables as if her life depended on it. " . . . happy together, unhappy together . . ."

Diana changed the subject. "Where's Rog?"

Hale didn't answer. Diana leaned up from the big leather chair. He had placed both hands flat on the ironing board.

He was leaning forward. His face had gone slack and his eyes were empty.

"Hale."

"What." He frowned.

"It's just a scratch."

"I don't think that's the point, Diana."

"Well, I do," she said. "I very much think it is the point."

He widened his eyes. "That the cuts weren't deep?"

"That she wasn't trying to kill herself. She said we'd probably be disappointed that she wasn't. And I don't know." She sat back in the chair. "Maybe she's right. Maybe we are."

"That's a shitty thing to say, Diana."

She switched back to whales.

Hale went to the kitchen.

Diana flipped to golf, baseball, commercials. Ninja on HBO. Right-wing preaching and faith healing on the Christian channels. Carmen McRae.

She felt bad about what she'd said. It was a low blow.

From the kitchen Hale shouted, "I'm going to feed." His voice was normal again.

Diana sat forward. "Wait," she said. "I'll go with you." Carmen McRae wound up her song with a flourish of fingers and keys.

"You don't have to." He was in the door again. To cut his losses he had shifted his mood from panic to resignation.

"I know I don't have to." With her thumb she flicked off the television set.

"Do you want to change clothes first?"

"No. I'm already a mess. I'll change after."

"I don't mind waiting." His tone was tender. She couldn't figure out what he wanted.

"No. Let's go. Where's Roger, by the way? I thought you two were going to fix fence."

"Austin. It's too hot. He went to Barton Springs for a swim."

"My B.T.'s are hanging heavy. I'm not sure I'll want a big dinner, how about you?"

"It's all planned. I wouldn't want to disappoint Roger."

"No."

Diana took off her sandals and set them on the coffee table. "Just let me get my shoes."

She went out on the deck and put on the running shoes she had worn to the garden that morning.

Rufus rose and stretched, readying himself for the trip.

· 27 ·

*H*ale whistled up the mares. There were twenty-two, about the same number of weanlings and yearlings: too much horse flesh for the amount of help and land he had. Unless he got rid of some, he needed to make a deal on the acreage across the road. He was ready to sell ten or fifteen head, but the market was so bad he hated to. The news was getting sleazier by the day. Now that horses were more valuable dead than alive, a scam had been discovered, in which men were hired to kill horses—by fire, injection or a plastic bag—in order to collect the insurance money. Word among horsemen was, prices were leveling off and the yearling sales in September would show improvement. Word among horsemen meant a great deal. Most sales were trade-offs only, a flashy show of paper, but no money. Hale would settle for a slow-down in the drop.

In the training barn, Diana followed Hale to the feed room.

Currently he had eight horses in training but that number would double in the fall when the babies came for breaking and then to prep for the futurities in the winter and early spring.

He had to go one way or another, borrow more money

from the bank, spend more to make more, or sell to be on the safe side. But sell to whom? Besides, the only way to make any real money was to sell the best of your stock. He wasn't ready to do that.

They came to the feed room, one wall of which was stacked to the ceiling with fifty-pound sacks of feed, the others with bales of wire-bound alfalfa and sweet hay. The room was large, airy and fragrant.

Hale lifted an open sack of feed from a wooden box he'd built to keep out squirrels and deer. He poured the sweet-smelling grains into a rusty wheelbarrow until the wheelbarrow was one-third full. From the same feedbox Diana took an empty plastic bucket and a round cardboard container of 707. She put the bucket and the vitamin supplement into the wheelbarrow with the feed and rolled the wheelbarrow down the center walkway.

Hale's father had given him the wheelbarrow. He was too old to use a wheelbarrow anymore, he'd said; Hale would put it to good use. Hale had been touched by the gift, the only sign his father ever gave him that he in any way approved of or understood his move to the country.

Hale stacked hay and alfalfa in another wheelbarrow.

Diana went from one stall to another, dipping out a small scoop of 707 and a bucket of feed for each horse. Hale stuffed netted bags with alfalfa and hay.

"Did you have any new ideas about Red?"

She took a bucket into the stall of a horse they were training for the owner of a hardware store in town. "Out of my way, Mitey Fine," she said. The horse curled his lip.

Diana drew back her arm. "Don't you dare," she told the vicious roan gelding. "Just don't you dare." Mitey Fine retreated. Hale came in, brushed against the horse, filled up his hay bag and went out.

"Don't let him bluff you out."

"Don't worry."

Cutting Mitey Fine hadn't done a bit of good; he was as

mean now as he'd ever been. One day he ran at some people with his teeth bared for no reason. Only a last-minute dodge kept a boy from getting bitten. He also kicked like a cow. Casey refused to have anything to do with a cow-kicker but so far Hale had refused to let Mitey Fine go. He liked the hardware store owner.

Diana made a wide arc around Mitey Fine's right hind leg.

She dumped 707 and feed into the gelding's trough. "You didn't answer my question."

"What?" Hale yelled from the other end of the barn.

Diana left the stall and entered the walkway.

"Oh," Hale said. "She's going Saturday, as planned. I haven't talked to Marvin but I don't see that we have any choice."

Diana latched Mitey Fine's stall door.

"I didn't mean Ruidoso. I meant her problem."

Hale took a hay bag into Ingratiating Sam's stall.

When he came out, he stopped and stood with his hands on his hips in the middle of the walkway. "Well," he said. "As a matter of fact I did. See what you think. I thought I might take her feed to the gates tomorrow morning and try to get her to stand in there to eat. If we do it every day until she leaves, who knows, maybe she'll begin to associate the gates with pleasure instead of pain." He took a hay bag from the next stall and attached it to two hooks to fill it. "Maybe. Maybe not. What do you think?" He put a slice of hay and one of alfalfa in the bag.

"At least it's a plan. Can I participate?"

Hale lowered his arms and came toward her. "If you're sweet to me."

"I'm always sweet to you."

At her wheelbarrow he stopped. "I don't want you to get hurt."

"Red wouldn't hurt me."

"She might."

"She won't."

He didn't answer.

"Let me just lead her to the gates the first time. You and the boys can do the rest."

He frowned. "I don't know, Diana. I have a lot at stake in that filly. She's not all mine, you know."

Diana scooped up 707 and a bucket of feed. "I know that, Hale. I do know that. But . . . Forget it. They're your horses."

Hale tied up another hay bag. The horses in training would stay in their stalls all night. The mares and weanlings grazed in the pasture and ate alfalfa from communal troughs.

"I'm going to feed the stallions. I'll meet you at the mare barn."

"See you there. Soon as I do Red."

While Diana filled her trough, Red waited in a corner of her stall. When the trough was filled the filly moved up to eat. With her nose, she shoved at the grain until it was piled up on one side. Some spilled. Diana had tried piling the grain herself, so that Red wouldn't lose any. Red had pushed the feed to the other side.

"See you in the morning, Reddo." Diana tossed the bucket into the wheelbarrow and rolled it back to the feed room. She put the 707 in the feed box and turned the wheelbarrow upside down.

· 28 ·

*H*ale gave Enlightened an extra portion of feed. Even though he had thoroughbred blood on both sides, Enlightened had a classic quarter-horse look, thick and blocky with the hindquarters of an ox. When Hale first got him, Enlightened was a smoky color. Now he was practically white, with gray dapples across his hips.

On his ninth birthday Hale's father had bought him his first horse, a sorrel gelding named Johnny. The gelding was gentle and fat as an elephant; to saddle Johnny, Hale had to take a kitchen chair to the barn. Every horse Claude ever owned was either sorrel or a bay; he said gray horses were good for nothing but to look at.

Hale brushed Enlightened's mane to one side. He had wanted a gray horse for as long as he could remember. Munching his feed, the horse turned around and looked at Hale, then went back to his business. For a stud horse, Enlightened was tame. Hale just naturally liked the horse, even though the trend now was away from the pure quarter-horse look, toward the finer-boned thoroughbred style. Enlightened had everything, looks, bloodlines, conformation, an excellent track record. Now if he would just turn out some race colts.

The stud barn had six stalls. Except for an occasional stallion leased for a season, Hale only had the two, but he and Marvin were keeping their eyes on a sorrel stud horse in Oklahoma named Man in the Moon. If the oilman who owned the stallion dropped the price another two thousand dollars Hale and Marvin were going to buy him. The horse had Go Man Go on one side and Dash for Cash on the other; at ten, he'd already turned out a high percentage of Register of Merit colts.

The stalls in the stud barn were like prison cells: iron bars were set into iron gates with iron latches. The lead shank hanging on the wall was made of thick chain. Breeding season went from February until June, and so the stallions were on holiday now. Every day, Casey led them to a high-walled iron pen to graze and exercise. On rainy days—when they occurred—the stallions made do with the walker.

Hale fed Dangerous Species and went to the mare barn to meet Diana.

In her stall, Pearl turned to Hale and nickered gently.

"I know, Pearl," he crooned. "I know. You're almost there."

He'd bought the mare in January. A fly-by-night trainer from Taylor had sold twelve good horses in one afternoon. Hale and Marvin had gone up to see the stock. After examining the papers and looking over the horses, Hale indicated to Marvin that he wanted Pearl. Her legs were sound, her lineage excellent, her conformation good. She was by Raise a Native out of My Secret by Ack Ack. She had her blue papers. In addition to which Hale just liked her. For one thing, Pearl was gray.

The horseman from Taylor was on the verge of bankruptcy. They knew they could get the mare for a good price. The only problem was, Pearl was bred, probably five months gone. She'd foal in July—too late in the season for the foal to have a chance as a racehorse, too late to be bred again that year.

"How'd it happen, partner?" Marvin asked the man from

Taylor, and he reached over to scratch Pearl's nose. When Pearl pulled away, the man from Taylor had let the lead rope go slack.

"Bitch," he said. He opened the latch on the lead shank and let Pearl go.

Marvin pressed his point. "I mean it don't matter much since there's nothing to do about it now, but I'm just wondering how a mare like this got bred way late in August?"

The anxious owner put his hands in his pockets. "She wanted it, I guess," and he laughed.

Marvin kept a steady eye on the edgy horse owner. "You pasture-breeding, partner?" he asked.

The owner from Taylor spat out a stream of tobacco juice and said nothing.

On the way home from Taylor, Marvin said, "Looks like a man afraid of horses wouldn't go in the business, don't it."

They'd gotten Pearl for half of what she was worth. She'd been wormy. Her red cell count was below thirty-four. Hale had been boosting her up with extra vitamins. She looked good now. Her coat had slicked off and her eyes were lively. After she foaled she'd get really healthy. In February Hale planned to breed her properly. He was thinking of taking her to Elgin where Dash Too now stood.

He knelt down and examined Pearl's milk bag.

"She ready?"

Diana swung the stall door open.

"A few days. Maybe the end of the week."

"Friday's a full moon."

"Maybe that'll do it."

The mares came up and they fed them, then went to the breezeway shelter where the yearlings ate, and to the other shelter where the weanlings were. Hale stuffed the communal troughs with alfalfa. Diana took care of the vitamins and feed.

Bits of alfalfa and sweet grains stuck to their damp skin.

The sun was still high, dusk some hours away. Rufus followed at a slow pace. On the road home the dog abruptly stopped and turned in the other direction.

"Roger."

The dark green Rabbit came slowly. Roger had the top down. Diana waved. Rufus wagged his tail. Roger stopped, turned down the music, took the Rabbit out of gear and got out.

He wore cut-offs, a purple T-shirt saying Jim's Gym, dark leather sandals. His hair was damp. From the trunk he took out a huge bouquet: rubrum lilies, anthurium, gerbera daisies. He held the flowers out.

"What a son. Look, Hale. Flowers." Diana gave Roger a kiss.

"You have a good time in Austin, son?"

"Terrific, just great. No place like Barton Springs. I'm going to the house to start supper. You want me to take those?"

"We're headed home. I'll carry them. I look like a bride?"

"No question about it. What's that?"

She covered the spot on her blouse with the flowers. "It's a long story."

"See you at the house."

Hale took her free hand.

Roger put the Rabbit in gear, eased up on the clutch and drove to the house. He had been to Cedar Hills to see Bethany himself that afternoon. He'd taken flowers, a palm-sized video game and the new *Rolling Stone*.

Bethany seemed glad to see him. They'd had a nice, if not exactly meaningful, talk. She showed him the place on her stomach.

"Say," Roger said when he saw the scratches, "conceptual art. Not bad. What were you going to write?" He'd asked it casually. " 'Mom'? Like the athletes?"

"No," she said. "Me."

"M-E?"

She pointed to her forehead. "That's the way to spell it, bro." And then her anger vanished. "Don't ask why. It's no big deal."

She seemed depressed. Roger asked why. Bethany said Sunday afternoon after parents went home was always depressing.

"Sometimes I think," she said, "it would be better if no one came at all."

She'd looked up at him and smiled her old sweet, smart-assy smile. "Not you. No offense, bro."

"None taken."

His parents were incredibly naive. They found a way to smooth out whatever she did. They didn't know Bethany the way he did. He had been with her when she'd stolen things—a flashlight from the glove compartment of a car of one of Hale's friends, a set of car keys someone had left at the checkout stand in a grocery store, a football left in a front yard. She took things she didn't need, just because they were there. Roger had told her to put the things back but the force of her conviction and her displeasure made him quickly back off.

In the kitchen, he set down the groceries. "I've got peaches from Fredericksburg," he told Hale and Diana when they came in. "I'm going to make incredible cobbler. Plus"—he took a bottle from the grocery sack—"a new, chilled chardonnay, recommended by Whole Foods."

Diana laid the flowers on the sink, took down a vase and plucked at her middle. "You'll make us all fat."

"Sure, Mom. You're a tub."

Diana stuck the flowers in the vase. The stems of the lilies were too long but she did not cut them. She filled the vase with water.

"Want to take a trip, Rog?"

Seeing Diana's surprised expression, Roger turned to Hale. Puzzled, he lied. "Sure," he said.

"To where?" said Diana.

"Ruidoso. Saturday morning. I'm sending Casey out with Red. I thought maybe you'd like to keep him company. It's a long drive, especially hauling a trailer. You can stay as long as you want and then . . ."

He put his hands on Roger's shoulders.

Roger set the peaches on the counter. "You trying to get rid of me?"

Hale dropped his hands. "You know better. You're welcome to stay as long as you want. But Mom and I will be fine here, you know. We *are* fine."

Water splashed out of the vase. Diana tipped it.

For once, Roger couldn't think of anything to say. As if in search of a punchline to cut the tension, he actually glanced behind himself, at the floor.

He blinked and shrugged. "Give me," he said, "a day to think about it?"

"Pito could drive your car to Ruidoso in a week or so. And consider this: it's cool in New Mexico." For a joke Hale wiggled his eyebrows. "A thousand feet up."

He was afraid the boy was going to cry. "That's a winner," Roger said. He gathered up a handful of peaches and set them on the counter.

The water from the faucet ran hard against the stainless steel sink. With her elbow, Diana turned it off.

Hale couldn't take the boy's discomfort much longer. He was on the verge of taking back the whole idea when Roger suddenly found within himself the buoyancy which rarely failed him. "Speaking of winners," he said, "how about them 'Stros?"

Hale sighed and held up his hand. "How about them 'Stros." They gave each other a high five.

Diana set the vase on the counter and said she was going to clean up and change her clothes. When she was gone, Hale cut the stems of the lilies so that they fit the vase. He arranged the flowers and put them on the table, washed his hands and ran cold water over a chicken he'd thawed.

On the butcher block Roger expertly kneaded butter into some flour for the cobbler crust. Hale took his portable radio from the drawer and turned on the news. Confused and surprised by his father's suggestion—even though Hale had not spelled out exactly what he meant—Roger thought of Benicia and how the water looked when the light changed. When he was finished with the crust he peeled peaches.

As dusk drew on and the light outside failed and the radio newscaster announced all the bad news he could come up with, each of the two men withdrew into a kind of dreamy state. Neither spoke. They did their work. Chopping, kneading, slicing.

After Hale had cut off the wishbone, he sliced the chicken in half. Roger measured out a cup of sugar and poured it over the peaches.

When Diana came down the kitchen was almost dark. "You two," she said, "have something against light?"

She'd showered and changed into a pale pink cotton shirt and matching drawstring trousers.

She whirled the rheostat to high.

Hale turned off the radio.

"Hey," he said to Diana, "you look great in that color."

She shook back her hair.

Roger opened the chardonnay.

·29·

"Roy Scheider." Roger mimicked the actor. " 'Show-time.' "

Diana wasn't paying much attention. Hale had taken his vodka martini and gone upstairs. Roger had cleaned up the dinner dishes. *Blue Thunder* was on HBO.

Rufus's nails clicked across the boards of the deck.

Diana slid her feet into her sandals. "My tomatoes."

"What tomatoes?"

"I'm going down. I forgot."

"It's dark, Mom. It's nighttime."

"Rufus just went down."

"He probably went to pee."

"Maybe." She stood.

"Let it rest, Mom."

"They work at night. I have to."

In the garage, she took the flashlight from behind the seat in Hale's truck and went down the slope. Midway up from the tips of the trees, the moon cast a pure white light across the pasture, turning the parched brown grass pure silver. Rufus's shadow as he sniffed the ground was as black and as clearly defined as it would be at noon.

Dinner had been delicious. Hale's fried chicken was crisp and spicy. "Not Popeye's," he declared. "But close." Roger fixed steamed asparagus with lemon butter sauce and an exotic salad made with oranges, new potatoes, radishes and cilantro. They drank the chardonnay before dinner. With the meal they'd shared a bottle of red Rioja. The crust on Roger's peach cobbler wasn't the best but the filling, with its opaque, sweet juices, was perfect. They'd convinced Hale not to make biscuits. There was food enough.

To create a more festive air they put new red candles in the tree-of-life candelabra, turned off the track lighting and ate by candlelight. They complimented one another profusely on the food, the flowers, the atmosphere. Hale and Roger discussed the coming football season. Diana spoke of Red's lessons.

"A plan," she said. "What a relief. We have a plan."

Finally the telephone rang. Rose Narcisco had sounded as falsely cheerful as ever. They had decided to give Bethany a week, to "demonstrate her willingness" to conform to Cedar Hills' behavior codes. They would have both private and group therapy sessions with her. The family, maybe even Roger, was to come for a session on Saturday. On Sunday the decision would be made whether she could stay or not.

"We are going the extra mile for Bethany," Rose Narcisco had said. "We want her to find out for herself how much she values Cedar Hills, do you understand. We are giving her the option to work her way back into the program if she proves she wants to be here."

"It's a trap," Diana said when she hung up. "How can a person demonstrate willingness? They're going to play around with her, then kick her out."

Roger said maybe not. Hale said nothing.

Even at night it was hot. No breeze, and the sky looked bored and puffy. Diana moved down the slope with exaggerated stealth, hoping to catch the intruder at work. As she got closer to the basil, she held up the flashlight. Nothing.

She stepped gingerly across a bed of arugula and, squatting on a pad of hay she'd put down for mulch, aimed the beam of light on the damaged herb. Around the plants, jagged pieces of cut-up basil leaves did a zigzagging dance, then marched drunkenly down the boundary bricks toward the deer fence and into the pasture.

Ants. Night-working cutter ants had stripped the plants last night and come back tonight to cut the leaves down to size. Cutter ants farmed underground, storing the foliage they collected until it turned to fungus, then feeding from their bounty. Cutter ants would not eat just anything. They liked basil but not peppers, chinaberry but not hackberry or oak. Overnight, they could strip a twenty-foot chinaberry tree to its branches.

Diana followed the parade to the fence. Another line of ants marched back toward the basil. The path was wide enough to walk down. She shined the light into the pasture. Cutter ants never died out completely. You could control them for a while with chemicals or gasoline, but they always came back.

Diana kept her gardening supplies in a shed under the deck. For the most part, she tried to avoid using chemicals but in the case of ants, the choice was clear: either the ants went or the garden did. The sack of 5% Diazinon was almost empty. Without using the flashlight—her eyes having become accustomed to the darkness—she took the Diazinon back down to the garden and sprinkled poisonous dust around the feet of the basil, then followed the trail of the ants, making a thick stream down their dancing path. As the chemical rained down, the leaf pieces wobbled and weaved. At the fence, she dumped the last of the sawdusty Diazinon on the ground where the trail disappeared into the pasture.

She should have known. Her first experience with cutter ants had been with roses. She'd planted three small bushes in February. In the beginning they'd done fine. One day she came out and they had all three been pared down to sticks.

A single rosebud drooped from one branch. She had used a mild insect poison and had fed the roses. By March they'd leafed out again, only to have the cutter ants strip them again.

That was when she got the Diazinon. Following the rose-leaf chips, she'd tracked the ants to their home and poured the poison directly down into the hole. The next day she found the poison spread out in a circle around the hole, the ants still at work. She read the instructions more carefully. To convince worker ants to gather the poison and take it to the queen, the poison had to be disguised as potential food. If it was poured into the hole, the workers died taking it back out again.

At the bedroom window, Hale watched her. Diana climbed the slope by the light of the moon. Her hands smelled of chemicals. On the porch Rufus did his flop.

By the time *Blue Thunder* was over and she went to bed, Hale was asleep. On tiptoe, she went to her desk, slipped on her reading glasses and turned on a tiny high-intensity lamp Hale had given her for Christmas. The lamp cast no more light than she needed to see the work immediately in front of her. Hale slept on her side of the bed, sheet tangled between his legs. The room smelled damp and vaporish. Whoever said vodka left no smell had never slept with a man who drank the stuff.

Diana took out her diary. Beneath her blue pen, the day unwound on the page before her, from riding Red to the ruined tomatoes to breakfast tacos, from Xanadu to Cedar Hills to the Big Wheel. Rose Narcisco's suit and bosoms, the haircut and earrings of the woman with the crewcut, Taylor Wayne's pink mouth glued to his mother's arm, dinner, the telephone call and the discovery of the ants.

· 30 ·

*F*rom the bed Hale watched her, head bent over her work like a schoolgirl. One of the most shameful things he'd done in his life was to read her diary. He'd never told her and would never, but he was glad he'd done it. The diary confirmed his suspicions. He knew the man she was writing about was not himself.

Rereading the passage about the telephone call to Jesse, Diana added a phrase, then paused. Remembering the sound of the girl's voice, she left her pen so long at the end of a sentence that it bled, making a big blue mark on the page.

In the moonlight the pasture looked like a field of snow. Somewhere deep down cutter ants were gathering, moving farther down away from the poisonous clouds of Diazinon, making a protective phalanx around their queen.

Silently, Diana made yet another vow to clean off her desk, the books, the papers, the junk of her life. On the wall, Virginia Woolf looked down through long limpid eyelids as if to say, Oh, really? Diana straightened the picture of Baryshnikov.

Beneath the picture, she'd pinned up a strip of yellow second-sheet paper. On the strip, this quotation: "And as usual, I am bored by narrative." At the bottom, the initials V. W.

Next to the typewriter was a worn copy of a volume of essays. Diana opened the book to her favorite, "Sketches of the Past." She had circled a section of the essay in pencil:

> I have already forgotten what Leonard and I talked about at lunch; and at tea; although it was a good day the goodness was embedded in a kind of nondescript cotton wool. This is always so. A great part of every day is not lived consciously. One walks, eats, sees things, deals with what has to be done: the broken vacuum cleaner; ordering dinner; writing orders to Mabel; washing; cooking dinner; bookbinding. When it is a bad day the proportion of non-being is much larger.

Non-being had its advantages; one foot in front of the other, the unexamined, blessedly uncomplicated life. Planting flowers, riding Red. She went on to another marked passage:

> From this, I reach what I might call a philosophy; at any rate it is a constant idea of mine; that behind the cotton wool is hidden a pattern; that we—I mean all human beings—are connected with this; that the whole world is a work of art; that we are parts of the work of art.

If life was a plot then who was the villain, where was the hero? And if there was pattern, what was it?

Hale turned over and groaned. He was not asleep—would not sleep more than two hours the entire night—but with Diana in the bed pulled close, he could at least relax.

She closed her book, took off her reading glasses and switched off the lamp. Her nightgown lay across the end of the bed. She lifted the gown and slipped it over her head. Lying on her side away from Hale, she put on her bedside reading glasses and clipped another reading lamp to the pages of a paperback mystery she'd bought in Austin at Half-Price Books.

When she finished the book and turned off her light Hale pulled her to him.

"It was ants. They're back."

"Cutter ants?"

"Yes."

"They never leave." He settled his hand on her breast. "They only pretend."

Downstairs, Roger smoked marijuana. Maybe, he thought, Cedar Hills would not kick Bethany out. Maybe Bethany would figure out how to demonstrate willingness. Hale's suggestion that he go back to California had pleased him more than he might have imagined. He had called Kim; she seemed glad to hear from him. He couldn't be sure she was telling the truth, but she said she hoped he'd come back soon.

He took out his notebook and began to make lists, pros and cons for and against the trip to Ruidoso, then Benicia.

At Cedar Hills, Bethany made her own plans. Beginning tomorrow she would alternate days of fasting with days of light meals.

"I have," she vowed, "eaten my last crumb of crap food."

Having not yet been told of Cedar Hills' decision, Bethany slept well, secure in the knowledge that whatever happened there was no scrape so deep she could not, with the help of her parents, get out of it. They had always rescued her before. There was no reason to think they would not this time.

Except for Tiffany Leberman's sobs, muffled by her pillow, Unit 14 was quiet. Sunday nights were always gloomy. After the high nervousness of parental visits, the kids plunged into a flat, woozy slump. Of all the inhabitants of the unit, only Bethany Caldwell looked forward to the morning.

Diana woke up imagining the kitten-like scratches had grown, and Bethany was coming apart at the seams, like a cheap blouse. Restaging the telephone conversation with Rose Narcisco, she became angry all over again.

Sensing her agitation, Hale stroked her thigh and told her to relax.

Closer to dawn Diana figured out what she was going to do. A plot lay before her, as linear a narrative as a hoed-up row of beans. All there was to it was to take the first step and then go on.

Monday

·31·

*R*ed shook her head. On tiptoe Diana reached up to slip the bridle over the filly's head, the bit between her teeth.

"Mrs. Coach."

She jumped. "Good morning, Pito. How was your Sunday?"

"Fine, Mrs. Coach. What you doing? You need maybe some help?"

Sometimes Pito spoke in broken rhythms, other times his English was quite good. Diana was about to refuse Pito's offer when the jockey pushed past her and buckled the bridle under Red's throat latch. He lifted her forelock out from under the head-strap.

Born and raised in Panama, Pito had pale yellowish skin. His features were choppy and he was naturally small—lighter than Diana without dieting. His eyes were black darts. Pito was never still. When there was nothing else to do, he fidgeted.

"Thanks," Diana murmured. Pito wore blue jeans and boots, a tight black western shirt, sleeves rolled to the elbow.

"Where's Coach?"

"The stud barn, I think."

"You going to ride Red?"

"No." She took the small leather saddle and laid it across Red's back. Pito began to tighten the girth. "Loose," Diana instructed. "It's only for a lesson. I'm not going to ride her."

Pito buckled the girth. He looked over the top of Red's back at Diana. "Good," he said.

Diana led Red out of the barn.

"Mrs. Coach."

"Yes."

"You planning to feed her?"

"Yes."

"You can't, Mrs. Coach, in that bridle."

Diana tightened her hold on the lead rope.

"You need," Pito said, "a hackamore. She can't eat much with that bit between her teeth." He grinned.

Diana blushed. "Oh, Pito," she said. "You're right. I forgot."

She turned Red around.

"Wait," Pito said. "I get it."

He came out of the tack room with the hackamore, took off the bridle and replaced it. As he worked he talked nonstop to Red.

Diana led Red down the road and then onto the path through the trees to the training track. They crossed the track and entered the infield. When Red saw the training gates, she began to snort and fuss. Through the lead rope Diana could feel the filly's nervousness.

"Hey, Red," she crooned. "It's all right. It's all right." She stopped and rubbed Red's velvety muzzle until the filly settled down. "Your breakfast is coming."

Red bowed her neck, lowered her chin and pulled back. Diana pulled the lead rope down, sharply but steadily, careful not to allow the filly any slack. Through the trees she could see Pito, watching her.

"Come on, girl. I won't let you get hurt."

Red raised her elegant head and whinnied. From the barn, one of her colleagues answered.

"I'll take care of you, Red. Thatta girl, yes. Come with me."

A red nylon hay bag filled with alfalfa hung from the side of the training gates. Diana took small steps toward the hay bag, making certain not to get too far in front of Red so that the filly had room to pull back against the rope.

If it came down to a contest of pure strength Red, of course, would win; size and speed were on her side. Diana's advantage was a bluff: the edge Red relinquished to intelligence, will and the terms of her training. Diana depended on Red's adherence to those terms. Without that common bond between them, Red might as well be a wild untrained filly all over again.

At the hay bag Diana stopped. Her other advantage was Red's appetite. Red was a gut; she never filled up. She nibbled at the sweet-smelling alfalfa, then nosed the hay bag and with her teeth, jerked out a larger swatch. Chewing, she looked over at Diana as if to say, "This far. No farther."

"You think." When Red wasn't paying attention, Diana tied the filly to the gates, using the sheep-shank knot Hale had gone to such pains to teach her.

Considering Hale's lack of enthusiasm about Diana's participation in this schooling lesson, she didn't know why he'd changed his mind. At five they'd given up trying to sleep and had gone downstairs for breakfast. She'd told Hale her new plan. Then he made his own announcement. He had decided, he said, it would be all right for her to saddle Red and take her to the gates to eat from the hay bag if she still wanted to.

"After all," he said, "you have as much time and energy invested in Red as the rest of us."

Diana sat on the bumper of the gates and looked back over at the trees. Pito was gone.

It was seven. At eleven she had an appointment with Gil. Late this afternoon, she wanted to get the tomato patch ready for replanting. Red spread her back legs and peed.

Hale had put a bucket of feed inside the gates. That was for him to deal with.

Empathy had been a temptation in the beginning, thinking horses felt the same as people, making even more specific comparisons, mares to women, men to stallions. Helping ride and train had changed all that. Sloppy thinking made for unruly horses. Red was a horse, Diana a human being and that was the end of it.

The first time she'd seen a mare palpated she'd been a little surprised. She'd come down to the pen and found Warren Burleson with his arm inside a mare's rectum to the elbow. " 'Morning, Diana," the vet said. "How you doing?" Hale was at the other end of the mare, keeping her quiet with a twitch. The mare stood drunkenly splayfooted, eyes glazed. After a while Warren Burleson pulled his arm out and said he was ninety-five percent certain the mare was still in foal. His arm was smeared with green. He went to the hose to wash it.

"Do they always go up the ass?" Diana asked Hale that night.

"Everyone I've ever seen."

"Why not the vagina?"

"Beats me. Fear of infection maybe. I don't know."

"You never asked?"

"No. That's how it's done."

Red snatched another wad of alfalfa from the bag.

Not that Diana didn't already know about gynecological examinations. But up the ass, to the elbow, out in the open, with men standing around? She couldn't help feeling mildly shocked. And sympathetic, from both points of view. The vet's. *And* the mare's.

The grass snapped in the direction of the trees.

"What do you think?" Hale called out. He was carrying the thermos and a cup.

"She's eating."

Hale poured her a cup of coffee. "It's a start."

"Thanks." He had already added cream. She took a sip. "What about you?"

"I've had enough." He smoothed Red's hip. "You can go on back to the house when you want to. I've cleared my schedule to stay with her all morning. I think we're going to have a rodeo when we try to put her in."

"Even with the feed?"

"Even with the feed. Casey's coming to help."

"I'm in no hurry."

"Whatever you want."

She sipped her coffee. "Once you get her in, then what?"

"Feed her, stroke her, make love talk to her. Whatever it takes. Make her think the gates are heaven on earth. We've got through Friday and that's it, Saturday she heads west."

"Who's going?"

"Casey. Pito wants to but I can't spare him. I told him he could drive Roger's Rabbit out in a week or so. I think Roger will go, don't you?"

"Maybe. I can't tell."

Hale picked a stick of alfalfa from Red's mane. "He seemed to like the idea," he said. "More than I had expected."

"I can't quite imagine Roger with Casey and Pito."

"Why not?"

"I don't know, I just can't."

The sun had come up out of its morning slump. Diana put on her sunglasses.

"He'll do fine," Hale said.

"You want some of this?" She passed her coffee to him.

He took a sip and made a face. "Cream," he said.

"You should have left it black. I could have drunk it. You could have had some."

"I made it for you." He handed the cup back. "Such a pretty girl." He gently pinched Red's nose. "Isn't she just the prettiest girl we've ever had?"

"No question about it."

"We have to clean her up and trim her feet before she

goes. We don't want her to go to New Mexico looking shabby."

In Hale's eyes excitement flickered like winking neon. He had awakened from his short sleep feeling irrationally optimistic. Mondays sometimes affected him that way.

"God, Hale," Diana said. "With everything else that's going on sometimes I forget. Ruidoso. It's exciting."

He ran his fingers through Red's mane, trying to untangle a knot.

"I have a feeling," he said. "Well . . . I hate to say it. But I do have this feeling."

"Don't hex it."

The knot wouldn't give. "You think we should roach her mane?"

"Absolutely not."

"Just kidding. You know I like long hair on girls."

Diana finished her coffee and went to the house.

·32·

"She cut herself."

"I heard."

"Has everybody?"

"They keep me up with . . ."

"Patients?"

"Clients. People I'm interested in."

Gil Barrientos was small and lithe with black hair graying at the temples, dark round eyes and an enviable mustache he liked to fool with.

Diana watched him closely.

The room was windowless, plain and tiny with one wall of bookshelves. Diana sat in the chair she liked, short, over-stuffed, covered with cheap, patterned upholstery in shades of mauve and Federal blue. The back of the chair was shaped like a shell, the scallops of which were hard as rocks.

Gil was in his usual place, beside his desk in a highly varnished, ladder-back oak chair with no arms. He folded his hands and waited. Beside him on his desk was a small digital clock and his notebook, open to today's date. The clock flicked forward to the next number.

He waited.

Six minutes in, Diana began. "I almost," she said, "called Jesse yesterday. In fact I did. A girl answered. I hung up."

Gil wove his hands into a basket. He disapproved of her liaison with Jesse, of course. He'd never said so but when Diana told him she could not imagine being faithful to Hale her whole life and he'd asked "Why not?" in his flattest tone of voice, she knew how his thinking went. For him the erotic was a commodity, there for the asking, without disguise and mystery. Diana wondered where he got his ideas, the hardware store?

"It had to do with its being our anniversary." She did a little sashay thing with her head. "Twenty-six years."

"Congratulations."

"Thank you. And going to see Bethany. I was mad at Hale for not going but I didn't say so. Then when I found out what Bethany had done it got to me. By the time I left Cedar Hills I felt, oh, high. Revved up." She looked away from Gil. Across the room a wallpaper picture provided the view: a grove of birch trees growing at odd angles, like pickup sticks. Sunlight worked its way down through the trees in softened slants. Diana had often wondered, why birch trees? There was not a birch tree in the state of Texas.

"It didn't mean anything. I wouldn't have gone over. I just wanted to talk to him. Or, really, not talk. Just make contact. I don't know."

She bit her lip. "I do hate to give him up." She took a Kleenex from the box on a nearby table and blew her nose. "Not just him, what he represents."

"Which is?"

"Hope, I guess."

"Rescue?"

"Maybe."

Diana plucked another Kleenex. There were three boxes at significant intervals around the room. The tissue was pink, the box boutique-style.

"I don't know. I need something out there to balance."

She pointed, as if to indicate where "out there" was; somewhere beyond the birch trees. "It's like being on a tightrope without a balancing pole."

"Did you call Jesse before or after seeing Bethany?"

"I told you. After." She wadded the Kleenex in her palm. "But I'm not going to torture myself about it, I didn't get him and that's that."

"You might have."

"Gil. I'm not going to let them kick her out. I'm going to get her myself. I've decided to wait until Friday. If I still want to by then, I'm going to spring her. I'm sick of Cedar Hills. Do you know what Rose Narcisco said to me? 'I share your pain.' My pain. If I wanted to share my pain I know one thing, it wouldn't be with her."

Gil lifted his hand to his face and lightly massaged his mustache.

"I don't believe in that place, Gil. I want Bethany out."

"That's natural."

"But?"

He shook his head. "I didn't . . ."

"Implied. You frowned."

He frowned again. "Now," he said, "perhaps I've got this wrong but my understanding is that they are not necessarily kicking her out."

"She's on reprieve. Did they tell you what she has to do in order to stay? 'Demonstrate willingness.' I mean, can you do that for me? Can you sit there and demonstrate willingness? It's a trap. They're going to keep her on a string all week, then tell her she's demonstrated oh, a little willingness, but definitely not enough. I can see the look on their faces when they tell her." She corrected herself. "Excuse me, not her, *us*. They'll bring us together and tell us what a pitiful excuse for willingness Bethany has demonstrated."

"When are you scheduled for a family session?"

"Saturday."

"And you propose to what, rescue Bethany before then?"

"You just said that."

"Said what?"

"Rescue. First about Jesse and now Bethany. Are you getting at something?"

"Only that the issue keeps surfacing. A way out. Something as you say 'out there.' A superior power, whether in yourself or someone else. 'The god in me, the god in you,' so to speak."

"The god in me, the god in you" had to be a quote from one of his fix-it manuals. Diana wished he read better books.

Gil shifted his weight. "Have you told Hale?"

"He won't interfere."

"What did he say?"

"He's not sure it's the thing to do. He's afraid of the law, of course. So am I. But he hates Cedar Hills more than I do."

"Diana, I have to tell you this seems a reversal to me. What do you think it's about?"

"Nothing is happening there. She *asked* me to get her out. They act like the weight gain is nothing and it's not nothing. It's something. In fact, it's a lot."

He waited.

"When she was at home at least she didn't have the fat to contend with. I can't help thinking if we love her enough . . . Look, it's me she has the problem with, you've said as much. The only way she can work out the problem is to be with me."

"All children ask to be taken home. She's not fat. Cedar Hills is not jail. You could have taken her out at any time."

"I know that."

"So why the fuss now?"

"Because . . . I don't know. Because I'm mad. She's unhappy. Because they're kicking her out."

"Maybe Bethany understands what they mean by 'demonstrate willingness.' Have you asked her?"

"I haven't had the chance. But how could she? It's impossible. It's not what *she* does but how *they* read it."

"Exactly."

"So?"

"So maybe the terminology is Greek to you but perfectly clear to her."

"I don't think so. I really don't think so, anyway . . ." She leveled her shoulders. "I've made up my mind."

He shrugged. "I'm not here to change your mind."

"Don't pander."

"Am I?"

"Not in so many words but yes."

He waited to see if she had anything else to add before going on. "And the police?"

She lifted her head too sharply. There was a twinge of pain in her neck, just below her ear. "What about them?" She rubbed her neck.

"Part of their leniency, as I recall, was based on Bethany's getting immediate and sustained help with her problems."

"Which she has received. Immediate. And sustained. December to July, that's one two three four, seven going on eight months."

He said nothing.

Diana counted on her fingers. "She was sixteen when they stole the car. She's seventeen now. The judge said when she turned seventeen that if she kept her nose clean they'd seal her juvenile records."

"Eighteen."

"Seventeen, I'm sure of it."

"The law works in favor of the law. Felonies committed by seventeen-year-olds are treated as adult offenses. But the treatment of juvenile records applies until the child is eighteen. She has five months to go. If she's kept her nose clean until then, they'll seal her records."

Diana waved the matter away. "Anyway . . ."

"What?"

"The police don't care enough to bother."

Gil unfolded his hands. "Right or wrong," he said, "that may be true. The question, of course, is not what will or will not happen but how Bethany sees all this." He uncrossed his legs, recrossed them.

"In the long run."

"Possibly even the short."

"It's a chance all right."

"Yes."

Diana waited.

"Tell me, Diana." His eyes were hard and bright. Sometimes she thought he was flirting, other times that he was gay. What she really thought was, he wasn't sexual at all. "Tell me what you want."

"Want? When?"

"If a fairy godmother came right now to grant you whatever you wished for, no strings, no recriminations, without your having to put forth any effort at all, what would you ask for?"

"You're asking me to answer a question that would never be asked."

"Try."

She stared at the floor.

"Don't think so hard. We're in dreamland."

"To start over. Have her again."

"Have her."

"Give birth, start over. Try to do better."

"You still have her. You've never let her go."

"I've had to."

"Not the point."

"I'm not trying to have her now."

"You're not."

"No. I'm not. I can't. But I want her to know that I know she's been wronged and that I take seriously her cries for help and that I am and will be there for her to the end. I have not always done that. This may not count for much right now but eventually it will. Don't you see? Eventually it has to."

"She doesn't need your life."

"I'm not offering it."

"You're not."

"Stop saying that!"

He leaned closer. Her anger was hard to prick; now that he'd done it he didn't want to lose it. "Try this. Yes, you are."

He sat back.

"Am what?"

"Offering her your life. Your marriage, your career. You've already told her—not in so many words, no, but in your actions—that there is nothing you won't sacrifice for her."

"No."

"Think about it. Children will do whatever they can to keep their parents from offering more than they can stand to take. Or even acknowledge."

"You mean like those silly books." She pointed to his shelves. *Getting Free, Setting Out, Breaking the Bonds*. "The gerundian road," she sneered, "to maturity."

Doubtless Gil Barrientos didn't know a gerund from a urinal. She scooted forward in her chair. "I will not be dissuaded, Gil. I know this is right. It's my first big idea in months."

He held up his hands. "Then do it. I'm not here to stop you."

Focusing once again on the birch trees, she avoided his dark eyes. "I know what you're thinking and I don't care." He said nothing. "The other thing I would wish . . ."

"Yes?"

"Is that she be thin again."

"Is fat the problem?"

Fatigue was making her cross-eyed. "It's not just a side effect."

"But is it the problem?"

"Not being fat would be the beginning of the beginning of a solution. Children are cruel. Fat people never fill up."

Gil looked off into the middle distance.

"I'm going to lay in diet food, toss out the chips and crackers. I'll poach fish and make diet Jell-O, clean out the custard cups of leftover grated cheese."

Gil glanced at the clock. "Well," he said. "Shall we stop here?" When he looked back at her his eyes were blank.

Diana unfolded her legs and dropped her damp Kleenex into the plastic wastebasket beside her chair. The wastebasket was empty.

"Call me," he said, "if you have second thoughts. Or if you want to talk."

"I don't think I will."

Gil closed his door softly. Outside the building, the boy on the red bicycle whose appointment came after Diana's pedaled up. The boy wore blue jeans, high-topped tennis shoes, a Jack Daniel's baseball cap and a red T-shirt that said "Fuck" in big letters.

Diana went to Poor Man's Grocery to buy diet food.

Sometimes she felt like murdering Gil Barrientos.

· 33 ·

"You want help?"

Roger knelt beside her. Though he worked out religiously and was in no way overweight, the boy exuded a sense of fleshiness which Diana found unpleasant.

"Sure." She scooted over.

He moved in close. "See?" he said. "It's possible. I'm indicating willingness, all over the place."

"Demonstrate."

"*Right,*" he popped his thumb and finger. "Demonstrate."

She attacked the dirt.

"Joke, Mom."

"I know. I'm just . . . I don't know what."

"Gotcha."

He was never sure how he stood with her or what she wanted. Her love was fluctuating, unpredictable; she passed it out in drips and drabbles to signs and rules he could never get a handle on. Sometimes she overwhelmed him with praise so lavish he knew better than to trust it. Other times, she shut him down.

"Here." She passed him her hand cultivator and picked up a trowel. "Turn it a little. It won't take much. It's been tilled already. We'll make mounds. Friday night I'll plant."

"Why not now?" Diana kept a close eye out. Roger had a heavy hand. Ask him to turn, he might dig to China.

"Go easy," she warned. "Watch the dill."

"I see it. Are you sure you want me to help?"

"Don't be silly. The moon is full on Friday. I like to plant," she said, "while it's rising."

With her trowel she began filling in the armadillo tracks.

Roger scratched at the dirt with the cultivator. "Why didn't he eat the plants?"

"The armadillo? They don't care about tomatoes. They make these holes with their feet, digging for bugs. You ever seen one up close?"

"Only at the zoo. And dead." He smacked the trowel against the ground. "Road pizza."

"They have these tiny feet, too small for their bodies. When they run they look like a fat lady in high heels trip-tripping down the sidewalk. It's pretty funny."

"What do I do with this?" He held up a weed.

"Here." She showed him. "For the compost."

Roger tossed the plant on the pile of weeds and leaves. "Maybe," he said, "you shouldn't fight it. How about an armadillo feed patch. Water it, mulch it, plant it. Throw in centipedes and roly-polies. Could be he'll feast there. Leave the good stuff alone."

"Assume he's coming, you mean. Give him what he's after."

"Well?" He gestured with his arm.

She spaded up a soft clot of earth. "Sounds like that fool theory at Cedar Hills."

"You mean paradox?"

"Yes. I mean paradox."

"What's wrong with paradox? Do it out here and everybody's happy, you, the tomatoes, the armadillos. The bugs lose out but it's a dog-eat-dog world."

Diana shoved her fingers down into the dirt.

"I'm sure," she said, "no self-respecting armadillo would

stoop to such shameless domestication." She dropped a patch of Bermuda grass on the compost pile.

"Nothing ventured. Where's Dad by the way?"

"I don't know, I've been waiting for him. I want to see what happened with Red. Anyway where would I put another bed?"

He shook his cultivator at her. "You're resisting."

"Don't be Freudian."

"Never read the stuff."

"It wouldn't work. It's too easy."

"You never think my ideas will work." He sulked.

She felt his disappointment. "Mothballs," she said, "are supposed to help."

"Rufus eats mothballs."

"One time he threw them up on Hale's boots."

"Hale must have loved that. Speaking of which."

"Yes?"

"I sold a pair today. Ostrich."

Diana shifted positions, bringing her legs out from under her to take the strain off her knees. She reached across him to pluck a clot of nutgrass. Roger waited. When he didn't speak she looked in his direction. He was staring at her.

She brushed her hair off her forehead. "What?"

"Just waiting."

He was too kind, too wide open, too available. She could not bear to take his vulnerability straight on. This, she was trying to tell him with her diffidence, is what the world will do to you. Protect yourself, arm yourself, be more suspicious. So far her strategies had not done much good. Roger was as obvious as an open window.

"So," she said. "That's great. Who'd you sell them to?"

"Garland Blair."

"Good for you. Garland Blair is a notorious tightwad."

Roger smoothed out an armadillo trench.

"Tightwad meets pro, tightwad yields."

He smiled broadly.

"Congratulations. We've had those boots forever. How much are they going for these days?"

"Three twenty-five. Cash on the you-know-what."

"Great," Diana said.

Three twenty-five was the old price for ostrich-skin boots. They now went for something closer to $400. But at least he'd sold them.

"So what else have you tried besides mothballs?"

Diana began making a new mound. "Oh, God, just everything. I think shooting them is the only answer."

"Blood on the tomatoes?"

"All right, Mr. Natural."

"Just saying."

"I know."

When he was little they used to make up acronyms together. W.F.D. meant what's for dinner, T.F.B., time for bed. They never missed. Sometimes even now that feeling of fusion returned. Those times, the chill in Roger's heart warmed and he felt fine. It happened rarely; these days for the most part his mother was gone as a ghost. She said she was proud of his cooking but that was a lie.

"So," he said, "what's the deal with the full moon?"

"I plant above-ground crops when the moon is waxing. It's an old idea. I like especially to do it at the last minute, just before the moon peaks. That's not what the books say. It's just what I like to do."

"This about right?"

"Looks good. Now mound up the dirt where the plants were. Then you can help me murder ants."

"Slaughter in the hill country."

"It's us or them. Hey, not such a big mound. Look at mine."

He fixed it. "So you were saying about the moon?"

"I like the friction of doing it at the last minute. It's exciting. I think it gives the plants a boost. They get the power direct."

"Talk about Mr. Natural."

"Well. It works. Until the armadillo decides to stage a night rout."

"Mother Fatalism."

"Mother Experience." She put down her trowel. "Hard-earned. I think that does it. Why don't you take this to the compost." She indicated the pile of weeds and dead plants. "I'll take up the tools and get the ant dope."

"Yes'm."

"Don't say yes'm."

"No'm.

"And thanks for the help."

"You're welcome."

He picked up the plants and went toward the compost pile. Diana admired their work: eighteen new mounds, evenly spaced even without a tape measure. She stood. The three six-packs of tomatoes, well watered, sat lined up on her red-brick border.

"Day after tomorrow," she said to the six-packs, "you dig in your toes."

She picked up her tools. As she went to get the Diazinon, Hale drove in. He parked the truck and jumped out.

"I think I've figured it out," he said, yelling down to her. "Marvin read about it in a book." He went to the bed of the pickup and took out a round wire cage. He held the cage up. "They're made," he said, "out of concrete reinforcing wire so the wind won't blow them down." The cage was about three feet around and two feet wide. "And look." Diana was beside him. He turned the cage upside-down. "We left long pieces to stick into the ground." He pushed the wire cage downward in the air to demonstrate. "So that rabbits and armadillos can't knock them over. Is that great or what?"

Diana was impressed. "It's great, all right. Now we don't have to shoot the animals *or* make Rufus sick."

His hands were pocked with small bloody marks, from working with the stiff rusty wire. When she touched one of the places, he did not flinch. "Did you make them at the gates?"

"We went to the hardware store to get the wire. We sat around down there doing it. But we stayed at the gates until after one."

"And?"

He held up crossed fingers. "So far," he said. His face was flushed.

He had left the pickup door ajar. On the seat were two pizza boxes. "That dinner?"

"Anchovies and onions for you and me, everything but the kitchen sink for Mr. California. Plus . . ."

"Yes?"

His wry good humor had returned. "I have a story for you. Oh, do I have a story."

On his way back up the slope Roger watched them. Hale held a wire cage in one hand. With the other, he massaged Diana's lower back. She pointed to her neck. He rubbed her there.

"All right, you guys," he said.

Hale and Diana came apart. Hale continued to massage Diana's neck.

"Pizza Man," she said, "has arrived."

There. The look Roger was looking for, the one he came for. He wondered if his parents would ever understand how much he loved them.

· 34 ·

*A*s Hale bit into his pizza a string of cheese followed his mouth. With his fingers, he broke it off.

"She did all right," he said, "as long as she was outside the gates. It was when I tried to put her in that she started acting a fool. I don't think until today Marvin actually believed there was a problem. I think he thought I was just being a wimp. Lord." He tossed the slice of pizza into the box. "That's all I can eat."

Roger cut himself another slice. He was eating too much again. In his parents' presence he stuffed himself, cleaning the food from everybody else's plates when he washed up, eating until the food was all gone. If he stayed much longer he'd be fat as a bear.

Diana pushed back from the table and propped her feet on an empty chair.

"I had told Casey to come down when he finished exercising the stallions. About ten he showed up. Until then I left her tied outside the gates, even after she'd finished the alfalfa. Marvin had driven up from San Antonio to see how she was doing and, well, you know Marvin, he kept trying to get me to put her in the gates right off. 'Hell,' he kept saying, 'I been

229

around horses all my damned life, Hale. If we can't handle her between the two of us how do you think a little jockey boy is going to?' "

Hale chuckled. "I told him no, we had to wait for Casey. Marvin didn't like that at all."

Casey Koenig was bone-thin and tireless. Hale had met him at an FFA horse show and rodeo. Casey was fifteen then, with arms that hung to his knees and long legs he could not get out of the way of. After watching the boy's graceful ride on a bucking bronco, Hale had offered him a job.

Casey started coming out after school and on weekends. He was twenty-three now, and worked full-time. Hale trusted him utterly. Casey had a way with horses that went beyond ordinary skill. He understood how they thought. Hale had never seen the least flicker of fear pass through the boy's eyes.

Marvin and Hale had been sitting there telling stories when Casey sauntered up in his baseball cap, a purple sleeveless T-shirt and jeans so tight they looked welded on. Casey tipped his hat. "Mr. Thoede," he said. Casey was never rude to Marvin Thoede, but he was cool. Thoedes and Koenigs had been unfriendly as far back as anybody could remember. The feud had to do with opportunity and money, which Thoedes seemed able to get their hands on while Koenigs never did.

Hale downed the last of his beer.

" 'You ready to rodeo?' I asked Casey. He said he was and we set in. Now you have to understand, Marvin was all the time pooh-poohing all this caution, because what he thought was that we didn't have the balls to go on and do the job right. His Cadillac of course was all the time running, the way he likes it, with country music going and the air conditioning on. So . . ." Hale went to get his martini from the refrigerator, where he'd left it while he ate. "So we finally untied the filly and started to lead her around, me talking my fool head off, Casey pushing at her, then we'd switch. Red wasn't fooled. She started going to town and I mean immediately. Well, you have never seen Marvin Thoede move so fast in your life. As soon as Red made her first little di-doh, Marvin fell out of the way like he'd been hit by a bolt of lightning. Which I'd told him to do in the first place, but of course he wouldn't. He hadn't seen Red act the fool the way Casey and I had. So Marvin went over and sat on the bumper of the Cadillac and Casey and I worked on Red. Soon as we'd get her in smelling distance of the gates she'd start carrying on, lowering her ears, raring, humping her back, dragging back until she was all the way on the ground, on her can. That was why I didn't want you even to try, Diana. She's a different filly around those gates."

He refilled his glass, adding ice.

Diana was trying to get the picture. "So were you, Red and Casey in front of the gates or behind?"

"Behind. Trying to get her to go in." He stirred his martini with his finger.

"And where was Marvin?"

He sucked his finger. "He'd gone back over to his car. Let me show you."

At the table, he moved the pizza box out of the way and pulled two of Diana's Mexican baubles closer. "The gates are here." He set a Day of the Dead carousel beside the pizza box. "And the Cadillac is here." He took a miniature figurine of a woman patting out tortillas and set it catty-corner to the carousel, about two inches away. "And Marvin"—he picked up a leftover crust of pizza—"is sitting on the fender"—he set the pizza crust across the lap of the tortilla maker—"of his Cadillac. Here."

"So Marvin," Roger said, "is the crust."

"He's the crust."

"And you, Casey and Red were here." Diana set an alabaster turnip, a carrot and a watermelon slice behind the Day of the Dead carousel.

"Correct."

"Looks like the car would have been too hot for Marvin to sit on, with the engine running."

"I don't know why it wasn't. Anyway . . ." Hale sipped his drink. "Casey and I, of course, have done this kind of thing a thousand times before. It's not pleasant but we do know what to do. Mostly you have to keep your strength up and wait the horse out. You can't get excited about any one thing the horse does or expect too much to happen too fast, you just have to stay in control and wait her out and"—he shook his head—"hope to God she tires out faster than you do. By the time we were finished, Red was wet from her topknot to her tail from all that carrying on."

"What was Marvin doing all this time?"

"Well, I don't know exactly. My attention was pretty well occupied, but I did hear him hollering a lot. I couldn't even hear what he was saying, but I got the message. He was making fun of us. Hee-hawing, hoo-rahing. Goddamn but it made me mad."

Diana picked up the last two slices of anchovy pizza and took them to the sink.

"You're not going to throw those away."

"No." She held the slices out toward Roger. "Did you want more? I thought you were finished."

He blushed. "I didn't mean I wanted any more. I just didn't want you to throw it away."

Diana got out the plastic wrap. "I was," she said, "going to wrap it up to save for tomorrow. Hale, were you finished?"

He said he was. She wrapped the slices of pizza and put them in the refrigerator, then came back to the table.

"So go on, Hale," she said.

"So this went on for I don't know, it seemed like two hours. Probably closer to one. We'd rodeo, she'd settle down, we'd inch her over a little. We'd rodeo, she'd settle, we'd inch. Rodeo. Settle. Inch. By then we'd given up on getting her inside the gates, we thought we'd just lead her around to the front of them where the feed was. So finally we started around the front of the gates." He took the watermelon slice and slid it around the side of the Day of the Dead carousel toward the pizza crust and the woman making tortillas.

"I think I'm beginning to get the picture. Marvin was in the way."

He aimed the watermelon slice at the crust. "Marvin and the El Dorado were dead-solid center in the way."

"And you started inching her around."

"We started inching her around to the front of the gates. Marvin kept yelling and laughing. I mean, I'd have been sorry about his damn car if he hadn't been making such fun of us. 'Ride 'em, cowboy,' he'd say, and he'd whoop like Slim Pickens in *Dr. Strangelove*. I wasn't paying a whole lot of attention, like I said, but he was starting to get on my nerves and if he was getting on mine you know how Casey must have felt. Plus by then he and I had about shot our wad. That was when it happened. At the point when we were on the very damn verge of giving it up, the situation turned."

"Are you sure it was the thing to do, pushing her that far?"

"Lord, Di, once we started we had to. We sure as hell couldn't let up. If she wore us down this time she'd do the same thing all over again the next. The turning point was the feed. You know what a gut she is. As I said, Casey and I had about had it. Casey's arms were running with sweat and you could have wrung his T-shirt out like a dishrag. He'd scratched himself when Red forced him back into a mesquite bush, and his cheek was bleeding. Oh, we were a mess. So we started to lead her over. And she was coming. One step. Another."

He slid the watermelon closer to the pizza crust and the woman making tortillas.

"This was where we were. I don't know what got into Red. She's so smart I almost think she knew what she was doing. Like it might have been the final humiliation for her, having Marvin over there laughing and shouting. Like she wanted to get her revenge before she gave in. Anyway, for whatever reason when her back legs got in line with the Cadillac . . ." He shifted the watermelon slice so that the tip end faced the tortilla maker. "She wheeled around." He swiveled the watermelon slice so that the other end hit the crust and knocked it to the table. "Her back legs shot out like a jackknife. Faster than Casey or I could do anything about. Marvin fell off his car like white off rice and Red knocked the teeth out of his El Dorado. *Wham!* I popped her with the rope and that was it. Reddo ate her feed from outside the gate, and later on when we tried her, she went in from the other end and stood there like a little lady." He chuckled to himself. "I mean," he said, "*inside* the fucking gates. Goddamn but that was a picture."

"What did Marvin say?"

"Lord. Poor Marvin. He called Illuminated Red 1 everything but a child of God."

"I wish I'd have been there."

"Well, he didn't like it, I can tell you that."

"I'm sure."

Hale chuckled again, remembering the look on Marvin's face. He sipped his drink. "You know I like Marvin," he said. "He's a hard-ass and a know-it-all but I can't help liking him. And you have to admit, he's got his good points. When I told him about your tomatoes, you'd have thought somebody died, Di, he was so aggrieved. He'd read about those cages in a magazine and nothing would do but what he had to go down to the hardware store and help me make them. Old Breeden tried to sell us that lightweight wire most people make tomato cages out of. Marvin wouldn't have anything but concrete reinforcing wire." Hale examined his hands. "Not that it wouldn't have been easier with the other but he was right, you have to hand it to him. Now God knows, Marvin and I have been down some rough roads together and I do like him but goddamn, it was funny as hell seeing him fall on his butt off that car to get out of the way of Red's feet. I thought Casey was going to bust a gut trying to keep from laughing. I bet when he got home he didn't stop for an hour."

Roger took a swig of beer. He closed the pizza box.

"I'll swear," Hale said. "I wish I'd had a camera."

He picked up the crust representing Marvin, reopened Roger's box and tossed the crust inside.

"How about his car?"

Hale turned to Roger. "Car?"

"Was the A.C. on all that time?"

"Oh, Lord, that was the last straw. The damn thing overheated. We had to get water. I don't know who was hotter, Marvin or the El Dorado. It was a sight, I'll tell you. A goddamn sight."

"What next?"

He ground his teeth. "We try it again. Hope today did her good instead of harm. You can't ever tell."

Diana threw the pizza box in the trash.

· 35 ·

"So what did they say?"

"Nothing, like always."

"Bee, you were in there an *hour,* they must have said something."

Now that it was Monday Bobby was his normal nervous self. Bethany concentrated on television. Permission to watch on weeknights was granted according to grades. Because her grades and Bobby's were high, they got two hours every night and as much as they wanted on the weekend.

Rose Narcisco had given Bethany the news, which Bethany was not feeling so great about. She wasn't sure why. She'd been wanting to get out of Cedar Hills since day one and now that it looked like she might, she was in a slump.

"I don't want to talk about it."

"Are they kicking you out?"

"Did I say I didn't want to talk about it or what? Do you have ears?"

Bobby moved to the other end of the couch. "Gah, Bee. You don't have to yell, I was just asking a question, you remember questions?"

"I didn't yell, I just said."

"Oh, sure. The fish practically died in their tracks."

Bethany looked at the aquarium despite knowing he was only trying to be cute. "Very funny," she said.

"Ha," Bobby said, rolling his eyes. "Ha."

"So funny I forgot to laugh."

Demonstrate willingness, the Cisco Kid said, now how was she supposed to do that? Especially since they were going to kick her out no matter what. Narcisco had that look. It didn't matter what Bethany did next, she was history at Cedar Hills Nutty Brown Fruitcake. Jail was next, probably Goree with lesbians putting no telling what up inside her, then the electric chair.

Everything happened to her, the wrong thing at the wrong time. She'd been pretty much true to her vow today. Not quite but pretty much. She used to be able to fast like a monk but not eating now made her feel like a train was coming at her. If she didn't eat the train would run over her. Even if she hadn't strictly kept her vow, she'd been good. One helping of eggs and orange juice this morning, no toast or bacon, a salad and an apple for lunch. In the afternoon she did have a graham cracker but she didn't think graham crackers had that many calories. Tonight she'd scraped the gravy off her meat and skipped potatoes.

She wondered if being on her own, self-prescribed diet demonstrated willingness. She wondered where she'd rather be, here or at home, really. Nobody wanted her either place, except Bobby Neuhaus. She wasn't even sure Alex would like it if she came to Del Rio. His grandmother probably blamed her for the whole thing.

She ran her hand across her midsection. The scratches didn't really hurt. But touching them gave her a crazy, shivery feeling.

"Bethany?"

Stephen Doty stood beside her with a black notebook under his arm. "You, uh, busy?"

Bobby was slumped in his chair watching an old Alfred

Hitchcock program about a mild-mannered bookkeeper and his trashy, complaining wife. Bethany hadn't seen the program but she knew what would happen. The wife was a dead duck.

"No. What do you need?"

Stephen Doty sighed. "I've been reading this stuff about squaring the hypotenuse and reading it and reading it. And I still don't get it."

Bethany liked problems with a definite answer. All you had to do was keep going. If you followed the rules far enough, the solution was there.

She moved over. Bobby got up and went to the wing chair. Stephen Doty sat beside Bethany so that she could show him how to do right-angle triangles.

When they were finished she went to bed.

The one thing she was sure of was that nothing was going to work out for her, not if she lived a thousand years. When the chips came down and she was up to her ears in wanting to be better, it would all go kaflooey on her all over again, no matter how hard she tried.

She wondered if helping Stephen Doty with squaring the hypotenuse was anything like what they meant by demonstrating willingness.

She turned over on her side and closed her eyes, hoping for instant sleep.

Maybe. Probably not. Probably not even close.

She hugged her knees to her chest.

Friday

·36·

"*I*s this wild or what?"

Jesse James rubbed his hand across the top of his head. He had a new haircut, squared off and punkish on top, high around the ears with long sideburns. He was also growing a beard.

"Looks punk, like Carl Lewis. You deserting rock and roll?"

He caressed his scraggly beard. "Time," he said, "rocks on."

It was no coincidence that Jesse liked Bruce Springsteen; he could have passed for the rock star's double. Short, dark— black eyes, strong nose—and wiry, with Springsteen's coiled, street-smart look, he dressed accordingly, in straight-legged, button-up blue jeans and a wide black belt with a plain buckle, a blue chambray workshirt and plain white Keds, the old kind.

"Come on in."

As Diana brushed past him, Jesse checked behind her, scanning the yard and street. As if the trees had ears. He closed the screen and locked the door. Diana went up. The stairway was dark but she knew the way. At the top of the

241

stairs was a long hall, living room, dining room and kitchen on one side, two bedrooms and a bath on the other. She went into the kitchen.

Jesse pulled the light cord. The kitchen was clean but shabby. The enamel on the sink was worn away in patches, the green linoleum floor badly torn. Over the stove, paint had peeled away in large patches. The furniture, standard Sears Formica and vinyl, was not Jesse's. It came with the apartment.

He put a pot of water on to boil, set a red plastic cone on top of a small brown ceramic pitcher, ground some beans, placed a paper filter in the cone, filled the filter with ground coffee and watched the water.

Diana said nothing. Until Jesse had his coffee and turned on his music he was a zombie.

He was thirty-seven, lived like a graduate student and probably always would. In Austin this was acceptable. All over the city at this moment, men pushing forty were standing on worn linoleum floors they would never own, grinding beans to pour through filter cones into ceramic pitchers not meant to be coffee pots. They would not dream of buying an electric pot or using coffee beans roasted any longer ago than last week, anywhere but Austin.

Jesse had grown up in Dallas. He'd lived in New Orleans for a while. He'd liked New Orleans, the music, the street life. But Texas was what he was used to and so he came back, always to the same neighborhood: ethnically mixed, poor but safe.

He lifted the pot and poured the water through the coffee. From outside the window overlooking the backyard, a dog yapped. Jesse went over to the open window and in a sharp voice told the dog to shut up.

"New neighbor?"

"I hate that dog. Yippity-yap."

Diana looked out. A small golden cocker spaniel with big feet looked up at her. The dog was leashed to a clothesline.

At the base of the iron pole on which the clothesline was strung was a large bowl of water and another of dry dog food. Diana made a clicking sound. The dog wagged its bobbed tail so hard its whole backside went back and forth.

"Jess, it's a pup. Puppies yap. Is it a he or a she?"

I don't care. I hate noise. A she. Do you know she sent off for it?"

"She who? What do you mean sent off?"

"I mean that stupid dog was shipped here from a convent in Massachusetts. Some nuns up there supposedly raise great cockers. A family of four could eat for a week on what she paid for that dog."

"Lord. Sociologists."

"What?"

"A survey for every occasion."

"Fuck you. It's true."

The yard behind Jesse's apartment looked like a jungle, overgrown with trees and tall junk grass. At the back of the lot was a row of bamboo eight or nine feet tall. The bamboo was spreading, moving closer to the house. Diana had asked Jesse what his landlady was going to do when Birnam Wood made it to Dunsinane; Jesse said it was no skin off his nose. Diana thought he really had no idea what she was talking about.

He poured the rest of the water through the cone. When the coffee had dripped through, he filled two thick white mugs, set the cups on the table and went to the refrigerator.

"I forgot," he said. "You take cream."

Diana drew her cup nearer. "Milk," she said, "is fine."

"I don't know about this," he said, peering into his refrigerator. Jesse had allergies. To help stem the flow of mucus induced by cedar pollen, he'd given up milk products. "I'm probably not going to have any. Oh, wait, yes I do."

Diana looked out the window. "What's her name?"

"Zelda."

He came back to the table. Diana crossed her feet and stretched her legs. Jesse set a pint of half-and-half by her cup. She drew her feet back under her.

"I had some after all."

His workshirt was unbuttoned to the nipples. In the middle of his chest were five scraggly hairs. Diana poured a dollop of cream into her cup and stirred. When she took the spoon out, islands of a buttery substance floated on the surface of the coffee.

"Oh," she said.

"What?"

"Nothing. The cream's just blinky. I've had enough anyway. I really don't drink much coffee anymore."

"Shit, Diana. I'm sorry." He leaned across the table. She put her hands over her cup.

"Never mind."

He sat back down. "Up to you," he said.

She'd asked him why his mother had named him Jesse James. At first he'd given her a cock-and-bull, Springsteen-like story about his father having been a thief who robbed gas stations to keep his family off the welfare rolls. When Diana pressed him for the truth, he said first off he didn't remember his mother much but he thought maybe she'd wanted to name him for somebody famous. He'd read a study on the effect of names on personality. His conclusion was that his name in combination with his size had had its effect.

"They came at me like I was a gunfighter," he said, "all through high school. I was always in a cast. Look at this nose. If my name had been Jack or Rudy, I don't think it would have happened."

He slid his cup across the table. "Share mine."

"Really," she said. "I've had enough. You just got up. Drink." She reached into her skirt pocket. "So let me show you why I came."

She had called from the Big Wheel to make sure he was alone. From her pocket she pulled out a small heavy object, loosely wrapped in the worn yellow tissue. She set the gift on the table. Against the Formica it made a muffled clink.

Jesse's eyes brightened.

"The bazooka?"

She shook her head. "There's a new junk and antique store in Dripping. I wandered in and there he was."

"The TNT?"

"No."

Jesse picked up the gift and set it in his palm. Testing its weight, he moved his hand up and down.

"It has to be . . ."

He began unwrapping. Before he could finish, Diana pressed her hand on top of his. "Wait," she said. "Tell me."

"The machine gun."

He lifted the soldier from its wrapping. He was right, of course. A small helmeted soldier, down on one knee, took aim at the world. The soldier was painted army brown. Across his shoulder and down over his chest was a belt of ammunition.

Jesse turned the soldier upside down and checked the sole of one shoe.

"Yes," he said. "Yes."

He got up and went into the bedroom. Diana followed.

Jesse was an orphan. His father had abandoned the family early on. Then his mother died. There was a brother. The two boys had been raised by an overburdened aunt with a number of other children. The aunt drank. As soon as he was old enough, the brother joined the army. At fifteen Jesse had gone to court to have his minorities removed, so that he could sign a lease on an apartment and buy a car. He'd worked as a haberdasher, a radio announcer, a street cleaner, a clerk at the 7-Eleven, a janitor. He'd gotten his undergraduate degree at Sam Houston State, then had stayed on to study criminology and deviant behavior. His aunt had died. Jesse hadn't seen his brother in years. He'd been living alone in garage apartments since he was sixteen.

He stood before a wall of shelves. On one side was his World War II collection: lead soldiers, tanks and airplanes, aircraft carriers, tiny ambulances, pup tents, men carrying stretchers . . . all mint condition, painted brown.

He held the new one by its head.

"I could move the hand grenader over here . . ."

On the other shelves were Jesse's amplifier and his prized record collection: rock and roll from the beginning, Little Willie John and Clyde McPhatter to Prince and the latest ZZ Top. Across from the amplifier, two huge black speakers sat on the floor, each one padlocked to a brass hook attached to the woodwork.

The bed was unmade. Dark brown sheets in a peacock print lay in a tumble at Diana's feet.

They had met at a faculty reception. To make ends meet, besides his community college class, Jesse taught nights in the UT adult education department. Jesse invited Diana over. She came that afternoon. Jesse put on a record, rolled a joint, they smoked, fell into bed and did not look up for an hour or more. When the effect of the weed wore off they smoked another joint. Jesse's walls had pulsated with the steady beat while the high notes, in their state, entered their earbones and made a home there.

He turned from the shelf. "Look," he said.

He had placed the new soldier beside one standing with a rifle slung over his shoulder. The standing soldier wasn't aiming the gun the way most of the others were; he was just standing there. The soldier with the machine gun aimed his weapon at Diana.

"Great."

"I have a present for you, too." He went to get it.

At the window Diana looked down into the yard. Zelda was still staring up at her, sitting on her tail and wagging it at the same time.

Diana checked the kitchen clock. She would have to leave soon. Lunch at Cedar Hills was over at twelve-thirty.

When Zelda ran along the clothesline, the clasp on her leash made a zippering noise against the metal clothesline. She looked up at Diana to see if she'd made an impression.

"Whose dog is she?"

Jesse glanced briefly out the window. "A girl in the house up front studying dance therapy, a real nut."

"It's not right to leave her tied up all day. She could get tangled up in the line."

"So take her."

"Oh, sure."

"Why not?"

"Just take her, how can I just take her?"

"She'd be happy at your place. The girl is a shithead. The dog drives me crazy. Make everybody happy." He made a wide gesture with his arm. "Liberate the possessor."

"The dance therapist wouldn't be happy."

"Forget her." He handed her a smooth brown sack. "Here. I figured I'd see you sooner or later."

"Bruce?"

"Anybody can buy Bruce. You've heard the new one, I presume."

Springsteen had a new album out, a best-seller the day it was issued. "No."

"Diana! I was in line the first day, the fifth person in Austin to get it. I can't believe it. How could you not?"

I can't because he reminds me of you. She did not say this. *I can't because everytime I hear his voice I'm stoned again, back in bed with you. And I'm finished with that.*

"I haven't gotten around to it." She looked at the sack, felt of the record. "Diana?"

"You're a hard girl to surprise."

She pulled the record out. It was the Supremes' first album, "Where Did Our Love Go?" She loved the sound of the early Diana Ross, her sweet high-pitched crooning on "Can't Hurry Love," and, in particular, "Baby Love." The record was an original pressing, in mint condition.

"It was at Half-Price Books, just sitting there. I couldn't believe it."

Diana looked at her watch. "Play one song," she said. "Then I have to go."

Another time, Jesse would have taken her statement as a ploy. This time he either believed her, preferred to be alone, or had somebody else coming. He slipped the cellophane wrapper from the album cover, took the record from the case and, holding it gingerly by the outer edges, set it on the turntable. Diana sat on the bed. On the wall behind her was a huge poster of Bruce Springsteen with Clarence Clemons. On the wall with the speakers Chryssie Hynde posed with the Pretenders. The lead singer looked mean enough to rip sheetrock with her teeth.

His head bent to the level of the turntable, Jesse set the needle carefully on a particular cut. A song Diana did not recognize came on.

He straightened. "This was their first," he said. "Even before 'Where Did Our Love Go.' Can you believe how brassy they were? They were much better before Motown got hold of them."

Diana listened. It was true, the Supremes had been brassier then. Diana, no purist, liked the soupy sound better. She looked back at the window at Zelda.

When they got Rufus, Bethany had asked for a poodle. Diana hated poodles; she said no. She'd made other suggestions, a husky, a shepherd. But Bethany wanted something small, to curl up in her lap.

Diana Ross hit a long high note. The song ended.

Jesse James lifted the needle. "Three minutes max," he said. "The old hit-song rule." He took the record from the turntable, put it back in the wrapper, the case, then the sack. He set the Plexiglas lid down over the turntable.

"So?"

"I'm going to take her."

"Zelda?"

"Bethany. I'm kidnapping her from the lunch table."

"You can't kidnap your own child."

"I'm taking her beyond the rules of the school and consideration of the law. It's not kidnapping. But it's not easy."

Jesse set the record on the bed.

"Who knows?" He meant, does Hale.

"I've told my family. They don't think it's great but they won't interfere."

"The family therapist? Old what's-his-name?"

"Gil. Him, too."

"He'll have warned the school."

"No. He won't say anything."

Jesse cocked his head. "But he's one of them."

"I told him in session. No. He wouldn't." She was pretty sure.

"Would you do me a favor? Would you let me know if I'm right? Will you promise me that?"

Diana picked up her record. "If *I* know. Yes."

He squinted. "Meaning?"

"Maybe he's told them and I'll never know. Maybe they're smarter than you think."

"I doubt it."

Jesse thought Diana should have kicked Bethany out the minute she realized the girl was a thief. Let her find out what it's like out there, he said. Let her experience what she thinks she's looking for. She'll straighten out soon enough. Or . . . he made a dimissive face . . . she won't.

He'd showed her charts, given her books to read. One of the studies on the socialization process had divided parents into four categories, cold-authoritative, warm-authoritative, cold-permissive and warm-permissive. Diana had recognized herself and Hale immediately as warm-permissive. "Like the womb," Jesse said. "Nothing to knock against, no inner policeman to tell her what to do and, more important, what not to."

Diana picked up her record. "But I was thinking, I might take *her*, too."

"The dog?"

"I was thinking about it."

This was the Diana Jesse admired. Sometimes, out of the blue, she did something totally rash, made a bold move this way or that when no one expected it.

"You teaching this fall?"

She held his gaze. "I think so."

"Pretty late to be making up your mind."

"I know."

He moved toward her.

She took a step back. "I have to go."

"Was I doing something to stop you?"

He pointed at her waist. Diana looked down. She was holding the Supremes record like a shield against her chest. She dropped her arms to her side and slid the record beneath one arm like a schoolbook.

"Well . . ."

"I'll help liberate the possessor."

The driveway was badly cracked. Diana stepped over a large rupture in the concrete.

As if knowing they were on their way, Zelda had come to the near end of the clothesline. When they got there she was looking around the corner of the garage, wagging her tail like crazy. Diana bent down. The pup lapped her face like a child at an ice cream cone.

"She's got ticks."

"I told you," he said. "She's a shithead. But don't get too exercised. Look at this." He clutched a fistful of the dog's flesh. "She gets fed."

Diana unhooked the clasp from the clothesline. Zelda ran in circles, wrapping her leash around Diana's ankles. Diana let go of the leash, unwrapped her legs, then re-gripped the leather strap.

"I have her," Diana said. "I don't think we need help."

Jesse stepped back. "All right," he said. "You're doing the right thing, Diana."

"I have to think so, otherwise I wouldn't."

"Thanks for the soldier."

"And the record."

He pointed at it. "You take care of it."

She scooped Zelda up in her arms. The dog whined happily and licked Diana's teeth.

Jesse made a face. "Jesus," he said.

"You don't have to come to the car," she said. "We're fine." Before she got there she heard Jesse's screen door slam.

There were garbage cans piled up by the curb. Picking her way between them, she bumped one and jarred the record from under her arm. The record bounced once, then slid to the ground.

"Shit." Diana looked back at the garage apartment to see if Jesse was looking. If he was, she couldn't see him. She unlocked her car.

"There you go," she said. She dumped Zelda into the backseat of the Buick and quickly closed the door. When she went back to get the record she heard Jesse's stereo crank up, the opening "*One, two, one two three four*" of "Born in the U.S.A.," followed by the *whop* of the drums.

Diana unlocked the door on the driver's side. Zelda licked the window. Diana shoved the pup over, threw the record in the back and cranked the car. She turned on the A.C.—which had been fixed—and quickly drove away. She hoped no one had seen her. It made her feel ridiculous to think back, of herself in Jesse's bed, high on smoke and passion, listening to a young man sing romantic songs about high school while her daughter hit the streets and ruined her life.

Zelda walked in small circles, then lay with her head in Diana's lap and fell immediately asleep. Fleas crawled between her golden curls.

At the interstate they turned south. Forecasters had announced a possibility of rain for the weekend, up to forty percent by Saturday night. Thunderstorms had been mentioned.

At Ben White, Diana turned west. She wondered whether by "the right thing" Jesse meant stealing Zelda or rescuing Bethany. She passed McDonald's, Wendy's, a boot store. Ben White was, as usual, jammed with traffic going both ways.

On its marquee, the South Forty Ballroom advertised twenty-five-cent tacos. The one-dollar movie was showing *Crocodile Dundee*. Zelda lightly snored. At Lamar, they took the spaghetti bowl onto 290.

· 37 ·

*L*unch at Cedar Hills was served cafeteria-style, not serious food, usually soups and salads, sandwiches, one hot dish, maybe a hamburger or enchiladas. Nobody cared how much you ate or which table you sat at. Staff went off to themselves to gossip and take a break.

In line, Bethany asked for fruit salad and cottage cheese.

Johnno waited to see what else Bethany wanted. She usually piled her plate high. When Bethany moved down the line, Johnno looked to the next kid.

From the drinks section she got a carton of low-fat milk, a glass of iced tea, one pre-wrapped package of two little graham crackers. Everybody was bound to notice how little she was eating; she just hoped they didn't say anything. She didn't have what it took to give it to anybody right now.

She went to her seat. Even though at lunch kids could sit anywhere, mostly they all took their regular places.

Bobby came over. On his tray was a plain hot dog, a diet Coke, two cookies and a piece of apple pie.

Bethany unfolded her napkin. "Jeez, Bobby," she said. "I don't see how you eat a wienie with nothing on it."

Bobby set his tray on the table and looked around the room. "You got it?"

"Got what?" She flipped her hair over her shoulder and put her napkin in her lap. Bobby sat down beside her.

"Napoleon."

"Maybe."

She had written a paper for Bobby on Napoleon's Russian campaign. The paper was tucked into her pants pocket.

She squeezed lemon juice in her tea and added three packets of Sweet 'n Low.

Bobby opened his fist and dropped a small white sack on her tray.

Bethany stirred her tea. "What's that?"

"Jelly Bellies." He licked his lips. "Nothing but the best." He scanned her tray. "You sick or something?"

"Or something." Bobby was a major thief of genius and that was all there was to it. He could steal things right out from under people's noses and nobody noticed. No telling where he got the Jelly Bellies.

Bethany took the Napoleon paper from her pocket and slipped it under the table.

"Thanks, Bee."

She slid the sack of candy in his direction. "That's okay about the jellybeans," she said.

"Not jellybeans," he reminded her.

"I know," she said. She couldn't seem to come up with her usual fast talk.

"But . . . " He looked bereft. "They're all piña colada."

"I know," she said. "I'm just not that hungry."

She sipped her tea. Keeping her left hand in her lap, she delicately speared a canned peach slice with her fork.

Stephen Doty and Priscilla Marchione sat down across the table. Bobby knew better than to say anything about Bethany's diet. He had stepped into that one before.

"It's probably an A-minus," she said in a low voice. "Maybe

even a B. I didn't want to make it too good or Egghead might notice."

She motioned with her head in the direction of the table where Staff sat. The history teacher at Cedar Hills, a man named Stanley Mears, was eating tacos. Kids thought Mears was more Nutty Brown than anybody. "You'd think history belonged to him," Bobby said, "the way he drools over it." Stanley Mears had hung a picture of Gandhi over the blackboard. Bobby swore the two looked alike if you gave Gandhi hair and took away Egghead's sneer. Bethany thought Bobby had been too influenced by the movie.

Bobby pulled his pie plate close. "So," he said, "what's up for the weekend. You hear anything yet?"

"Not yet." Bethany tugged at the red strip on the graham cracker package. "You going to eat that pie first?"

The red strip broke. "Why not?" Bobby said. "I always eat my dessert first, you know that."

"I hate these things," Bethany said. "I really hate these stupid things." It took all the strength she had to keep from pounding the graham crackers to a pulp.

"So let me do it."

"No!" She felt like killing him

"So ease up, Bee. *Gah!*"

Tiffany Leberman took her seat, then Tiny Saunders and Jason Michaels. Bethany asked Stephen Doty how he'd done on the hypotenuses. Tiffy looked wet about the eyes. Jason's mouth was a tight line. Stephen said he'd passed, thanks to Bethany. Prissy wiped her mouth.

When Bobby finished his pie he started in on the hot dog, eating cookies along with it, like chips.

The noise in the cafeteria increased, as the rest of the Cedar Hills wackos arrived.

· 38 ·

*D*iana drove into the parking lot, exactly on time. Zelda stood on the passenger seat beside her, nose out the window. Not knowing what the dog might do, Diana had only cracked the window and so Zelda paced, sniffing at the tiny slice of air, making snot tracks on the glass.

"I won't be long." Diana patted Zelda's silky head. When she opened the door Zelda made a sharp darting move. Diana barely caught the dog in time.

"Hey," she said. "You're fast." She held the dog by the nape of the neck with her right hand while with her left she opened the door. "The nuns," she said, "breed for early speed."

She pulled her arm out and closed the door. Zelda stood on her hind legs and pressed her paws against the glass, scraping her claws against the window.

Diana tickled the glass. Zelda sniffed the place where her hand was and began to whimper. When Diana dropped her hand and turned away, the whines turned into moans and yelps of misery. Diana took two steps away and then went back.

"I told you I'd be right back," she yelled through the window. "You'll learn to trust me. I'll be right back."

She tucked her purse beneath her arm. From behind her, Zelda shrieked. Diana did not turn around. She picked her way through the rocky footpath around the administration building, then turned down the curving path leading to the cafeteria.

Anyway, she thought, still fixed on Jesse James, why venerate Bruce Springsteen? High school was horrible. Given a choice, Diana would have skipped right over that time and gone straight to adulthood.

She opened the cafeteria door. The noise came at her in a rush, all the young voices. The cafeteria smelled of sweat, chalk, wet trays and reheated food. School cafeterias were all the same.

Surveying the room, she spotted Bethany sitting at a corner table against the back wall, next to Bobby Neuhaus. Her chair was tilted back. Leaning against the wall, she nibbled a cracker.

Diana let the cool air of Cedar Hills' computer-controlled environment blow in her face. She could not hesitate or she would lose her momentum, not to mention her taste for heroics; she only needed a second or two to gather her strength. Having noticed her, a woman at the Staff table came over. The woman wore white jeans, a cerise Mexican blouse, and Birkenstocks. She had brought her paper napkin with her.

As the woman made her way toward Diana, other people took notice. One student nudged another. The noise of the cafeteria lessened in waves as word was passed: someone was there without permission, it was Friday, someone had broken the rules. By the time the woman in the Birkenstocks got to Diana, silence had washed across the length of the cafeteria.

"May I help you?"

Diana stepped back. "No, thank you," she said. "I don't need help."

Her voice was steady but a little shrill.

"I'm afraid"—the woman in the Birkenstocks was trying to muscle Diana back out the door—"the cafeteria is off-limits to visitors. I feel I've met you. Are you a relative of someone here?"

"My daughter." Bethany had set the legs of her chair back on the floor. She was looking at Diana.

The woman glanced in Bethany's direction. "Oh, yes," she said. "Then you do know the rules."

"Yes." Diana met the woman's gaze. "I know the rules."

"Is there an emergency? A death in the family?"

"What? No. Everything is fine."

Bethany had risen from her chair.

"You're Bethany Caldwell's mother, I believe. From Buda."

"Not Buda. I don't live in Buda. I live near Driftwood." Like a girl entranced, Bethany moved toward her mother. Bobby tugged at her sleeve, but Bethany kept coming.

The woman in the Birkenstocks grasped Diana's elbow. Diana shook her away.

"Leave me alone," she said. "I've come to take Bethany home."

"You're free to do that, of course, but have you spoken with Dr. Narcisco?"

"No."

"Then you could be doing great damage. We have a plan. The process . . ."

"Please." Diana held up her hand. "It's over."

When Bethany was close enough, Diana reached for her. "Come on, Bee," she said. "Let's go home." Her voice was thin.

Bethany stopped in her tracks. She was not sure what to do next. Every wacko at Nutty Brown Fruitcake and all the Staff were staring at her. She wanted to go home but Diana scared her. She had that look.

Diana stepped forward and took Bethany's hand.

Bethany pulled back. "Did somebody die?"

It hadn't occurred to her that Bethany might think she'd come with bad news. Diana pulled at her. "No, Bee, nothing is wrong. I've come to take you home, is all. I've come to get you."

Bethany's resistance melted like wax. She let her mother lead her away.

At the door, another member of Staff was waiting.

"Mrs. Caldwell . . ." Diana thought the man bore a faint resemblance to Gandhi with hair.

"Never mind," she said to the man. "It's over." The man moved out of their way.

Just outside the door, Bethany stopped. "Wait," she said. She went back in. " 'Bye, Bobby," she called out to her friend.

"Bee," Bobby screamed. "Don't go!"

His chair had fallen on the floor and he was standing up, looking as M as he did on Sundays. He held up the Jelly Bellies. Across the table Tiffany Boo-hoo was doing her act and Stephen Doty looked as if somebody had smacked him in the face.

"Don't leave, Bee." He was really screaming.

Bethany turned around and went out the door.

"Gah," she said. "It's hot out here."

Diana released the breath it seemed she had held the entire time she was in the cafeteria. Being a hero wasn't so hard. It was the anticipation and planning that rattled your mind and raked at your confidence. This was the easy part.

"Wait," Diana said.

"Now what?"

"I have to go back and get something."

"If you mean the chicken forget it."

"Why?"

"We already got it."

"Who?"

"Bobby saw you put it there. We're keeping it in the living room by the fish. The kids went nuts over it."

"They did?"

"Not the plant. The chicken. What'd you do that for, just leave it like that?"

"I don't know, Bee. I really don't know."

By the time they got to the footpath around the administration building they could hear the screams.

"What is that?" Bethany asked. "Somebody into torture?"

"You'll see."

Zelda's plump little body began to quiver all over when she saw Diana. She jumped from the front seat to the back and back to the front again. When Diana opened the door, the pup fell out onto the parking lot and hit square on her nose.

"Where did you get it? Is it mine?"

Diana nodded.

Bethany picked up the puppy. "Da pooch," she said in falsetto baby talk. "Da baby, da pooch."

"She'd been neglected. Somebody I know at the college wanted her to have a good home. So . . ." She shrugged. "Here she is."

Diana stuck her head into the car.

"Oh, Lord," she said.

In the middle of the backseat was a neat pile of turds.

"Do you," she said to Bethany, "have a Kleenex?"

Bethany looked blank. "I don't have anything," she said.

Rescue was more complicated than Diana thought. She had neglected to remember Bethany's things. Her clothes, purse, everything.

"Well," she said. "I'll come back and get them Sunday. We don't want to go back in there now."

"I'm not ever going back, that's for sure." Bethany put Zelda down on the concrete and began to tease her, feinting this way and that. Zelda took immediately to the game. Diana pulled out the Supremes record and, using the sack for a broom, cleaned up the mess.

She threw the turds into the parking lot, tossed the sack in a trash basket, put the record in the backseat.

"What's her name?"

"Zelda. It may stink in here but we're ready."

"Let's hit it, Zelda." Bethany carried the pup to the passenger side of the car and got in. "*P.U.*, Zelda," she moaned. "Oh, my God, I can't stand it." Bethany held her nose. "I can't stand it, Zelda, I can't stand it." Zelda was all over her, jumping up and down in her lap, licking her mouth, her cheeks, her nose.

Diana cranked the car and pushed the button to let down the top.

"Hold her," she told Bethany. "We won't be able to smell it after a while."

She looked up at the gold windows of Cedar Hills and wondered if anyone was watching. Although she could not see her, she was certain Rose Narcisco was at the front door tapping her foot, short arms crossed over her healthy chest.

Just past the real Nutty Brown, at the cutoff through the hills, Diana turned west off 290. They drove home slowly, giggling like schoolgirls at Zelda's antics. To the south, a line of dark blue clouds boiled up over the hills, making the possibility of rain seem even more likely.

·39·

*H*ale drew the brush from the middle of the filly's back to her tail. A cloud of dust rose from Red's hip.

"You can't go to Ruidoso looking like a scumbag, Miss Illuminated Red 1," he said. "I won't let you."

Tuesday, Red had gone into the gates like a lamb. She'd stood, eaten her feed, come on out. Wednesday Hale fed her in the barn, then took her to the gates. Once in, she'd turned around and looked long and hard at him, as if to say, "How long do we have to play this game?" Pito wanted to get on her but Hale made him wait. Thursday he'd let him ride her into the gates and sit on her there. This morning they'd broken her out. Red fell out of the gate as if breaking were her heart's desire.

"I'm so proud of you, girl." Red turned around and looked at Hale. "You are the smartest girl I ever had." He ran the brush down her leg. "I'm really proud of you."

"Dad?"

"In here."

Roger stepped into the light at the end of the barn. At first Hale could see only his dark silhouette, his hopeful walk—

a slight bounce, up on his toes, then down—against the sun-light. The light of the setting sun on his curls made his head look like it was on fire.

"What's up, Dad, the beauty treatment?"

"I can't let her go to New Mexico looking scuzzy."

Without enthusiasm Roger rubbed Red's blaze. Red looked quizzically at him. There was no reason for Roger to know how to act around horses; he had grown up in special schools, drawing pictures. With the horses he tried too hard. Hale had once caught him running at a weanling, as if at a dog.

"What's going on at the store?"

"Not much. I left Buddy in charge. He has to get used to it some time."

"*Whoa,* girl," Hale said to Red. Keeping one hand on her hip, he walked around behind her.

"I'm not going to Ruidoso, Dad."

Hale froze. "Why not?"

"One thing and another. I need to get back to my job. I called last night. They can't hold it for me much longer. They found another cook but she hasn't worked out."

"Can't you go out after Ruidoso?"

"Dad, why do you want me to go to Ruidoso?"

"I don't know. I just thought . . ."

"What?"

Hale dropped his arm. "You could be there when we . . ." He shook his head. "I don't know, Roger. I don't know. I am so tired of trying to figure out why I do what I do and what I really mean when I say something, I feel like . . . I don't even know what I feel like. A rat in a maze. A big fat nothing. I can't do it anymore. I'm too old and too tired."

Roger moved down to Red's other flank and leaned across the filly's back toward his father.

"Hey," he said.

Hale looked up.

"I don't want to make it hard on you, Dad. I want to

help." His chin quivered. A tear welled up, hung there. "But I'm only making things worse." The tear rolled out. "And Dad . . ."

Hale took off his glasses.

"I'm not a cowboy. Those guys don't want me along. I like Casey fine. Pito too. But they think I'm a wimp, you know? I'm not, but I keep trying to prove it to them and, well, it's their world and their game and I don't even know the rules."

Hale started to interrupt.

"They do, Dad. I'm telling you, they think I'm a California wimp, and you know it. And . . ." The matching tear from the other eye rolled down his cheek. "Who knows, maybe I am. Maybe I have to live with that. All I know is, I can't fight it."

Hale wiggled the brush back and forth on Red's backside to scratch her. Red relaxed her hip. "Son," he said, "I don't want you to be anything but what you are. My daddy put down everything I ever tried to do in my life. God knows I've meant to do differently by you."

Roger wiped his eyes with his shirtsleeve.

"I didn't mean you. Please don't twist up what I'm trying to say."

"I don't mean to."

"I know. But it makes me feel bad for saying anything."

Hale set his glasses back on his nose.

Roger did a comic thing with his shoulders. "I know, you know, we both know. But . . ." He took a breath. "I just don't want to have to feel bad about what I'm telling you. On top of everything else?"

Hale nodded, even though he wasn't at all certain he understood.

"I've made up my mind. I'm going to start back tomorrow."

"By yourself? To California? In the Rabbit? What about the transmission, did you have it looked at?"

"Dad. It got me here. I'll be fine."

"It's supposed to storm."

"I'll be fine."

"I just worry."

"I wish you had a little more faith."

When Roger moved away from the filly, Hale began to brush her once again, stroking her from the middle of her back up over her hip and down to her tail, pressing hard to get to the dirt.

"What makes you think I don't?"

"Well, I mean this is just for instance. When we were talking about my going to Ruidoso with the guys, every time I mentioned driving, you said no, Casey would do it."

"But, Rog, that's silly. Hauling a trailer's not easy. Turning around's a real bitch. You have to have experience."

"But if I was going I needed to do something besides sit shotgun and look pretty. Look, I don't know . . ." He picked a burr from Red's belly. "I don't particularly want to go into all this. There's a point, I think, when talk does damage instead of good."

"Amen."

"But . . ." Once again, he moved away from the horse. "I mean, I'd like you to be proud of me, you and Mom both. And I'm not sure how to do that but I know I can't do it here. I thought I could help out with Bethany but I'm not even sure about that anymore. And so I think I'd better go back to my job and my friends and figure out what to do next myself."

"If you wanted to go back to school . . ."

"I might. I don't want to go back to Santa Cruz but I could get my degree at Berkeley. There's something else, now that we're having confession time. Do you know why I didn't finish? Really?"

"No."

"Because when I'm done with my course work I'll have to do a senior project. It's something like a thesis at the undergraduate level. It can be a research project or a creative one, it doesn't matter which. Just so it's approved by your project director. But you knew that. I told you."

Hale set the brush on a stool. "But the ten credits. You have to get the ten credits first."

"Right."

"And then?"

"I've had these ideas. I was going to do a film. Mom helped me pick out a story. I was going to write a script and shoot the movie. I had a crew, a cast. I didn't like the story much. I went along because I didn't have any better ideas. I did a treatment. People—friends—were anxious to help, then I don't know, I lost it. I wrote three lines of dialogue, then nothing. I tried again a few times but really, I never went back. I can get the ten credits anytime. It's the project beyond the credits I'm avoiding."

"Why not just get the credits and see what happens?"

"Why not fly to the moon, that's what I'm trying to tell you, I don't know. But I don't want you to think I'm not thinking about it because I am. And I don't want you to think I don't worry about it because I do. And I don't want you to think I also don't worry about being a bum my whole life because I worry about it a lot. But I'm not like you. I can't seem to figure things out, then go take care of them. I don't know why, I just can't. I keep making lists. Then nothing."

Hale smoothed Red's mane. "Does Bethany coming home have anything to do with your decision?"

Roger shook his head. "It's wrong, Dad. Bethany's got to take her lumps and Mom's never going to let her. I love Bethany but I'm scared for her. And for you guys. I can't stand to sit around here and see it happen all over again."

Hale picked up his brush. "She's doing what she thinks is best. I don't like that place either."

"That's not the point."

"Wait until you have children. Until then you can't know. Nobody can."

"I don't mean to be a smartass."

"No. I know."

"I'm going up to the house and wash some clothes. I just wanted to tell you."

As Roger walked around behind Red, Red shifted her backside.

"Son, don't . . ."

"I was paying attention, Dad. She was shifting her weight."

"I didn't think you were watching close enough."

"As Mom always says, look to the adverb. 'Enough' is the key."

Roger went to his father and hugged him. Hale felt like a child in his son's arms. When Roger started to pull away, Hale drew him closer before he let him go. He asked the boy to come back to the barn when he was through washing clothes.

"It's supposed to rain tonight," he said. "Or at least let's hope so. I need to get feed before then. I can use your back and shoulders, unloading."

Roger held up his fist. "Anytime," he said. "An hour about right?"

"About. Yes."

Roger left and Hale went back to Red, wondering as he continued his grooming why he could not find the grace within himself to believe that decency and goodness were enough. There were plenty of ambitious creeps in the world. Roger was sensitive and generous; he could weep in front of his father without feeling ashamed. Hale ought to be satisfied with that. He didn't know why he was not.

Roger drove to the house. Confession was supposed to be good for the soul. He wasn't at all certain he'd done the right thing.

Good for his soul maybe. Not his dad's.

· 40 ·

*I*n Hale's wing-back chair Bethany sat with her feet on the table reading an article in *Vanity Fair*, about a fourteen-year-old girl who'd gone off with one of the Rolling Stones.

Diana put six veal chops in the broiler pan. Roger had left a note. He and Hale had gone to Kyle for feed. They were due back any minute. To keep the evening from getting out of hand, Diana had decided to set up a strict schedule. Preparations for the meal at six, dinner at seven . . . even though they rarely ate before eight or nine these days, when darkness was so late in coming and there was always some outside chore to take care of.

She had typed out a list of house rules. Bethany had looked briefly at the list, then gone back to her room. She had made written comments on the rules, "Okay" by some, "We'll see" by others, "No way" by a few. She had signed the paper with a flourishing signature.

Diana read the comments, then gave the paper back. "It's for you," she said. "I didn't ask for comments." Bethany had shoved the list inside her magazine.

She sat forward. "Listen to this, Mom," she said. " ' "This is your big chance," the mother said.' Gah. How sick can you get. He's thirty-eight and her mom wants her to go off with him. Gross."

Diana sprinkled tarragon on the chops and turned the oven to broil. With a paring knife she began to peel broccoli stems.

Bethany's hair was over her face. She looked as if she might gobble up the *Vanity Fair*. Diana turned down the burner under the steamer pan. It felt right, having Bethany home. She'd done the right thing, she was sure of it.

Not that everything had gone smoothly. When they'd first arrived, Bethany had sauntered into the house as if she'd been gone an hour. When Diana asked her to help carry groceries in, she said she wanted to fix Zelda a place to sleep first but she would if she really had to. Diana said no, it was all right, she could do it.

Bethany had taken Zelda to meet Rufus. Rufus sniffed at the dog's behind and growled. When Bethany scolded Rufus, Rufus took off and had not been seen since. Zelda was asleep on Bethany's bed. So far the pup had shit twice and peed three times in the house.

Bethany read another paragraph. "Can you believe that?"

Diana was not listening. "What was that again," she said. "I missed it."

There was a sound from outside, a crunch of tires, men's voices. Bethany kept reading. She came to the end of the paragraph. Tossing her hair from her eyes, she turned the page.

"Anybody home? Di?"

Roger and Hale had stopped at a Sac 'n Pac on the way home from Kyle for a beer. Their first glimpse of Bethany was her hair, fanning over the wing of Hale's chair.

"In here," Diana called out. When Hale saw the hair, he came to a dead halt. Roger rolled into him.

"Hi, guys," she said, peering around the wing of the chair. "I can tell by the look on your faces how thrilled you are to see me."

She settled back in with her magazine. Not that she was reading it anymore.

She knew what Hale and Roger were thinking and it was fine with her. Someday she'd show them. When she got out of her teenage years she would straighten up, go to college, not do any more bad things. Most of her problems had to do with being a teenager. "It's the teenage life," she often said to herself and others.

Hale bent down and kissed Bethany on her cheek. Diana was right; the girl had gained weight. But she was not really fat, the way Diana said.

"I'm in your chair." Bethany started to get up.

"Keep your seat."

"No," she said. "I insist." She stood. "This is the daddy bear seat and I'm the big bad wolf. Hi, Rog. How's tricks?"

"Can't complain." Roger also gave her a quick kiss. He indicated the magazine with his finger. "You reading about the chick who went off with the Stone?"

"Isn't it a blast?"

"A blast all right."

"I've got something to show you guys. A surprise." She dropped her magazine on the table and bustled out of the room.

Diana picked up another stalk of broccoli.

"Diana," Hale said. "Where's Rufus? It's his dinnertime and I can't call him up."

"Look." In Bethany's arms, Zelda wagged her rear end and blinked. She was still half-asleep. "Her name is Zelda. And she's an inside dog."

"But I thought . . ." Hale turned to Diana.

"She's a baby, Hale," Diana explained. "We'll put her out after she gets used to us. I was afraid she might run off."

Hale patted the puppy's head. "She's got ticks."

"We sprayed her. The ticks aren't all dead yet. They will be."

"Where'd you get her?"

Diana opened the oven door and basted the chops. "Somebody in Austin left her. I took her."

"Just took her?"

"She'd been abandoned. Like I said."

Roger peered over Diana's shoulder at the chops. "I wouldn't cook those too long."

Diana pushed the broiler pan back under the heating element. "Would you like to take over?"

Roger held his hands up like a robber in a cowboy movie. "Hey," he said, "I'm out of here." He went down the hall toward his room. "When's dinner?" he called back over his shoulder.

"Seven," Diana said. "On the dot."

"*Seven?*" Roger went into his room and closed the door.

"What about Rufus?" Hale took Roger's place next to Diana.

"Oh," Diana said, placing stalks of broccoli in the steamer basket, "Rufus got a little skitzy about Zelda. But he'll be back."

"How can you be sure?"

"Where would he go? Hale, please."

Hale took a glass from the cabinet. "Please what?" he said. "I'm not doing anything to you, Diana. I am not doing a goddamn thing." He filled the glass with ice and reached for the vodka.

"Here we go," Bethany said in a singsong voice. "Welcome home. Here we go again."

She took Zelda to her room.

Hale fixed his drink in silence. "I'm going upstairs to change my shoes," he said. Martini in hand, he left.

When the broccoli and the chops were done, there Diana stood, in the middle of the kitchen, broiler pan in one hand, spatula in the other. The chops looked overcooked.

"Soup's on," she said in so low a voice not even the broccoli could have heard her.

·41·

*H*ale and Roger had checked out *Pale Rider* from a video store in Kyle. Roger took the movie from its case. Diana opened the new *Harper's*. Hale was ironing.

"This is a big mistake, Mom. I promised myself I wouldn't say anything but I can't help it. It's a big mistake."

Diana looked up over her reading glasses. "What is?"

"Bringing her home. Like she was a hero."

"Who said she was a hero?"

They could hear Bethany in her room chattering away on the telephone. She was telling her chums how awful Cedar Hills had been and how glad she was to be home and that the mysterious gland disorder which had caused her weight gain had been diagnosed and cured, and that not only would she be back in school in September but now that she had her pills, the extra weight was simply going to melt.

Diana's first house rule had been "No lying."

"Or what?" Hale had asked when Diana showed him the list. He had tossed the paper on the table. "This means nothing without some kind of reinforcement. If she doesn't do these things, then what?"

Diana took the list back. "It didn't seem right to say if she didn't behave we'd send her back to Cedar Hills. Anyway we don't know that they'd take her."

"But that's what we'd try to do. There or someplace else."

"We have to figure it out, Hale. Not just blat out the truth."

"I like blatting out the truth."

"Anyway we don't know what they'd do."

"I expect at four thousand dollars a month they'd be happy to have her back. I'd be willing to bet that nut schools for kids are having their problems just like everybody else."

"Money's not everything."

"It's close." He wanted to bite his tongue but he could not stop. "It's damn close."

Bethany was making no attempt to keep her voice down. "Glands," she said, "can you believe it. I don't know where they are, somewhere in the neck I think." Hale loudly cleared his throat and nodded his head in Bethany's direction.

"Oh, Hale," Diana said. "That's not the kind of lying I was talking about."

"Okay, guys," Roger said. "Here we go." When he pressed Play, the screen remained staticky and blank. They watched it for a while. Finally Roger ejected the cassette.

"I hate it," he said, "when people do that." They watched the blank screen as the reels whipped the movie back to the beginning.

Diana took off her half-glasses. "Nobody said she was a hero, Roger."

"But look at us, Mom. She hasn't been home six hours and already we're kowtowing to her, eating at *her* time, *her* food. The veal chops were lousy. Not because of anything you did. Veal just won't broil unless it's really really thick. And I'm still hungry."

"Then eat. Nobody's putting you on a diet."

"That's not the point. Besides, you threw out the ice cream. And the leftover lasagne."

"We could all stand to diet."

"Sure, Mom, you're really fat. Isn't it a little radical to throw everything out?"

"If it stays around she'll eat it."

"You ever hear of A.A.? It doesn't do any good to pour the liquor down the sink."

"It's not the same."

The cassette clicked, signaling the end of the tape. Roger pushed Play once again.

Hale turned his shirt over.

Diana put her half-glasses on her nose and opened her magazine. "In a way, Roger," she said. "It's none of your business."

Roger fast-forwarded through the government warning.

"I know that," he said, keeping his eye on the screen so as not to miss the credits. "Boy, do I know that."

He let go of the fast-forward button and fell back into the deep leather chair. Resting his cheekbone on his fist, he turned his attention to the television screen. Soon he had forgotten about his family.

Diana stared at her magazine.

Hale ironed the back side of his shirt, looking up at the television screen from time to time to keep up with the plot.

"Great shot," Roger said. "Day for night is great."

Diana went to the window. In the distance, at the edge of the horizon, a sliver of white emerged from behind a bank of rolling dark clouds.

"The moon," she said. "I forgot."

Hale set the iron on its heel.

"Diana," he said. "It's past nine."

"I don't care. The tomatoes have to go in before it peaks. The almanac said nine fifty-two. I'll take a flashlight."

"Get the Coleman. It's brighter."

"Whatever."

She left the room in a rush.

·42·

*T*he plants sat lined up like small children waiting to be told what to do.

"Rufus," Diana called into the night. "Are you out there, Rufus?"

She thought she heard a whimper, but Rufus did not appear. She looked up at the sky. Dark clouds hung low. Rain was still in the forecast. She hoped it waited until after Roger left.

She had unhooked the hose from the drip system and turned the water on. Carefully, she directed the water into each of the eighteen holes she and Roger had made. When the earth had soaked the water up, she filled the holes again. On the ground beside her, the blue-white light of the Coleman lantern made the garden look like a neon-lit laboratory.

When the water had drained the third time she threw the hose behind her, put a tablespoonful of Tomato Booster into each hole, then mixed the organic fertilizer with the wet dirt.

The drought had broken in some parts of the state. Houston was getting afternoon thunderstorms. To the south, around Victoria and Corpus, there had been heavy rain.

Diana took a seedling from its container, bent it and set

it in a hole at an angle, so that the rootball was at an L-shaped angle to the rest of the plant. Quickly, she surrounded the rootball, then covered the plant past its first leaves, so that the stem would be strong enough to hold the fruit. From a tub she scooped out a handful of sterilized potting soil and packed it around the roots and lower stem of the plant.

She worked quickly and carefully, making sure that air pockets did not develop or roots dry out. The moon had risen but she could no longer see it. Dark clouds had swathed it in smoky darkness.

From the pasture a horse snorted. Hale had said Pearl's colt might come tonight. He had given her a stall next to a fenced-in pen, so that she had room to move around.

From behind her a footstep crunched in the dry grass.

"Hale?"

"No. Tomato man."

He knelt beside her. "You're crazy," he said.

"Can you believe it? I've turned into a night gardener, first the ants, now this. I'm out of control."

He moved into the light.

"We have to hurry," she said. "It's rising fast."

"What can I do to help? Any tricks?"

"Plant them at an angle, like this." She move the Coleman lantern closer so that he could see. "Make sure there are no air pockets around the roots. You can help me put in the cages when we're finished."

The water from the hose had trickled down the hill. The right side of Diana's skirt was wet. When she stood, the skirt stuck to her leg.

"Also," she said, "I want to put out these mothballs."

"I thought you weren't going to. We have the cages."

"The mothballs will be double protection."

She opened the box and shook some mothballs onto the ground. The smell of camphor rose through the night. From the house they could hear the sound of Bethany's laughter.

When the plants were in, Hale began setting the cages in

place, pressing the bottom spikes into the wet soil. When he got close enough, he said, "You smell like a winter sweater."

She tossed out the last of the mothballs. They looked like bouncing balls of ice on the dark ground.

"Did you see Rufus?"

"No, but he's out there."

"How do you know?"

"He snores. He's asleep out behind the garage. He'll be back. He's just staging a small revolt."

"I hope so."

Hale fixed another cage. "She's a really cute dog. But we said no inside dogs. I think we ought to put her out."

"Wait," Diana said. "Shine the lantern over here."

He moved it. She counted.

"We forgot some."

She bent down to set the last two tomatoes in. Hale firmed the earth around them.

"Hurry," she said. "You can't see the moon but I know. It's happening fast."

They got the seedlings in just in time, before waxing peaked and turned into waning and the time arrived to plant below-ground crops.

· 43 ·

*I*n the night the predicted rain clouds arrived.

"Feast or famine," Hale said in the dark.

It was as if the sky had opened up and all the water it had gathered in the past months was coming down at once.

He reached for Diana. It was two-fifteen. "You asleep?"

"I'm thinking about getting up. I can't stand just lying here. I guess there go my tomatoes."

"Maybe not."

"A rain this heavy will beat them to the ground. Plus the mothballs will be ruined. And the Diazinon."

She sat up.

"Don't get up." He pulled her closer.

"I wasn't. It's starting to get funny."

"What is?"

"All this. I checked the calendar after we came up. I had it wrong."

"What?"

"The full moon. It's not tonight."

"It looked full."

"It always does the night before. Now the rain is blamming the Jackpots and Bingos into the ground."

"Don't complain about the rain."

"I wasn't but . . ." She turned on her side in his direction. "Don't you think it's funny?"

He didn't say anything. He pulled her close. Her body shook. She pressed her mouth against his chest so that the children could not hear.

"Shh," Hale said as if she were crying. "Shh. It's all right."

Roger had tuned to HBO, a comedy special featuring a comedian named Gallagher. Bethany never liked the same funny stuff as Roger. She was waiting for a commercial, when she'd flip to MTV.

Gallagher was doing something with a watermelon. He raised a sledge hammer over his head.

"Watch this," Roger said.

"You've seen it?"

"Watch. This is great."

The comedian brought the sledge hammer down and split the watermelon. Juice, meat and seeds went all over the stage and into the audience. People were wearing plastic raincoats and rainhats. They opened small umbrellas.

"God*dang*," Bethany said. The people getting hit with watermelon juice laughed their heads off.

"Can you believe it?"

"Goddang that's great."

"I told you."

When Zelda shit in the house the fifth time, they put her on the porch. Sometime after midnight they heard the Rufus Flop. Once Rufus showed up, Zelda stopped crying.

At six when Hale came down, he found Rufus asleep on his rug in the workroom of the garage, Zelda curled in a ball between his front and hind legs.

It was still raining. He checked the rain gauge. Two inches already.

He went to get Red ready to go to Ruidoso. In the mare barn he found that Pearl had foaled during the night, a dark sorrel stud colt, sickly but intact. The colt had four white feet. Pearl seemed fine.

"Great," Hale said to nobody in particular. "Four white feet, just great."

Saturday

· 44 ·

Marvin moved out of the way. "I thought she was trailer broke."

"She is trailer broke. She knows something's going on."

"Aw, Hale, hell. She's just a horse."

For a big man Marvin Thoede carried himself well. He did a sidestep-skip to his left, out of Red's path.

Once again, Hale led Red to the end of the walkway. He'd backed the trailer into the barn so that nobody had to get wet. Red was well trailer-broke but she'd suddenly gone spooky.

The other horses munched their feed. The rain beat hard against the barn roof.

"Where's that boy of yours?"

"Roger?"

"The slinky one. With the arms."

"Casey. He's on his way. So is Pito. It's only six-thirty, Marvin. They'll be along."

Marvin had awakened with the rain. He had not been able to go back to sleep. At five-thirty he'd driven out to see if Hale was up. When he saw the lights on in the upstairs bedroom, he'd gone to the barn. Hale was doing everything he could to keep Marvin from helping.

"What time are they due to leave?"

"Seven."

"Should be here by now."

"They will be, Marv. They will."

Marvin had a crewcut and a beer belly. Shifting his weight, he sucked in his cheeks like a shy boy preparing to make a speech.

"I'm going too," he said.

Hale frowned. "With Pito and Casey?"

"Shit, Hale. You know I couldn't stand to drive that slow. No, there's a chili cook-off up north of Santa Fe next weekend, in Red River. I thought I'd go on up. Chili cooks up different in the mountains. Thought I'd experiment a few days before the contest. Plus," he nodded toward Red, "keep an eye on our girl. We wouldn't want nothing to happen."

Marvin went to a chili cook-off every weekend. Fridays he hooked up to his car a small trailer filled with pots and herbs and spices, an ice chest of his special-cut sirloin and his portable stove.

Rufus wandered up, followed by the pup, chasing Rufus's tail. "Shit," Hale said.

"Now what?"

"Oh, Diana brought that puppy home yesterday. She's never been around horses."

"You want me to hold her?"

"I think you'd better."

Red lowered her ears and snorted at the dogs. She pawed the ground. "Here now, Red," Hale said, to calm the filly.

Marvin went for the pup.

"Come here gal, she a girl?"

"Zelda. Yes."

"Yeah, she's cute. All little girls are cute. Useless and cute." He reached for Zelda; Zelda dodged. "Come here, you," Marvin said. The dog dodged again. Marvin made another move in her direction but the pup slid out from under his grasp. Marvin took off his hat and threw it at Zelda, who yelped and ran and then came back and picked up the hat with her teeth. Marvin grabbed his hat away just in time.

Hale and Red stood at the end of the walkway watching the show. "I swear, Marvin," Hale said. "You're the first person she's done that to. I've never seen a dog move so fast. You just don't have the touch, I guess."

"Shut up, Hale. Just shut up." He grabbed for the dog again. Zelda ran out from under his hand and stood by a stall door. Her eyes flashed and she wagged her hind end. A bolt of lightning cut across the sky. The pup yapped.

"Maybe you should get Diana."

"You think it's necessary?"

Hale thought if he got rid of Marvin he might be able to walk Red into the trailer. "We don't need any more trouble than we've got. And the pup's crazy about Diana."

Marvin pressed his cowboy hat lower on his head and, sloshing through the mud, went to his car. He hadn't had the grille replaced. The Cadillac dealer said it would cost $250. Marvin figured it could wait until after Ruidoso. He got in and without turning on his headlights drove the fifty or so feet to the house.

Hale led Red once again down the walkway toward the trailer. Red came obediently along beside him until she got to within a few feet of the ramp leading into the trailer. Then she started to snort and whinny. Hale coaxed her on. "All right, Mama," he said. "Yes, Red, yes." Red took one more step. But when her feet hit the ramp and she heard that hollow sound, she went crazy again, wheeling and raring and lowering her weight against her hind legs.

"God*damn* you, Red," Hale said, pulling on the rope to get her to stand full down on all four legs.

Zelda whimpered and ran back out of the way.

It was the barn making her crazy; the rain, the strange sounds. Red was used to getting into a trailer in the open. In here, the sound of her hoofs on the ramp echoed. Finished with their breakfast, some of the other horses hung their heads over their stall doors, to watch what was going on and contribute an occasional snort or whinny. Once again, Hale led Red away from the trailer, back down the walkway toward the other end of the barn.

Rufus lay curled by the tack room out of harm's way. Zelda sniffed the floor and ran in circles, peeing every few feet to mark her spots.

"Hi, Coach. Trouble?"

Pito and Casey came in.

"I don't know what's come over her. All of a sudden she won't go in the trailer. I think it's the barn. She's used to getting in a trailer in the open."

"She knows something's up," Casey said in a flat, matter-of-fact tone. "She ain't nobody's fool. She don't want to take that long of a trip, that's all."

"You get behind her, Case," Hale said. "I'll lead."

Casey got a length of rope and walked past Red.

"Pearl foal?"

"A damned stud colt. With four damned white feet."

"Any good?"

"Not much. He's pretty ugly."

"You never can tell. Especially a catch colt. Sometimes they'll fool you." Casey got around behind Red's left hip. He smoothed her tail and stroked her hindquarters. "You remember that Light Up the Sky colt we had for a while? Out of Red Rider by The Flag Is Up? Remember how ugly he was, with that dish face and them skinny little bottleneck hips? Remember how he used to dig in and fly?"

Hale remembered.

"I mean," Casey reminded Hale, "a horse will fool you."

Pito put in his two cents' worth. "That's no lie, Coach," he said. He made a clicking sound with his teeth.

Casey held up the rope. "Okay," he said. "Ready when you are."

He flicked at Red's hindquarters. Pito went along beside the filly, whistling his warm-up "Star-Spangled Banner." Red bowed her head. She took a step. Hale crooned to the filly, the neck of the lead shank grasped firmly in his right hand. Nobody noticed Zelda in the walkway just to the right of dead center, picking pieces of hay and seeds from the mound of manure Red had left there. The men were on the left of the horse, as the horse was used to. Only Hale—who was in front of Red—saw the dog. He yelled out her name. The dog turned around. Pito and Casey had not seen Zelda and so Casey kept flicking the rope and Pito whistled his tune. They did not know who Hale was yelling at when he called her name and they could not see her.

Zelda looked up from the mound of manure and, seeing Red practically on top of her, went into a state of passive resistance. With the sudden speed she'd shown earlier dodging Marvin, she turned over on her back, closed her eyes and pawed the air with her front feet, begging for mercy. Hale dug in his heels and pulled down on the lead rope. He kicked at Zelda but missed. Red kept coming, eyes fixed on the hay bag hung in the front end of the trailer. She was moving now, drawn on toward the promise of food. She picked her right foreleg up high and before Hale could do anything about it set her foot down square on the puppy's neck.

Zelda shrieked, not loudly. Nobody heard it but Hale. She began to turn full somersaults, like a trick dog in a circus.

"She's broken her neck," Hale said. "She's dead. Red's killed her. Goddammit to hell, she's dead."

Pito and Casey heard what Hale said but, not knowing what he meant, went on about their business. Red was on a roll. When her feet hit the ramp and made the hollow sound, the filly nickered but did not stop. Casey popped his rope, Pito whistled and Red went on in. Hale slammed the doors behind her. Pito closed the latch.

"All *right*," Casey said, and he pocketed the rope.

Zelda lay like a fancy red throw pillow in the shavings.

"Oh, Lord," Hale said, standing over the dog. "Diana is going to have a fit. She was crazy about that dog."

"Coach," Pito said. "I never saw her." He went over to the dog. "Poor little thing. I never saw her before in my life."

"Me neither." Casey shook his head. "A dog. I never even saw her." He squatted down and stroked Zelda's fur. "I hate to see something like that," he said.

"You couldn't have seen her," Hale said. "She was on the right-hand side of Red picking at a pile of manure. There was no way for you to see her."

In the trailer, Red stomped her foot and munched her feed. Ingratiating Sam nickered and then sent a mighty stream of urine into the shavings of his stall.

"I'll bury her," Casey said.

"It's raining like a son of a bitch, Case," Hale replied. "You'll get soaked."

"I don't care," Casey said. "I can dry off. I just hate to see something like that." Gently, he picked up the pup and, cradling her to his chest, went to the tack room to get an old towel to wrap her in and a shovel to dig her grave. Then he took Zelda out into the dark wet morning.

Not two minutes after he left, Marvin drove up with Diana.

"Oh, Lord," Hale said. "I dread this."

· 45 ·

*D*iana was out of breath. "Sorry it took so long," she said. "I was making the guys coffee for the road and . . . I see you got her in."

Red stamped her foot and whinnied. One of the other horses answered her.

"Diana."

"Mrs. Coach, we couldn't help it. It wasn't Hale's fault."

"Where's Casey?" She looked around. Rufus stood by the door to the barn, looking out. "Where's Zelda?"

"She's dead, Di."

"Dead. What do you mean?"

"There was an accident."

"She can't be dead. I just got her."

Hale told her what happened.

The men stood in a half-circle around her. Marvin took off his hat, mumbled "Shit," and shifted his feet.

"Here," Diana said, holding out the thermos of coffee.

Pito took it. "Thanks, Mrs. Coach," he said. He patted the thermos. "We're going to need it, that's for sure."

Hale pulled Diana close so that the others couldn't see her face. "I should have left her where she was," she whispered.

"Now I'll have to tell Bethany." She pulled back and looked at him. "Where is she?"

"The pup?"

She nodded.

"Casey's burying her."

"In this?"

"Casey said he didn't mind. You know how tender-hearted he is. Hey."

He pressed close. There was not even a spot on the floor of the barn to show where the dog had died. There was nothing.

Soaked and shivering, Casey came back in. He returned the shovel to its place in the tack room.

"Lord, boy," Marvin said. "You don't have enough meat on you to keep you warm."

Diana moved out of Hale's embrace and wiped her eyes. Casey could not keep his teeth from chattering. "I've got dry clothes in my suitcase," he said. "I just need to get it out of my truck."

"I'll go," Pito said. He was out the door before Casey could protest.

Hale got a horse blanket and wrapped it around Casey's shoulders. He poured him some coffee from the thermos. Casey's hand was shaking so hard he spilled it.

Diana spoke up. "Bring him to the house, Marvin. He needs a hot shower."

"No ma'am, that's all right. I'll be fine."

"Don't be silly, Casey. Come on."

"Wait until Pito gets my things."

Pito came in carrying an old blue Samsonite suitcase with a squeaky handle. He handed the suitcase to Casey. Marvin and Diana drove Casey to the house.

Inside, Diana went to the downstairs bathroom and flicked on the heat. "Stay as long as you want," she yelled through the door after Casey locked it.

A dog, she kept telling herself. She was only a dog.

·46·

"*T*ake me with you."

Folding a shirt, Roger looked up.

"To California?"

"I know it's not on your way. But it's raining too hard to hitch."

"You want to go back to Cedar Hills?"

When she poked out her stomach she could feel the tiny scabs pop off, like ripped thread. She pulled a hunk of flesh from her cheek between her back teeth to keep from crying.

"I don't know, not really. I know I don't want to go to jail. I mean, it's easy for everybody else to make these big gestures. Not me."

"Mom said you asked her to take you out."

Bethany fooled with her hair. "I didn't think she'd do it."

"I'm out of here in ten minutes."

She shrugged. "I don't have anything to pack. We didn't get any of my stuff. We just left. I mean nothing works out. The whole thing's a rip."

Roger put the shirt in his suitcase. "What are you going to tell them?"

"Mom and Dad? I don't know."

"You have to tell them."

"Don't tell me what to do. You're not the boss of me."

"It's my car."

Bethany screwed her round little face up in a pucker and she rolled her eyes to the ceiling. "Just please this one time," she said, "don't let him lecture me. One person. Just one."

Roger looked down at his neatly folded clothes. She was right. He should either give her a ride or tell her no.

"Mom and Hale are at the barn with Pearl. I'm going to stop by to tell them good-bye. They'll see you."

"I'll hide. It's raining like an idiot. There's no way they'll come out to the car."

"Listen, I'm not trying to tell you what to do but will you at least leave them a note?"

"Don't tell me what to do."

"I just don't want them to be hurt anymore." She was starting to get to him again. "I'll tell you what. I'm going to call home an hour after I let you off to make sure they know. Just to clear things in my own head. I mean if I take you, I'm in on it. All right? Do you believe I'm not kidding?"

"Yes, *mein Führer*." Bethany clicked her heels.

"I'll be ready in fifteen minutes."

"So will I."

Stuffed animals lounged in restful positions around Bethany's room. Some were in chairs, others in the window looking out. A few were on the bed. One, a monkey, had been her first, bought when she was only six months old. The monkey had a funny, pinched-up face. Why a monkey? Bethany had asked. Why not a teddy bear? Oh, Diana had replied, we were trying to be different.

She took Diana's list of house rules and turned the paper over. Sitting at the drafting table they'd bought when she'd said she liked to draw, she looked out her window.

There wasn't much to see. Gray rain made lakes in the pasture. Black storm clouds turned morning into night.

It was seven-thirty, Saturday. Bobby would have signed in for breakfast, then gone back to his room to sleep until cartoons were off and reruns came on. Bobby would shit to see her. If she wasn't there tonight he'd go even more M than usual. By tomorrow when The Vice came he'd be totally nuts. It was Bethany's turn to be P.U.

Whether she went or stayed it was all a made-up story. There wasn't any more reason to go back to Cedar Hills than stay here, but there were things to do there. The only thing she could accomplish here was to sit around and watch Diana go crazy cooking diet food. Pretty soon she'd be taking Bethany to Weight Watchers. Then jail. Hale would turn into a martini rock. She might as well go back.

She sat with her pen poised over her paper. Roger said he was ready. Bethany said so was she.

While he waited she wrote the note, signed it, drew a heart beside her name, set the note on the stuffed monkey's belly and wrapped the monkey's arms around it.

"You should have made up your bed," Roger said. "That would have really surprised them."

"Bug off, white swan. If you don't want to take me I can hitch. I'm not afraid of a little water."

"No, come on. I'm sorry. I didn't mean anything."

"Yes, you did."

"Just please. Let's don't fight anymore."

"Who's fighting? Not me, bro. The black swan is peaceful as a rat."

She stormed past. Roger took a deep breath. He didn't mean to fight with Bethany. He meant to love her, help her and keep his mouth shut. But when the time came he said things.

They ran through the rain and jumped into his car.

"Scrunch down in your seat if you don't want them to see

you," he told Bethany. "You're right. They're not going to come out in this."

Bethany scooted down until her knees were on the floor of the Rabbit and her head lay on the seat.

"Try not to take too long," she said. "I can't believe I'm saying this, after as hot as it's been, but I'm cold."

"I'll do my best."

·47·

At the mare barn he cut the motor, opened the door and got out. The truck and trailer were gone. He sloshed through the mud to the barn.

"In here, Rog. Come on back."

Roger went to the open stall next to the pen where Hale shut up his foaling mares.

Diana was smiling. "Come see the baby," she said.

The colt stood beside his mother on wobbly legs. Pearl seemed calm. She was eating alfalfa from a hay bag and not paying attention to her baby at all, except occasionally to turn back and look at him. Some mares went crazy when they had a colt and would not let you near their babies for days. Pearl seemed to be a modern mother, lax and nonintrusive. When Hale went over and touched the colt on his hindquarters, neither mother nor baby flinched.

The colt went to his mama to suck. His tongue was bright red. He made some awkward sucking sounds. Milk dribbled down the sides of his mouth.

"I thought they were born knowing how to do that."

"It takes a while to get the drill down pat."

The colt's back legs seemed about to give way beneath

him. He raised his short little tail. Three hard black drops came out.

"That's good," Hale said. "He's not plugged up."

The colt was a brownish-red color, nothing like Pearl.

"What color do you think he'll be?"

"Sorrel, I imagine. Look. Four white feet."

"What difference does that make?"

"White feet are soft. They get infections. You have to be careful trimming their hooves. Daddy used to say with four white feet you throw them to the jaybirds. But what the hell, with the blaze face, he'll be flashy. I can always sell him to a South American dictator to ride in parades."

Diana squatted. "Oh, Hale," she said. "He's cute."

"You always think they're cute."

"They always are."

Roger remembered Bethany. "So . . . ," he said. "I'm on my way."

Diana stood. "Oh, Roger, in this weather. Why not wait until tomorrow, see if it breaks?"

"I'll be okay, Mom. I can get to Benicia by Monday lunch, if I'm lucky. Time I get to Fredericksburg the sun will be shining."

Diana hugged him, then stepped away. "Did Hale tell you about Zelda?"

"Yes. I'm sorry."

"It was stupid of me to bring her home."

"It's not your fault."

"I know but still."

"Son."

Roger looked at his father.

"Do you have plenty of money?"

"Dad. You gave me two hundred last night."

"I know but . . ." He reached for his wallet. "Here. Maybe you'd better take this."

"Dad." Roger laid his hand on his father's arm. "It's enough. I'm fine. Really."

"Fifty more?"

"I said I was fine."

"Well, you do have the Exxon card."

"I'll send it back when I get there."

"You can keep it."

"I'll send it back. I can handle the gas."

"If you won't keep the card, then at least take this." He took a fifty-dollar bill from his wallet. "Put it in your wallet and save it for something special if you don't need it on the trip."

Diana took the bill from Hale and handed it to Roger. "Take it," she said. "He wants you to have it."

Roger raised his arms to the ceiling. "You saw me, God," he said. "You saw me try." He took the money. They all laughed.

"We'll miss you, Rog."

"Especially my cooking."

"That, too. It's been fun. Thanks for coming."

"We probably won't sell another pair of ostrich boots until you get back."

"You get a potential buyer, send for me."

"Well."

"I guess it's time."

A brief tooting sound came from the road.

Diana frowned. "What was that?"

"What was what?"

"I thought I heard a car horn."

"I don't think so."

The horn tooted again.

"There. Am I crazy?"

"No, I heard it too."

"Probably that stupid peacock. Now really, as we say in California, I'm history, folks."

Roger hugged his parents. "I love you both," he said. " 'Bye, kid," he said to the colt. "You know what you're going to name him?"

"Maybe The Chisos Kid. Pearl's full name is The Pearl of the Chisos."

"How about Jaybird?"

"Not bad. We'll see."

Roger went down the walkway toward the road. "How about A Break in the Weather?" He called over his shoulder. "You can call him Break?"

"Too many letters. But nice try."

" 'Bye. Good-bye. I love you, good-bye."

"Roger."

Roger turned around. Diana was in the walkway.

"Don't worry about Bethany," she said. "I'm sure she'll be fine."

"Yes'm," he said with a salute.

"Don't say yes'm."

"No'm."

He ducked his head and ran out into the rain. Hale and Diana came with him, all the way to the barn door. They stood there until the little red lights of the Rabbit had made the final turn in the road and disappeared.

Bethany unfolded.

"How come you honked?"

"Do you know what it's like down here on this stupid floor?"

"No, but . . ."

"Then never mind."

Because of the weather, Roger took the freeway instead of the back roads. When he turned on Ben White, Bethany crossed her arms and stared hard out the windshield, watching the wipers push the water back and forth. A feather of fear tickled her throat. "They better let me back in," she said. "If this isn't demonstrating fucking willingness I don't know what is."

When Roger pulled into the Cedar Hills parking lot she said it again. "If this isn't willingness, I don't know what is."

He stopped the car but left the motor running. "You rather go to California?"

Bethany leaned forward into the light, to see his face better. Roger looked back at her without blinking.

"Well?"

Bethany swallowed hard.

His hand was on the gear shift. She covered it with her own. "No, bro," she said. "I better not. But thanks." She withdrew her hand and lifted up on the door handle. "It means a lot."

She opened the door. "Pray for me," she said.

He pointed in the direction of his forehead. "Good thoughts," he said, "as we say in California. The whole way."

"I need them."

She ran through the rain. The last Roger saw of her, she was disappearing behind a gold door.

In the Rabbit, Roger headed west.

·48·

When Hale and Diana got back to the house, Diana went to Bethany's room. In the monkey's arms she found the note.

Dear Mom and Dad,
   I'm going back to Cedar Hills. Roger is taking me. He didn't want to but I begged.
   Please don't be mad. I don't want to go to jail. Thanks for putting up with my shit.
   Love, Bethany.

Beside her name she'd drawn a heart.
Diana took the note to Hale.
"I knew I heard a horn," she said.

Sunday

· 49 ·

*H*ale came out of the bathroom. He was fully dressed. "You awake?"

"Barely." She meant to get up with him, go check on the colt; instead she'd burrowed in. The rain had slackened. She thought of Zelda, cold in the wet cold ground.

"How about coming down and bringing the camera. I want to take some pictures."

A new colt never failed to excite Hale, no matter how many were born or how unpromising they looked.

"I'm coming."

It was strange to have the house to themselves. During the night Diana kept waking up, thinking she heard the door close, a car drive up, the comforting breath of another person in some other part of the house. When it happened she lay concocting new events in her mind. When she had convinced herself no one had left she could sleep.

She got up, went to the bathroom, got dressed. She had picked up the camera and was checking it for film when Hale came back in. He was yelling. Diana dropped the camera at the top of the stairs and went down.

In the kitchen, Hale was frantic. "He's dying!" he said. "He was outside the fence when I got there, on the pasture side. He's cold and hungry and he's dying. I need a jar to milk the mare into, something small." He opened the jar drawer, which was jammed, took a pint-size mason jar from the top of the pile and turned to run back out again. "Call Warren," he said. "Tell him to come. Then I need you."

He ran out.

Diana dialed Warren Burleson's home number. "Dr. Burleson's out of town," a woman announced in a nasal, hill-country twang. "Dr. Armour Hooten is taking his calls. Do you wish the number?"

Diana said yes. She'd never heard of Armour Hooten.

Hooten answered the phone himself. He sounded like a boy. He said he'd be right out, meantime they should keep the colt warm. "I know it's been hot," he said, "but hypothermia's a danger. That baby could have gotten a chill in this rain. I'll bring liquids."

Diana ran to the barn. The colt lay on a bed of shavings, shivering. His eyes were glazed, his tongue now a very pale, grayish pink. Hale sat on a bale of hay with the mason jar between his knees, his head against Pearl's flank. Very little milk was coming out. "If she was a cow," he said, "I could do better."

He brought the jar to where the colt lay.

"Don't you have a nipple?"

"He's too weak to suck. I'm going to try to pour it down his throat. Here, little fellow . . ."

He went down on one knee, held the colt's head up, propped it on the other knee, and poured a small amount of milk down his throat. The pale tongue rose and fell. The colt swallowed a little of the liquid, but he was too weak and listless to pursue the swallowing with any vigor or even to care. When a drop or two dribbled out on the ground, Hale cursed.

Diana rubbed the colt down his spine and across his hips.

A deep shiver ran through him. "Warren's out of town," she said.

"Shit. Who'd you get?"

"Somebody named Armour Hooten."

"Christ. He's a kid. Graduated from A. and M. the day before yesterday."

Diana moved closer to Hale. "He said the main thing was to keep him warm. He said maybe we should bring him to the garage or the laundry room. We could run the dryer."

Hale went back to the hay bale. "Not yet. I don't want to move him." He milked the mare. Pearl dozed.

Diana rubbed the baby's neck. "I'm just telling you what he said."

"Diana, I know it's . . ."

"I'm just telling you."

"Newspapers."

"Newspapers?"

"They're a good insulator. Casey keeps a stack in the tack room. I've always said they were a fire hazard but . . ."

She ran down the walkway. Water poured from the storm drains of the barn in a gush, but the heavy rains of the night before had become a normal summer drizzle. Rufus lay by the barn door looking out, as if for Zelda. Just inside the door to the tack room was a knee-high stack of newspapers. Diana grabbed a good six inches' worth, along with two saddle blankets folded on a shelf.

In the stall, she lifted the colt's head and placed a number of *Austin American-Statesmen*s beneath it. She slid another copy of the paper beneath his neck, several *Houston Post*s under his shoulders. "I can't lift him in the middle," she told Hale. "You'll have to help."

Hale propped up the jar and came to where Diana was. He lifted the colt's stomach and legs. Diana slid a pad of newspapers beneath the colt's hind section, then spread the two blankets over him. From his shirt pocket Hale took out a thermometer.

"Stroke his ears," he said, "to distract him. Although in his state, I doubt he'll notice."

Diana rubbed the baby's soft ears and talked to him while Hale inserted the thermometer in his rectum.

The colt shut his eyes. Diana fanned them back open. "Hey," she said. "Don't go to sleep."

"He may need to."

"If he goes to sleep he won't wake up. Hey, little guy, wake up." He opened his big eyes. They did not seem to focus.

Hale pulled the thermometer out.

"Two degrees below normal. I'm going to get an IV. You try this." He handed Diana the jar of milk and a small scrap of cloth. "Dip the rag in the milk and put it in his mouth. Maybe he'll suck it. Hold it in his mouth until it's dry, then do it again."

He left.

Diana slid her knees up under the colt's head. She dipped the rag in the milk, squeezed it a little, then slid it past the baby's lips into his mouth. She felt the back of his tongue rise listlessly against the wet rag. As he sucked, his pale smooth gums wobbled.

"Hey," Diana said. "Come on now, you have to do this." She shoved at his head. The colt's eyelids lifted, then shut. His head dropped.

Diana slid her hand beneath the colt to feel his heart. She had no idea how fast a colt's heart should beat but his was pounding. She dipped the rag into the jar of milk and placed it in the colt's mouth. Again his tongue responded and his jaw muscles worked, neither with any enthusiasm.

All the new mornings. Bethany back at Cedar Hills, Roger on his way west, Red heading for the mountains, Zelda in the ground. This new dying baby. Diana withdrew her knees and replaced them with the corner of one of the blankets.

She checked the barn door. No Hale. She lay down on the bed of shavings beside the colt, stretching out until her midsection was against his spine. She pressed her chest and stomach against his back the full length of him, the way she and Hale slept, then lifted her leg and laid it over the colt, pressing her knee into his stomach. With her free hand she rubbed the colt's belly and with the flat of her hand reached down between his front legs to rub him there. The colt no longer shivered at her touch.

This close she could feel him going. He had enough energy to keep from dying and that was all. Soon that would go. Diana pushed her torso even closer. Outside, the rain drizzled slowly. Against the tin roof of Hale's home-made mare barn it sounded like a thousand falling pin-heads.

She felt the colt's heart once again. Still racing. She put her mouth to his ear and hummed a few notes. The colt flicked his ear as if to bat at a fly. Diana crooned at him some more. The colt's eyelashes fluttered. Encouraged, she began to sing, "Good Night, Irene" and then "The Tennessee Waltz." The three-quarter beat felt right, as if it might tune into the colt's heartbeat and keep it pumping. For resonance, she pitched her voice low. The colt's eyelids fluttered again. Pearl glanced down at the colt, then turned away and munched alfalfa.

"He take anything?"

Hale's hands were full. He had a needle and syringe, a box and an IV bottle. "I had to go to the training barn."

Diana lifted her head.

"I figured."

"Did he take anything?"

"Almost nothing. He's going, Hale. I think we should take him to the laundry room. We'll run the dryer. You can give him the IV there. Armour Hooten should be here soon."

'Armour Hooten doesn't know his ass from third base."

"He's all we have."

Hale looked back toward the house, then at Diana. The IV bottle swung in his grasp. He frowned.

"Maybe you're right," he said.

Diana slid her arm from beneath the colt, uncurled and

stood. "I don't know much about horses," she said, "but I do know a little bit about babies. If we don't do something this baby is going to die. Pearl's given up on him."

"If we had any sense so would we."

"We can't."

"Oh, I know. You bring all this. I'll get him."

"Don't you want help?"

"It's easier if I do it by myself."

"Don't kill yourself just to prove a point."

Hale's face turned red.

"Good Christ, Diana," he said. "You have a bad back. I'll be all right. Now would you please not fight me on this and just *help*?" He shook his head. "I'm sorry."

"Never mind."

She took the IV bottle, the tube and syringes, and lifted the blankets off the colt. She piled the supplies in the blanket and carried it like laundry.

"After we get the glucose going, we'll need to give him an enema. He'll shit in the laundry room."

"So?"

"Well, horseshit in the house, that's all."

"Tile, remember? It mops."

To keep the colt from kicking, Hale gathered his soft hooves together in one hand, as if taking a bouquet of flowers by the stem. He squatted and put the other arm under the colt's body.

"You go ahead," he told Diana. "Open the laundry room door. He's going to be heavy to get that far. I won't be able to stop once I've started. Make sure Rufus is out of the way for God's sake. I just wish Roger was here."

Clasping his hands beneath the colt's belly, he took a deep breath. Gathering up his strength, he thrust his pelvis forward to take the strain off his back. He drew the colt to him and in one motion stood, grunting as he straightened, holding the colt the way he would a load of firewood. The colt's head and feet dangled. Hale could barely see over his back. His tail flopped over one arm.

"Go on," he said to Diana, motioning impatiently with his head toward the house.

Diana ran backwards. Hale came at a trot, breathing heavily. The colt's head bobbed. Curious, Rufus wandered up, sniffed Hale's foot. Diana made a move toward the dog. Before she could get there, Hale had kicked Rufus in the head. The dog ran off whimpering.

At the turnaround, Hale paused. The colt's head hung down dangerously, pulling on his neck. Diana opened the door to the laundry room. Hale started coming again. He'd slowed his pace to a fast walk. He kept his knees flexed. At the door to the laundry room he turned sideways.

"Newspapers," he grunted.

Roger had taken them all out. Diana went to the garbage cans, came back to the laundry room and spread the papers on the tile floor to make a pallet. Hale all but fell with the colt. The colt sighed, shuddered and lay still.

"Lord," Hale said. "I'm too old for that." He took several deep breaths. He could feel the blood pounding in his head. Sweat and rain ran down his face into his shirt. Under his arms, an itchy place had begun to spread. He was, Hale was convinced, allergic to himself, to his own sweat.

"You want some water?"

"No, I'm all right. Let's get started."

Diana went to the kitchen to warm the glucose under hot running water. Needle in one hand, Hale knelt down beside the colt.

"It'll take me a while," he said, "to find his vein."

At the sink, Diana looked out the windows. A line of pink clouds were stretched along the peaks of the hills. To the east she could see the first light of the sun. The sky was clearing. By noon they'd have summer again.

Diana opened the bottle and stuck her finger in. They

needed a miracle now. If not a miracle then magic. The glucose felt right, about skin temperature.

In the laundry room, Hale was rubbing his thumb in an upward movement along the colt's neck.

"Hold on," he said to Diana. "I've almost got it." A lump popped up. "I had it," he said. "And I lost it." In a sudden fluid motion he plunged the needle into the colt's neck. "There," he said. Blood dribbled from around the needle across Hale's hand and down the colt's neck.

They attached the tube to the needle, the glucose to the tube. "After this we'll give him Foal-lac."

"In a bottle?"

"He doesn't have the energy. We'll have to tube him."

When the glucose bottle was empty, Hale mixed the powdered milk substitute with water in another bottle.

"Hold him," he said, and he inserted a clear plastic tube in the colt's nose and shoved.

"You see how apathetic he is," Hale said, still unrolling the plastic tube. "Ordinarily he'd fight this like the devil."

The colt made a whining sound. His nostrils quivered.

When the tube was in, Hale connected it to the bottle and held the bottle high. He rubbed the colt's topknot. "I'm afraid we're going to lose this one, Diana," he said. "I think this is not our weekend for holding on to babies."

The Foal-lac ran for a time and then stopped. Hale disconnected the bottle from the tube and, placing the tube in his mouth, blew hard. His face reddened. When he reconnected the tube, the level of the liquid at once began to drop.

"Sometimes," he said, "you have to get it started."

When the bottle was empty, he unhooked it.

"We'll leave the tube," he said. "We may need it again."

The infusions had an immediate effect. Within minutes, the colt lifted his head. Color began to return to his mouth and gums and he scraped his feet against the floor, pulling them in toward one another, as if trying to stand.

Diana turned the dryer on, expecting to hear the bump of clothes whirling around inside. But Roger had folded all the clothes before he left. "I just thought of something," she said. "I'll be right back."

"What would we do," she said when she returned, "without Vidal Sassoon." She held up her hair dryer.

The colt had lifted his head. He was looking around, as if amazed to find himself alive at all, much less inside the house.

Diana plugged in the hair dryer and, aiming the hot air against the colt's spine, rubbed his coat, making sure the barrel of the dryer did not get close enough to burn.

The colt stirred. He stretched his neck and trembled. His ears were up. Diana scratched his back.

"He likes it."

The colt nickered. Surprised, Diana drew back. "Hey," she said. "He can talk." She ran the dryer up and down his back, watching as the hot air made a path through the hairs of his coat. The colt stirred again.

"He's trying to get up, Diana. Move back."

He stretched his legs, rolled toward his spine, then over, trying to get his feet under him. He couldn't make it. "He's cast himself," Hale said. Diana stood back, still aiming the hot air from the dryer on the colt.

"Come on, Buddy," Hale said. "Try again." He squatted by the colt's head.

The colt rolled so far over he seemed about to turn on his spine, then pushed back in the other direction until his feet were beneath him, forelegs bent, hooves down on the floor. He paused. His head went up and down, not so much a nodding gesture as one of lifting and dropping on its own as he gathered strength and then lost it. His eyes were wide open and for the first time, alert. He fixed his gaze on the door to the kitchen, but did not exactly seem to see.

In one swift movement he pulled himself up. When his forelegs were settled he drew his hind legs up. His back legs buckled and seemed about to give. Hale pushed on the lower part of his hips. The colt's head dropped. He looked dispirited. And then he raised his head and looked around.

"While he's up let's do this." Standing with his shoulder against the colt's hindquarters for support, Hale opened a box and took out a large rubber-bulb syringe. He threw the box aside. "The only thing I can think of is, he's plugged. He had a stool last night and one yesterday morning. But he may still be plugged."

Diana set the hair dryer down and went to hold the colt, clasping her hands around his midsection the way she had seen Hale do. Hale inserted the lesser end of the tube in the colt's rectum and slowly squeezed the bulb. The colt did not flinch.

The telephone rang.

"Let it go."

"I was going to."

It rang six times and then stopped.

"Rose Narcisco, I'll bet."

"Now look, Di, when I'm finished I'll hold him. You go get some old sheets."

"He can go on the floor. It's nothing to clean up."

Hale took Diana's place. He held the colt around the stomach. "I wonder where that vet is."

"I thought you didn't want him. Anyway, haven't we turned the corner?"

"It may not last."

The colt spread his back legs and lowered his buttocks.

"Come on, fellow," Hale said. "Get it out."

The colt pressed so hard his legs buckled. Hale held him tighter. The colt shivered and pushed. A hard black lump came out, followed by another. "Good boy," Hale said. "Anymore?" The colt pressed down. One more lump came, smaller than the others.

"Good boy," Hale said, stroking the colt. As he relaxed from the effort the colt tilted back and straightened himself.

"So. Is it over?" Diana said hopefully.

"We still need to get him to suck. If he can't suck he won't live. It doesn't have to be his mama, it can be a bottle, but he has to suck."

"Why?"

"If he lost oxygen during the birthing process he won't be able to. We need to know that. If he can't suck he's a dummy foal, brain-damaged. It's nature's way of culling out the rejects."

"What if he is brain-damaged?"

"He'll die, Diana. Look, I wouldn't have involved you in this at all, except that everybody else is gone. He may die. We may have to let him. An idiot horse is of no earthly use to anyone, least of all himself. Now help me."

"That may be why Pearl gave up on him."

"It may be. Now do you think you can get her?"

"Pearl? I think so."

"She has a halter on. You know where the lead ropes are."

"I'll be right back."

·50·

*P*earl stared dumbly at her hay bag. Her back foot was cocked. She shifted her weight to the other foot.

"Easy, Mama." Diana reached up and with a movement she hoped the mare interpreted as confident latched the lead rope to her halter.

Pearl offered no resistance. Diana turned her in a wide circle, then led her down the road toward the house.

The rain had stopped. Water dripped from the trees. The usual humid stillness was setting in. Diana talked to Pearl. The mare seemed to trust her. When they got to the garage, Hale came out with the baby, inching the colt along by wrapping his arms around him from his shoulders to his hips and pushing. When Pearl saw the colt, she reared. Diana pulled down on the rope but the mare lifted her front feet higher. Diana pulled again. The rope flew through her palm.

"Let go," Hale yelled. He let the colt go and ran toward Diana. "Let go of the rope."

Diana drew back her hand.

"Crazy bitch." Hale jerked hard at the lead rope, pulling the mare down by force.

Diana's palms were torn and red, the outer layer of skin

ripped away. She reached down and grabbed a handful of mud in each hand.

"You all right?"

"Yes." She kept her fists behind her.

Hale led Pearl into the garage and tied her to his riding lawnmower. The colt had remained standing when Hale left her, though his legs wobbled and shook.

"Let's see what happens."

They pushed the colt to Pearl's side and under her belly, shoving his nose into her bag. The colt seemed to get the idea. He put his mouth on his mother's teat, made a few half-hearted attempts to suck, then pulled away.

"Damn," Hale said. The plastic tube dangled from the colt's nose like a drop of snot.

"Let's try again." Diana tossed the mud away. She took the colt's nose and pressed it into his mother's bag. Hale helped.

A truck drove up in the driveway.

"Diana, go get that idiot. I'll keep on here."

The vet had parked his truck—small, white and Japanese, with a NO NUKES EVER sticker on the front bumper—next to the Buick. Armour Hooten jumped down out of the cab, carrying a black leather case. He was small and thin. He wore round, metal-rimmed glasses. His straight blond hair was cut Prince Valiant–style, bangs across the forehead. He wore blue jeans and an open-collar shirt.

"Love your car," he said. "What year is it?"

" 'Seventy-two. We're in the garage."

"All righty," he said.

Diana rolled her eyes. She'd asked for a miracle. What she got was Armour Hooten.

The colt staggered. He looked confused.

"He's failing again," Hale said. "We gave him glucose with an IV, tubed him with Foal-lac, then gave him a Fleet's. He had a rocky stool and rallied for a while, but I still can't get him to suck."

The colt looked around at the vet. His eyes went soft and he got that dreamy look again, as if he had gone off in space. His hind legs buckled, his forelegs quivered and he did his collapsing trick, like a dropped handkerchief. His head bobbled, then drooped.

The young vet stood back observing. He set his bag down.

"I think he's a goner," Hale said. "He won't suck."

" 'Morning," the vet said pleasantly. "I'm Armour Hooten."

"Hale Caldwell." Hale held out his hand. "My wife, Diana." The two men shook hands. Armour Hooten came to where Diana was and shook hers. "Nice to meet you," he said.

He knelt down beside the colt.

The colt's lids lowered. Armour Hooten snapped his fingers at his ear. The colt opened his eyes and blinked. Hooten passed his hand in front of the colt's eyes and moved it back and forth, snapping his fingers and saying "Hey-*UH*. Hey-*UH*." The colt's eyelids fluttered; he looked annoyed.

The vet stood. "I don't think he's a dummy," he said. "He's too alert. I'm going to give him something to reduce any swelling he might have in his brain anyway, then we need to get him back on his feet. I think he's just plugged."

Hale shook his head. "He had a stool last night, Hooten. And again when we gave him the Fleet's."

"I still think he's plugged. Sometimes it takes drastic measures."

Hooten took a needle and syringe from his case. He filled the syringe. As he worked he hummed a little tune.

"We've been keeping him warm with blankets and papers and a hair dryer," Diana said to the vet. "We even had him in the house."

"You did the right thing." Armour Hooten slapped the colt's neck to dull the sensation of the shot. "You know what they say. Keep a cool head and a warm patient." He plunged the needle in the colt's neck, released the fluid, pulled the needle out. He stood and looked up over his head.

"We need to make a harness," he said, "to go under his belly. We'll attach it there." He pointed to a beam in the ceiling. "I want him standing. It'll be easier on us all if he's got help."

He took three bottles of mineral oil from his black bag. With three fingers he combed his bangs out of his eyes. "Come on, son," he said to the colt. Armour Hooten was stronger than he looked. In one easy motion he had the baby on his feet. He turned to Hale. "Can you rig me up something?" he asked pleasantly. "A sling to go under his belly?"

"You going to give him that? Plain mineral oil?"

"You bet. Pepto-Bismol for colic. Mineral oil for constipation. Works for us, works for them." He leaned against the colt to hold him and opened the bottle. "Diana," he said. "If you'd lean in the other direction?"

Diana followed the vet's instructions. Hale grumbled, then went off to the barn to get the requested materials. He had some old burlap sacks feed used to come in. With those and some ropes and baling wire he thought he could rig something up. Although he had no confidence in Armour Hooten, he was happy to hand the responsibility over to him. More than likely the colt was a goner. Hooten would charge a hundred dollars for the house call, more for the medications, fifty dollars to bury the colt. He'd be out a couple hundred and then it would be over.

He looked behind to see if Rufus was following but Rufus was off in the woods, nursing his hurt feelings.

When the first bottle of mineral oil was empty, Armour Hooten attached another to the tube in the baby's nose.

"You had your car since 'seventy-two? Or did you buy it restored?"

"Both. We've had it the whole time and have had it restored. It's got two hundred thousand miles on it."

He shook the bottle to keep the liquid moving. " 'Seventy-two was a great year for GM. I have an Oldsmobile Cutlass from that year. I keep it in the garage, drive it to car shows. We have a blast." The second bottle had been drained. "I think we'll do one more."

"Bottle?"

He reached for it. "He's bigger than we are." He hitched up the third bottle of mineral oil. "But mine's not a ragtop," he said. "You ever want to sell yours you let me know."

"Not likely." The colt started to buckle. Diana pressed at him. She wasn't contributing much. For the most part Armour Hooten was holding up the colt on his own.

Hale returned with burlap bags, ropes and wire. He attached the wire to either end of two burlap bags, threading the wire through the openings in the burlap to wire the two together, making sure the open ends of the wire were on the underside so that they did not scratch the colt's belly. He wrapped the ends of the wire around the ends of two lengths of rope and slid the burlap bags under the colt's belly.

"Pearl's asleep," Diana said.

"You'll need a ladder."

"I know." Everytime Hooten gave instructions the itching in Hale's underarms heated up and spread. Hale took an aluminum stepladder from the storeroom at the back of the garage. The storeroom was now in perfect order, Roger having spent an entire afternoon cleaning it. Diana held the burlap bags in place under the colt's belly while Hale climbed the ladder and attached one end of the rope to a beam.

"The second one," he said, "will be trickier." He climbed down and moved the ladder.

Armour Hooten checked the colt's pulse. "We need to be fairly swift," he said. "The oil should take effect pretty quickly."

"I know." Like hired help, Hale obediently climbed back up the ladder. Diana held the burlap bag in place. Hale began to tie another knot.

"Wait."

He let go. "What?"

She laughed. "It was too high. He was in the air."

Hale was on the top step of the ladder, reaching above his head. "All right," he said, "now I can't see up here. You have to tell me when it's right." he pulled. A stream of sweat skirted one eye. "Now?"

"Not yet."

"Now."

"A little more."

"Now."

"*Whoa.*"

Diana giggled. "Too far."

Hale slid the rope across the beam. He wasn't sure how much more of this he could take. He let out some slack. "Now?"

"What do you think, Armour?"

"Perfect. Exactly right, Hale. Now tie it. That's great."

Hale tied the rope to the beam and climbed back down the ladder. He took his cap off and wiped his forehead with his handkerchief, then put his hands on his hips to keep his arms away from his side. Used to be, he could stand on the top step of a ladder without a thought.

"Now," Hooten said. "We wait." He rubbed his hands together like a magician about to perform a trick. "You folks by chance got some coffee?"

"I'll make some. You take anything in it?"

"I like it black. Black as my heart."

Armour Hooten shook his head, settled his scholar's glasses in the groove in his nose and grinned.

Diana went into the kitchen. The telephone was ringing again.

·51·

"Mom? It's me."

"Bethany. Are you all right? Did they let you in?"

"Mom, I didn't mean to hurt your feelings but . . ." Before she dialed she'd taken ten deep breaths, held each one five seconds, let it out through her nose. Bobby was wrong; deep-breathing didn't help. ". . . Oh, Mom, I'm so afraid of going to jail."

"I know, baby."

"Is it okay? I mean, will you and Daddy pay?"

Diana inspected the blisters in her palm. She tore off a piece of skin. "Of course we'll pay, Bee. That was never in question." She tore too far, down into the pink part. She licked her hand and shook it.

"Well, I didn't know. Did you see my note?"

"I did."

"The kids were really glad to see me, Mom. Even Tiffy Boo-hoo and Prissy Marching-on. I mean it wasn't an act, I could tell. They were really really glad."

"That's great, Bee."

"Rog told me about Zelda."

"It wasn't anybody's fault. It just happened."

"I know, Mom. But poor thing."

"I know."

"So, I have to go. I'm P.U. today."

"No deodorant?"

"What?"

"Joke, Bee, small joke. You're what?"

"Parental Unit, the A.F. I get to say when my table eats. Rosy wants to see you."

"I'm sure."

"But she said I did it."

"Did what?"

"The big D.W. You helped, Mom. I did the impossible, I mean I demonstrated the eyes out of stupid willingness. It all worked out."

"For once."

"Gotta go."

"Bee."

"What?"

"Your dad's proud of you. He thinks you did the right thing. He's really proud."

"Really? What do you know, me, the black swan. How about you?"

Diana pushed down on the scar on her chest. "Oh, I'm too busy missing you right now. But I will be. Give me time."

"I have to go."

"I love you."

"Me, too."

"Congratulations on the big D.W."

But Bethany had hung up.

When Diana went out with the coffee, Armour Hooten and Hale were waving their hats in the air.

"More, baby, more," Hooten shouted.

From the colt's behind, brown liquid poured out in a stream.

"I'll have to hand it to you, Hooten," Hale said. "I never would have thought it. I never in a rat's-ass coon age would have thought it."

Diana handed them each a cup of coffee. When the colt was empty, his rectum made a snorting sound. The colt sighed, then nickered.

From her position at the riding lawnmower Pearl nickered back.

Armour downed his coffee. "I think he's finished," he said.

The colt lifted his head. Pearl stamped her feet. Armour Hooten and Hale began the intricate business of unhooking the colt from his harness.

"You really think this was necessary?" Hale asked the vet. "We barely got him hitched up before it was time to take him down again."

"It works better," Hooten said, "if he's standing. Better still if he's doing it on his own." He unthreaded a section of wire from a burlap bag. "Yes. I think it was necessary. Otherwise we'd all three of us be coated. I don't know about you, but that's a treat I'd rather not enjoy."

Hale told Hooten the joke about the monkey making love to the skunk. Hooten laughed loudly. He'd have to remember that one, he said, for other such occasions.

When they were finished, they led the colt to Pearl. He pulled so hard at the mare's bag he almost choked. Pearl stomped her foot. The colt flipped his tail.

"Plugged up," Hale said. "I'd have never thought it."

Diana looked from one man to the other. "So," she said, "*now* is it over?"

The men turned to her.

"I mean, is it?"

Armour Hooten smiled pleasantly at her.

"Sometimes it is that easy, Diana," he said, combing back his bangs with his fingers. "Sometimes Rome gets built in a minute."

Diana hoped she believed him.

When the young vet left, Hale's skepticism returned. Taking Pearl and the colt back to the mare barn, he talked to himself.

"Good God," he said, "I must be crazy. All that trouble for an ugly little white-footed bastard catch colt."

Rufus came from the woods. In the barn Hale let the dog jump up on him and put his paws at his waist, even though they'd taught him not to, to show Rufus he was not mad.

· 52 ·

*D*iana let her nightgown fall over her shoulders. She pressed the silk down over her breasts. In bed, Hale held his elbows high, letting the ointment he had put on his underarms dry. He was reading about gold fever. Diana picked up a paperback written by a British mystery writer new to her, climbed in next to him, turned on her reading light, put on her glasses and stared at the opening paragraph.

"Let's go somewhere."

Hale closed his book.

"Where do you want to go?"

"I don't know." She took off her glasses. "How long before you plan on leaving for Ruidoso?"

"A few weeks."

"Maybe we won't wait that long. Maybe we'll go on out and see Red sooner. Take a long drive, listen to music, watch west Texas go by. Go for hikes in New Mexico. Maybe I'll unbox that computer and who knows, write something."

Hale set his book aside. "We'll have to wait until Pito gets back. Somebody has to take care of things here."

Diana placed her own book on the bedside table. "That," she said, "shouldn't take long."

"A week."

"It will take us that long to get ready."

"What about your teaching?"

"I'm thinking about getting a greenhouse. Is that a good idea?"

"It is."

"But I don't know." She turned to him. "Hale."

"What."

"I had to do it."

"I know."

"And I guess so did she."

"I think she did."

She bit her lip. "But Hale," she said. And then she stopped.

"What."

"I hate Cedar Hills. I really hate it."

"So do I."

He waited for her to speak again.

After a few seconds she did. "And you know what else?"

"What?"

"I hate California, too."

"Me, too."

"And Zelda having to die."

He touched her shoulder. "Same here."

"And I wish white feet were great and I want Red to win."

"Yes."

"It's all so *hard*."

He took off his glasses. She'd closed her eyes. "Look at me," he said.

He cupped her chin. When her eyes were puffy she looked her age. She frowned.

"You gotta be a pro," Hale said. "We have to hold on."

"Maybe I'm not a pro. Maybe I'm a sissy."

"You have no choice. You have to be a pro."

"Maybe."

He turned off their reading lights. They lay on their sides, facing each other.

In the dark, Diana whispered. "Hale," she said.

"What," he whispered back.

"Do you think she has a shot?"

He waited a long time before answering. "I hate to say it." He was speaking so low she could barely hear him. "But you know, I do. If she breaks okay I think she might."

They held each other and hoped the night would not be too long. Believing they had failed the two people in the world for whom they had most wanted to be heroes they came together and held each other in sadness. There seemed little else to do.